About the Author

Kevin Bailey was born in Newtown, Wales in 1975 and grew up with his 3 younger siblings in and around the town of Ludlow, Shropshire, (which the fictional town of Chelmesbury is based on). He has been married twice and has 3 wonderful children.

He has been writing fiction for over 30 years and ideas come to him in the strangest of places; for example, when he is delivering bathroom equipment around the country he has to pull up and write them down on scraps of paper, much to his wife's annoyance at finding them in his clothes in the washing basket.

He lives at present in his little house in the city of Worcester, where he balances writing, being a husband and a dad and driving around the midlands delivering bathrooms.

His ambition is to be a success and maybe one day write a James Bond novel.

As well as his Simon Eliote continuation Mysteries, he is currently working with his auntie Patricia Heath on a series of Sci-fi Spoofs....

Also by the Author

THE DEATHLY ANGEL
The first Simon Eliote mystery

The brutal slaying of Jamie Tweeting in Lovers Lane turns out to be the start of a series of violent attacks on the unsuspecting people of a Shropshire town by a psychopath known only by his alias 'The Deathly Angel.'

But the historic picture postcard town holds darker secrets than a man seeking revenge, as the recently demoted Detective Chief Inspector Simon Eliote soon finds out when he is sent back from the smog of London to his ancestral home after being framed for the shooting of an un-armed man.

Upon arrival, he finds himself straight into a confrontation with two of his team; a grouchy, old fashioned Pathologist, and a Detective Inspector who resents him for taking a job which he feels was his.

Can the 'Angels', macabre killing spree shock the team into working together to catch him before it is too late…?

Available from Amazon.co.uk & Amazon.com in electronic format and Paperback

WHEN ANGELS FEAST

By
Kevin Bailey

Copyright © 2016 Kevin John Bailey
All Rights Reserved

Cover Photo © Adam Selwood
Used by kind permission

Edited by Heather Osborne

Cover designed and © ShipRex Designs

This book is dedicated to Katt, Ben and Abi.
Three bright lights in a dark world.

This is a work of fiction. Names, characters, places and incidents are the product of the author's imagination. Any resemblance to actual people, alive or dead, business establishments, locales, or events is entirely coincidental.
Any reference to real events, businesses, or organisations is intended to give the fiction a sense of realism and authenticity.

All rights reserved. No part of this publication may be reproduced, stored in a retrieval system, or transmitted by any means-electronic, mechanical, photographic (photocopying,) recording or otherwise- without prior permission in writing from the author.

WHEN ANGELS FEAST

By
Kevin Bailey

PROLOGUE

The night descended on the small Worcestershire market town of Tenbury Wells, like a blanket falling gracefully onto a bed.

At a secluded spot away from the centre of town and the prying eyes of the law, a group of black-suited minders surrounded a small man who was watching children playing. He was dressed in the attire of a country gentleman, wearing a tweed jacket which overlaid a pressed cotton white shirt and a green striped tie. Smouldering in his mouth was a large cigar that dropped ash onto his green trousers and brown shoes.

Before long, one of the minders whispered in to his boss's ear, informing him a younger man in a smart black suit and red tie was approaching. Taking out the cigar, he ordered, "Let him through." He returned the cigar to his mouth, watching as this visitor arrived, and sat down beside him.

The two men sat silently for a while, until the older statesmen turned to his associate who was studying his iPad. Returning his attention to the fast-flowing River Teme in the distance, the statesman remarked. "I always think of this river like our organization, speeding quickly towards its destiny." He turned and looked at his younger companion. "What have you to report?"

The junior counterpart danced his hands over the device, and then spoke with a posh accent. "It would seem London have sent us a copper who does things by the book. I mean, look at this." He showed the cigar smoking man the information on his screen. "In the last month alone, his department has arrested two of our clients and the others up at the house are worried that they will be next."

Taking a couple more puffs on his cigar, the elder man simply replied, "Then, we add him to the payroll."

His younger associate shook his head. "The officer is incorruptible."

The older man pulled out a hip flask and passed it to his compatriot who took a small swig, the liquid burning his throat. "Any person can be brought for the right price," the middle aged man said, continuing to look at the water. "We just have to find his price."

Passing the hipflask back, the other man stated. "You know I would usually agree, but this man doesn't really need to be a copper. He is sitting on a small fortune, and is heir to a large family estate on the outskirts of Chelmesbury."

The older man took a large swig, almost consuming all of the contents of the flask, and replaced it back inside his jacket. Once again, the two men were silent. The only sound was the fast-flowing water and the children playing.

Looking towards his mentor, the younger man could see the veins in the elder man's neck rising, and he watched as his superior took another couple of puffs. "How could they be so fucking stupid," he said angrily as he threw the cigar on the floor, and stamping on it with his leather boot. "After all the hard work I have done for them! This is how I am treated? It's a bloody disgrace." The younger man tried to calm him down, but was hushed up. "I asked them for a copper, one who would turn a blind eye to our affairs, not someone who would go around arresting our clients." He walked to one of his minders. "Contact the hub," he looked over at his companion. "It is time we knocked London off their fucking perch."

The minder spoke into his Bluetooth earpiece, and a female voice erupted from the speakers.

"Ask our father what he would like us to do?" The minder relayed the question to the elder statesman who seemed lost in his anger.

"Tell her I want to know why they have done this to me?" He took out the hip flask once more and drank the remaining liquid straight back. "I think it's about time we became the number one crime syndicate in this country."

His companion looked at him with admiration. "So what do you think we should do about this detective?"

The older man smiled. "You're to keep him under surveillance, but if he steps out of line, we…" He placed his finger on his throat and pretended to slit it. "…get the idea?"

The younger man nodded. "I wouldn't worry too much about him at the moment. I understand from our contact at the station there may be someone there who we could corrupt." He handed over the iPad, and the elder man smiled at the picture on the screen. "Let's just say things haven't been going to well for them." He received the device back and was given his orders.

"The planning, I'll leave to you," the older gentleman said, lighting a new cigar. "For now." He took another drag. "And this other officer," he waved his hands, "we will keep them in mind."

The younger man took a series of deep breaths. "I don't want to seem like I am treading on your toes, but this matter of taking over the country, let us not be too hasty." He tried not to look at the other man. "Plans you set in motion are afoot, which I'm sure will keep London and all our other friends quite busy for a while."

The elder man stood up. "Agreed. I want this to be a shrine to my brilliance. Make sure it comes to fruition."

The younger man nodded. "It will. Our contact hasn't let us down before. He has discovered the perfect place."

The elder statesman smiled and stood up as one of his grandchildren ran up and handed him a daisy, which he took with gratitude. "Thank you, sweetheart," he said, and the child ran back to play. He turned and showed his associate the gift. "These children are our future. They must be moulded to our way of thinking, but for now. They're young and innocent." He smiled warmly at his companion.

The younger man stood. "Until they grow up, Father." With those final words, he turned and walked away, leaving the older man to enjoy his time with his grandchildren.

***

Several miles away in Chelmesbury, a crimson moon shone brightly in the night sky, illuminating the historic market square and imposing castle ruin. In the distance, the ancient stone church of St Bartholomew seemed to be the only structure in the vicinity not encased in the radiant eerie light, as if some unseen force had encircled the building, protecting those inside.

It was from the main door of the large sanctuary to God the church warden Richard Jackson, or Rick as he was affectionately known, emerged into the unprotected glare. Closing the large oak door behind him, he pulled his long blue coat together, and headed quickly towards the Dog and Duck Pub, staying hidden in the shadows as if fearing the red light may take him to an evil place.

As Rick neared the opening that would take him down into the old drinking establishment, he heard the sound of rustling behind him. He slowly turned around and found nothing, apart from several shadowy figures in the distance going about their wares. He felt a shiver run down his spine. The night was so eerie, and he turned back toward the black and white building in his eyesight, savouring the idea of a hot meal and a nice pint or two. It was then he felt it.

At first, Rick thought something had bitten him in the arm, and was still there sucking the blood from his veins. So, he tried to push whatever it was away, but found nothing. Squinting to see anything on his arm, he spotted a red puncture wound, and began to feel strange. His left side drooped, and he began to stumble around as if drunk.

Rick suddenly felt two strong arms catch him from falling. Before he had chance to thank the person, he fell unconscious, and was dragged away.

Slowly and groggily, Rick opened his eyes. Where was he, and how had he got here? He didn't know, and squinted trying to see anything, but apart from something moving up and down near him there was nothing. The only sound he could hear was heavy breathing, which seemed to be emanating from somewhere in the dark

As his eyes got accustomed to the dark, he realised that what was moving in front of his eyes was the unmistakable image of two beautiful breasts, bobbing around in the dark. With his sweating hands, he could feel the flesh of a woman, and as he moved down the silky skin, she groaned loudly. The women became more rigorous, and he could feel himself thrusting harder and deeper inside of her. Rick's hands moved up and caressed those wonderful breasts, grabbing and cradling them.

Her breathing became ecstatic, and she began moving harder up and down on top of him. The feelings coming from his groin were ones of sheer satisfaction, and he knew he wouldn't be long. His breathing intensified, but to stop his pleasure, she smacked him across the face.

"Don't you dare, if you want to live," she ordered, punching him again and again in the face. He closed his bludgeoned eyes and concentrated harder than he had ever done before.

Her movement increased as did the strength of the women's thrusts on his body. It became quite painful, and as he cried out in agony, she screamed out in pleasure. Finally, she released a scream, which could have shattered glass within a mile radius.

She softly and quickly got off, and moved away without saying anything. She wouldn't even allow him to finish. Even though Rick was in pain, he was also feeling a little frustrated. He begged into the darkness for her to come back, but the place became quiet, still.

Suddenly, as if by magic, the lights came on, and he squinted to look around. His realised he was in some form of basement, lying naked on a fold up bed. The room felt cold and uninviting. The walls were grey and bare, apart from frenzied patches of what looked like red paint.
When his eyes finally got used to the light, he surveyed his location, but his gaze was drawn to one of the corners, and an object hanging down from what appeared to be a meat hook. Sheer terror ran through every part of his body as he realised what he had discovered. It was the torso of a man, in all his glory, blood trickling from a hidden wound down the naked grey flesh and into a shabby bucket on the floor.

Feeling nauseous, Rick quickly looked away. In his heart, he knew full well he was going to end up on the same meat hook. His only chance of survival was to scream as loud as he could, hoping, praying some passer-by would call for help, and he would be saved.

But that hope was short-lived, because as soon as he began screaming, the wailing sound from his mouth was silenced by the sound of a sharp blade quickly slicing through his neck.

WHEN ANGELS FEAST

By
Kevin Bailey

CHAPTER ONE

Brendon Evans and his best friend, Elizabeth Cordon, walked casually away from Brendon's home in the small village of Bottly. Along the path, they could see the red brick public-house, 'The Old Tin Cutter,' and decided to go for a drink.

It was a relaxing Sunday jaunt, giving them time to talk about life, as well as taking in their picturesque surroundings. They laughed together at memories of time spent in the fields and trees. Elizabeth looked over the hedge to an old motte and bailey castle.

"I remember me and you playing knights up there." She paused. "Wasn't I Guinevere, and you were Arthur?"

Brendon nodded. "We used to have so much fun, Lizzie." He looked over to the mound. "Do you wish we were still those two children? Life was so much easier then."

She nodded and replied, "Sometimes." The two friends walked down the street arm-in-arm.

As people passed the pair, they assumed they were any other couple. They had been friends since childhood, the joy of living next door to each other. When they grew up, they'd tried dating, but to them, it had seemed wrong. So they made a pact to stay firm friends; a pact they had never broken.

Elizabeth had begun dating a copper called Steve, and as they neared their destination, Brendon was giving her advice. "Just take each day as it comes, babe, and I'm sure if he is the right one, it will work out fine." This seemed to cheer her up somewhat.

"I hope he is, hun." She paused before continuing, "He's a perfect man and a gentleman."

Brendon smiled, but as they walked down the country lane, the smiles were wiped off their faces by a large object in a ditch. At first, Brendon thought it was rubbish dumped there by some litter lout.

"Bastards! Why can't they take their rubbish to the tip like the rest of…" But as they got closer, they realised it was a more gruesome object.

Emanating from an old blanket was blonde hair, matted and dirty. Brendan went a little closer, and with both hands shaking, slowly lifted the material. What he found was a female, her head face-down to the earth.

Elizabeth watched the scene unfold, and seeing the dead women, she let out a blood-curdling scream.

From every house in the village, people flocked to their location, wondering what was going on.

***

Detective Sergeant Miranda Day sat at her desk in a smart grey trouser suit with a cream blouse. In her hands was a buddle of paperwork she would need for a court hearing. Chelmesbury's Criminal Investigation Department had been helping the Serious Crimes Squad, and they had arrested two, long term criminals. Both teams knew they had information leading to the organization they worked for, but both suspects had kept quiet.

As Miranda was reading the statements, preparing for any questions she may be asked to answer, the phone rang on her desk disturbing her thoughts. Pushing her long blonde hair away from her ear, she picked it up. "Day." She listened to the operator, and using the pencil and notebook on her desk, she began to write down the particulars. She thanked the operator, and after taking a couple of gulps, she dialled her boss's number.

***

Detective Chief Inspector Simon Eliote drove the black Saab 95 Turbo down the dismal back roads towards the station. He'd had the car for years. It was really time for it to go, but Eliote loved it. It was the only reminder of his old life, and he knew how to handle her around corners. Today was no exception.

But as he swung the car around a large, white Mercedes van parked delivering bathrooms, his thoughts were not on the road, but on the twenty-four word warning he had received from Charlotte:

"I must warn you, Chief Inspector, don't trust those around you, because one will betray you, and that betrayal will lead to your death."

It kept going around in his head, almost burning his mind, in addition to all the reports and statistics Superintendent Dorothy Brightly had bestowed upon him since the 'Deathly Angel' case. The culmination of both had kept him away from the rest of CID.

If what Charlotte had said was true, it was perhaps better he stayed away from the members of CID and bury himself in all the 'paperwork' he was going through.

His thoughts were disturbed by his iPhone ringing, and after contemplating whether to answer it, he took out a Bluetooth headset. "Eliote," he almost snapped, and heard the soft voice of his sergeant.

"Sorry to bother you, Gov, but a body has been found in a ditch. Officers who were first at the scene wondered…"

Eliote butted in. "…Why aren't they dealing with it?"

"Well it's an unexplained death, Gov." She became sarcastic. "Our department."

Eliote sighed. "Yeah, so?"

Day had been getting annoyed at Eliote's lack of enthusiasm to a job she loved, but he was still her superior. So after taking a couple of deep breaths, she replied, "They just wondered if we could send someone to take a look."

Her response was met with silence, before Eliote spoke again. "Can't you deal with this, Sergeant?"

The disrespect in Day's voice was evident. "No, Gov, I am at court all day."

Eliote cursed under his breath. "Okay, send the details to my phone!" he snapped bluntly.

Eliote drove the black Saab hard to the crime scene, and finally came to a violent stop, just in front of the tape. The car roared and fell silent. He got out, onlookers watched him. After locking the car, he approached a tall, imposing officer. "Morning, Potter."

The officer nodded at Eliote. "You should be more careful at the way you drive, Gov. One day, somebody could get hurt."

Eliote pushed the criticism away and looked over at the white tent which had been set up over the ditch. "Who's here from CID? I never did ask Day."

The tall officer sighed and pointed to Philip Pickington, who had grown a black goatee since they had last worked together. "Thanks, Potter." Eliote patted the officer on the back and approached the CID officer, who was eating a chocolate bar.

"Gov," he said, wiping the chocolate from around his mouth and the beard.

"No breakfast this morning, Constable?"

Pickington shock his head. "No, Gov. I was up most of the night with the little nipper."

Eliote sort of smiled, remembering the times well. "So, what have we got?"

Pickington pulled out an iPad and pressed notes. "Young women and two children found…"

Eliote butted in. "…There are two children as well?"

Pickington nodded as the two officers approached the tent. "Yeah, Gov."

Eliote beckoned him to carry on with his report.

"Yeah, em," he looked at the iPad and continued to read his notes. "They were found by a Mr. Brendan Evans and his friend, Elizabeth Cordon." He pointed at a squad car, and Eliote could see a man in the back seat.

"Go on," Eliote ordered.

"They were out for a walk to a local public house, when they made the gruesome discovery. Miss Cordon was in hysterics, and had to be sedated and taken to hospital. We have, at present, no ID on the victims."

"Well, let's go and take a look shall we Constable?" Pickington nodded.

When they got to the entrance to the tent, a female forensics officer handed the two detectives some protective clothing. After they had got changed, they entered the tent.

Doctors Richard Strong and Penny Hardcastle were crouched down on the floor examining the bodies when the two officers entered. Strong stood up and removed his mask, revealing the ginger handlebar moustache.
"I'm sorry for you, Simon." He seemed remorseful. "This may bring back sad memories of the past."

Eliote sort of smiled. "Let's just get on with it, shall we, Doctor!" he ordered bluntly.

Strong nodded. "Okay, no problem." He looked over at the bodies. "At this moment, I cannot see any external injuries, but a thorough examination will be carried out at the lab. All I can say is, she has been here all night."

Pickington looked up from the iPad and asked. "What makes you think that, Doc?"

Strong looked at him and rubbed his ginger moustache. "The temperature fell well below freezing last night. Also, when we got here, her body was starting to thaw out. The children are stuck to her."

Eliote walked up to the bodies. "Poor bugger. I wonder why she was out with her children all night. Maybe she was running from someone?" He looked at Pickington first, who shrugged his shoulders and then at the doctor. "Could she have been dumped here?"

Penny who had been listening, answered. "Sorry to butt in Doctor." She looked at the detectives. "I don't think so, Chief Inspector. We have found a small blanket." She showed the flower coated item. "It wouldn't have kept them warm."

Eliote watched a photographer take some stills of the blanket. "Anything else, Strong?"

The doctor shook his head. "Nothing else Simon. As I said before, we will know more when I do the post mortem and find out how they died."

Eliote nodded. "Okay. Full report ASAP." He turned, and the two detectives left the tent.

Walking from the tent to the squad car, Eliote prepared himself to interview the witness. Pickington followed behind, his iPad in hand. When they got to the car, the officer who was sat in the back got out to allow Eliote to sit next to Brendon. "Hi, I am Detective Chief Inspector Simon Eliote and this is my colleague, Detective Constable Philip Pickington. I understand you found the body?"

Brendon sort of smiled. "It's not something I want to discover again, Chief Inspector." Eliote would have to agree with him there. "I'm just in shock. When I close my eyes, I can see them lying there." He paused, before stuttering, "How did they die?"

Eliote looked sombrely at him. "We plan to discover that, sir. I know it's a long shot, but do you recognize the women?"

Brendon shook his head. "Sorry, I don't. I tend to keep myself to myself." He looked into the detective's eyes. "You see, Chief Inspector, I don't make friends easily."

Eliote knew the feeling well. "It was just a thought." He got out of the backseat and glanced back to Brendon. "I'll get someone to take you home."

Brendon nodded. "Thank you!" The two officers left the vehicle.

When the detectives returned to CID later on the day, Eliote made his first trip to the observation room in months. He had almost left the department to run itself. As the room filled up with members of CID, he began placing the pictures he had received from Strong onto the lectern and scanned them onto the computer. He then turned and looked at the officers, their eyes fixed on him.

"Right, listen up, people." Eliote directed their attention to the large screen, and pointed at the women and her two children. "Three things I want to know. One: who is this woman; two: what was she doing here in a ditch; and finally, why hasn't anyone registered that she is missing." He peered around at the faces staring back at him. Some had written notes. "I want you to do door-to-door, and circulate that picture. Somebody out there knows who she is." There was chattering coming from the group of officers.

Eliote turned his attention to Detective Sergeant Day. "Day, get onto the rags, see if they can put an article in their papers about an unknown women being found dead." She nodded, and he continued, "Don't say anything at the moment about the children." Eliote turned back to address the gathered officers. "Okay, to work, people. If you need me, I'll be in my…"

Just then, the door to the observation room opened, and in walked Superintendent Brightly. "Ah, Chief Inspector, may I have a word with you, please?" she ordered, walking out of the room. All the team watched as Eliote reluctantly made his way to Brightly's office, his imaginary tail between his legs.

Once they were in the confines of her office, the Superintendent exploded, all her anger vented at him. "WHAT THE HELL IS WRONG WITH YOU, CHIEF INSPECTOR?" Eliote just shrugged, like a school boy being told off by a headmaster. "Since Frashier was seconded to the Firearms Unit, you have been distant with your team. They are all but running themselves! This makes me wonder why I have a department head at all!" She paused, sitting down at her desk with a serious expression. "Your team needs you to show them the way. Look what happened last month.

You had Day and Pickington investigating a murder enquiry, while you hid away in your office!"

Now, it was Eliote's turn to get angry. "With all due respect, ma'am, I knew Sergeant Day could handle the case, and I haven't been 'hiding away in my office,' as you say. I have been looking through statistics and crime sheets, trying to balance the bloody budget you gave me!" Eliote took a breath, trying to compose himself. "If I had more admin assistants, I wouldn't be in my office as much. I would be out in the field, doing the job I was paid to do!"

Brightly threw him a folder, and he looked at the title. 'Station Budgets.' "I can't give you the things you need, or want. The whole force has had to deal with these austerity cuts from the government. I have had to lay off ten auxiliary staff this month alone, but still find the staff to keep this station running." She snatched the folder back from his outstretched hand. "You're just going to have to get on with what you have, and lump it."

"Lump it?" he remarked angrily. "You're sounding like a ruddy politician, more interested in budgets and costs than what we are paid for. To hell with you, and your bloody budgets! We are just lucky we haven't got a murder investigation on, or we wouldn't have the money to deal with it!"

Brightly glared at him. "I don't like your insubordination, Chief Inspector…"

"…And I don't like the way the service is run," he snapped back.

"We are both police officers, Chief Inspector. We do our jobs to the best of our abilities. Maybe you should go home for a few days, and evaluate your future with the force. Not all of us have rich backgrounds to fall back on." As soon as Brightly had said it, she regretted her words.

Eliote turned and stormed out of the office, slamming the door behind him, the force nearly breaking the frame. "Shit." Brightly cursed under her breath. A part of her wanted to run after him, but she knew the best way to deal with angry people was to let them calm down.

Eliote opened his office door, grabbed his coat and briefcase, and began to head out of CID. Day ran after him, and was about to ask him something, when he spun and snapped at her.

"Deal with it yourself, Sergeant, or go and ask the Budget Queen in there!" He gestured towards Brightly's office. Day was left in shock at his outburst, and watched as he walked out of CID.

Eliote stormed out of the building, just as a little middle-aged lady walked up to the desk and rang the bell.

The officer on duty approached the desk. "Hello there, how can I help you?" The lady handed him a photograph, and the officer examined it. "Who is this?"

"It's my son, Rick. I've not seen him for days."

The officer placed the photo onto the desk, and then took out his notebook and pencil. "How long has he been missing?"

"About a week," she replied, and began sobbing. "I am so worried something bad has happened to him."

The officer smiled reassuringly. "Don't worry. I'll take down some particulars, and then I'll get someone to come and talk with you."

The woman did her best to return the smile through the tears. "Thank you," she said.

***

Blood boiling in anger, Eliote approached his car, banging the roof with his fist. Breathing heavily, he turned in time to see a grey BMW pull into the lot, and park next to his Saab. Throwing the briefcase and coat onto the backseat, Eliote saw his number two get out of the car and look over.

"Gov, are you alright?"

Eliote didn't answer, but simply jumped into the front seat and drove off.

***

Detective Inspector William Frashier watched him leave with bemusement. After locking his car, he walked into the station, and headed for CID a slight smile on his face. Was it his time to take over the unit?

Still a little dumbfounded by Eliote's actions, he opened the door to CID, and found Sergeant Day still stood looking at the door in shock.

Seeing him made her a little happier. "Hey, I thought you had been seconded to the Firearms Unit?"

Frashier nodded. "I was, but Brightly thought Eliote needed help." He turned and looked at the door. "And from what I just witnessed in the car park, I think he does." Frashier said placing his blue trench coat on a coat peg and returned to Day, now seated back at her desk. "What's wrong with him?"

"Him and Brightly had a little lovers tiff." She smirked. "And I think she has sent him home to get his head straight!"

"Why?"

Day looked solemnly at him. "Where do I start?"

Frashier sat down on the top of an empty desk. "Start at the beginning."

"Okay," she said, getting comfy. "It began when the Gov was informed the guy who killed his wife is appealing against his conviction and jail term."

"Well, that would piss a lot of people off," Frashier remarked.

Day continued, "And then there is the case against Mathew Davies!"

"What, the 'Deathly Angel'?" Frashier asked. "I thought that case was home and dry. The bloke admitted to it."

Day nodded. "So did the Chief Inspector, but Mathew's defence lawyer says his client was forced into admitting the crimes."

Frashier was about to respond, when something on a white board on the wall above Day's desk made him stop. "What's that up here for?" he queried, pointing at an A4 sized photo.

Day looked up at the image. "That's our main case at the moment. An unexplained death." Frashier was fixated on the photo. Something about the women looked familiar. Day continued with her report. "They were found dead in a ditch. I guess since Eliote's gone, it means you're in charge, Gov!"

Frashier continued to stare intently at the photo. "Where is the body now?" he demanded.

Day answered quickly. "It's down in the lab." Before Day could say any more, Frashier got up and strode out of the unit.

WHEN ANGELS FEAST
By
Kevin Bailey

CHAPTER TWO

Frashier walked into the disinfectant-smelling, sterile lab, making his way to Strong's office. Upon entering, he found Richard examining some slides. Peering up at Frashier, Strong smiled warmly at his friend.

"Hello! I didn't think I would see you in here for a while. It's not the 28th yet, is it?"

Frashier peered around the room, eyes landing on the fridges. "Em, no. Where are the bodies from the family found in the ditch?"

Strong walked out to a cold, protected area where several large metal tables were in a row. On three of the tables were bodies with white sheets over the top. Strong pointed at them. "You're a little early for the post mortem. I was going to do it when Penny gets back. Just getting a few things ready."

Frashier put on some surgical gloves and lifted the sheet over the woman. "Okay." As he stared down at the woman's cold features, Frashier was overcome with sadness.

Strong walked up to him. "I understand they haven't been identified yet, but I'm sure it won't be…"

Frashier let out an extended sigh. "This was Jane Lock, and the two children are…" he paused, holding back the emotions, "Eve and Amy."

Strong looked at Frashier and spotted a small tear trickle down his friend's cheek. "Was?"

Frashier leaned against the table for support and nodded. "Yeah, she married a lad called Alexander Boyd." He smiled, remembering his old friend in arms. "Alex Boyd was a bit of a jack the lad. He had moved from Birmingham to Shrewsbury in my last year of secondary school, and we hit it off. We went everywhere together." He laughed slightly. "Our teachers and parents called us the 'Troublesome Twins.' We sort of drifted apart after we left school, especially as I went off to be a copper." Frashier stopped and stared at the women.

Strong could sense seeing Jane was upsetting, so he grabbed the sheet from his friend, re-covered the body, and beckoned the detective into his office. Once there, the doctor opened a filing cabinet and pulled out a bottle of Teacher's whisky, pouring some into a cup. "This is, of course, for medicinal purposes only." He passed the cup to Frashier. "I don't want DCI Eliote throwing us off another crime scene." Strong slightly smiled, but Frashier just took it and sat down on a chair. Strong sat opposite, and the men consumed their drinks in silence.

***

Even though it was spring, a strong wind howled through the giant structure erected in the market square. It was put in place for the annual music show, now in its fifth year. The people behind the scenes wanted this show to be one of the best, an event that would never be forgotten.

Nicolas Waite walked past the structure and stopped to admire the view. Nick was approximately thirty-five years of age, with a receding hair line. His boyish good looks were still visible though, and his blue eyes had most women blushing when he looked at them. He also had a flare for getting himself into trouble, and, on this night, it was no different.

"Can you move out of the way, Sir? This area is off limits." A security guard observed him coldly.

"Hey, mate, I'm only looking at it. It's not as if I am going to take it to pieces."

The security guard frowned at him. "Are you being funny, Sir?"

This seemed to trigger something in Nick. "Why, what you going to do about it?"

The security guard walked up to him, looked into the blue eyes, and coldly replied, "Well, if you are being funny, then I'm going to drag you away from prying eyes and break every bone in your body. So, go on, piss off."

Nicky smirked and looked back at his oppressor. With a quick movement, he kneed the guard in the groin, who winced in pain and fell to the floor holding his sensitive area. Nicky looked around, and seeing that no one was in the vicinity, he kicked the guard in the head. The guard fell back onto the ground, blood gushed from the open head wound. Nicky spat at the guard and briskly walked away.

***

Frashier had finished his drink and looked over at Strong. "Thanks."

The doctor smiled. "No problem, isn't that what friends are for?" Frashier stared into space. Strong placed his own cup on the desk and asked, "You were telling me about Alex Boyd?"

Frashier nodded. "I hadn't heard anything of him for years. Then, my mother redirected a letter that she had received from him. He had met the deceased at college. She had also gone to the same school as us. They were planning on getting married, and were moving down to London to run one of his dad's, Jim's, plumbing shops." Frashier paused in thought. "That was the last thing I heard about him, until I bumped into his dad last year. He told me Alex, his wife Jane, and his grandchildren, Eve and Amy, had returned. Jim had finally retired, and Alex was now coming to run the whole business. I was going to arrange to meet up, but I never got around to it."

Strong looked at him. "Maybe we should let Eliote know, and have you removed from the case?"

Frashier regarded the doctor with a cold expression. "No, I think he has too much on his plate at the moment, especially as he has just been sent home."

Strong looked shocked. "Sent home?"

Frashier nodded. "Yep." After a moment, he stood up and returned to the tables, looking at the white sheets. "How did they die?"

The doctor looked over at the tables. "Well, my first impressions are hyperthermia."

Frashier stared at Jane, hidden from view on the examination table, and tried not to think about his friend cutting into her. Feeling a little nauseous, he turned and looked over at the Doctor. "Be gentle with her, old friend, she meant a lot to me, and when you've finished, let me know." Strong patted him on the shoulder and then watched as he left the morgue.

After first stopping at the toilet to freshen up, Frashier headed back into the heart of CID, where he moved the photograph above Day's desk to the large board which overlooked all the room. Taking out a marker pen, he hastily scrawled underneath the picture:

-Jane *Boyd and Eve and Amy Boyd*-

He placed the pen on a ledge and looked at the names.

Day saw what he was doing and walked over. "You okay, Gov?" Frashier saw her approach and replied simply with a nod. "How did you find out who they were?" she asked.

Frashier merely touched his nose and sarcastically quipped, "I have my sources!"

Day looked at him with a beady eye. "Let me know who they are. I wouldn't mind having them working for me." She looked at the names. "You want me to find out some info on her?" She pointed at the picture of Jane, but Frashier shook his head.

"There is no need; I already have all the info I need." Before Day could say anything else, Frashier was gone.

***

The next morning, Nicolas Waite sat in his car at a set of traffic lights. Workers were digging up the road, one of them was using a jack-hammer to dig through the concrete. A cream-coloured Jaguar XJS pulled up alongside him, and the engine roared. Nick turned and looked at the car, admiring it.

He tried to look in through the window to say 'nice car,' but couldn't because the car had tinted glass. Before the lights changed to green, the window opened, and he could see a pair of leather-gloved hands. Nick was shocked to discover tightly gripped in the hands was a silenced pistol, and it was aimed at him.

As the worker used the jack-hammer once again, Nicolas tried to protest, and mouthed, "No!" The driver ignored the pleading and pulled the trigger, shooting the scared man five times before speeding away into the town.

***

In a quiet and peaceful cemetery, located in the principal London borough town of Hounslow, a black marble gravestone emerged from the mist, like a beacon of hope to all those lost souls traversing the living world. All around the place spring was descending, and the birds began to sing their morning chorus, as the warm sun began to disperse the mist. Walking towards the black headstone was the ghostly figure of a tall, skinny man wearing a long black coat and carrying a bouquet of fresh flowers, the dew still attached to the rose petals.

A little worse for wear, Eliote placed the roses onto the mounded earth and looked up at the gold letters, which were burnt into his memory.
Crouching down on the wet grass, Eliote fitted three of the red flowers into the slots beneath the stone. As he did, a tear trickled down his cheek. He took out a tissue from his coat and wiped the tear away, before touching the surface of the grave.

"I told you I would be back. Can't get away from me that easily," he said to his beloved family. "Thought I would tell you how my life has been without you." He started to recount his last investigation and his argument with Brightly. "I am thinking of giving up the service, and becoming a hermit. Maybe write a book on my family's history." He bowed his head. "Wouldn't that be fun?"

As Eliote talked to his family, he didn't realise he was being watched by a figure on the Hanworth road. A set of clippers were perched on top of the hedge. A man was looking over it at him through binoculars, whilst writing down what Eliote was doing and saying.

Back at the grave, Simon had finished his recounting and touched the cold stone once more. "I had better get back to Chelmesbury, settle my debts, and find something else to do with my life." Simon touched the grass and smiled at the names on the stone. "I just don't want to go, but I know I must." He got up and solemnly walked back to the Saab. After getting in, he took a last glance at the grave and drove away, passing a man cutting a hedge, beginning the long drive back to Chelmesbury.

The shadowy figure watched the car disappear into the distance, and then, replacing the clippers and binoculars into a bag, walked towards the stone, he laid one red rose on to the soil before walking to an awaiting black Mercedes. The back door closed, and it drove away.

***

Back at his modest apartment in Chelmesbury, Frashier had been up all night, attempting to find a number for Jane's husband, Alexander Boyd. He'd had little luck, as each person he contacted did not seem to have one. After having a little breakfast, Frashier gave up. He got dressed, headed to his garage, started his BMW, and headed for Glayton.

Upon arriving at Glayton Plumbing, Bathrooms, and Heating Supplies, Frashier observed several company vans parked outside the large, two-storey building. The bottom level was occupied by the main shop, whilst the top floor housed a bathroom showroom. Frashier parked his car alongside the building, and headed into the main shop. The employees regarded him carefully, probably thinking he was an unknown sales rep.

At the counter, a tall man with silver-streaked, black hair was laughing in a contagious way, and Frashier smiled. After finishing laughing with his co-workers, the man looked up at the detective. "Can I help you, sir?"

Frashier took out his warrant card, showing it to the man who gulped when he saw the West Mercia Constabulary Insignia, in addition to the face, name and rank of the man stood in front of him. "How can I help you, Officer?"

"I'm looking for Alexander Boyd."

The man answered, "Unfortunately, Alex isn't here at the moment."

Frashier looked a little gutted. "It is important I speak with him."

The man nodded and asked the detective to wait for a second, disappearing through a door. Frashier could see him through a window into a large office, talking with another man with glasses. The other man picked up the phone, speaking hurriedly into the receiver. Jotting down some information on a piece of paper, he handed it back to his colleague, who returned to Frashier.

"Sorry for the delay, Alex has authorized us to give you his address."

Frashier thanked the man and left, heading for his BMW. He touched a control on his dashboard and a Sat-Nav appeared. Typing in the address, Frashier drove away.

***

Brightly had just entered her office when the call came in for the shooting in the town. She picked up her internal line and dialled CID.

"Day."

Brightly spoke commandingly, "Sergeant, is DI Frashier down there?"

"No, ma'am. He's investigating the unexplained death. Seems he has a lead."

Brightly smiled feeling happy she had at least done something right by bringing Frashier back to CID. She returned her attention to Day. "Right then Sergeant. I want you to take Pickington and get to the town centre. Seems a man has been shot in his car."

"You want me to start the investigation until either Frashier or Eliote returns?"

With a sense of pride, Brightly ordered, "No, I want you to lead this. I was impressed with the way you dealt with that murder enquiry last month."

Brightly could hear the pleasure in Day's tone. "Thank you, ma'am." The line went dead. Brightly replaced the receiver, and looked out towards the round CID building and watched as Day grabbed her long red leather coat. With Pickington in tow like a stray dog, she headed out of the building and walked hurriedly towards Day's silver Vectra. She could see Day beaming with pride, and this made the Superintendent extremely happy.

Returning to her desk and the mountain of files, she sighed and then sadly quipped, "No rest for me." Opening one of the files, she began reading its content.

***

When Day and Pickington arrived at the scene, it had been taped off, and there were several police vehicles and an ambulance. Potter walked towards them, and Day spoke up. "What've we got, Sergeant?"

The officer looked at his notebook. "Male, approximately thirty-five years of age. Shot five times in the head at close range."

The two officers walked towards the white tent, which had been erected around a grey Vauxhall Nova. Day looked around the site, and saw the men who had been working being interviewed by officers. One of them looked rather annoyed at the interruption. It was obvious to Day he must have been the foreman of the work crew.

"Good morning, Sergeant Day, Constable Pickington." Day glanced back over at the suited pathologist, who was beckoning the two of them to enter the tent. When they did, Strong bent over to look into the car. "As Potter has no doubt told you, the victim was shot five times in the head. The last bullet went straight through his head and skull, and has imbedded itself into the seat of the car." He paused to show the hole in the seat.

"What kind of calibre weapon could do this type of damage?" Pickington asked.

Strong shrugged his shoulders and looked over at Penny. "My esteemed colleague is the gun expert, what do you think?"

Penny was examining the entrance wound, "Looks to me like it came from a handgun, maybe a Berretta. I am guessing it may have had a silencer, or some form of quieting device fitted. We are in a well-populated town."

Pickington nodded, but Day remarked, "I don't think it needed a silencer on, Doctor. The killer could have pulled the trigger whilst they were digging up the road with those jack-hammers." She pointed at the equipment. "What with health and safety these days, the workers would have no doubt been wearing ear protection, and wouldn't have heard the shots."

Pickington was typing the conversation into his electronic device, as Day bent down and looked into the car's interior. It was a mess.

She noted to Pickington that the seat had been coated in blood, and parts of the man's face were missing. She looked up as a member of Strong's team was sorting out the mess and placing evidence into plastic bags. Day was about to get up, when she noticed a brown leather wallet. Protruding from it was a ticket for a night club. After putting on a glove, she picked it up and handed it to Strong, who carefully opened it to reveal its contents.

Seeing the driving licence, he took it from its protective sleeve and handed it to Day, who scrutinized the picture. The dark eyes looked up at her from the licence, as if introducing himself. "This identifies the victim as one Nicolas Waite of Newlands Gardens, Chelmesbury." She handed the license back to Strong. He placed it into an evidence bag. Then, he handed both the wallet and the licence over to Pickington, who was examining the ticket.

"Thanks. These should give us something to go on."

Day went to walk out of the tent, "I'll need your report on my desk, as soon as possible."

The doctor smiled warmly at Day. "Just like the others do." Strong shot the detective an intense stare. "You have come a long way from one of those officers who would have asked those above them for advice."

Day stopped and smiled back. "I grew up, Doctor. I now stand on my own two feet." She beckoned Pickington outside. "Come on, Constable. We have to inform the family." Pickington nodded, and the two officers departed the crime scene.

***

Frashier parked his car outside the Edwardian townhouse. It was in what people would call the 'posh' area of town, and its bay windows made it look quite imposing. He looked at the piece of paper which he had received from Alex's co-worker, and after checking to see if it was the right place, he got out of the BMW. Walking up to the fence, Frashier opened the gate and walked up to the main door. A buzzer was attached to the side, and he rang the bell.

After a while, a small, balding, muscular man in a white tracksuit with a gold chain and a Rolex watch answered, and he looked at Frashier who showed his warrant card. "Ah, Officer…" He stopped, and gave Frashier the once over, grinning as he recognized his old friend. "Blimey, if it isn't me old scallywag, 'Willy' Frashier!" The two men shook hands. "Please come in." He beckoned Frashier through the door and into a large, open-plan sitting area.

Frashier was about to sit down when he heard noises coming from upstairs. A very attractive big bosomed woman, with flowing black hair seemed to glide down the stairs, a towel protecting her modesty.

"Oh, I am so sorry, Mr. Boyd," she said in a Russian accent. "I didn't realize you had a guest!" She paused, placing her hand on her front, and gestured back up the stairs. "I'll go and get dressed, and make you some tea."

Alex smiled. "No rush, Tatyana, we haven't seen each other for…" He looked over at Frashier. "How long?"

Frashier smiled and answered quickly, "A while."

Alex winked, and Frashier sat down. "So, what brings you to my door? Is there another one of those damn reunions coming up?"

Frashier shook his head. "It's purely a business matter."

Alex nodded and pointed at the bulging pocket that contained Frashier's wallet. "Yeah, I never thought you'd be a copper. Always thought you'd do other things."

Frashier glanced around the lavishly decorated room. "Things, and people, change I'm afraid." He looked back at Alex. "I see you haven't done too badly for yourself. I never thought I would see you in a place like this, maybe an apartment."

Alex surveyed the room for himself. "It is merely a shell, Willy." Frashier cringed at the old name. "Somewhere to live. Besides, I've been there, and done that. Thought it was time for a change, a place to bring up my family away from the hustle and bustle of city…life." Alex quickly observed the saddened look in Frashier's eyes. "What's wrong, and why are you here?" he cautiously questioned.

Frashier gulped. This was the one part of the job he had always hated; letting a loved one know of a death. He had always tried to prepare himself physically for the news he must bring, but no matter how hard he tried, it was still painful. "Alex, there is no easy way of saying this, so here goes." He took a deep breath. "We've found Jane and the kids, and, unfortunately, they're all dead."

***

WHEN ANGELS FEAST

By
Kevin Bailey

CHAPTER THREE

Pickington turned the Vectra into Newlands Gardens. It was a fairly modern estate, which had been recently developed and built by Chelmesbury's new housing association, in connection with a local businesses and the council. Its homes were different in design to all the other association estates. Elegant in design, the dwellings were ideal for bringing up children in a clean and tidy environment.

Pickington slowed down, and followed the numbers until he reached number twenty. Pulling up outside, the two officers got out of the car and walked up towards the blue door. Day pressed the doorbell and waited.

A few seconds later, the door opened, and a brunette stood in the doorway, wearing a dressing gown and a towel covered her wet hair. "Yeah, what do you want me to buy?"

Day pulled out his wallet and showed the women her warrant card. "Hi, I am Detective Sergeant Miranda Day, and this is my colleague, Detective Constable Phillip Pickington. Does a Nicolas Waite live here?"

She nodded. "What's he done now?"

Day maintained a stoic expression. "I think it may be advisable if we could come in, Miss…"

"Gittings, Mary Gittings. What's happened?"

"Miss Gittings, I think we really should speak inside."

Miss Gittings allowed them to enter, and took them into a large sitting room with open patio doors. A black-haired, towering man stood at the door, having a cup of tea, and watching some children play in the garden. He turned around when they entered the room. "Who was it, Mares?"

Day recognized the man immediately. "Johnny Gittings, long time no see."

Johnny smiled at her. "It's Constable Day, isn't it?"

"Sergeant now, Mr. Gittings," she rebuked.

He drank some more of the tea and smiled coldly. "Congratulations on your promotion, and yes, it has indeed been a while. So, what brings you to my sister's house?"

Day glanced back at Mary and answered, "Miss Gittings, I am afraid I have some bad news for you. I am here to inform you Nicolas Waite has been found dead in town."

Mary looked shocked, and so did Johnny. "This is a joke, isn't it?"

The two officers shook their heads. "I am afraid I am not joking," Day acknowledged. "He was found early this morning."

Mary began crying, and ran straight to her brother's outstretched arms. He began rubbing her back as she cried out, almost screaming. Pickington approached the patio doors and pulled them together, to stop the children hearing that their mother was upset. Day sympathetically glanced at them both, and then over at constable Pickington. "Can you call for the Family Support Officer to come to this address?" Pickington nodded and left the room.

"Dead, I can't believe it," Johnny said, holding back the tears. "He was my best friend," he stared straight at Day, but still comforted Mary. "These two were planning to marry next year." Finally, he could no longer stop the emotions he felt, and the flood gates opened. He began crying, shouting at the heavens above. "Why?"

Pickington re-entered the room, and spoke softly to Day, "The support officer is on her way."

Day nodded. "When she gets here, ask her to come in, will you?" Pickington acknowledged the request, and walked out of the room again. Day looked back at the two grieving people. "I am sorry to ask this, but did Nicolas have any enemies?"

"Why do you ask that?" Johnny demanded.

"Because we believe he may have been murdered!"

The room fell silent, except for the whimpering of Mary and the happy sounds of children playing in the garden.

Johnny glared at the Sergeant. "I can't think of anyone who would want him dead!"

Mary released her grasp on her brother, and turned to Day. "He had a bad temper, and was always getting into scraps, but when he'd calmed down, he would go and apologise. He hated it if anyone held a grudge against him."

Day made a few notes in her ledger.

The door opened, and in walked a small blonde haired lady in a suit. She acknowledged Day, who then turned and looked at the sad couple. "Mary, Johnny, this is DC Georgina Hayes. She is our Family Support Officer. She will help you in any way she can."

With red swollen eyes, Mary thanked her.

"We will do our best to find out who caused Nicolas's death, Miss Gittings." Day said abruptly, and with that final sentence, she left the room and headed out towards Pickington, who was eating a KitKat next to the car.

"How did you know Johnny, Sergeant?" Pickington asked with a mouthful of chocolate, as they both jumped into the car.

"Johnny was a high-flying London accountant, who owned several firms in the area. A police sting on one of his businesses caused suspicion, and after several interviews, he was convicted of fraud, and sent down for five years. But it turned out that one of his customers was a gang leader, and he turned snitch to grab the leader. This gang would pick on the homeless and elderly, the latter by breaking into their homes. If any of their victims resisted, they would beat them up, then they would sell the items at car-boot sales or on Ebay."

Pickington started the car. "Not nice people, then?"

Day shook her head. "No, they weren't. I was a constable at the time, and I was partnered up with, then Sergeant Frashier. We arrested the leader, after Mr. Gittings, and several other accountants came forward. We sent Johnny to a rehabilitation centre, and he came out a changed man. People assumed he had been to prison, and he was promised no one would say different."

Pickington started the car. "So, where to, Sergeant?"

Day took out the plastic evidence bag, and looked at the ticket for the club. "Glossies' Night Club, the one down from the church."

Pickington placed the car in gear and drove away.

***

Meanwhile, Frashier sat in silence, looking at his old friend. The man just stared at the floor. His eyes were bloodshot and full of tears. When he did speak, it was full of mistakes. "When, where, how…"

Frashier replied, "We are still investigating the death, but all I can say, at the moment, is that we are not treating the death as suspicious…"

Alex jumped in. "…I want to see her, them!"

Frashier raised his hands. "Like I said, we are investigating…"

"I WANT TO FUCKING SEE THEM!" he shouted at Frashier with gritted teeth.

Frashier looked at the man, and, with sadness in his eyes, answered, "When we have concluded our preliminary investigations, we will need a relative to make a positive ID of the bodies. That is when you can see them." This seemed to calm Alex down a little. "I need to ask when you last saw your wife?"

Alex looked up at him with anger in his eyes. "Can't it wait, Inspector? You have just told me that my family is dead, and you want to ask me some questions?"

Frashier apologised and stood up to leave. "I'll leave you to grieve, but I'll be in contact." He took out a card from his inside pocket and placed it on the mantel piece. "Here are my contact details, if you need me."

Alex didn't even look up, he just sat on the chair, looking at the floor. When Frashier left, Alex slid off the chair and collapsed into a heap on the floor.

Frashier entered the hallway, and was about to leave, when the Russian woman came rushing down the stairs. She must have heard Alex crying. "What have you said to Alexander?" she demanded.

Frashier replied, "I had some sad news concerning his wife and children. They were found dead yesterday morning."

She appeared to go slightly white. "Oh."

He scrutinized her. "How long have you and Alex been seeing each other?"

The woman looked angry, and he could see that she was restraining herself from hitting him. "Me and Alex, no, I am the nanny stroke housekeeper." She froze to the spot, anger flaring in her eyes when she stared at him. "How dare you think that? How dare you? You're just like the others!"

Frashier was sympathetic to her. "I'm sorry it is my job to ask these questions, Miss…?"

"Tatyana Avilov."

"Miss Avilov, as the lead investigator of…"

Tatyana interrupted him before he could finish, "…I know what your job is, Inspector. I was a police officer in my country before I came here, but comments like that can get people into trouble, so please go. I have to go and look after Alexander. The family were kind to me when I came here." She opened the front door, and motioned for Frashier to leave, which he did, and then, she slammed the door in his face.

Frashier walked to his BMW, and then stopped to survey the house. He placed one of his fingers to his lip, as if pondering. He wondered what Day was up to. She could get onto records, and find out everything about Tatyana Avilov. He jumped into the car and sped away.

***

Glossies' had caused an outcry when it had brought the old vicarage and turned it into a night club. Its owner was an Arabian business woman, and she had transformed the building from a rundown, old house to an elegant, black marble-fronted hotspot.

Pickington turned the car off the main street and headed towards the club. Passing the church and pulling up outside the building, the two officers got out.

Both officers looked at the club and could understand why some of the residents of the town had called it an eyesore, especially as it was near the beautiful and majestic St. Bartholomew church.

The building itself was covered from roof to floor in black marble, which reflected its surroundings like a mirror. Small, blacked out windows lined the upper floor, their frames painted black to match the rest of the building. There was no sign on the building, just several tables and chairs outside in the smoking area, the parasols swaying in the wind, the name of the club printed in large letters on the cloth.

The constable looked at Day and asked, "How in hell did they get this through planning?"

"Money talks, Constable," she replied. "Anyway we're not here to sightsee." She walked towards the large black doors. "Come on."

When they got to the threshold of the building, Day pressed the intercom button. A voice erupted through a speaker, "Yes?"

Day pressed the button again, "Detective Sergeant Miranda Day and Constable Phillip Pickington, Chelmesbury CID." They showed their warrant cards to the camera above their heads, and she continued, "We would like to ask the manager some questions?"

The voice spoke back, "I am on my way." The door opened, and they stepped inside a room. It was similar in design to the front of the building with the black marble walls, which seemed to flow into the distant dance hall beyond a door. The only thing that stood out was a single, white marble-topped desk, where a till was fastened to the surface.

A few seconds later, a strong muscular red-haired man with green eyes, emerged from some steps. He was wearing designer clothes and gold rings. "Hi," he spoke in an overly flamboyant voice, which both officers were surprised at, considering his muscular appearance. "I am Tom Walker, Glossies' Bar Manager, and how may I help the police?"

Pickington took out the picture of Nicolas Waite. "Do you recognise this man?"

Tom took the picture and studied it for a few moments. "Yeah, I have seen him around. I had to turn him away on Saturday night because he was drunk."

"What was his behaviour like?"

"He was ok, until he was insulted or hurt. Then, he would get violent, but usually people left him alone."

Pickington placed the photo back into his pocket. "What time did he arrive?"

Tom thought for a few more seconds. "It was about eight-thirty. I had just opened the door when he turned up in that car of his, nearly knocked over one of my staff parking it."

"What happened then?" Day queried.

"Well, of course, he demanded to come in, when I refused, he gave me this!" He touched his left eye where both officers could see signs of make-up to hide bruising. "A couple of my bouncers threw him out into the street, and he left quickly in his car, wheel-spinning down the road."

"Was it reported?" Pickington asked.

Tom scoffed. "What, report it to you lot? Ha! What would you have done? Give him a slap on the wrist? Told him off for drinking?" He turned away and touched his bruised face. "He will be punished, if I ever get my hands on him in a dark alley."

Day almost glared at him. "Mr. Walker, Johnny Gittings was shot dead in the high street this morning."

Tom went white and seemed to be a little shaken by the information passed to him. "Shot?"

Day nodded "So, I need to ask where you were this morning, at around eight-o-clock?"

Still shaking he replied confidently. "I was at home in bed with my partner, I can give you his name if you want," Day nodded, "Its Martin Phillips I've got his number do you want that as well?"

"Please," Tom read out a number, and Pickington typed it into his iPad, before urging, "Can you think of anything else that could help us with our enquirers?"

Tom remembered something. "I did hear he was involved in a sort of tussle up at the market square. My sister works for the security firm, Gold Security. One of their guards was beaten up by him."

Pickington prepared to type something into the iPad. "Have you got the address?" Tom took the iPad from the constable and typed in the address, before handing it back to him. "Thank you"

"Not at all, anything to help the police," Tom said, almost sarcastic.

Day scanned Tom's face, trying to see anything that would identify whether he was telling the truth, or not. "Thank you for sparing us some of your time." She handed him a business card. "If you can think of any more information, please feel free to phone the number on the card, and ask for me or constable Pickington."

Tom took the card, and showed the two officers out of the building. After they had gone, he went to his office and rang his sister. "Hi hun, it's me. The police are on their way to you. They are investigating some shooting involving Nicky." He nodded, as if agreeing with his sister, and hung up, then opened the door and entered the heart of his marble empire.

In the car on the way back to the station, Day looked at the constable. "Phil, I want you to go to Records and find out if our Nicolas Waite had a criminal record. Then, find out where he works, and see if anyone there knows anything."

Once they returned to the station, Pickington went to work. After getting into the relevant section on his computer terminal, he typed in 'Nicolas Waite.'

> *Nicolas Waite, date of birth 17th October 1980*
> *Convicted of Aggravated Bodily Harm, served five out of seven years, released on good behaviour, March 9th 2010.*
> *Complaint made on 28th January 2012 against Waite by Glossies' Bar Manager, Mr. Tom Walker. Waite accused of menacing behaviour, and a prior sexual assault. Charges dropped due to lack of witnesses.*
> *Currently employed at Glayton Plumbing, Bathroom, and Heating Supplies.*

The part about Tom Walker interested the constable. During their earlier encounter with the bar manager, he had not mentioned the incident.
Pickington wrote this down on his iPad, and phoned through to Day. "Sergeant, I have discovered Tom knows Nicolas a little more than he let on."

Day cursed under her breath. "Okay, Pickington. We'll get to Gold Security first, find out about this security guard, and then we will find out why Tom lied to us."

"Right, I'll get the car ready." The line went dead.

Just as Day was about to leave her desk, an internal call came through.

Brightly was at her desk when Day walked in. "You wanted to see me, ma'am?"

The superintendent glanced up from her paperwork. "Yes, please sit down." She beckoned the sergeant to a seat, and regarded her seriously. "I am pleased to say that you have passed your Inspector's Exam." Day smiled, quite proud of herself, as Brightly continued, "I am also aware you have put in for a transfer to Birmingham, which I am saddened to say, has been accepted."

This gave Day a disheartened feeling. She had not wanted to put in the transfer, but she'd got fed up of Eliote not being very responsive over the last couple of months. "Ma'am, I will leave when this investigation is finished."

Brightly nodded. "I will let Eliote know of your departure." She then silently remarked to herself, 'when he comes back.'

Day got up from the seat. "Ma'am, I would be grateful if you didn't let Inspector Frashier know, just yet. I feel like I am betraying him."

Brightly was sympathetic. "Of course. The apprentice leaving the master."

Day grabbed her belongings, and glanced at her superior. "Is there anything else, ma'am?"

Brightly shook her head, and Day left the office.

As they travelled to Gold Security, Day had mixed emotions. She was elated at having been awarded the rank of Inspector, but the excitement was overshadowed by her pending departure from the station, a place she had called home since becoming a constable.

Pickington knew something was wrong. Usually on the way to interview a potential witness, they would talk about the case, or anything else for that matter, but the journey to Whatling Street was travelled in silence.

"Are you okay, Miranda?" Pickington's voice brought Day out of her thoughts.

"Pardon?"

"I was asking if you were alright."

Day hurriedly nodded. "I'm fine, Phil. Just got a lot on my mind."

Pickington wasn't convinced, but didn't want to push the matter. He turned the car on to Whatling Street, and looked for Gold Security. They passed a few office buildings, a supermarket, and several other business units. After travelling down the road for a while, they found the site. They were met with puzzled gazes, and a few angry stares.

Pickington parked the car in a space, and the two officers got out and headed for the reception area. Upon entering the main building, they were greeted with the same puzzled glares. Day took out her warrant card and walked up to a desk area. After showing the lady her card, she spoke to the receptionist. "Hi, I would like to speak to the owner, please."

The lady looked curiously at her, whilst replying, "I'll see if I can find her for you, Sergeant." She picked up the phone and dialled a number, speaking to whoever was on the other end. "I have two detectives here in reception who want to speak to you." She nodded and hung up. "Rachael will be with you shortly, if you'd like to take a seat."

A couple of minutes later, a woman entered reception in a designer business suit. She had flowing red hair down her slim back, and piercing green eyes. "Good day, Sergeant. I am Rachael Walker."

Pickington piped up. "Tom's..."

The redhead finished his sentence for him. "...sister, yes."

Day smiled at the woman. "Your brother told us that one of your guards was beaten up by a Mr. Nicolas Waite. Is this true, Miss Walker?"

She nodded. "Horrid man. I hope one day he will get his comeuppance."

The two detectives looked strangely at her, before Day put her in the picture. "Miss Walker, we are investigating Mr. Waite's death."

Rachael froze, shocked at the revelation. "He's, he's died, dead, from, from what?"

Pickington spoke, "He was shot dead at a set of traffic lights this morning." The two officer's watched Rachael change. Her eyes filled with tears, and looked a little bloodshot. She moved to a chair and slid into it. The receptionist walked up to Rachael, a tissue in her hand.

Day crouched down in front of her. "I have to ask. How well did you know the deceased, Miss Walker?"

The receptionist answered for her boss, and Day sensed a little venom in her voice. "They knew each other extremely well, Sergeant. They were planning on running away together, but then, that slag of a girlfriend got pregnant, and he had to stay with her out of some loyalty to the family."

Day looked at Rachael. "Is this true?"

Rachael replied, "Yes."

Day stood up and asked the receptionist, "Who was the guard that was beaten up?"

The receptionist had her hand on Rachael's shoulder, comforting her boss, but answered courteously, "His name is Edward Pierce. His family rang up this morning to say he was being released from hospital."

Pickington typed this info into his iPad. "Could you tell me where Mr. Pierce lives, please?"

She released her boss and walked to her desk. Withdrawing an address book, she flipped to the relevant page. "He lives at 25 Hectors Close."

"Is that the road with the Farmyard Pub at the top, on the left?"

"That's the one."

Day turned her attention back to Rachael. "We will be in touch." As almost an afterthought, Day asked, "Rachael, records show your brother was beaten up by Mr. Waite, amid accusations of sexual assault. Is this true?"

Rachael gnawed on her lower lip nervously. "Yes and no." She hesitated. "Nicky beat up Tom because Tom felt that Nicky was using me. For the sake of his pregnant girlfriend, we made up that story that Tom had tried it on with Nicky."

Day looked seriously at her. "You do know I could arrest you and Tom for perverting the course of justice?"

Rachael no longer worked to conceal her emotions on the matter. "Carry on, Sergeant. He's dead. What's the point of going on?"

Day beckoned Pickington towards the door. "We will leave you now, but we may return if we have more questions."

The two officers walked out and headed back to the car.

Rachael watched them go and then the emotions which had been building burst out once more, the receptionist grabbed another tissue and comforted her again.

When Day got into the car, she glared back at the building. "Constable, when we get back to the station, I want you dig very deep into this company and Miss Walker, their finances, property deeds everything. She's hiding something."

"Yes, Gov," he said, sounding positive.

"Then, I want you to get the original records for Waite's conviction. I want everything checked out." She paused. "But first, let's go and visit Hectors Close."

Pickington was happy. This was the Sergeant Day he had got to know, not the brooding detective he had been dealing with for the last few hours,

"Constable!" She snapped him out of his thoughts and glared at him.

"Yeah Hectors close, em, right, Gov." They drove out of the estate, and headed for Edward Pierce's property.

***

About eight miles from Chelmesbury was the picturesque village of Loughton on Teme. It was a place where the elderly came to spend the rest of their lives in peace and tranquillity.

At a rundown bungalow near the medieval church, a family group were starting to tidy up the mess that years of neglect had imposed on a possible beautiful place. They were steaming the walls and ripping up the shabby carpets that had been laid years before.

In the sitting room, a forty-year-old, red-haired, skinny woman in a shabby, old, football top and grey leggings was throwing out the old, large television which was sat on a brick built unit, incorporated into the fireplace. If it had been up to her, she'd have ripped the whole lot out, but, due to cost, they were forced into just tiding it up.

When she returned for the outdated video recorder which was in an alcove, she noticed something peculiar at the back. It looked like someone had fixed an extra socket, and had hidden it well into the back wall. Attached was a dirty looking plug, wires disappearing into the ground.
"Hey, Trev," she shouted to someone outside the room. "Are there any electrical appliances in any of the other rooms?" She heard a noise of someone moving about outside the room.

Trevor was about the same age as the women with black hair. He wore a tatty boiler-suit, and was rubbing his beard as he inspected the fuse box. "All the rooms are empty, but looking at this, something is on Carol!" he shouted towards the front room. "This dial is going crazy. Why do you ask?"

Back in the front room, Carol looked at what she had found. "There's a hidden socket with a plug in. The wire disappears under the floorboards." She stared down at the floor and asked, "The cellar doesn't come this far into the place, does it?"

Trevor answered quickly, "Nope, I think it comes to the bathroom."

Carol looked at the plug and turned it off. She waited for a while to see if anything happened, but apart from her breathing, there was nothing. "Okay," She unplugged the plug, and tried to pull the attached wire from the floor. It was only after several attempts and the help of her husband that the wire came loose. Both fell onto the floor in a heap and began laughing.

After a couple of minutes, they had controlled the laughter, and they both looked at the end of the wire. Apart from a few cobwebs, the wires gave no clue as to what had been attached.

Before continuing with their tidying of the place, they began exploring each room in the cellar, checking for any electrical equipment. Eventually, they gave up, conceding in their effort to find out where this wire had been attached to.

"Oh well. It was probably for some outside equipment that no longer works," Trevor remarked.

Carol nodded. "I wonder why they didn't turn it off?"

"Maybe they forgot. Who knows, love? It can't have been for anything important." He surveyed the rest of the building. "Let's just get this place done for your mum, okay?" Carol nodded, and they continued working.

Behind a hidden, dark room in the cellar, an electrical motor came to a stop.

When Angels Feast

By
Kevin Bailey

CHAPTER FOUR

Charlotte Steel was sat in the town's library, looking through an old microfilm reader, as well as glancing at her own laptop. Turning the wheel of the ancient looking device and using short hand, she wrote down as much of the information contained from the local newspapers matching a group of cases she was studying.

It had begun as it always did for her, at home. This time, she'd been in the kitchen making a ham sandwich when suddenly, she had a vision…

> …David Fox walked quickly out of the darkness and headed towards his lift. He carried a large grey rucksack on his back which crumpled up his navy boiler-suit.
>
> As he walked towards his destination, he stumbled upon a large, metal structure being erected on the market square. It looked like twisted evil creatures which could come to life at any point. His friend, Lesley, had told him about the building work. It was for some big music event which the town of Chelmesbury was hosting for the first time. He had said some big names had been signed to come, and the people of the town were getting rather excited.

"I must get some tickets," he murmured to himself as he headed towards an old supermarket car park, and the battered old blue ford escort which was pumping out black smoke from the exhaust. How many times had he told his friend the car should be at a scrapyard. He smiled and pretended to cough a couple of times as he neared. The occupant in the driver's seat smirked and beckoned him to get in.

David approached the rear of the car, placed his rucksack into the boot, and closed it…

Three Years Previously

Lesley Jones, an unfit, chubby man with receding brown hair, felt the back of his car drop down. He prepared to move off and turned over the local radio station to Radio Two. Chris Evans was just starting his breakfast show, and was talking to his team about his fantastic weekend. As Lesley listened, he glanced down at a headline on the front cover of the Chelmesbury Chronicle. It was an article about the local football team's win, and whilst waiting for his friend to get in, he started to read.

After reading a couple of paragraphs, he glanced out of the side window. The sun was beginning to rise. Looking in the rear view mirror, he spotted the large rucksack protruding out from behind the rear seat. He peered out of the car, expecting to see David talking to a passer-by, but there wasn't any movement.

"Perhaps he's just popped over to the newsagent," he said worryingly, but when he looked across, he only observed the assistants putting the morning papers out on their appropriate stands.

After placing his own paper on to the dashboard, he got out of the car and looked around. There was no one there. He closed the door and walked around the square, scanning the backstreets that descended in all directions. He began shouting out his friend's name, but apart from a few people heading to the local newsagent, there was no sign of David. It was as if he had simply vanished into the shadows.

When he returned to his car, and after grabbing his mobile, he rang David's number. He listened as it rang and rang. Lesley jumped back in the car and rang the number again. Somewhere behind him, he could hear a muffled ringing tone, emanating from the back of the car.
Stepping out of the car, Lesley approached the back of the car and opened the boot. He could tell the ringing was coming from the bag. "Where the hell is he?" he said to himself, and took one more look around the area, before jumping back into the driver's seat and driving away.

One Week Later

Carla Thomas made her way into the centre of town, her three children in tow. She could see the outline of a derelict building in the distance, long abandoned by the bankrupt company several years ago. Now, the only people who used the structure were drug addicts and drunks, taking advantage of it as a public convenience on their way home from the bars and clubs.

As they neared the buildings, Carla bumped into her school friend, Mary Gittings. The two exchanged pleasantries and continued to walk together.

It was a nice, warm day, and the two friend's children played happily together, but when they passed the building, Clara's smallest child ran up to her mother, holding her nose. "Mummy, what is that horrible smell?"

Her mother didn't know. Mary grumbled angrily, "I've been on to the council about this eyesore for months, and have they done anything? No!" Her temper rose. "I'm thinking of going to the press, just need a few more people to back me up…"

Out of nowhere, they heard a scream, and Carla saw one of her children next to a syringe. She quickly rushed up to her child. "Don't touch that!" Then she turned to Mary. "I'll support you, and I'll take some photos, if you want?" Mary nodded, and Carla took out her new smart phone.

She began by taking images of the syringes and then ordered her children, "Stay here with Mary." The three children nodded, and watched their mother move to the building to snap a few shots of the crumbling façade. She knew she had to tread carefully, as she didn't want to step in any of the human and animal waste which was littered around.

By the time she approached the front of the building, her camera phone was almost full of pictures. Spying a broken window, she peered in with the phone. As she was taking the photo, something made her do a double take.

A shiver descended down her spine, and Carla wondered if she really saw what she thought she saw. "What the hell…?" she muttered to herself. Squinting through the darkness, she could make out something dangling from two hooks. At first, Carla thought it was an old sack, maybe left by the company. Repositioning herself, she attempted to get a better look. Once Carla viewed what it actually was, she immediately wished she hadn't.

A macabre display lay before her. It wasn't a sack at all, but the torso of a man. The skin around his skull had been methodically cut away. The eyes were missing, and the hooks poked through the empty sockets. She threw up on the ground, and as Carla hurried back to her friend and children, the memory of the man's mutilated corpse stuck in her head.

"Are you alright, Carla? You look like you've seen a ghost!" Mary anxiously questioned her pale-faced friend. "Carla?"

After a few moments, Carla was able to answer. "Could you take the kids to your house? I need to phone the police."

Present Day

In the swirling mists that was Charlotte's mind, the dissected man turned to face her, and she could see the hollow sockets where the eyes used to be. A lonely maggot wriggled excitingly. This made her feel slightly nauseous.

The man spoke continuously, with a deep sorrow voice, "Please help me." She saw the white door appear, and she approached and stepped through it.

But instead of being back at the library, where she thought she would be, she suddenly began to feel drowsy, as if drunk, and she saw the spinning whirlpool, and the voice echoing from the swirling mass. "Lotte, loopy Lotte, come in and play!" She allowed herself to fall into the whirlpool, no longer afraid of it.

When she emerged, she found herself in an ancient stone transept, and could feel the presence of several monks, moving slowly through the structure. As she stood and listened to the sounds of the monks chanting, a strange site surprised her. Across from her was a woman in modern clothes. Charlotte looked closely at the women, but as she did, the women turned and walked into a dark space and vanished.

Curiously, Charlotte walked towards the space, and was catapulted forwards in time. The first thing she spied when she emerged was an elderly man in a black suit, carrying a large vase of flowers towards the picture of a beautiful lady adorning a wall. As she watched, he replaced the decaying flowers with fresh new ones, and then he adoringly glanced at the lady and blew her a kiss.

Something behind her made her turn, and it was then she saw the women from before. After smiling, this spectre turned once again, and disappeared through a door. Charlotte followed, and came into a large study. A man was slumped over the desk, and she could smell the undeniable stench of alcohol mixed with sick. Next to him was a half full glass of whiskey; two large empty bottles had been thrown in the bin.

The woman was standing next to the man, her arms trying to comfort him, but unable to do so. When Charlotte looked at the women, she had tears in her eyes. She recognised the woman, and this new information sent a shiver down her spine. This protector was a ghost, and she now knew who the man was, and what she must do.
She saw the white door appear again in the corner, and when she opened it, she was back in the warm library. People looking over worryingly at her, but before anyone could ask, she'd grabbed her belongings, and was racing to her car.

***

Simon Eliote sat in his study, looking at a photo of his family, tears trickling down his chin. He felt now he had left the station, he had nothing left to cling on to. Opening the bottom drawer, he pulled out one of the unopened bottles of Chivas Regal Blended Scotch whisky and a large crystal tumbler, pouring himself a large amount.

Since that painful night when his family had died in the car crash, and he had tried and failed to take his own life, he had refrained from drinking alcohol. But now, he felt the bottle was all he had. It hadn't helped seeing Day working hard on a case. She didn't seem to need his advice. Seeing William Frashier walking happily towards him as he left, almost stepping into his shoes, had cemented the perspective in his head.

The realisation hit him hard. He was no longer needed on the force. He went to take a swig from the glass when he heard his phone ringing.
He placed the glass on the desk and answered, "Yes?" It was Henry.

"Sorry to bother you, Simon, but I have a Miss Charlotte Steele to see you!" Eliote wondered why she was here. "Shall I prepare some tea for you, Simon?"

Eliote smiled happy that someone needed him. "Yes, please." He carefully poured the drink back into the bottle and replaced it in his drawer.

"Very good, Simon," Henry replied and hung up.

Henry escorted Charlotte through the house and past the vase of dead flowers by the painting.
"Excuse me, who is that lady?" Henry stopped and looked at the painting.

"That, ma'am, is Simon's mother, the late Mrs. Julianne Eliote, a woman I loved dearly."

Charlotte smiled and acknowledged her. This made Henry smile. "I think you need to replace those flowers!"

Henry nodded. "I was just about to pick some from the garden when you arrived. I'll get you and the master..." He smirked. "Don't tell him I said 'master.' He gets upset with me."

Charlotte shook her head. "I won't, if you don't."

Henry smiled warmly, brightening the room. "Please come this way."

When they walked into the study, Simon had moved from the desk, and was now sat on a comfy, cream-coloured leather chair looking into the unlit fireplace. To her, he appeared dishevelled, wearing an old, blue polo shirt and ragged, black trousers. It was miles away from the smart navy blue suits he usually wore. Glancing around the wood-panelled room, a wedding photo on the mantelpiece caught her eye. Taking a closer look, she saw the woman who was haunting her visions. A chill ran down her spine, and she quickly went and sat down opposite Eliote.

"I'll go and get the tea," Henry remarked, preparing to leave them alone, until Charlotte, who stayed staring at Simon, spoke to him, making the old butler glance back at her.

"Go and get some flowers first for your mistress. She hates the dead ones."

Henry was taken aback a little. "Yes, of course and," he stuttered, "then, I'll get you some tea, M…" He quickly left the room.

Eliote looked confused. "What was that all about?"

Charlotte stared at him, and didn't answer his question. "I'm sorry for what I said to you about those around you. It was a mistake on my behalf."

Eliote nodded. "It has been going around in my head since then. I've been scared to work with any of them, just in case they stab me in the back." He paused and walked to the fireplace, gazing longingly at the picture of his wife. "Why are you here, Charlotte? I thought you were on a break?"

Charlotte stared up at the picture as well. "Let's just say, I need your help."

Eliote returned to the chair. "What kind of help?"

Charlotte placed a large file in front of him and several notebooks. "I've been having a recurring vision of a man asking for help in identifying his killer…"

Eliote interrupted her. "…I am on indefinite leave. Couldn't you ask Frashier or Day?"

Charlotte glanced at him and replied, "I tried them both, and was told they are investigating their own cases. So, I came to you."

Eliote sighed heavily. "So, I am third time lucky?" he scoffed, and then stood up and walked towards the patio doors. "I am thinking of leaving the police. They don't need me anymore."

Charlotte took one of the notebooks. "I feel the problem is, after the 'Deathly Angel' case, you needed something to get your teeth into, not sitting behind a desk, moping."

Eliote glared angrily at her. "I was not moping."

Charlotte snapped back, "Yes, you were, Simon, and you know it. You are fed up with office work, and I don't blame you, but that is part and parcel of the job." She held out the notebook. "But, this time, all the paperwork is done."

At that precise moment, there was a knock at the door, and Henry walked in carrying a silver tray with a pot of tea, a cafetiere, and a plate of biscuits. He set the tray down and looked at the two friends. "Is everything okay?"

Eliote nodded curtly. "We are fine, Henry. Charlotte has an interesting cold case for me to investigate, and I told her I was on indefinite le…"

Henry interrupted with enthusiasm, "Sounds like you are going to need more tea!" He turned and winked at Charlotte, then hurried off.

"Okay, give me that notebook, and I'll take a look…"

After what seemed like hours, Simon finally closed the file and stared over at her in mild disbelief. "There's a-hellava lot of information in there. Where did you get it all from?"

"Well, after the vision, I went to the local library and went through all the local newspapers. There were snippets everywhere." She grabbed another folder from her bag and pulled out a wad of newspaper articles. "It was then I found this!"

Eliote took the paper and read it.

MUM IN SHOCK AT GRUESOME FIND IN BUILDING

Detectives have linked this case with the case of missing person, David Fox.

Police are investigating the old Murphy's site after the discovery by Mrs. Carla Thomas of a mutilated torso, who the police believe is that of David Fox, last seen by his friend Lesley Jones the week before.

Simon looked up at Charlotte, and then at the photo of the building. "Hasn't Murphy's been pulled down, replaced by a Co-op supermarket and a new housing estate?" He poured some tea for himself and Charlotte, continuing, "I'll bet this is probably being investigated by the cold case unit now?"

Charlotte nodded. "I know that, but wait, there's more." She took out the other notebook. "Look at this. I liked the headline."

POLICE IN A HOLE AFTER BODY FOUND

POLICE HAVE TODAY CORNERED OFF CHELMESBURY'S MUNICIPAL GOLF COURSE AFTER GOLFERS MADE AN UNEXPECTED FIND.

The body of a woman has been found on the seventh green at Castleview Golf club, when brothers Arron, Martin, and Kieran Holmes were out playing a round.

Kieran discovered a stone marker, after he lost his ball in a thicket, and when he went in to retrieve it, he tripped over the marker and twisted his ankle. When he shouted for his brothers, they saw the marker had writing on it and tipped off the police.

A police source stated that the writing said,

BENEATH THIS STONE
IS THE ANSWER TO THE QUESTION.

Police forensics and archaeologists led by Chelmesbury's own pathologist, Doctor Richard Strong, excavated the site, and found the remains of a female skeleton. They deduced that the body had been in the ground for about ten to fifteen years.

On examining the body, the doctor's team discovered that the woman had died from her throat being cut. Further study of the skeleton revealed cut marks similar to butchery:

"It would seem," Doctor Strong reported to the inquest into the cause of her death, "that the body had been stripped of meat for purposes unknown."

Simon stopped reading the article. "You're not going to tell me you believe these cases are linked are you?"

"These, and at least three other cases of body parts being found in Chelmesbury, are, in my opinion, linked. Before you say how, I have gone through these notes several times, and the connection isn't just the cut marks, which have been surgically done, it is the markers!"

"Markers?"

"Yes, the first marker was the stone which asked the question." Raising her hands and shrugging her shoulders, she continued, "What that question is, is known only to the killer."

Eliote drank some of the tea. "Was there a second marker?"

Charlotte nodded. "Oh, there was a second marker alright." She opened the large file once again, and showed Simon the picture of the old Murphy's building. She handed him a magnifying glass and pointed to a sign on the wall. Simon read the sign:

BEWARE ALL THOSE
THAT ENTER BEYOND THIS POINT

"That's not a marker. I have seen loads of those on buildings."

Charlotte smiled proudly. "Look at the other signs. They are all the same."

Simon nodded. "My God. You're right. The others are very in-your-face, but this one looks almost made up."

Charlotte drank some of the coffee. "This was the second marker. No one would ever think it was out of sync with the other signs."

Eliote stood up and walked to the door. He shouted to the butler, "Henry, I am off to the station."

Somewhere in the great house, he heard the butler shout back, "Damn! I've made some lunch for you and your friend."

Eliote sighed. "I'll have some when I get back."

He heard Henry curse and then reply, "Okay, Simon. See you later."

Eliote grabbed his coat from the cloakroom and returned to Charlotte.

"Are we going somewhere, Simon?"

Eliote inclined his head in the affirmative. "Yes. I think Superintendent Brightly needs to see this." He stopped, smiling warmly at her. "By the way, you were right. I did need something to get my teeth into." He smirked slightly at his own pun, and they both headed out towards his Saab and drove to the station.

WHEN ANGELS FEAST
By
Kevin Bailey

CHAPTER FIVE

DC Pickington parked the car outside Hectors Close, and both officers got out and headed for the house. When they rang the bell, there was no answer.

They returned to the car, and Pickington asked, "What now, ma'am?"

Day looked at the house. It looked like it hadn't been lived in for weeks, let alone days.

"First, we go to Nicolas's place of work. Then, after that, we get back to the station, and see if we can get information on Edward Pierce, find out if he has family in Chelmesbury or Glayton he could have been staying with."

Pickington agreed, and they drove away.

Upstairs on the landing, Edward Pierce lay still. He'd heard the car drive away, and approached the front bedroom window and peered out. He saw the Insignia turning a corner. "Bloody salespeople. Why can't they just leave me alone?" He exited the bedroom.

***

Frashier had returned to the station, and was informed Day and Pickington were investigating a shooting in the high street. He went to his office and sat at his desk. He typed in his password and checked up on the police records database: Tatyana Avilov.

TATYANA NATALYA AVILOV

Born November 17th 1977, in Leningradsky Prospect, a suburb of Moscow to Dmitri and Natalya Avilov.

Educated at a local school before joining the police, rising to the rank of Sergeant.

For a time, she was an undercover officer, but left the force in shame when it was discovered that she had family in a local crime syndicate.

She moved to Chelmesbury where she resides at...

Frashier wrote down the notes, and then touched the screen at a different point. He was about to check something else when the phone rang on his desk. "Frashier."

He heard the distinctive Shropshire tones of the chief pathologist. "Inspector, I have finished my report, and my findings confirm death of the family by hypothermia."

Frashier wrote this down. "Anything else, Strong?"

"Yes, I've had the toxicology reports back, and they discovered a chemical in the blood samples."

Frashier was intrigued. "Go on."

"In all three victims, the blood samples contained a product which is given to beef cattle in the states to gain weight." Frashier heard the rummaging of paper, "Ah, here it is. It's called 'Zilpaterol Hydrochloride.' As I said, it is used in the states, and is often called 'Zilmax.'"

"Okay," Frashier said, surprised at the findings.

"Do you know if Jane, or her children, had asthma?"

Frashier thought about it for a while. "Not that I am aware of. Why?" He heard the rummaging again, and could imagine Strong's desk, strewn with medical papers and books.

"Well, you might want to check that out, because the only reason for the chemical to be in the body was if they had asthma." He paused, and Frashier could hear him turning a page. "I have done some research on the drug. It is a beta-agonist, and was used to treat the condition in humans. The drug was an absolute failure, but was found to be a repartitioning agent. It changes the body metabolism so more muscles are produced instead of fat. The World Anti-Doping Agency banned the drug for human consumption, but like I said before, it is still used in cattle."

Frashier was indeed surprised. Where had someone picked up an American drug? He would have to find out. After writing all the information down, he spoke back to Strong, "Okay, we can now get a relative in to identify the victims, once that's done, we can release the bodies to them for burial." When Strong answered in the affirmative, Frashier ordered, "Report on my desk ASAP."

He heard Strong sigh. "It's on its way."

Frashier smiled. "Thank you." The line went dead. Frashier stared into space for a while before withdrawing the paper he had been given earlier with Alex's phone number. He dialled the number, and after several rings, a voice answered, "Hello?" It was Tatyana.

"Hi, Miss Avilov, it's Inspector William Frashier. Is Alex in?"

She was silent for a second, and then replied, "He has had to go into work. They seem to be having problems with a supplier. You can find him there."

"Okay," Frashier replied, placing the phone down and grabbing his coat.

When he arrived at the plumbing shop, he was surprised to find Pickington standing outside, smoking. The constable gulped when he saw Frashier. "Relax, Constable." Seeing Pickington's packet of cigarettes on a pallet, Frashier took one and lit it. "What are you doing here?" he asked, taking a long drag.

"The guy shot at the traffic lights worked here." Pickington contemplated his next question before carefully asking, "Why are you here, Gov?"

"I'm here to interview the owner. The bodies in the ditch were his wife and children." They both stubbed their cigarettes out, and Pickington escorted Frashier inside where Day was interviewing the workers.

"So, what was Nicolas like to work with?"

A skinny, bald headed man, with several tattoos on his arms answered "He was okay. Could be a bit of a prick sometimes, but a good worker." Everyone agreed, then the office door opened and out stormed Alex Boyd.

"What the hell do I pay you all for?" The workers turned, indicating to Day. "Who the hell are you?" he snapped.

"Detective Sergeant Day, Chelmesbury Police. I am investigating the murder of Nicolas Waite."

Alex shrugged his shoulders. "So that gives you the right to disrupt my business, does it?"

Day was about to answer, when she heard Frashier's voice. "Yes, it does."

The two men glared at each other, and Alex threw his hands in the air. Spinning, he walked back into the office, muttering as he went,

"So be it." Alex slammed the door behind him, leaving all the staff wondering what to do.

Day glanced suspiciously at Frashier. "What are you doing here? Come to check up on me, have you?"

Frashier shook his head. "No, I want words with Mr. Boyd." She seemed contented with his answer and he headed for the office door, knocking.

"Come in!" He heard his old friend snap. Frashier opened the door and walked in. "What do you want, William?"

"I'm here to inform you Jane's body is ready to be identified."

Alex shuffled some paperwork on his desk. "Couldn't you do it? You did know her as well."

Frashier shook his head. "Unfortunately, I am not her next of kin. So, therefore, you need to come."

His friend sighed. "Okay William. Is that all?"

"No, I still need to ask you some questions…"

"Can't it wait? I'm one man down, suppliers aren't delivering the right stock, and I've got customers wondering where their goods are." Unable to keep up his business-like composure any longer, Alex's head fell to the desk, and he banged it several times onto the hard, wooden surface, crying out in pain.

Frashier felt a great deal of empathy for the crumbling man. "Stop that," Frashier demanded. "Come on, old friend. Let's go and grab a coffee somewhere."

Alex's sobbing subsided briefly as he stared at Frashier though puffy eyes. "Okay." The pair headed out of the office, past the dumbstruck staff.

***

Day and Pickington headed back to CID. Day didn't appear overly happy, and Pickington glanced worryingly at her, asking, "You okay, ma'am?"

She snapped back, "No, I am fucking pissed off." Then she speculated, "Frashier will persuade Brightly our case and his are connected, and he will take charge, and, as usual, I'll be his fucking go-between. The sooner I leave this place the better."

Without further comment, Pickington turned the car into the station. The two detectives were surprised to see Eliote's Saab parked in his space.

***

Alex and Frashier were sat in a posh café on the high street. Alex was drinking a mocha, and Frashier had a cappuccino. "I am sorry for the way I have been, Will. It's just I still can't get my head around the fact they are gone. I half-expect to see them come through the door at any moment." More tears rolled down his cheek, and Frashier handed him a tissue.

"I do think it's time we talked, Alex."

The man nodded. "Perhaps you're right, Will."

Frashier put on a serious expression. "But first I need you to come and identify the bodies, and then we will talk."

His friend wiped tears from his eyes. "You want me to do it now?"

Frashier considered his friend's current state, and came to a decision. "Maybe after we've had coffee." To take Alex's mind off the forthcoming duty, he started to reminisce about the good days when they'd been children.

***

When Day and Pickington entered the CID offices, they could see Eliote sat in the observation room with Charlotte. On the screen were the front covers of newspapers and images of a factory building Day instantly recognised. She opened the door and walked in. Eliote looked up at her and smiled. "Hi, Sergeant."

Day gestured to the images. "Gov, isn't that the old Murphy's Building? I was part of the team that…" She stopped to remember the incident. "Why are you looking into that case?"

Eliote stood up and walked up to her, handing her the file Charlotte had given to him. "Because of this." he said bluntly.

Day opened the file and started to go through it, when another case made her look up. "The body on the golf course. That was a strange case." Eliote showed her the pictures of the other markers. "That's just a co-incidence, Gov!" But deep in her sub-conscious, it intrigued her.

"That it may be, Sergeant, but it has tickled my senses, and I feel it needs to be re-investigated. I was just about to…"

The door to the room opened, and Brightly looked at Day. "Ah there you are, Serg…" She stopped cold when she saw Eliote and Charlotte in the room. "Chief Inspector, I wasn't expecting you back."

Eliote sort of smiled at her. "I needed time to think about what you said, and now, I have thought about it, and I'm here," She looked at him and responded,

"Well then, can I have a word with you, please?" she demanded.

Day looked at Charlotte. "Want a coffee, Miss Steel?"

Charlotte nodded, and both of them left Eliote to get a roasting from his superior, closing the door behind them.

***

Frashier and Alex had finished talking about childhood adventures. When Frashier managed to bring the conversation back to Jane, Alex began to really open up. "When did you meet Jane again?"

Alex drank some coffee and answered, as if on cue, "I'd gone to college, and then to Uni, studying business management, and I bumped into her in the canteen. We talked for hours, missing several lectures. We just didn't care." He slurped some coffee, a smile appearing on his face as he reminisced. "When I came back to Chelmesbury, we met up, and one thing led to another. We were inseparable, like me and you used to be."

Frashier looked at him and drank his cappuccino. "When was the last time you saw them?"

Alex's expression sobered as he was catapulted back into reality. "About two weeks ago, I'd discovered she was having an affair and told her to go, which she did. But, unbeknownst to me, she took my kids with her." He started to lose his composure again, and Frashier handed him a tissue. Alex blew his nose.

"Do you know the name of the fella?"

Alex's facial expression was blank. "She never told me his name. If she had, I'd have gone and killed him," he said with venom.

Frashier didn't doubt this. "Can you think of anywhere she could have gone to?"

Alex, again, indicated in the negative. "I expected her to be at her mother's, or at his!" Malice dripped from his words.
"So, you tried her mother's?"

"Yes, but she wasn't there." He drank some of his coffee. "Either that, or she didn't want to talk to me." He implored his friend, "Have you tried her mother's house?"

"Not yet, that will be my next port of call." Frashier finished his coffee, took out his mobile, and phoned Strong. "Hi, Doctor, it's me. Can you get things ready? I am bringing in the husband." He hung up and turned to Alex. "It's time."

***

The observation room was silent, both officers not wanting to say the first word. But, finally, Brightly broke the deadlock by examining the image of the factory on the screen. "What is this, Chief Inspector?"

Eliote walked to the screen. "This was the old Murphy's building. A few years ago, a mother and her children were out walking when they made a gruesome discovery. I think there is a link between this case, and another one."

Brightly's expression remained blank. "What other case?"

Eliote moved the pen, and the pointer moved on the screen to a file. He opened it. "Three brothers were playing golf, when one of them made this discovery." He brought up the images.

Brightly didn't even look at them, but stared coldly at him. "What is the link?"

Eliote pointed at the screen. "The link is on the screen, ma'am. Please look."

She glanced at them. "A scratched piece of stone. So what?" she said bluntly and unimpressed.

He pointed back at the image of Murphy's. "You just can't see it, can you?" He walked to the image and physically touched the screen. "The two incidents have markers: the stone at the golf course and a different sign at the side of the building. I would like to go through both cases with a fine-tooth comb, and explore the possibility there may be other unsolved cases matching these."

Brightly turned red, spinning and glaring at Eliote. "I get it. This is because of what I said about budgets. You're seeing shadows and putting them together to make me suffer, is that it?" She barely paused in her tirade, "I suppose Miss Steel had one of her so called 'visions,' again, and you're running after her."

Eliote threw the pen at a wall. "No, Dorothy! It's got nothing to do with that. It's about bringing to justice a killer who has murdered two, possible more, people. I have told you many times. I don't care for money. I just want to do my job, a job that I am good at, and if you can't see that, then please, go to hell." It was his turn to glare at her, and Brightly could see something that scared her in his eyes.

"Okay, *Chief Inspector*," she said sarcastically. "I'll give you the resources you need to investigate these cases, but only if you get the cold case unit's permission. This type of investigation is their turf, so to speak."

Eliote nodded. "I'd like to use Day for this investigation."

Brightly approached and informed him, "Just so you know, Miranda Day is now an Inspector. Also, she has put in a transfer to Birmingham, which has been successful. At the moment, she doesn't want Frashier to know."

Eliote felt ashamed, and as she turned, he asked, "Is the transfer because of me, because of the way I have been?"

Brightly didn't answer.

"I'll take that as a yes then, ma'am." Brightly didn't say another word, and left the observation room, leaving Eliote to his thoughts.

WHEN ANGELS FEAST
By
Kevin Bailey

CHAPTER SIX

Detective Inspector Frashier and Alexander Boyd walked into the Princess of Wales Hospital and headed for the chapel of rest. The room they entered was calm and quiet, and Frashier felt like he'd entered a church.

The two men cautiously approached a curtained screen, and the Inspector turned to look back at Alex, who was running his shaking hands over the Bible, obviously nervous at what was behind the screen.

"Are you ready for this?"

His friend took a few deep breaths and then nodded at Frashier, who spoke into the microphone. "Okay, Doctor Strong. We are ready when you are." Soft music started to play as the curtains opened to reveal a beautiful women lying on a bed. She had been made up to look like she was asleep.

Alex began sobbing. "That's her." He grabbed a tissue. "That's Jane." Frashier placed his hand on his friend's shoulder, and they both stared at the woman.

***

Day and Charlotte returned to find Eliote writing out his notes. "Everything okay, Gov?"

He turned and smiled at her. "I understand congratulations are in order, Inspector."

She blushed and looked away. "Thank you, Gov." Eliote felt so guilty, but maybe he deserved having his star detective jump ship. She brought him out of his thoughts. "I would like to tell Frashier the news myself, if I can, Gov, and the forthcoming move to Birmingham?"

Eliote gave her a curt nod, and then changed the subject. "How is your investigation into the shooting of Nicolas Waite going?"

"No suspects yet, but it's coming along nicely. I am having a problem trying to interview Edward Pierce, a man who was beaten up by Waite, and could be a suspect."

"Good. I know you are investigating the shooting, but I am going to need you on this case." He pointed to the screen. "That is, if the Cold Case Unit allows me to investigate."

Concern passed over Day's face. "The CCU? Oh, that means you have to deal with the 'Ice Queen.'"

Eliote looked strangely at her. "The 'Ice Queen?'"

"Detective Inspector Tracey Downes. We call her the Ice Queen because of her white complexion and cold exterior. She tends to stay away from the other departments, and keeps the unit running with an almost iron fist."

Eliote rubbed his hands together and smirked. "My kind of woman then?"

Day rolled her eyes and smirked right back at him.

***

Frashier watched Strong retract the curtains. He walked back over to Alex, who was sitting on one of the pews, staring at the floor, tears trickling down his chin. "Do you want to be alone, Alex?"

Alex glanced upward at Frashier. "What I want is answers from you, Will. Who was the bloke she was seeing, and where has she been for the last two weeks?"

Frashier shrugged his shoulders. "I will find out, Alex…"

His friend's expression turned cold. "…Then you will come and tell me who, and where he is, so I can make a home-visit." Alex made a fist and punched it hard into the palm of his other hand.

"Calm down, Alex. You know I can't do that."

Alex jumped to his feet, squaring up to Frashier. "Calm down?" he snapped. "That was my fucking wife in there!" He gestured at the window. "And you're telling me to calm down? I want a name. That's all!" He pointed directly at Frashier. "You owe me that, Will."

Frashier backed down slightly. "I know I owe you. God, I've never forgotten, but I am a police officer, sworn to protect. I cannot divulge information which could endanger the lives of others!" Alex went to protest, but Frashier put up his hand. "All I can do is work my hardest to find the information which will bring this case to a close. That is all I will swear to you, no more, no less."

The two old friends stood facing each other, both not backing down, but eventually, the stalemate broke. "Look, I'm sorry," Alex said, placing a hand on Frashier's shoulder. "It's just seeing the woman I love, looking all peaceful, and me suffering, wondering what happened to her and my kids in the last two weeks…it's eating away at me."

Frashier forgave his friend, knowing emotions were running high. "Don't mention it. I am feeling it, too, but I will do my job, and get back to you."

Alex slightly smiled. "You were, and still are, a good friend, Will."

Frashier nodded. "Same with you, old friend." He turned and walked to the door. "Time to knock off, and go for a drink."

Alex declined, "I don't drink anymore."

Frashier smiled warmly. "Then I'll have a beer, and you can have a soft drink." The agreement made, both men left the small chapel room.

***

Eliote approached a part of the station he had never been to before. It was in the older part, and as he descended into the belly of the station, the temperature began to lower, and he shivered. He arrived at the bottom of the stairs, and after walking through a corridor with pipes above his head, he approached an imposing door. He knocked and waited.

A muscular black officer opened the door. He was wearing casual clothes, and was holding an iPad in his hand. Eliote smiled, and the man studied him curiously. "Can I help you?"

Eliote showed him his card, and the man beckoned him in. "Sorry, Chief Inspector. We don't get many people down here in the basement. I am DS Denver Delaney, second-in-command of this." He opened a second door, and they walked into a large, white-walled room that had several doors and corridors going off in all directions. Eliote surveyed the main room. It contained row upon row of shelf units. On each shelf, from the floor to ceiling, were stacked large boxes and files. He could not see any natural light in the room, so spotlights lit the boxes to an extent.

Denver approached a door and motioned for him to go through into a smaller room with several officers sitting at desks typing. "How can we help you?"

Still in awe at the size of the unit, he stuttered, "Well, after some new evidence has come to my attention concerning two old cases, it has got me wondering whether there are other cases where a marker of such has been found near a mutilated body."

Denver was about to reply, when a door opened, and the temperature dropped again. Standing in the doorway was a short woman, with tied back, black hair. She was wearing baggy clothes, and stared at Eliote with cold blue eyes. "Who are you?" she said, almost raising her nose.

Eliote noticed that the officers at the desks were typing quicker. He looked up at the woman. "DI Tracey Downes?" She nodded. "Hi there, I am Detective Chief Inspector Simon Eliote."

She didn't even bat an eyelid from beneath the glasses. She reminded him of a school teacher he'd once had. "So, what brings you to my domain, Chief Inspector?"

Eliote looked at Denver and then back at her. "As I have just told the Sergeant here, I have received some new evidence concerning two old cold cases, which I have come to ask be reopened and investigated."

She peered over her glasses at Denver and then back at Eliote. "Give the information to the detective, and we'll look into it." She turned to walk back into what Eliote could only imagine was her office.

Eliote was slightly irritated by her dismissive attitude. "Look here, Inspector. I have come down here with respect, and I expect that same respect from you, or do I have to place you on a charge?" The room fell silent.

"How dare you come in here, and threaten me?" She too was getting angry. "This is my department, a place I have built from a rundown unit into a hard working place, where cold cases are re-examined, and criminals who have eluded the mighty CID," as she said 'CID,' she made speech marks with her fingers, and continued, "are finally brought to justice."

Eliote reacted adversarial. "Excuse me?" Downes stared into his eyes, and for the first time in her life, she felt afraid. There was darkness there. "I came here as a friend, a colleague, but it would seem that I am leaving here as an enemy." Without letting her say another word, he handed Denver a USB stick, and after thanking him for his time, he turned.

"Chief Inspector Eliote, I must…"

Eliote turned and swiftly cut her off. "Good day, madam," he said, and left the unit.

As he walked into CID, he was greeted by Day. "How was your trip to hell?"

He glanced at the door. "I think we had better turn the heaters down. I've got a feeling the 'Ice Queen' will be paying us a visit."

Day sort of smiled. "I'll prepare the warm jackets then, Gov?"

Eliote saw a glimpse of the happy Day he had been welcomed by on his first day, and it made him feel guilty. He decided he would make it up to her. "Right then, whilst we wait for something to happen, I'll help you in trying to track down this Edward Pierce."

Day seemed a little shell-shocked. "Okay, Gov. I was just about to try again. You could always join me." He nodded, and both officers left the unit, heading for the Saab.

When they arrived back at the Pierce address, both officers got out and walked to the front door, but once again, the house was dark. Eliote decided to try the house next door and rang the doorbell. Unlike the neighbouring house, this one was tidy. The gardens were well-kept and looked like they had been mowed recently. Deep within the house, he heard a door open, and footsteps approached the front door. He looked at Day, and then the door opened, and a bruised, bald headed man stood in the doorway. "Can I help you?"

Eliote took out his badge. "Hi, I am Detective Chief Inspec…"

Before he could finish saying his name, the bald headed man eagerly piped up. "I know who you are, Mr. Eliote. You saved my life a couple of years ago, when I was pushed into a river in London."

Eliote paused for a second. After looking at Day with a puzzled look, he turned and scanned the man's face. "I remember." He pointed at the man. "You were having a few problems with some hooligans, as I recall, at a football match. I was driving past, jumped in after you."

"That's right! If it weren't for you, I would be dead! I never learnt to swim, you see." He smiled and then asked, "What can I do for you, Mr. Eliote?"

"We are trying to trace a Mr. Edward Pierce who lives next door."

The man looked at Eliote hard. "You don't remember me, do you? I am Edward Pierce." Both officers were clearly confused.

"Okay, Mr. Pierce," Day said. "Can we come in?" Edward allowed them into the house, and into a brightly lit sitting room. It had magnolia walls, and a large television in one corner, a beige sofa and chair opposite. They all sat down, and Edward looked at Eliote. A warm glow filled him; the man who had saved his life was in his home.

"I understand you didn't accept the bravery award that was offered to you."

Eliote shook his head. "It's not that I didn't want it, I was just doing my job, and, secondly, it would have made my job harder to do."

Edward was admiring his hero when Day asked, "Mr. Pierce, can I ask why your work has your home address as next door?"

Edward looked at her. "I own both houses, Sergeant. This house belonged to my mother, and I lived next door. When she died, I was left it in her will. I moved in here, but kept up the pretence of living there." Eliote thought this was a weird arrangement, but Edward elaborated, "I didn't want anyone living in either house. Memories are hard to erase." He looked at the two detectives. "So, what brings you to my door?"

Eliote allowed Day to answer; this was her case. "Mr. Pierce, we are investigating the fatal shooting of a man who was accused of a violent attack on you."

"Shot dead?" At first, he was shocked, but then his reaction changed. "Good. That son of a bitch got what he deserved. All I asked him to do was to move away, and the bastard hit me in the groin, and kicked me in the head, and then walked away." He had bitterness in his mouth. "I was found by other security personnel and rushed to hospital."

"Do you own a gun, Mr. Pierce?" Eliote queried.

Edward shook his head. "I did own one, but when my dear wife was killed by one a couple of years ago, I got rid of it."

"What make of gun was it?" Day piped up.

"What mine or the one used to murder my wife?" Edward said angrily.

Day replied, "Your weapon, Mr Pierce?"

"Beretta," he paused. "Got it on leave while I was in America."

"You were in the armed forces?" Eliote asked.

Edward nodded. "Ten years serving Queen and country, but that was before I met my wife."

"What happened to the gun?" Day probed.

"Sold it to the gun shop on the corner. You know. Andows."

Eliote glanced sideways at Day who replied, "Thank you for your help." She stood up, and Eliote followed suit.

"Ok." Eliote turned to Edward. "Thank you for seeing us, Mr. Pierce, and we'll be staying in touch." Both officers got up and headed for the door.

Once outside, Day looked at Eliote. "Thanks for coming with me, Gov. It has given me more questions than answers, but it's a start."

Eliote smiled. "I'll get you back to the station, and you can continue with your hard work."

She nodded and both officers jumped in the car. Day glanced over at her boss. "Can we stop at Andows first, Gov? If he lied about where he lived, what else could he be lying about?" Eliote nodded and started the car, driving away.

Both officers knew that Andows Gun Merchant had been a family run business for as long as the town had been in existence, and had owned the same plot for just as long. Eliote pulled into a small shabby run down car park and once again both officers departed the car, and headed for the shop.

When they entered, the first thing they noticed was the smell of gun oil. The Chief Inspector looked around the cases of riffles while Day approached the counter, where a handful of handguns and bullets were displayed in a security glass cabinet.

A woman came from a back room and approached Sergeant Day. "Can I help you?" she inquired.

Day showed her warrant card. "I am wondering if a Mr Edward Pierce sold you a Berretta?"

She grabbed a large A4 notebook from beneath the till, and using the tabs on the side, she opened a page. There, in detail, was Edward's handgun. "A Berretta 92fs Pistol, sold to us for a few hundred quid, a few marks and rust on the gun. I think it's still around somewhere."

Day asked her to find the item, which she did, and after both officers had examined the weapon, both were quite happy. Day addressed the clerk again. "Is it alright, for the time being, you don't sell this? Also, could we get a photo of the gun?" The female assistant nodded, and Day took out her mobile phone and snapped several pictures. After thanking the clerk for her time, the two detectives left the shop. "So, Gov, that knocks Edward off the list."

Eliote opened the car door and pushed his hand through his hair. "I would still do a bit more digging on Edward. I have a gut feeling that something isn't right. Check on his service record, and the death of his wife."

Day nodded in agreement, and the two drove back to the station.

WHEN ANGELS FEAST

By
Kevin Bailey

CHAPTER SEVEN

The next week went too quickly for all the officers at CID. Eliote, Day, and Charlotte continued with their prospective cases. Day had discovered Edward had served in the army since he was nineteen, risen through the ranks, and left as a Captain. His wife had been shot by an unknown assailant whilst heading to work. The weapon and killer were never found. She would continue to dig into his past while Frashier and Pickington prepared themselves for Jane's funeral.

Frashier was, of course, feeling anxious. He'd always had a soft spot for Jane. Deep down, he had hated that Alex had married the women of his dreams. This was a fact he had not told those around him, fearing maybe they would take him off the case, and he wanted to learn what had happened to her.

The day of the funeral came, and Frashier stood sombrely in the shower, allowing the water to trickle down his muscular body. It was as if the pain of her death was being washed away. After getting into a black suit, he made his way to the small village church in Loughton.

Outside the main gate, he was met by Pickington, and before they both joined the party of family and friends, Frashier gave Pickington his orders. "Right, Constable, eyes and ears open. Any information you think is relevant to the case, note it down, and we will investigate it later, okay?" Pickington nodded, and they walked through the gate, following others into the small church.

They sat near the back of the church and surveyed the guests. Most were either crying, or telling their nearest and dearest it had been a shock to find out about Jane and the children's deaths. Frashier looked down to the front of the church where the family had placed three large smiling photos of Jane and her two children. As he scanned the pictures, it took every ounce of strength in him to not break down himself.

But his feelings of loss were disturbed by a commotion outside, and when the two officers went to investigate, they could see a group of people near the main gate, surrounding two men who were being restrained. Frashier could make out that one of the two men was Alex, but he couldn't identify the other man.

Frashier and Pickington walked to the group, and both officers stood in the middle and looked at the gathering. "What the hell is going on?" Frashier asked, looking at both men, and then at his old friend. "Alex?"

His friend was looking aggressively at the other man, and then at a woman who was sobbing uncontrollably. Frashier could see that below the black netting covering her face was Tatyana, and he could make out her bloodshot eyes.

"He," Alex pointed at the other man, "won't let Tatyana in to the service. She has a right to mourn as well."

"I ain't gonna allow that Russian slag in to my sister's funeral. If it weren't for her and him," the man gestured to Alex, "my sister would still be alive."

Frashier looked at both men. "This is not the time, or the place, for this to happen. Jane is dead. Let's leave this until after the funeral, or shall we continue this down at the station?"

The group dispersed, and both warring parties were escorted to opposite sides of the church, with Pickington and Frashier stewarding.

The service began as the song, 'Who Wants to Live Forever?' by Queen played as the entourage of one large white and two small, brightly-coloured coffins were brought into the church. As the saddening procession approached the front, the sound of sobbing echoed around the church.

The Vicar approached the coffins, and after doing a sign of the cross, she faced the congregation and raised her arms to welcome everyone to the church. "We are gathered here today to say farewell to our sisters, Jane, Eve, and Amy, and to commit them into the hands of God." She began to read from the bible.

Frashier turned and looked at Alex, who was being consoled lovingly by Tatyana. She held him close to her, and was kissing him on the head. Frashier scowled at the outward display of emotion, and then looked over at Pickington. Using his head directed him in the direction of Alex and Tatyana. The Inspector glanced around at Jane's brother who too was looking at the show opposite and was shaking his head in disgust, but when he saw Frashier looking at him, he turned back quickly to look at the vicar.

After a while, the vicar looked at the man, and beckoned him to the front. "Jane's brother, Greg, will now say a few words."

Greg stood, and after glaring at Alex, he patted the larger coffin, and began his eulogy. "Hello, I feel sad that some of you didn't know my sister Jane as I did. She was a loving, caring, and thoughtful individual, who I loved dearly. She was unique."

Greg held back the tears as he read from an A4 sheet, Frashier started to feel the loss, and tried very successfully to stop himself from crying. "Even though when we were children, we didn't really get on. I hated the fact that she always got the biggest and best-dressed toys."

There was a small giggle from somewhere in the church.

"But as we grew older, I came to realise that my big sister had a heart of gold, and if you had a problem, she would try and help. If you needed comforting, her shoulder was always there. She was the best sister any man could ever have, and I was proud to call her mine."

Greg turned to the next sheet, and all the congregation could see the red eyes looking at the words, which he had written from the heart. "She was also the best mother in the world, who adored her children, and tried to protect them always, and I know will do so in heaven. To Eve and Amy, what can I say about two of the most adorable children, gone before their…"

He stopped and bowed his head, Frashier could hear him say to himself, "You can do this. Hold it together, Greg." He looked up.

"…Gone before their time. I remember when Eve, the eldest, came to my house with Jane. I offered her a biscuit out of the tin, and after a while, she came back to ask if she could have another and then another. This went on for ages until there was none left. Then just before she went, she asked if she could have a bag, I asked why she wanted a bag and she innocently replied. "To take the biscuits she had saved for her sister Amy, so they could eat them later," She'd been stock piling them."

There was a lot of laughter, and people were talking amongst themselves, remembering the same past encounters. "They both gave their love completely, and with their mother, made our lives complete. Thanks Sis, for being my sister and my friend."

He walked back to his seat and burst into tears. A woman, whom Frashier assumed was his wife, comforted him.

After the service and the internment, everyone headed for a local pub. Both officers followed, mingling with the bereaved. Alex and

Tatyana hadn't come to the pub. It was obvious to Frashier they didn't want any more confrontations. After talking with some of Jane's family, the inspector took his orange juice outside, and saw Greg sat on a bench, looking out towards the town of Chelmesbury. He turned when he saw Frashier approach. "Sorry, can I join you?"

Greg beckoned him to sit down. "Please." Frashier sat down. "I understand you're a police officer." He nodded. "Come to arrest Alex?"

Frashier raised an eyebrow in curiosity. "Why, what's he done?"

Greg smiled wryly. "I'm sure I could make stuff up, Detective…"

"Sorry, DI William Frashier."

Greg looked puzzlingly at him. "You were Alex's mate at school?"

"I was," Frashier said, drinking some of his orange juice. "But I am here on a purely business matter. I would like to ask why you were at loggerheads, before the service?"

Greg took a long swig of his glass and sat forward to look at the Inspector. "This on record?"

"Do you want it to be?" Frashier asked.

"It should be. Jane left because of Alex and that Russian Slut."

Frashier was intrigued. "Go on."

"All right. Jane and Alex's marriage had been on the rocks for a while. He'd been born into money, she hadn't. Some people said she'd only married him for the money."

Frashier interrupted him. "I wouldn't say that. When I knew them, they were very much in love."

Greg looked deep into Frashier's eyes. "At the beginning, maybe." He looked back at his half full glass. "Then came the children, and the arguments started. Small ones first, and then, they became vicious on both sides." Greg paused, taking a sip of his drink. "All I heard was something happened before the children came along, something so bad, that every time they'd have an argument, he would bring it up, and she would leave. Days later, they would get back together, and they would be loved up again."

"Is that why she and the kids left him?"

Greg shook his head. "No, Jane and Alex were going to Germany to see some friends, and the day before they were planning on going, Alex had to stay because of a deal, which he couldn't get out of. So she'd gone with the kids alone, but to surprise him, she'd come back early. Asked me to have the kids under the pretence she was going to spend a nice couple of hours together, you know, just the two of them." He took another swig. "But she told me later, she'd got there, and had heard groans from the bedroom, and found him in bed with that slut," he said vehemently. "She ran out, screaming, and came here for a night. He didn't stop ringing her mobile and the house phone. He even tried mine, and I told him to f... go away. She ignored him, but then, I heard her talking to someone. The next day, they all left, and that was the last time I saw them."

Frashier was angry. Alex had lied to him, and he would find out why. However, at this moment, he could do nothing but watch, as Greg swelled up with tears, so he asked, "Do you know who this person was?"

"She just said it was a friend, and wouldn't tell me their name." Greg drank the last bit of his pint, and after excusing himself, he left the detective to his thoughts.

Detective Constable Pickington walked over to the brooding Inspector, who on his approach, turned and looked at him. "What did you find out, Constable?"

He sat down and began his report. "The gist of what people have said about Jane, mirrors what her brother said in his eulogy, but if you talk about her husband, you get a different reaction, one of hatred," he paused, "I get the impression he wasn't well liked, and it was him, not her, who was a cheat, and it was with that Russian bird." Now it was confirmed, Frashier stood up, anger filling his veins.

"Come on. I think it's time we left this family to grieve. I have a few questions I need answered."

WHEN ANGELS FEAST

By
Kevin Bailey

CHAPTER EIGHT

Over the previous week, Charlotte had been feeling very exhausted. Even though working with Eliote was always fun, it could be extremely draining. When she returned to her home, and after she had done her usual rituals, she'd got into bed, and fell into a deep sleep.

Charlotte dreamt she was on a starship, travelling amongst the stars, sitting in the command chair giving orders to the crew, when one of the crew approached her, and when he opened his mouth to report, the words that came out surprised her.

"Lotte, little Lotte, come out and play." She saw on the large viewer a whirlpool. Looking around, Charlotte realized none of the crew saw the image. They continued with their jobs. She tried to get their attention, but they ignored her.

She looked back at the whirlpool, just as an airlock blew open, and everyone on the bridge was sucked out into space. She was overcome with the familiar feeling she always had when she fell through the swirling mists of her mind.

She then found herself in an overgrown cemetery. She could see and hear the town of Chelmesbury, with its blinking lights and the moving vehicles. Suddenly she could hear the sound of stone moving, and a dark shadow appeared behind her. She could hear her heart beating faster as she turned slowly to see what was behind her.

There, pointing to somewhere in the town, was the stone angel. It had moved from its base, and was stood smiling at her. She realised that it was her face on the angel.
She froze, fixated on it. The face changed to Simon's, and he didn't look happy. The arm kept beckoning her to the town, and at a point. Turning once again to look at Chelmesbury, she was suddenly transported to somewhere in the town, a part she didn't recognize, but she realised she had also been transported in time.

People in nineties-style clothing walked past her, towels under their arms, heading for a swimming pool. Some way in the distance, others travelled in what Charlotte could make out were old cars, but these looked brand new.

Looking back up to the graveyard, she saw the Angel pointing to a path which rose up into the castle grounds. There, she spotted two strange looking people; both were frozen to the spot. On closer inspection, she could see one was a middle-aged man, and the other was an attractive younger woman. Their faces were blank, and she could see that their throats had been cut.

When Charlotte approached their location, the people disappeared quickly, and she turned to look back at the Angel, but it had gone. In its place was an open door. Before leaving, she looked around, trying to remember the location so that she could tell Simon, when a noise made her stop and look up.

It came from a woman who was walking towards her, a bag under her hand. She had a beautiful smile on her face. Charlotte could hear the sweet sound as this woman hummed to herself. The face looked very familiar, but she couldn't recount where from. Turning back, she watched the lady as she approached the old swimming pool.

It was then Charlotte remembered the old pool. It had been closed for many years, replaced by a newer, bigger one at the secondary modern school. She had spent many a summer here with her friends. Charlotte looked down the road at the sports field, and saw children and parents playing and having picnics on the grass. Maybe, if she went there, she would see herself playing, being watched by her beloved father.

As if to distract her, she became aware of the presence of a man, who had appeared from the footpath. Seconds later, he dragged the women down an alleyway next to the pool. The women tried to scream, but she was stopped from doing so by the man putting his hand around her mouth.

Charlotte tried in vain to call for help, but no one could hear her. She walked slowly down the alleyway, and came out next to the river. Water rushed over the weir loudly. The area used to be the site of a corn mill. She stared out at the weir and remembered sliding dangerously down into the cold water below on numerous occasions.

Again, she was distracted by a loud whistle, and the sounds of people inside the pool having fun with their friends. She walked alongside the water's edge, and brushing past bramble bushes and nettles, she emerged underneath the stone bridge.

The soft sound of groaning came from some bushes beyond, and she walked towards them. There, she found the man had pushed the women to the floor, and was raping her. He was obviously enjoying the sensation, groaning with pleasure. When Charlotte looked at the women, her eyes were dull, as if she had switched off, and was blanking the ordeal.

Charlotte went to speak, in the hope it might disturb the rapist, but before she could say a word and without warning, she found herself sat upright in her bed. The sweat from the vision soaked her nightie, which clung to her body. She knew what she must do, so she went and got changed, and headed for her car, not realizing it was two in the morning.

***

The sound of a buzzer going off somewhere in the house awoke Eliote from his slumber. After getting up and turning on the bedside light, he approached the front window and looked out. He saw a small vehicle at the gate, and knew it could not be the office. They would have rung first.
He saw the gate open, and the small car come up the drive, pulling up next to his Saab. Eliote was about to put on his dressing gown, when there was a knock at the door. He found Henry there, looking a little tired. "Who was at the door, Henry?"

"Not to worry, Simon. It's just Miss Steel again." Eliote looked at his wristwatch, and then looked back at the old face. "She wants to talk to you, says it's urgent." The last word came out as a yawn.

"Okay, where is she now?" Henry pointed to the drawing room. Eliote nodded and ordered, "You go back to bed, old friend. I'll deal with Miss Steel, and escort her out."

The old man smiled. "Very good, Simon." He left, and Eliote walked down the old staircase, opening the door to the drawing room.

He found an extremely pale Charlotte. "Is everything okay?"

She shook her head. "I had another vision." Eliote sat down and beckoned her to do the same. "It was of a couple, a middle-aged man and a younger woman, both had had their throats cut…"

"I know you want to keep me busy Charlotte," Eliote said, interrupting her, "but don't I have enough to deal with?"

She jumped to her feet, and paced around the room. "I know, Simon, but I believe this is connected somehow to the cases we are dealing with."

"How do you know that? Did you see a stone marker?"

"Not in so many words, but since we began collaborating, Simon, the visions have always been connected to the case we were working on. This, I believe, was no exception."

Eliote looked warmly at her. "Okay, where was the location of this vision?"

Charlotte's relief crossed her face. "Somewhere I spent a lot of time at when I was a kid. Do you remember the old swimming baths?"

Eliote leaned back onto the couch cushions. "I spent all my summers either at my father's parents' house in London, or here at the Priory. I learnt to swim in our small lake."

Charlotte nodded and imagined the scene as Colin Firth, who played Mr. Darcy in *Pride and Prejudice*, but it was Eliote jumping into the lake. She groaned quietly.

Eliote brought her out of her daydream. "Charlotte, are you alright?"

She started to blush and walked quickly to a set of curtains which covered one of the large bay windows and pulled them open, looking out into the courtyard. "Yes, I'm fine," she lied.

"Where were the old swimming baths?" he asked, still concerned.

"They were situated just down from the castle, not far away from…" She froze and then spoke, "The angel smiled at me and told me where to go!"

"You saw the killer this time?"

"No, I saw the stone angel." He looked puzzled. "You know Mathew's Angel, the one in the old St. Mathews graveyard?"

"Oh, that one." Eliote contemplated the meaning of the vision before standing. "I'd better go and get some drinks on; we may have a long time to wait."

"I'm ready now. So get dressed, and we can go."

Eliote raised an eyebrow incredulously. "Charlotte, it's nearly three in the morning, and it's still dark out there."

She looked at her watch, and after shaking it for a few seconds, realised that it had stopped working. Eliote gestured to the large grandfather clock, which began striking three. "Ah, okay." She sat down, and he went and got ready.

As she waited, Charlotte scanned the pictures on the fireplace, and came to one of a happy woman on a bike. She did a double take, and shouted for Eliote, who came running in. "You okay?"

She showed him the photograph. "Who is this?"

He didn't have to think about it. "That's my mother, it was taken in Chelmesbury somewhere. Henry says it was taken in the eighties, before she began aging quickly." Eliote took the photo from her and looked at his mother, who seemed happy and radiant. "I don't remember my mother like this. To me, she was always miserable, distant and grumpy. When I see her in my mind, it's the woman in the large painting in the hall, not this."

Charlotte could see the hurt this picture gave him. "I am so sorry, Simon."

He looked at her, and she could see his eyes were red. "Why are you sorry?"

Charlotte sadly stared at Simon's pail coloured eyes "I think your mother was raped. I saw this lady," she pointed at the photo in Eliote's cradling hands, "being dragged behind the old swimming baths and raped."

Eliote began to get angry. "That's not true. She was raped, but by my father on their wedding night." Lurking just outside the door and listening to the two friends arguing, Henry walked quietly to the doorway and spoke.

"You are correct, Simon, but," he glared at Charlotte, angry that she had revealed a dark secret to Eliote. "Miss Steel is also correct."

***

Scott Morris, the driver of a yellow Mercedes Atego, turned into a parking space next to the Millennium Green, or as the people called it, the Chelmesbury Beach. After turning off the engine, he and his team of labourers got out and approached the back of the truck. Perusing his work sheet, he ordered his team to grab the pick-axe, a couple of spades, a bag of quick mix concrete, some water, and one of the posts. They made their way up the path and stopped.

Scott looked back with his blue eyes over at the green, and saw that some staff were preparing the café, which once housed the old swimming pool's pumping machines. He addressed the youngest member of his team. "Hey Sean, go and ask if we can order a couple of brekkies and some tea." He gave the young lad a twenty-pound note. "And I want the change this time."

The lad sighed. "All right, Dad." The boy walked back towards the old swimming pool. Scott moved back to the other members of his team.

"Right then, Bob, let's get this done. We've got about eighteen of these bloody signs to put up before lunch." The balding man nodded. Scott had lit a cigarette, and the two men began to dig a hole. It was hard graft, so Bob grabbed the pick-axe, and began to try and soften the ground.

Suddenly, Bob stopped. "What the fuck's that?" he demanded and looked at the end of the pick-axe.

Scott examined it, and realised it was a Rolex watch. "Blimey that's a find. What else is in there?" The two men looked into the hole they had just dug, and really wished they hadn't.

At that moment, Sean came back to tell his dad breakfast was on its way. He found the two men looking at the ground.

"What up, Dad?" Scott looked white.

"To hell with the breakfast, you'd better go and ring the police."

Sean peered down, and saw what his father was looking at. "Is, is," he stuttered, "is that a…"

Scott nodded, and shooed his son away to make the call.

***

"What do you mean by that statement?" Simon demanded. Henry walked solemnly into the room and looked out of the window. "She was raped twice, once by your father, and then by another man."

Simon approached his mentor. "I suppose this rape was hushed up as well?"

Henry nodded. "Yes, the family thought it best it never came out, so the second rape was never reported."

Simon walked away, the anger raging in every part of his body. "You're telling me that my mother was savagely raped, and no one was brought to justice? What is it with our family? Everything is so bloody secretive!" He spun and glared at Henry, the anger reaching fever pitch. He could feel himself hyperventilating. "Is it the so-called 'blue blood' that runs through the family veins?"

Henry approached quickly and squared up to Simon. "That blue blood, as you call it, runs through you too, Master Simon."

Eliote walked away from Henry to look out of the window. "If I had my way, I'd drain out the bloody lot, and fill it with common blood," he paused, trying so hard to calm himself down before he said anything he would later regret. "But I'll tell you this," he said, looking back at Henry. "One of the best things that my grandfather ever did for me was to give the family title and lands to my uncle. I have never seen myself as Lord of the Manor."

Henry pointed at him. "That is still your family heritage, Master Simon, and you should be proud of it, but as always, you deny it."

Eliote smashed his hand down on the top of a chair, and both Charlotte and Henry could see real anger in his eyes. The change in emotions had Charlotte feeling afraid, and she cowered away slightly, but Henry stood his ground as Eliote walked towards him, his fist clenched. "I escaped that heritage, if it was up to me," he said with gritted teeth. "I'd bulldoze the lot, and sell every last bit of my family's heritage, and have the normal life I always sought after."

He faced Charlotte. "When I was a child, that heritage he speaks off, paid for friends to come and play with me, paid for expensive toys and games, stuff that I did not want, paid for birthday parties, where the children in the village were paid to come. I would sit there and watch them all be smiles and friendly to me, but at school, they wouldn't come near me. Some did, but only to bully."

Eliote focussed back on Henry. "So I am going to bulldoze the secrecy, and let the secrets come out. Do you hear me, Henry?" The elder man just stood there, looking at his master. Eliote could see no movement in him, he just maintained a stoic expression. "I want the facts!" Eliote demanded.

"I cannot give you any facts, Master Simon," Henry said calmly but with an air of sarcasm. "I was only told many years later. All she said was she was heading to the pool to have her morning swim, when she was grabbed from behind, and pulled kicking and screaming into some bushes, and then raped. Because of the first rape, she blanked out the pain, and the man who raped her," he paused, obviously in emotional pain. "She never described her attacker, and afterwards, she continued with the little life she had, hoping that she would never see him."

Simon frowned. "So, she did know her attacker?"

Henry nodded. "Yes, she knew him, but also knew if she told me, I would have killed him. She didn't want to lose me."

"I was a police constable. She could have come to me, and I would have brought this perpetrator to justice."

Henry sadly looked at him. "I did beg her on numerous occasions to come forward, but she refused. I kept it up until the day she died, but she was adamant she would take the secret to the grave."

Simon was about to say something when the phone rang, and he answered, almost snapping, "Hello?"

It was Day who was apologetic, "Sorry to disturb you, Gov, but we have been called to the Millennium Green. Some council workers who were putting up some signs nearby have found a hand buried in the ground."

Eliote sighed and looked at Charlotte. "I'll collect Miss Steel, and be there ASAP." He hung up and spoke to Charlotte, "Where did you say that vision was situated?"

"Near the old Chelmesbury swimming baths. Why?"

"Workers have just unearthed a skeleton near that location."

Charlotte seemed a little delighted by this turn of events, perhaps glad she was leaving the arguments. "I'll wait for you in the car."

Eliote nodded, and she left the two men alone. Henry walked up to Simon, and solemnly said, "You'll have my resignation on your desk by the end of the day."

Eliote stood frozen for a while, but replied, "If that is your wish." Henry nodded. "Then so be it." He walked out of the room, leaving Henry to take one final look around the stately surroundings.

**

Alex Boyd woke from his dream and stared at the empty room. He remembered his children bouncing on the bed, and him nearly tickling them to death. He was just about to try and get some more sleep, when his alarm on his phone went off, and he saw he had a text. Reading the message, he clicked cancel and clicked on contacts, scrolling down until he reached the desired number. He heard it ringing, and a female voice answered, "Hi."

He smiled. "Hello, is the deal still on?"

After some hesitation, the woman responded, "Of course."

"Good. We will meet in the usual place." Waiting for her confirmation, Alex hung up the phone. Stretching, he got up and put on his dressing gown. He went out of his bedroom and down to the kitchen where classical music was playing.

Tatyana was making him a full English breakfast. She smiled warmly at him when he entered, and she approached the CD player, pressing stop.

He did not smile at her, but simply said, "I'm sorry, but I'm going to have to let you go."

She turned from the cooker and stood there, shocked, a wooden spoon in her hand. "Let me go? But why? After everything I have done for you?"

Alex had no remorse for what he was doing. "I have no children anymore, so I don't require a nanny, and as I am selling this place, I don't need a housekeeper." He turned, and as he moved out of the kitchen, he remarked, "You'll be paid until the end of the month, plus two months for all you hard work. Then, you're on your own." He went to walk away, when he heard her shout a few words in Russian, and the pan containing baked beans come hurtling towards him, missing him by inches.

Angry at her outburst, he screamed, "GET OUT OF MY HOUSE!" She tried to apologise, but he pointed at the door. "OUT!" She bowed her head in shame, and headed for the door, as she was about to leave, she looked at him.

"You'll be sorry." She slammed the door shut behind her.

Alex smiled evilly. "That was easy. Now to get on with my life!" He went back upstairs and got dressed.

WHEN ANGELS FEAST
By
Kevin Bailey

CHAPTER NINE

Simon was quiet as they headed for the scene of crime. He'd told Charlotte of Henry's resignation and this she knew was hurting him badly. Still, as they passed the open playing field everyone in the town called the 'Linney,' they could see flashing blue lights in the distance, and his whole demeanour changed. He sat up straight in his seat and remarked, "Here we go again." It was as if the blue light ignited him, and he felt at peace.

Without warning, Charlotte lapsed into a vision, feeling herself being transported to an open field, the cows grazed, and the world tranquil. She felt the grass between her toes, and breathed in the sweet smell of roses, which emanated from a large bush next to her.

Gazing around, she saw a woman smiling at her, and she realised it was the woman in the wedding pictures, the one who had warned her to go to Simon, and get him back to work. Fixating on her, she saw the woman began to walk towards her.

When she got close, Charlotte could see that the woman was extremely beautiful. When the apparition finally spoke, it was like angels singing, and Charlotte was mesmerized by her. "Simon is not ready to be alone."

Charlotte didn't understand. "You want me to be with him?"

The woman shook her head. "No!" she snapped. "Your paths go in separate ways. He must be with the protector."

Charlotte was shocked. "Protector…are you referring to Henry?"

The woman nodded. "Yes, but there will come a day when my beloved will find love again, and he will no longer need Henry. The protector will then re-join his love."

Charlotte was slightly horrified. "Are you saying, the day Simon's new love comes, Henry will die?"

"Like I said, he will re-join his loved one, and have eternal peace, his reward for protecting our," Charlotte saw another women approach, and she recognised the women as Simon's mother.

"Simon," they both spoke at the same time. The first women smiled at the other women, and then she turned back to Charlotte.

"When that day comes, this new love will protect him until the day he dies, and then we will be able to rest in peace." Simon's mother spoke to her.

"You must join them back together, will you do this for us?"

Charlotte looked away from the women. "I will try, but he is stubborn!"

Simon's mother smiled and nodded. "You will find a way, Charlotte. You always do." She smiled dotingly. "Your father is very proud of you."

Charlotte gazed at the spectre with tears brimming in her eyes. "My father!"

The woman touched her cheek, as a mother would to her child and wiped the tears away. "You will see him again one day, until then…"

Charlotte felt somebody prodding her and turning away, she half expected to see a cow nudging her…

"Charlotte, we are here. You can get out if you want to." She was a little dazed and confused, but the sight of Simon, looking worryingly towards her, brought her out of her confusion.

"Yeah, sorry, I was in a world of my own."

He looked scared. "Do I have to be worried?"

She smiled. "No, it was a pleasant dream."

He opened his car and remarked casually, "That's a relief. I thought maybe this case was going to get a little more complex."

The two of them got out, and while she mingled with the uniformed officers, he walked to a taped off area and got kitted up.
Placing on covers to protect his shoes, he trundled under the tape and approached a white tent, which had been erected some way up the path and into the undergrowth. Two people were waiting for him, and he identified them as Strong and Day.

"Morning," he barked, making them look in his direction.

"Gov," Day replied.

"So, report please, Doctor!"

Strong looked at his notes, and pulled back the tent flaps to reveal several Scene of Crime Officers, Socos for short, scraping away the soil, layer by layer, like archaeologists on some historic site.

"Since we arrived, we have discovered there are two human skeletons, one male and one female. The male has signs of arthritis in his joints, so I'd say he was in his late fifties when he died. The female looks younger, probably late twenties, early thirties, hard to tell."

Eliote looked into the grave. "How did they die?"

Strong pointed to several parts that were visible. "That is the easy bit, from cut marks around the cervical vertebrae, it would appear that they've had their throats cut." He pointed to deep cuts on both skeletons, and then walking behind Day. "Sorry, Day." Strong mimicked coming up behind her and slashing the neck area.

"No problems," she lied, scowling.

Strong consulted his notes. "Right then, there are also signs of butchery around the female's genital area."

Eliote was given a magnifying glass, and the doctor circled the area around the hips of the smaller skeleton with his pen. "This whole section, from this leg to this leg, has been cut away. You can see there are deeper cut marks in both legs and hips."

"Gruesome," Day remarked.

"Very, Sergeant," he paused. "Whoever killed these poor bastards is one sick killer, and whatever he used to kill them, the blade must have been extremely sharp."

"Could it have been a robbery gone wrong?" Day asked.

Doctor Penny Hardcastle shook her head. "If this was a robbery, why did we found a Rolex, along with a wallet full of old twenty-pound notes, a few very expensive pieces of jewellery, and a couple of gold rings."

Eliote looked at the evidence tray. "It still could be robbery. Maybe the perpetrator planned to come back later?"

Strong stepped back. "With all this stuff up for grabs, I don't think so. Something isn't right with that hypothesis. Would you leave all this?"

Eliote shrugged his shoulders. "Probably not, but someone left them as a clue." He saw Charlotte looking at him from beyond the tent. "I know it's a long shot, but you haven't found a stone with engraving on, have you?"

Strong was shocked. "How did you know about our star find?" Penny lifted a tray, and there, in the ground, was an iPad-sized piece of rock. Eliote and Day could see words had been scratched onto its surface, and it read:

'BETRAYERS BEWARE. FOR TONIGHT, THE ANGELS FEAST'

Eliote watched as Penny replaced the tray over the find. "Whoever this man was, he wasn't short of a few bob. We found pieces of clothing indicating he shopped in Saville row in London, and a wallet with, unfortunately, no ID, that came from an upmarket gentleman's outfitters in Worcester."

Eliote remarked, "Got around a bit, didn't he? What can you tell about the woman?"

"From the fabrics found on her, I'd say she also wore high end clothing, as well as an expensive matching set of pearl earrings and necklace, in addition to another smaller necklace, which this was attached to." She pulled out an evidence bag containing a heart-shaped locket.

Eliote looked at Strong. "Have you looked inside?"

Strong nodded and handed Eliote another evidence bag which held a faded picture of a face. Eliote beckoned Day to have a look, but both officers couldn't tell whether the subject was male or female. "Anything else, doctors?" Eliote asked, and handed Penny the evidence bags.

"Nothing at the moment, but when the skeletons are back at the lab, we will be able to do a better examination of them."

Eliote nodded. "Okay, report as, and when, you can!" Both he and Day walked towards the tape. Eliote took off his protective clothing, and after handing them to an officer, he asked Day, "Have you taken statements from all the witnesses?"

"Did it just before you arrived." She pointed to three men who were sat at a bench, drinking hot tea. "They are the ones who found the bodies. They were putting up 'No Litter' signs along the paths."

"Excellent work, Inspector." Everyone looked at Day, who was blushing. Eliote raised his hands to apologise. "I'm sorry, Miranda. I'm an idiot."

Day looked around the officers. "It had to come out sometime, Gov," she said, coldly. "I just wanted to tell everyone."

Eliote felt like a fool, but maybe he deserved it. He had been a miserable oaf for months. "Okay, people. Back to work." They did as was ordered, and he looked at the blushing detective. "Right, you have a choice. You can either help me with this enquiry, or you can deal with the shooting of Nicolas Waite."

Day seemed a little peeved at this question. "Why do I have choices, Gov?"

"I now have two inspectors in my department, so therefore, I am going to need one of them to work with me. As my relationship with Frashier isn't perfect, I would like it to be you! He can deal with the other cases."

She cursed under her breath. She'd had an inkling this was going to happen. "Okay, Gov. I'll fill Frashier in with my cases. He can do it, as well as the body in the ditch case."

Eliote looked confused. "I thought that case was finished. I mean, what with Doctor Strong proving that they died of hyperthermia, that should have been an end of it being a CID case, and it should have been passed to uniform."

Day agreed, but replied, "He still feels there are more questions than answers, like what was she doing out late with her children?"

"Okay," Eliote said bluntly, "but tell him I want the loose ends cleared up and the case closed ASAP. The shooting of Nicolas Waite is to be his top priority."

Day nodded and stormed off. Eliote watched her leave, and knew she was angry at the choices he had just given her, but he had his reasons.

The smell of bacon cooking wafted up Eliote's nose, and he felt hungry. Heading back over to Charlotte, who was drinking a cup of tea, she handed him a second cup.

"Thanks, I needed this." He looked up at a waitress who was loitering around. He got her attention, and asked for a bacon sandwich. The waitress headed off to get his order, and he took a swig of the tea, smiling. "That's better." Charlotte was staring off at the bridge in the distance. "I'm sorry to ask this, Charlotte, but I'm going to need a statement off you, everything you saw in the vision."

She barely shifted her gaze back to him. "Everything, Simon?"

"At this present time, the rape might be linked."

Charlotte wrapped her arms around her chest. "I'll try."

The waitress returned, and he took a large bite of the sandwich. "That's lovely. Do you want some?" Eliote tried handing it over to Charlotte, but she held up her hand to refuse. "Suit yourself," he said, taking another mouthful. She was looking puzzled. "What's up?" he queried, as he drank some of his tea.

"It's the vision; they usually mean something. So what about Mathew's Angel? I saw that as well."

"You couldn't have. If you had been at St. Mathews, you wouldn't have seen this, as it's on the other side of the town."

Charlotte glanced over to where she saw the angel, and it was just trees. "Right, but I still think there is a connection. Why would I have seen it?"

"I don't know how your mind works, and I don't think I ever will." After finishing off his sandwich and placing a crisp twenty pound note on the table, Eliote got up and walked towards the water's edge. He stared at the flowing river, deep in thought as the water flowed over the weir.

Charlotte sat watching him as she drank the remainder of her tea, wondered whether he was thinking about his mother. She could see he was looking at the bridge. She placed her cup on the table and turned her attention to the hill overlooking them. She wondered why the angel had come to her.

Standing up, she walked over the bridge, and headed for the place where, in her vision, she had seen the angel.

***

Loughton-on-Teme, England

Mrs. Pamela Griffiths loved her new home. Her children had done a grand job of getting the bungalow ready for her, but the garden needed a lot of work. She had decided to plant some flowers in the borders, ready for the summer, which was a mere few months away.

Taking a spade and a trowel from the small shed, she approached the borders and began work. Her golden retriever, Meg, lay on the ground next to her. As she dug, she found a selection of small bones in the ground, but not knowing what animal they were from, she threw them in the direction of Meg, who got up, and devoured them.

Not far from where she crouched, behind a secret wall, flies began to circle the room.

WHEN ANGELS FEAST
By
Kevin Bailey

CHAPTER TEN

Charlotte approached the spot where the Angel had brought her to and she looked down and could see the police officers working hard below, scurrying around like ants. Simon was right. The angel could not see the site as she couldn't see anything, as most of the town of Chelmesbury was hidden behind the imposing walls of the medieval castle which dominated the landscape.

Turning from the Castle, she looked out across the fields and recognised the buildings of the secondary school, the bells ringing for morning break. She could also see the small hamlet of Loughton-on-Teme, its bungalows and houses doting around a central green, but as she gazed in awe of the beautiful Shropshire countryside, she could not see why the angel had brought her here.

"You wanna be careful, miss!" Charlotte turned and saw a man observing at her. He was wearing what could only be described as shabby clothes, and had a raggedy grey beard and balding hairline. He was carrying a rucksack.

"Excuse me?" she enquired.

"I was just warning you that you are getting a little close to the edge. The ground has a tendency to give way in certain areas."

Charlotte could see pain in his eyes, but didn't want to ask why, so she moved away. "Thank you, Mr…?"

"Swinburne, Harry."

"Thank you for warning me, Harry." She walked towards him. "What brings you to this spot?"

Harry took off his rucksack and pulled out a flask. "I always come here. It's where me and my late wife used to come when we were courting."

"What happened to her?"

He poured a drink from the flask, and she could smell the alcohol in the coffee. "She left me for another man. Never found out where she went. I have only just come back to the area; so thought I would revisit old haunts." A tear trickled down his cheek. She handed him a tissue, and he wiped away the tears. "So," he drank some of the hot coffee, "what brings you to this place?"

She pointed down at the police activity. "I'm with them!"

Harry looked down at the scene. "Okay, so you're a copper."

"No, I am helping them with their enquiries."

"So, what have they found down there?"

"They have found the remains of a couple, both have had their…" she froze, "I'm sorry, I really shouldn't be telling you."

He just shrugged his shoulders and drank more of the coffee. "I don't care." He put the flask back in the bag and smiled at her. "It was pleasant to talk with you."

Charlotte smiled back. "Maybe we can talk again."

Harry walked back towards the path, and the trees beyond. As he did, he answered her, but the words echoed around the area like the wind, "Maybe!"

Simon had been watching Charlotte talking to Harry and wondered who the man was. He was distracted by the approach of a confident Strong.

"We have found a piece of paper with a name on it."

Eliote took the evidence bag and read out the name, "Rebecca Swinburne." He beckoned one of his officers over to him. "Can you get onto the station and check on this name?" The female officer nodded, and as she left, Charlotte returned and walked over to him.

"How's it going?"

"We have a possible name of the woman. I have sent DS Wright off to get some info on her, and we'll see where it goes."

Wright came back some time later, and approached Simon and Charlotte. "Rebecca Swinburne, went missing from her home fifteen years ago. Husband, Harry, reported she had left him for another man. The case became stagnated until it was reported Harry had rung his wife's mother, just after she had left, and threatened if he found them, he would kill them both."

Charlotte looked up at the spot where she had just talked to Harry.

Simon glanced over at her. "Are you alright?"

"Yeah, I'm fine," she lied.

"Who was that guy you were just talking to?"

Charlotte blushed. "Oh, him. He was just a backpacker, wondering what was going on."

Eliote could tell something was up, but he wasn't going to push her. "Okay," he said, and addressed Wright, "Find out where this Harry Swinburne lives. We may need to ask him a few questions. Also, get on to records. I want everything on the original case." DS Wright nodded and left.

Strong walked up to the group. "Just to inform you, the bones are being lifted."

Eliote thanked him and turning to Charlotte, who was still looking up into the woods. "Seeing something else, Charlotte?"

She regarded him indifferently. "No, I'm just looking," she snapped, and walked towards the café. Eliote now knew something was wrong. Who was that man? But he had a gut feeling, he already knew.

***

Detective Inspector Frashier walked into a very quiet CID. He spoke to an officer who was answering phones, "Where is everyone?"

"There all at the Millennium Green. Two skeletons have been found, possible murder investigation."

'Good,' he thought, 'If Eliote is up there, he could do what he wanted to do.'

As Frashier walked into his office, he heard the main door to CID slam shut. He spied an angry, red-faced Day come storming towards him.

"What's up with you, Miranda?"

"Two things." She pointed at him. "One, your bloody attitude. It's about time you buried the bloody hatchet with Eliote. I'm fed up with it."

Frashier felt like a school boy being reprimanded by a head teacher. "And, because of that animosity, I have been taken off my case, and placed on this murder investigation. You're to take control of my shooting case. It's just not fair. I just can't bloody wait to leave this station, then I can be the inspector I should be!" She slumped into a chair.

"You're leaving?" Frashier was shocked and saddened by the admission.

Day looked angrily at him. "Yeah, I got my promotion, and I leave for Birmingham when this case is over." She crossed her arms. "Whenever that is!"

"You're leaving?" he said again, sitting down in his chair. Day finally processed his question, and froze. She had hoped to tell him in different circumstances. Now, the two officers stared at each other for a few minutes, both wanting to say something.

It was Frashier who broke the deadlock. "Right then," he said, sitting up in his chair, keeping eye contact with Day. "I want all the case notes concerning your shooting." He wrote something on a notepad next to him. "I will join my case to that one, especially as both cases do have a slight connection." He picked up a phone and dialled Pickington. "Constable, I want you to liaise with Day. I want a detailed report of her case." He put the phone down, and she was about to say something, when he snapped at her, "Dismissed, Inspector!"

Day waited for a few moments, trying to get his attention, but he carried on writing. She got up and left the office. Frashier looked up, a slight sadness in his eyes, as he watched her go. He solemnly stood up and closed his door.

***

Detective Constable Wright walked up to Eliote, handing him the address of Harry Swinburne. He placed the note into his inside pocket, and both headed for the Saab.

Charlotte watched the two officers leave, and then asked a female constable who was watching the car drive away, "Where are they off too?"

"A suspect's house, one Harry Swinburne." Before she could say anymore, Charlotte hurried away.

Eliote drove the Saab into the town and approached what could be described as a rundown, townhouse. It had obviously been a beautiful dwelling at some point in its life. Eliote imagined in the late 1900s, it had probably belonged to a rich banker.

He pulled up outside the brick built house and gazed at a makeshift shed which was attached to the side. He could hear the sound of wood working tools being used. Both officers got out and opened a gate, entering a large driveway, which led down a path to the front door. Eliote rang the bell, and heard a dog bark. A Rottweiler looked at them from behind the blurred window in the door.

"Can I help you?" a voice said from behind them. They turned to see a small, chubby man, with greyish black hair and round glasses, peering at them.

"Hi, we are looking for Harry Swinburne."

The man stared at them. "Why do you want Harry?" Eliote pulled out his warrant card. "Coppers," he sighed. "Can't you lot leave the poor bugger alone? Hasn't he suffered enough? You sent him down for a crime he didn't commit, and now, you're pestering him again."

"We just need to…"

Another man came to the attention of Simon. "I'm Harry, what can I do for you?"

Eliote looked at the shabbily dressed man. He realised that it was the same man he had seen Charlotte talking to. "I would like you to come to the station."

Harry looked a little angry. "What for, you gonna pin something else on me?"

Eliote just looked at the man. "Please," he beckoned him to go with them. Harry sighed heavily and walked towards the gate.

"This is police harassment." He walked with Wright, who led him to the Saab and got in next to him. Eliote got into the driver's side and drove away.

As they drove away, the man from the shed shouted his wife, "SANDRA, SANDRA!"

A petite woman opened the front door. "What's up, Pete?"

Pete glared at her. "Get Giles on the phone. Inform him the police have taken Harry in for questioning, and tell him we don't know why!"

***

Giles Edwards sat at his desk, and was looking at some of the notes from a court case he was involved in, when the call came through from Sandra. "They've what?" He listened intently. "Okay, leave it with me." He slammed the phone down and grabbed his coat, heading out of the door.

His secretary stopped him. "Is everything okay, Giles?"

Giles shook his head. "Get me all the information we have on Harry Swinburne. He has just been arrested. I have to get to the station." The efficient woman went to a cupboard, and, after searching for a while, she handed him a folder, and he disappeared out the door.

***

Eliote called a meeting of all his staff upon their return to CID. All the officers filed into the room, carrying iPads and notebooks. Once everyone was assembled, he began, "Right, listen up people. I am splitting the team into two." He pointed at Frashier and a few officers who were hunched around the inspector. "You lot will be working alongside Frashier on the shooting of Nicolas Waite…"

Frashier piped up, "…and the death of Jane Boyd, we still have a few questions to answer."

Eliote glared at him. "I want the case of Jane Boyd handed over to uniform. They can deal with it."

Frashier's face darkened. "But…"

It was Eliote's turn to butt in. "…Do I make myself clear Inspector?"

Frashier bowed his head, trying to conceal the rage rising inside him. "Crystal clear, Gov."

Eliote returned to look at the rest of the team. "Good. The rest are going to work with me on this." He pointed at the screen as a picture of two skeletons appeared. "These were found in the castle grounds this morning. We have reason to believe the victims are linked to two possible cold cases. So, therefore, I'd like to introduce Detective Sergeant Denver Delaney, who will be helping us with the investigations."

Delaney stood up and took a small bow. "Right then, we have this man in custody." He pointed the pen-like device at the screen, and Harry's image appeared. "Harry Swinburne, arrested and charged with the murder of his wife, Rebecca."

A member of the team asked, "If he was found guilty of the murder, he can't be charged again, can he?"

Eliote shook his head. "No, he is here to answer a few questions. If he did murder his wife, then we need to know where he was when the other two people died. Strong says the murders were probably committed by the same person or persons." The team began writing down stuff on paper or their iPads.

There was suddenly a knock at the door, and a uniformed officer walked in looking sheepish. "Sorry to disturb you, Gov."

"What is it, Sergeant Wells?"

The sergeant walked towards him and informed him, "We have a Giles Edwards in reception. He wants to see you at once. He says he's Harry Swinburne's parole officer."

"Okay, Sergeant Wells. Place him in Holding Room 2. I'll be there as soon as I can." Without objection, the officer moved to follow Eliote's orders.

Watching the sergeant leave, Eliote addressed the room again, "I want Day and Wright to look into the original case against Swinburne." Day looked reluctant, but Wright seemed like she was chomping at the bit to get started. "I want the rest of us, and that includes myself, to go through some old cases, which DS Delaney has brought up from the depths of the station, including these two." He, once again, pointed at the screen with the pen device, and two images flashed up. One was the man hanging by hooks, and the other was of the body found on the golf course. "DS Delaney?"

The black officer stood and approached the front. "The cold-case unit has, in its files, about twelve cases which match the cases you are investigating. They became cold cases when the original investigations hit a dead end."

"How many contain a stone marker?" Eliote probed.

Delaney glanced at Eliote. "Four." He checked his notes. "Yeah, four, but the other eight have a few similarities to the others."

"Okay, it sounds like we may have another serial killer on the loose."

"It would seem so sir." Delaney grimaced in agreement.

Eliote looked concerned. "I think I had better go and inform Brightly of the situation so that she can plan her budgets!" he said sarcastically.

The briefing concluded, the officers dispersed, leaving only Frashier and his team to begin their meeting. Eliote nodded at the Inspector, and retired.

When Angels Feast

By
Kevin Bailey

CHAPTER ELEVEN

Frashier was so glad Eliote had gone, and as soon as it became quiet, he began his meeting. "Right, people. Edward Pierce. What information did you get about his wife?"

Pickington stood and read from his iPad, "Mrs. Pierce left her home at about eight, and headed for her job as a barmaid at the old pub called 'The Castle.' It was the one that used to be located in the high street, down from the Buttercross. As she walked from her home, she was shot dead by an unknown assassin, and her body was dumped on the common."

Frashier wrote a few notes. "Where was her husband at the time?"

"Edward was in London," Pickington raised his eyebrow, "as a royal bodyguard!"

"So, the Queen was his alibi," Frashier mocked. "How did he take it?"

One of the other detectives in the group read from a file, "When the investigating officer informed him, he went into utter shock, couldn't work and had to be sent home." Frashier made a snide comment. Ignoring his remarks, the female detective continued, "The file says..." She turned a page. "Later, he was admitted to hospital, and was placed on suicide watch. Social Services got involved, and this resulted in his two young children being put into foster care."

Frashier continued taking notes. "So, he was in a bad way." The team collectively nodded. "He seems to have made an okay recovery, owning two houses." Frashier scanned the room until he found the team member he sought. "Constable Dawes, get on to the insurance company. See if Mrs Pierce had an insurance policy, and if so, who the benefactor was. My money is on Edward."

The team seemed to look shocked at his comments. Pickington said what the others were thinking, "A little harsh, Gov. The man lost his wife. He has a watertight alibi, and you're making him prime suspect to a shooting we aren't even investigating. Shouldn't we be dealing with Nicolas's death?"

Frashier glared at him. "Okay, Constable," he said, irritated, "you're right." Pickington sort of smiled, as Frashier continued with the briefing, "The bullet that killed Mrs. Pierce, what did ballistics record as the murder weapon?"

Dawes turned the page and consulted the report. "They were inconclusive, Gov."

Frashier rubbed his chin. "Are there any theories in the file?"

"According to their findings, it could have been a berretta, but no weapon was found." She shrugged her shoulders.

Frashier observed the group of officers. "The bullets found in Nicolas Waite, do they match Mrs. Pierce's?"

Pickington sighed. "Gov, Edward was in a hospital bed, bruised and battered." He looked bemused at his superior. "You think he crept quietly out of hospital, killed Nicky, and snuck back in when no one was looking?"

Once again, Frashier glared at him, but the constable didn't seem frightened by his superior. "He could have, Constable!"

The tension between the two men reached a fevered pitch. The others felt, at any moment, the two were going to start fighting.

"I just don't buy it, Gov!" Dawes said, trying to settle the argument. "Edward has got an airtight alibi to both shootings, especially as one of those alibis just happens to be our Chief Inspector."

Both Pickington and Frashier looked at her. "Eliote?" they said in unison. She nodded and read the report. At the end, Frashier bowed his head in defeat.

"I still want you to get in touch with the insurance company." Pickington swore under his breath as Frashier continued, "And check with ballistics. See if the bullet found in Nicolas Waite was the same as the one used to kill Mrs. Pierce!"

Pickington shrugged his shoulder. "Once this meeting is finished, I will get on to them."

"No time like the present," Frashier remarked disdainfully, but Pickington wasn't listening. Instead, he was writing something down on his notepad. He looked up when he didn't hear anything, and saw Frashier looking glumly at him. "So, go on. What are you waiting for?"

"You want me to go now?"

Frashier narrowed his eyes, and Pickington got the message and left the room. Frashier then addressed the rest of the team, "I am setting off to re-interview Edward Pierce. I'll see if I can get anything else out of him." He gave the others their orders, and ended the meeting.

***

Eliote walked into Holding Room 2, and met Giles Edwards. The two men made polite introductions, and the meeting began.

"Chief Inspector, I am Harry Swinburne's probation officer. I've looked after him since he was released from prison last month." The two men sat down at the table.

"If you don't mind me asking," Eliote said, sitting back in the chair and placing his index finger to his lips. "How have you helped him?"

Giles smiled warmly. "We started by finding him somewhere to live. We have several safe houses we can call upon to house ex-cons," he said, almost gloating. "This permanent home gives him some stability, and a residence which allows him to find a job. We, of course, vet these new jobs," he sniggered. "We can't have a thief working in bank, or a paedophile working with children."

"So what job could you find a murderer?" Eliote asked bluntly, which made Giles look slightly annoyed.

"Harry has served his time. Shouldn't we let bygones be bygones?"

"I'll be sure to let his victim's family know he is happy and doing well."

Giles sat forward in his chair and stared intensely at Eliote. "Harry is well aware of the victim's family, Chief Inspector. He has written to them on numerous occasions, expressing his compassion for them, and informing them he is innocent and determined to clear his name."

Eliote opened the file in front of him, and Giles examined the visible pages. "What is that?"

"Oh, this. It's just Harry's original case notes and his confession." Eliote turned over the page. "DCI Christopher Reynolds, the officer leading the investigation into Rebecca's murder, asked Harry," He read the lines from the transcript, "'Did you kill your wife?' Harry replied, 'Yes!' Reynolds then asked, 'Where is the body, son?' 'I cut her up, and flushed her down the river.'"

"Chief Inspector, can I ask why you arrested Harry?" Giles tapped his fingers on the table impatiently.

Eliote paused in his recitation of the transcript. "He was not arrested. He was brought here to answer some more questions."

"What questions?" Aggravation dripped into Giles' tone.

"Let me ask you a question, Mr. Edwards. Do you think he killed his wife?"

Giles squirmed on the chair, disarmed by the question. "I cannot answer that. My job is to help them integrate back into society, whether he killed her or not."

Eliote smiled. "Of course, I'm sorry for asking you a difficult question. Let's get back to Harry. Where is he employed?"

"He is working as a night porter at The Three Feathers Hotel."

Eliote nodded. "Thank you." He closed the file and stood up. "I think it's time we had a chat with Harry, don't you?"

***

Pickington walked into CID, and headed for Frashier's office. He knocked at the door, and he heard the inspector shout, "Come in!" Frashier glared up at Pickington as he entered the room. "What is it, Constable?"

Pickington handed him the email he had received from ballistics. "I received that just now, Gov. They are saying there are similarities between the bullet that killed Nicolas Waite and the one that killed Mrs Pierce."

Frashier scanned the piece of paper. "Similarities…so, no solid proof?"

Pickington shook his head. "As you can see…"

"I can see, Pickington!" Frashier snapped at him, ensuring everyone in CID stopped what they were doing and glanced curiously towards the office. "I would also like to remind you I am your superior officer. I do not like your attitude and insubordination." He handed Pickington a note. "I have, therefore, sent Eliote a request to have you removed from my team, but, unlucky for you, he has denied my request."

Pickington slightly smiled, and said under his breath, "A little hypocritical."

Frashier stood up quickly, and dashed to stand in front of him, pointing his index finger at the obstinate officer. "I've warned you before about this, Constable! This is your final warning. I want you to go from this office, and be silent. I do not want to hear a peep from you. Do I make myself clear?"

Pickington sneered slightly, lacking all respect for Frashier. "Crystal, Gov!"

"Go and help Dawes with her work. She knows how to follow orders. Go on! Get out of my sight!"

Pickington turned and left the office red-faced, slamming the door shut as he did so.

"Little prick," Frashier grumbled, returning to his desk. He opened the file, and saw a picture of Jane smiling back at him. "Now, to finish off what I started." He touched her face, and closed the file. Grabbing his coat, he walked out of his office, and approached Dawes, who was copying some documents. "I'm popping out to see

Emelia Lock. I'll be back in a couple of hours, if anyone needs me." Before Dawes could acknowledge Frashier, he had left CID.

***

Eliote asked Giles to wait with Day outside Interview Room 1 while he headed for his office. He had left some notes, where he'd scrawled some question marks on, that he wanted to ask Harry. When he entered CID, he found the officers busy. Pickington had a disgruntled expression, but since Eliote had read Frashier's request, he made the assumption that was the reason, and ignored him.

As he passed Frashier's dark office, he stopped, glancing back at Pickington and Dawes. "Where's DI Frashier?"

"Gone to talk to Edward Pierce, Gov." The lie spilled from Dawes' lips before she could prevent it.

"What, without Pickington, or another officer?" He looked down thinking aloud, "I must have a word with him about police procedures." He turned, and still thinking, left their vicinity.

Pickington stared incredulously at Dawes. "Why did you lie to the Gov?"

"You do know who Emilia Lock is, don't you?"

He shrugged his shoulders. "Should I?"

"Emilia Lock is Jane's mother. Eliote would have his guts for garters, if he knew that."

Pickington snorted derisively. "Maybe he deserves it, the fucking wanker." He punched his fist on the table, spilling a tea over the desk.

"Maybe he does, but he is still our superior, and we have to follow his orders."

After Pickington had cleaned up the split tea, he sat down. "You're right, as usual, but one day, he will get his comeuppance."

Eliote was stood, just out of vision around a corner, and had heard Pickington's outburst. "So!" he said quietly to himself. "Frashier hasn't done what I asked." He glanced at the vacant office. "Don't worry, Constable. He will get his comeuppance, mark my words." With a dark promise made, Eliote resumed his trek to his office.

***

Frashier drove his grey BMW to the sleepy village of Loughton, and turned into a small drive, parking in front of a green garage door. He studied the neat looking bungalow, and saw a grey-haired woman looking out of a side window. She smiled when he got out, and he approached the door.

"Hello, stranger," the woman said, as she opened the door.

"Hi, Mrs. Lock."

She tapped him in the chest. "How many times have I told you? It's Emilia, or as my friends call me, Em." She beckoned him in, and he found himself in a large, well-presented kitchen. "Tea, coffee or something else?" she said, almost flirting with him.

"Tea, two sugars." Frashier ignored the blatant come-on.

Emilia switched on the kettle. "So, what brings you to my door?"

"Unfortunately, it's business." Frashier pulled out his warrant card.

She half-smiled. "Thought it might be, especially as you ignored me at the funeral."

Frashier apologised profusely, "Had to keep my distance. Haven't told my friends and colleagues at the station exactly how well I know the family."

Emilia made the drinks and walked into a large front room. "So, why have you come?"

"At the funeral, Greg told me Jane went to his house for a few days. Do you know where she went afterwards?"

Emilia drank some of her tea. "She rang and asked if she could come here for a few days. I agreed, and she came here. Alex kept ringing and ringing. She was scared he would show up. You know what he is like." Frashier nodded as Em continued, "She said she had to get away. She grabbed a few items and left!"

"Any idea where she went?"

"None." After a brief second, a light dawned in her eyes. "Wait, she made a phone call to somebody." She stood up and approached the phone. Notes were strewn over a small table. "I wrote the number down somewhere after she had gone, thinking maybe I could contact her there." She found the paper and handed it to him.

"Have you tried to ring it?"

"No. When I didn't hear from her, I did contemplate ringing it, but then she was…" Tears started to trickle down her chin.

"It's alright, Em." Frashier put his arms around her and comforted her.

After a while, he let go, and asked if he could borrow the phone. She nodded, and he dialled the number. It rang for a while, until a male voice answered, "St. Augustus Nursing Home, Daniel speaking."

"Hi there, Daniel. This is Detective Inspector William Frashier, Chelmesbury CID. I am enquiring if anyone there knew a Mrs. Jane Boyd?"

Daniel seemed to sigh. "I'll go and check with the home manager." There was a silent pause, and Frashier covered the mouthpiece, looking over at Emilia.

"Have you heard of St. Augustus Nursing Home?"

Emilia nodded. "Yes, Jane worked there, years ago, before she went to college. I don't know why she would…"

Frashier held up a finger as he heard a female voice on the other end of the receiver. "Hello, Inspector. I am Mrs. Gladys Cook. I understand from Daniel you are looking for anyone who knew a Jane Boyd?"

"That is correct!"

The woman was blunt. "I have checked with my staff, and no one here knows anyone called Jane Boyd."

Frashier cursed under his breath and quickly asked, "What about a Jane Lock?"

The woman's voice seemed to change at this new surname. "Of course, we all knew Jane Lock! How is she?"

"Would it be okay if I came and spoke with you?" Frashier knew he would have to break the news of Jane's death to the woman.

Mrs. Cook sounded worried. "That doesn't sound good?"

Frashier elaborated no further, and briskly arranged a meeting before hanging up. Emilia looked over at Frashier, and beckoned him to sit next to her. She had something to show him. He sat down on the sofa, and she took an old looking photo album from the sideboard, bringing it to where Frashier was sitting. It looked like it would fall apart if opened, but somehow, she managed to safely open the book, and turn to the right place.

"I was going over these yesterday, and I found these." Em pointed at a young girl, standing next to a rather handsome lad. Frashier recognised the lad immediately.

"How young we looked." He smiled at his younger self, and then at the girl. "I forgot how long Jane's hair was."

She held his hand under the album. "She did love you, Will."

A tear trickled down his cheek, and he wiped it away. "We were young, foolish."

Emilia turned the page, and he saw himself in a smart suit. Jane was wearing a beautiful, emerald green dress, and looked every bit as radiant as he remembered.

"Ah," Emilia recounted. "That was the night you asked her to the ball, the night she met…"

Frashier said his friend's name with utter disdain. "…Alex, the man who could give her anything. What could I give her?" He stood up and walked to a window, looking at the freshly mowed grass. He remembered playing in that garden as a child, watching his best friend grow into a woman. A woman he fell in love with. He could feel the emotions rising from inside, the same ones he had managed to hold in at the funeral.

Emilia put down the album and walked to him. She looked into his bloodshot eyes. "You gave her what he couldn't. Remember that."

"I know, and it's destroying me." Frashier raked his fingers through his hair.

Emilia touched him gently on the arm, in a motherly fashion. "So, let it go."

Frashier collapsed on the floor, his emotions erupted, and he screamed at the top of his voice. Emilia knelt next to him, rocking him, and letting the heartbroken man find release.

WHEN ANGELS FEAST

By
Kevin Bailey

CHAPTER TWELVE

Simon was still fuming when he entered the interview room. He found Harry and Giles talking.

"I hope I am not interrupting anything," he said derisively. Both men shook their heads, and he approached the desk. Seconds later, Day entered and sat down next to Simon. Both looked over at the two men. "Shall we begin?"

"Before we begin, I would like to state Mr. Swinburne is not under arrest, and, for the record, he is here to assist us." Eliote looked over at the microphone, and at Giles, who nodded. "We would like to ask him a few questions."

Harry glanced at Eliote. "That is fair."

Eliote nodded slightly, and got down to business. He opened his file and pulled out a photo of the two skeletons.

Harry gazed curiously down at them, and back at Simon. "Who's this?"

"The smaller of the skeletons has been identified as Rebecca Swinbourne."

Upon the revelation of this information, Harry started to cry. "So you found her? It is about bloody time."

Eliote and Day were slightly taken back by this outburst. "Can you explain that statement?" Day requested.

Harry just stared at the picture, touching the bones of his loved one. He glared coldly at the two officers. "Years ago, in what seems like another lifetime, I was charged with the murder of my wife. According to the detective at the time, he accused me of burying her in a pit full of quick lime in the woods; even though I joked I had cut her up and dumped her in the river." Harry kept touching the picture sensually. "He kept on and on about it, even said he would plant something on me, if I didn't confess."

Eliote could sense the anger emanating from Harry. "So, why did you confess?" He took out a piece of paper, "I have your confession here." He took out some reading glasses and put them on. "This is the rushed version," he paused, clearing his throat. "I, Harry Swinburne, killed my wife, because I caught her cheating. In a fit of rage, I strangled her and placed her in quick lime." He placed the paper and glasses on the table.

Harry bluntly asked, "Does it also say that a pair of woman's shoes were found in my bag, as well as a receipt for quick lime?"

Eliote picked up his glasses and read the report. "Yes, it does."

Harry let out a big sigh, as if fed up with telling the same story. "Like I said to DCI Reynolds, they were a gift from a female friend of Rebecca's, and I owned a home that needed a lime render." He sighed again. "And, like him, you don't believe me either, do you, Chief Inspector?" He slumped down on the chair, dejected.

Eliote opened the file again, and showed him the image of the woman found on the golf course. Raising his head with a great deal of effort, Harry queried, "What's this? More images of my Rebecca?"

Eliote shook his head. "This skeleton was found at the Chelmesbury Municipal Golf Course, and as there are similarities between this murder and your wife's, I have to ask…"

Harry looked horrified at the two detectives. "Whoa, hold your horses for a second. Are you accusing me of killing this woman as well? Because if you are, then I am going to need my solicitor present." He sat up straight in the chair, and wouldn't budge.

"We are not accusing you of anything, Mr. Swinburne," Day said calmly.

"It sounds like it," he protested.

"It's just that we have two murder scenes, and three bodies that match each other."

Harry glared at her. "In that case, you should be worried, Miss. I am obviously a woman killer." Harry smirked slightly.

Eliote shifted in his chair, casually crossing one leg over the other and pressing his index fingers to his lips. "I know you didn't kill them, Mr. Swinburne. It's just a little odd. On the day that we found your wife, you were spotted nearby with a colleague…"

Harry cut Eliote off. "So that's what you were up to by the Millennium Green." He looked at the mirrored glass on one wall. "Is Charlotte behind that glass, watching this? I've seen the dramas on the telly. Psychiatrist, is she?" He looked back at Eliote, hoping he would be smiling, but he wasn't.

"I was the one who saw you talking to Charlotte. What were you doing there?"

Harry answered quickly, "Like I told her, it was somewhere me and Beccy used to go when we were courting." He smiled, remembering happy times.

Day brought him out of his daydream. "You can see what it looks like to us, Mr. Swinburne."

Harry glared at her. "Yeah, I can see clear enough, Miss." He looked sombrely at the table. "When I was in prison, I wished I had killed her. It would've made it all worthwhile, being there, watching my back all the time." He looked up with bloodshot eyes. "Waiting to be free and find her. Promise her the world, if she'd have me back." He shifted his gaze to the picture of the couple in the grave. "Not gonna get a chance now, am I?"

Eliote shook his head and perused the file in front of him, with his glasses perched on his nose. "We found a locket containing a picture. Can you tell us who this was?"

Harry smiled. "It was of her dear mother, who died not long after Beccy went missing."

"For the record, can you give us a name of the lady?" Day was poised to write down the name.

Harry nodded. "Nora Fitzpatrick was as batty as a fruitcake, but Beccy loved her dearly. She liked me at first, but then, as she got ill, her attitude towards me changed. She spat at me in court, and wasn't there at my sentencing."

Day thanked him and then asked, "It says that Rebecca worked for the council?"

Harry nodded. "Yeah, she was a PA."

Eliote looked at him. "PA to whom?"

Again, Harry sighed heavily. "Like I told Reynolds, she worked for a guy called Clive Jenkins. He was some big-wig."

Day looked through the notes of the original conviction, but couldn't find the name. She turned and whispered into Eliote's ear,

"If Reynolds was convinced he had his man, he wouldn't have checked anything out."

Eliote nodded and returned his attention back at Harry. "Okay, Harry, I want you to tell me about the last time you saw Rebecca alive. Every detail that you can, please?"

Harry sat back and recounted the story whilst Day left the room.

***

The old lime-rendered house sat next to a stream, and was beauty itself, picturesque. In the old farmhouse style kitchen, Harry sat at the table, reading the local rag. He looked up at his wife, who was wearing a smart suit, and was putting on some pearl earrings, making sure Harry didn't see them.

"I see from the paper the new Bond film is at the cinema. Thought we might go and see it?"

She looked cruelly at him. "You said you didn't like Bond."

He persevered. "I know I don't, but you do. Thought we might go to the pictures, and then go for a meal afterwards. Make a night of it. What do you think?"

"When do you want to do that" she said, putting on the nice perfume he had brought her for Christmas.

"Maybe tonight?"

She picked up a small carrycase and sadly said, "Can't tonight. Working late for Clive. We've got the auditors in, and he needs me."

Harry stood and walked towards her. "I need you," he said pleadingly. "You do realise that today is our anniversary?"

She stopped and looked at the calendar on the wall, and saw the small writing. "Oh." She kissed him on the cheek. "I'll make it up to you, I promise," she said, lying to him. "But you know what these auditors are like."

He nodded dolefully and sat back down on the chair, watching her walk out of the kitchen. "Love you," he said, but she exited the house without replying, and he heard her jump in to the Audi and drive away.

***

"In the outhouse was a big bouquet of flowers and two tickets to Paris. I'd already rang her boss and booked the day off." Harry wistfully glanced up at Eliote. "Now I knew she was having an affair." He looked at the picture. "But I never got to find out who it was she was seeing." His demeanour shifted to anger. "If I'd found out who it was, believe me, I would have killed him." His voice broke. "She was everything to me."

While Eliote was talking to Harry, Day was at her desk, talking to someone at the council. "Can you give me his address?" She wrote the info down and thanked the caller. "Loughton Green…" She looked around, and saw Dawes writing some information up. "Dawes, you got anyone near Loughton Green?"

Without looking up, the officer said, "Inspector Frashier is near there. Contact him."

"Thanks." Day grabbed her mobile and walked out of the station. After lighting a cigarette, she phoned Frashier. When he answered, she could tell he was upset, but without questioning if he was alright, she asked if he would do her a small favour.

After explaining what she wanted, Day finished her cigarette and walked back inside, putting on some perfume to hide the smell. She re-entered the interview room, and spoke directly to Eliote, "I've found Mr. Jenkins, and have sent someone round to speak to him." She didn't tell him it was Frashier.

Eliote nodded and looked at Harry. "Okay, Mr. Swinburne. I would like you to come back tomorrow, it would give us time to corroborate your story with Mr. Jenkins." He stood up. "Until then!" Eliote turned and walked out of the door. Day escorted both Harry and Giles out of CID.

***

Frashier watched the Sat Nav as it directed him to a farm gate, and he got out. A pack of dogs came running to the gate, barking madly. Frashier stepped back slightly from the gate, and saw a man with a large cane walk tall towards the howling pack of dogs.

"Shut up!" he ordered. The dogs cowered around him, and he looked at the detective. "Can I help you?" he said in a posh manner.

Frashier took out his warrant card, and showed it to the man. "I'm looking for Clive Jenkins."

The man smiled. "You have just found him." He put out his hand, and Frashier shook it.

"Mr. Jenkins, I would like to talk to you about Rebecca Swinburne."

The man hesitated, and called the dogs to the house. "You'd better come in then!" He pressed a remote in his pocket to open the gate to allow the detective to drive his car up to the house.

After parking the BMW next to a Bentley Continental, Frashier followed the stately postured, grey-haired man into the house, and into a posh open-planed living place. Frashier noticed a picture of Clive and a group of people surrounding him on an oak sideboard "That's Rebecca and her husband Harry at my birthday," he remarked pointing at a couple who looked uncomfortable.

Frashier examined the couple. He seemed happy, but her face showed disgust at being photographed. "She seems like a beautiful and confident woman," Frashier commented.

"She was, and she knew it." Clive heard a bleeping noise coming from the kitchen and decided to investigate. On discovering it was the dishwasher finishing, he gazed at the kettle and enquired. "Can I offer you a drink, Inspector? Tea? Coffee?"

Frashier nodded, still gazing at the photo. "Thank you, a tea would be nice."

Clive walked towards a sink and filled a steel kettle and switched it on.

"So," Frashier meandered away from the sideboard and sat down at a breakfast bar. "What can you tell me about Rebecca Swinburne?"

Clive took out a milk jar from a fridge and placed it near the kettle. "She was one of the best PAs I ever had," he said, as he grabbed two cups from a cupboard and placed them on the side. "She knew what I was up to, before I did, kept my office in ship-shape. It was a loss when she left."

Frashier was confused. "Left? I thought she went missing?"

Clive turned and looked at Frashier. "My dear boy, the weekend she went missing, she'd handed in her resignation. Her husband had rung to ask for the Friday and Monday off. Seems he'd planned for them to go to Paris."

Frashier wrote this information down, and glanced up, watching Clive making tea the old-fashioned way. "Resignation?"

"I'm guessing from your question, Inspector, Harry didn't know that."

Frashier shrugged his shoulders. "I honestly don't know the answer to that." Frashier said, as Clive handed him a cup. "If Harry didn't know about the resignation..." he paused. "How do you think Harry would have taken the news?"

Clive handed Frashier the cup and sat down next to him. "From what I remember of Harry, he wouldn't have taken it very well." He drank some of his own drink. "I remember the two having an argument at my birthday party." He pointed back at the photo. "His eyes were so red, they were almost glowing, and he was shaking with anger." They drank some more tea. "We were worried she would come back on the Monday morning with black eyes and bruises."

Whilst Frashier sipped some of the hot tea, he queried, "And did she?"

Clive shook his head. "No, she came back all apologetic."

Frashier looked seriously at him. "Do you think he killed his wife?"

Clive nodded. "Well, the court thought he did, or they would not have found him guilty." Frashier watched the man and listened to him. "According to what I can remember, he buried her body in quick lime in the woods. Her body was never found."

Frashier remarked quickly, "We have found the body, and from what my colleagues have told me over the phone, before I came here, it's looking like Harry didn't kill his wife."

"You're joking, right?" Clive blinked in shock.

Frashier shook his head. "The new enquiry has uncovered new evidence that quashes the original conviction."

Clive looked concerned. "It can't have. DCI Reynolds personally told me he had bagged the right man."

"He personally told you?" Surprise leaked into Frashier's tone.

"Yes, the whole department were in shock at the disappearance. He came and told everyone it was her husband who had killed and buried her."

"Well, unfortunately, my superior believes she, as well as another man…" Clive abruptly turned away, causing Frashier to stop his statement abruptly. "Sir, do you know something about this other man? Anything you say may help us with our enquiries?"

Clive turned and looked at him. "I didn't know his name, but I guessed she was seeing someone…"

"Elaborate please, Mr. Jenkins?" Frashier demanded.

"Well," he began, "she started coming in dressed in posh clothes, nicer jewellery. We thought, at first, she had won some money, but when Harry would turn up in his usual clothes, we put two and two together." Clive poured himself some more tea and offered some to Frashier, who declined. "Then came the phone calls from an older man. We just assumed it was an old relative. She would go for lunch, and come back flustered. She would finish work early, and Harry would ring the office, and she would beg us to say she was in a meeting." He drank from the cup.

"So she never gave you a name?" Frashier asked.

Clive shook his head. "I'm afraid not, Inspector." He ran his hand over the surface of the table. "I do miss her." he said, looking up, tears in his eyes.

Frashier placed the cup back on the table. "Thank you for your time, Mr. Jenkins." Frashier rose and headed for the door, leaving the older man to his thoughts.

As he headed back to Chelmesbury CID to report to Day, she phoned him. "Hi, Will. How did it go?"

"I was just coming back in to report." He could hear glasses being collected in the background. "Where are you?"

"I am in the Dog and Duck. Thought we could meet there?"

Frashier smiled to himself. "Is that a date?"

Day laughed low, and flirtingly replied, "You should be so lucky." The call ended, and Frashier turned the car around, heading for the pub.

***

That evening, Eliote walked into the priory to found it in complete darkness. As he walked past the picture of his mother, he smiled at her as he always did. He felt it was his way of erasing the pain of not being there when she had died. The rest of his guilt he could never erase. Keeping those thoughts, he approached the door that would take him into the long gallery to Henry's part of the house. When he got near, he could hear classical music playing, and he smiled remembering when he was younger, going to school in Henry's old car, and that same music blaring through the speakers.

He quietly opened the door at the end to find the only light emanating from the room was the fire in the grate. "Henry?"

There was a saddened answer. "Simon." Eliote entered and sat down opposite his old friend and mentor. Henry was holding a large red photo album, and had obviously been crying. He looked up from the book and asked, "Can I help you, Simon?"

Eliote looked glumly at him. "I came to apologise. I was a complete idiot."

Henry nodded. "Yes you were, but I, too, am sorry, Simon." Eliote was surprised at the mutual apology. "I'm sorry I keep forgetting you did not want this life. You turned away from the life your family hoped you would welcome. I will not forget you when I am gone."

Eliote stared into the fire. "I don't want you to go, Henry."

Henry sat forward in his chair and placed a log onto the burning ambers. "I think it is for the best, Simon." He paused. "After all, we are from two different worlds."

Eliote peered over at him. "Maybe we are, Henry, but this house is your home. No," he said bluntly. "It should be me who leaves."

Henry sat forward. "But you own this place."

"Yes I know." He spotted the photo of his mother on the mantelpiece, smiling at him. "She would want you here, and so do I. You are the heart of this place, so please, I beg you, don't go."

WHEN ANGELS FEAST

By
Kevin Bailey

CHAPTER THIRTEEN

Frashier parked the BMW in a side street and headed for the pub. As he walked, he didn't see a shadowy figure watching him from afar, following his every footstep, and waiting for the right time to pounce.

Unaware of the figure creeping up behind him, he just continued to walk; his thoughts of Jane blinded his senses, but then again, since her death, he had been distracted by his pain.

Even at the meeting with Clive Jenkins, her image kept coming to him, like a ghost taunting him.

"Pull yourself together, ma..." He felt a cold chill which sent a shiver down his spine. Stopping, Frashier pulled his lapels together and squinted into the darkness, but he could not see anyone. "Just your imagination, Inspector," he said, laughing at himself. 'It's probably Day cursing me,' he thought and headed for his rendezvous.

The shadowy figure stopped and pulled back. The mention of his prey being a police officer obviously shocked the stalker, and the figure watched from a vantage point as the detective past the once majestic cottage hospital, where a series of posh retirement apartments now occupied the place where patients once waited in its walls for treatment. The stalker waited as Frashier climbed up some steps and out into the open churchyard, where the gravestones of past townsfolk had been removed and placed against the wall of the giant parish church of St. Bartholomew.

Both the figure and Frashier spotted a group of drunk youths urinating against one of the gravestones. The detective shouted at them, and they ran down a passageway, laughing. He sped up to catch them, but when he circled the church, emerging near the Glossies Nightclub, they had disappeared.

"Damn and blast," he panted.

He saw two bouncers looking over at him. "Everything alright, sir?" one of them questioned. He shook his head and took out his wallet to show he was a police officer.

"You didn't see some youths run past did, you?" They both shook their heads, and he cursed again and thanked them, "Cheers." He began wandering back, thinking what his next course of action should be. "I'll have to get on to control." He took another series of breaths. "See if they can catch the dirty little bastards." He then remembered his meeting with Day. Frashier hurried across the open area, through a hole in a wall, and into the courtyard of the public house.

One of the youths had doubled back, and had watched the detective leave the graveyard and walk down the steps.
He made a masturbation sign and smirked, but his smile was short-lived as he felt the presence of something behind him. Thinking it was one of his friends, he remarked, "He's go…" He felt a prick in his arm. Looking down, he saw a large hypodermic needle sticking out, a hand wrapped around it, pushing the colourless liquid into his arm.

His attacker was the figure that had been stalking the detective. The killer had found a new prey. This new 'Deathly Angel' had no facial features to recognise, but the whole world was becoming disorientated and blurred. "Far out…" he said as he passed out, his only memory of the event was his name being shouted.

***

Unaware of the incident going on near her, Miranda Day sat in the corner of the public house and waited for her mentor to turn up, a lemon-flavoured Bicardi Breezer in her hand, and a glass of whiskey and ice on the table. Soft music echoed throughout the bar-area, and she tapped the table to the beat. Every time someone walked into the bar, she would look up, expecting to see his smile, but was disappointed when it wasn't him. She looked at her watch, and saw time was slowly passing on.

Just as she was about to give up, drink her drink and leave, the door opened, and Frashier walked in.

"You're late," she said, glaring at him.

"Sorry, I had to go somewhere first," he said, remembering the graveyard and the small bouquet of flowers he had just placed on the freshly-covered grave. "Then, as I was walking through St. Bartholomew's graveyard, some little shits were taking a bloody leak on the stones, so I chased after the little bas…"

She raised her hand. "…I'll let you off this time, if you can forgive me?"

Frashier sat down and took the glass from the table. "Why have I got to forgive you? You haven't done anything." He raised his eyebrows. "Have you?"

She took a swig of the bottle and nodded. "I entered the Inspector's exams without telling you, and then, I applied for a transfer to another station."

"Look Miranda," he said, drinking some of the whiskey. "I am not going to say it wasn't a shock when I heard. You are, and always will be, my golden girl." She blushed. "I am very proud of the way you have turned out," he said, almost like a father to a child. "And even though I hoped you wouldn't, I knew that you couldn't stay here forever, and that maybe someday, you'd spread your wings and reach the top of the ladder, like you always wanted."

She smiled at him. "Thanks, Will."

Frashier lifted the glass and looked happily at her. "So, I hope you succeed in your new posting in Birmingham, Miranda. I really do." He toasted her new success. "Here's to you, kid." They clinked glasses, and he swigged the liquid straight down. He felt it burn his throat, and he shivered. "Whoa, I needed that!"

Day contemplated him with a worried expression. "If I was your golden girl, why aren't you telling me what's wrong?"

"There is nothing wrong, Miranda," he said bluntly.

"Oh, come on, Will! You've been going around with a face like a slapped arse."

Frashier chuckled lightly and managed a smile. "That's what I like about you, Miranda. Direct and straight to the point."

She beamed back at him. "Well, I learnt from the best."

Frashier was glad for the more relaxed atmosphere, and stood to head to the bar. "What are you drinking?"

"I was drinking this stuff." Day lifted the bottle. "But as I am on call tonight, I'll just have a coke."

Frashier shifted away from the table, angling himself towards the bartender. "Two large cokes, please." The barman nodded, and started to pour the drinks. Turning back to Day, Frashier remarked, "I am on duty tonight too, and I don't want that wanker to throw me off another crime scene. One more bad mark, and I'll be joining you in Birmingham."

Day laughed and shook her head, as Frashier waited for their drinks.

***

Stanley Ford had been site security officer for about twelve years. He knew every business, and who to contact when an alarm was going off. As he drove his fiesta van down Whatling Street, he passed the businesses he protected. His thoughts were on the weekend's football match, between his team, the Chelmesbury Rangers, and the Glayton Tigers. As he contemplated the match, Stanley was distracted by the flickering flames rising above the buildings. Acting fast, he knew he had to get there quickly. Changing down a gear, he put his foot to the floor.

Upon arriving at the site, he saw that the main building was up in flames, and the reception area was just starting to take. He took out his phone and dialled the emergency services.

***

Frashier returned to the table and placed the glasses down. "You never answered my question!" Day pulled her glass over, taking a drink of the icy coke.

Likewise, he took a swig of the liquid and shifted his attention from the glass to her. "Maybe there's nothing wrong." She gave him a weird look, and he gave up. "Never could lie to you, Miranda."

"Nope! That's why we were good partners." He smirked at her, but she stood her ground. "So, why are you persisting with this death in the ditch?"

He took another swig and looked seriously at her. "Okay, the deceased, Jane Lock, was my first true love, Miranda. We had been childhood sweethearts. We went through school together, and she was the first."

Day appeared confused by the last statement. "The first?"

"You know, my first!"

It clicked. "Oh, that first."

He nodded. "When we were about fifteen, there was a school disco…"

"…You don't have to tell me all the personal details, Will."

He rolled his eyes. "Don't be daft." She raised her hands to apologise, and he continued, "At that disco, I asked her to marry me, but as the night progressed, I realised I was too young to get married, and we agreed, in the future, we would eventually be together."

Miranda's expression grew sombre. "Oh, Will, now, I can see why you've been acting the way you have. I am so sorry."

Frashier swallowed some more coke, and frowned. "That's not the end of the matter, Miranda…"

***

Detective Sergeant Frashier and a junior officer, Detective Constable Hollins, jumped into the Vauxhall Carlton and headed towards the town of Glayton. He had been sent by DCI Christopher Reynolds to investigate a series of thefts at a local plumber's merchant.

Castle View Bathrooms and Plumbing Supplies were concerned a member of their staff was taking money and stock from its branch in Chelmesbury, and as the CEO of the company was a friend of Reynolds, his team were assigned the task.

As they approached the town of Glayton and the branch, Frashier received a phone call from Reynolds, informing him that the perpetrator had been apprehended, and they were to meet the Assistant CEO at the branch…

Day's eyes gazed at Frashier from behind her glass of coke, and she asked, "I am guessing that Castle View Bathrooms and Plumbing Supplies became Glayton Plumbing, Bathrooms, and Heating Supplies?"

"Yeah, that company went into liquidation, and the assistant CEO brought the buildings, stock, and vehicles of the old company. Because C.V.B.P.S was a limited company, he started the new company, and based his headquarters in Glayton."

"Alex Boyd's father's company?"

"The very same." Frashier continued his story, "Well, when me and Hollins arrived, we were met up by Alex's father, Jim, and he immediately recognised me, and told me Alex and his wife were in town and they'd love to see me. So…" He drank some more liquid. "After me and Hollins had brought the accused person back to the station, I arranged a couple of days off and met up with them."

Day watched him intensely. "That must have been a painful experience?"

"It was. The woman I had always loved, married to my best friend. The pain was unbearable, but I went along for old times' sake. We ended up in a hotel in Rouquetas de Mar in Spain, just the three of us, and we had a pretty good time, drinking at night, sleeping in the daytime. When we returned home, we vowed that we would do it again."

"Did you do it again?"

"No, that was the last time I saw Jane, but not Alex. I'll get to that in a minute."

Day was surprised. "There was more to the holiday than meets the eye?"

Frashier nodded. "We went back to Alex and Jane's rented apartment in Chelmesbury, and we drank into the night. Before long, we had nearly drunk the place dry. Alex said he would go to the local off licence and buy some more. I offered to go with him, but he said stay with Jane, and he would be back soon."

"You didn't?" Day asked, and Frashier raised his eyebrows.

"No, well, not then!"

Day smirked. "You dirty beggar, and with your friend's wife?"

Frashier lowered his head, and slumped down in his chair. "I'm not proud of what I did, Miranda."

"So, what happened?"

He peeked out from his slouching position and responded, "Alex got arrested for assaulting a police officer while he was getting more booze. The officer had only asked him if he was alright, and he became aggressive."

"The officer or Alex?"

Frashier looked up. "Alex. He was taken to the nick, and thrown in a cell for the night. The duty sergeant rang Jane to let her know, and she was told he wouldn't be released until morning…"

> *Jane got off the phone and looked at Frashier, who was slightly slumped on the floor. She approached him and fell*

down beside him. "That stupid beggar has been arrested. He's being detained till morning."

Frashier went to stand up. "I should get there. I may be able to help him get out."

She placed her hand on his chest. "You are in no fit state to go anywhere. Besides, he won't be much good until he's slept it off." Jane tried to get up. He helped her up, and she did the same for him. When they stood, they looked at each other and nearly kissed, but Frashier placed his hand between them.

"We can't, Jane. Alex is my friend."

"I'm sorry, Will." She changed the subject, "I'll get the spare room ready for you." Frashier nodded, and she left him for a while.

He walked to the window, and opened the curtains slightly. Looking out over the market square, Frashier could see couples departing the local pubs and heading home after a good night out. He turned as he heard Jane shout from the back of the flat that the room was ready. He closed the curtains and headed for the back passage and the room. Just as Jane was running holding her mouth in the direction of the bathroom and started to throw up.

He banged on the door and asked, "Are you alright?"

She softly said, "Too much drink. I'll be alright in the," she heaved, "morning."

Frashier turned and looked at his room. "I'll bid you goodnight." He turned and walked into the room, closing the door behind him.

As he lay in bed, he reminisced about the night, and the moment they almost kissed. He cursed to himself that he hadn't done the deed.

He heard her come out of the bathroom, and after a while, he heard her creep down the corridor and shut the door. He turned over in bed and placed the pillow over his head, cursing.

He fell asleep, but was woken an hour later by the door opening. Through his blurred vision, he saw Jane standing there in a see-through nightie. She approached the bed, slipped the nightie off, and got in beside him. She held her finger to his mouth to silence him, and then she pulled the blanket over them and they passionately made ...

Day was about to say something, when she felt the phone in her pocket vibrating.

After getting off the phone, she looked at Frashier. "We will talk again, but for the moment, we have to go. Someone has torched Gold Security."

WHEN ANGELS FEAST

By
Kevin Bailey

CHAPTER FOURTEEN

They arrived to the usual welcome of several police cars, the fire brigade, and a few reporters. Day drove the Vauxhall to a spot, and the two friends got out. A uniformed officer acknowledged them, and lifted the tape to allow them to enter the crime scene. Pickington had arrived prior to them, and was talking to the fire fighters. He looked up and acknowledged the arriving inspectors, but not in his usual greeting.

"Evening," he said glumly.

"So, Constable, what happened?"

Pickington explained the police had been called to the scene by the security officer, who had seen flames coming from the offices.

"The fire brigade have managed to douse the flames in the reception area, and have the fire under control in the main building. Once it's out, they will begin their investigating into how the fire started."

About an hour later, the fire was completely doused, and the investigations started. Day and Frashier were in the fire support vehicle, talking to the chief firefighter, when one of the investigators burst into the vehicle and looked at his superior and the two detectives. "Sir, I think you and the detectives had better come and have a look at what we have found."

Frashier and Day shared a glance and then followed them into the office, and approached a downstairs room. In one corner, it looked like the examiners had been digging a hole.

The investigator faced the two detectives and reported, "We now believe this area is where the fire started. Blueprints of this building show there was a gas pipe situated in this basement, so we thought we would check to see if it was there." He gulped. "It was then we discovered this." One of the others moved to one side to reveal a human skull.

Day looked at her superior. "I think we had better contact Eliote…"

Frashier furrowed his brow. "…Why?"

She gave him an incredulous stare. "He is our Chief Inspector and head of CID."

Frashier frowned, conceding to her point, "Okay, you'd better get Strong to get the SOCOs up here as well."

Day nodded and then looked at the examiners. "You are to stay where you are. This is now a crime scene."

***

Eliote was in his study, going over the folders Charlotte had given him. He still had to admit they were thorough, and he was impressed with them. 'She would have made a good copper,' he thought to himself, and turned the page to look at some more articles.

He was just about to read them when the phone on his desk rang. It was strange it wasn't an internal call, but he had given Henry the night off, and so he picked it up. "Hello?" It was Day, and she informed him of the fire and the body found. "Okay, I'll be there ASAP." He changed and headed for his Saab.

***

Back in Chelmesbury, Frashier had left Day and the fire investigators, and was heading toward the main office of Gold Security. When he entered, he saw a safe which had been opened. He put on some white gloves and opened the door.

Inside was a burnt mess. He rummaged through the charred papers and felt a hard object. Pulling it out, Frashier saw that it was a berretta. He grabbed a plastic bag from out of his pocket and placed the gun into it. After he sealed it, he scrutinized it more closely. Could this have been the murder weapon used to kill Nicolas Waite? He took the bag and walked back towards the downstairs office. Day and some other officers were taping off the area. Leaving her to do her work, he walked outside to the awaiting officers who were kitted up for a thorough search.

"When the SOCOs get here, I want you lot to help them search the whole area. As usual, if you find anything, place it in a bag and inform the Doctor's team." The officers nodded and waited, while Frashier headed back to Day.

It wasn't long before Doctor Strong arrived, and set to work on the discovery. The rest of his SOCOs worked with the officers on searching the site. Frashier handed Penny the berretta, and she returned to the station to check it.

Eliote drove his black Saab down Whatling Street, and saw the commotion ahead. It was gridlock as residents had come to investigate the flames. He parked his car in another business car park and walked to the sealed off area.

Potter was patrolling the tape, and when he saw Eliote, he stood tall. "Evening, Gov. They are waiting for you in the main building."

Eliote smiled. "Thanks Potter." The lanky officer lifted the tape, and Eliote walked underneath. "Get some of your friends, and move this lot on." He pointed at the queue. Potter was about to shout some officers when Eliote turned and looked back, throwing his keys at the officer. "Oh, and my car is parked in Hughes Cash and Carry. Can you have someone move it to a safer place?" he said cheekily.

Potter nodded. "It will be a pleasure, Gov." Eliote smiled and made his way over to the designated office building.

Frashier was talking to Day when his phone rang. He grabbed it out of his pocket and answered, "Frashier."

It was Dawes back at the station. "Sir, DS Day asked me to check up on Gold Security. It was started ten years ago by four people." He read out their names, "Rachael Walker, her brother Tom, Nicolas Waite, and a Nigel Pugh."

Frashier stopped and looked at Day, and informed her of Dawes's findings. Day looked a little angry. "Interesting."

Frashier glanced at her. "Why do you say that?"

Day looked back at him. "Rachael never told us Nicolas was a partner in the business. It now makes me wonder what else she is lying about."

Frashier handed her his mobile, and she spoke back to Dawes. "Hi, it's Day. Where does this Nigel Pugh live?" She could hear the detective turning pages in her notebook.

"According to records, he lives at 20 Hectors Close."

Day's mouth dropped open in disbelief. "Did I hear that correctly, you said 20 Hectors Close?"

Eliote walked in at that precise moment, and had heard the address. "Inspector, isn't that's where Edward Pierce lives?" Day nodded, and after thanking Dawes, hung up and passed the phone back to Frashier.

"Strong is in the basement, Gov," Frashier informed Eliote. Eliote thanked him, and after placing on protective clothing, he headed for Strong

On arriving, he found Strong crouched down in the corner, and two of his team were examining the body. Eliote stayed behind the tape. "Evening, Strong. I understand you have another body for me."

Strong turned and nodded. "Yes, I have Chief Inspector, but unlike the others, this one is more typical."

Eliote was confused. "More typical, Doctor?"

"Yes. The others had their throats cut, and the meat butchered off their bodies. This one was killed by a gunshot wound to the left temple. I'll know what calibre the weapon was once we get back to the lab."

Eliote looked at the skeleton as Strong stood up to approach him. It was almost crouched, as if the person had been huddled in a ball.

"Is it a man or a woman?" Eliote asked inquisitively.

Strong answered without hesitation. "Oh, it is defiantly a man. I'd say he was tall and from the look of the bones which are in a good state of health, I'd say he was mid to late thirties."

Eliote studied the skeleton, and then addressed Strong, "Full report on Frashier's desk as soon as is possible."

The doctors seemed surprised. "On Will's desk?"

Eliote nodded. "Yes, Doctor. He is the one who is dealing with Nicolas Waite's death."

"Right you are, Chief Inspector."

Eliote stood up and walked back to the others. As he re-joined Day and Frashier, Eliote issued his commands. "I want you two to work on this." Motioning to the pair, he requested, "I want you to get to Hectors Close, and re-interview Mr. Pierce. See if he knows where this Nigel Pugh has moved to. Also, get on to records see if they can find any information on Nigel Pugh, and any missing persons who have been involved at some time with Gold Security."

They walked with him to Day's Vauxhall Insignia where he gave more orders, "Of all the people who started this business, the only living ones now are Rachael and her brother, Tom. I want them brought in for questioning. They must know who this skeleton could be." He turned his head towards the chard building, "That basement was very clean, as if no one used it. Find out why."

"Yes, Gov," they said in unison, and headed off in the car. Eliote watched them go, and after speaking to Strong a final time, headed back to the station.

Day arrived at Hectors Close and parked the Vauxhall outside. She looked at the house, and saw a curtain move. The two officers got out and headed for the front door, where Day rang the bell, and Edward answered, "What can I do for you at this time, Sergeant?"

Frashier answered from the shadows, "Can you tell me where Nigel Pugh is, Mr. Pierce?"

Edward squinted in the darkness to meet Frashier's glare. "Nigel Pugh," he said with utter disdain. "He moved to Hastings Row, I think. Yes, I remember. It was number sixty-eight."

"You're sure about that, Mr. Pierce?" Day asked, and Edward nodded.

"Pretty sure," he said, and allowed the two detectives into the house. They followed him into a front room, and watched him as he walked over to a photo on the mantel piece. "You see that woman?" The two officers looked at the picture. "She was a good woman, and I miss her a lot. That bastard, Pugh," he once again became aggressive, "murdered her, but like all weasels, he slimed away. You see, he had an alibi." He replaced the photo onto the mantel piece. "I hope the bastard is a long way away from here, and is in a hellava lot of pain, cause when I find him, I will cut out his heart, like he did to me."

Both officers believed his threat. "We are sorry to disturb you this late at night," Frashier lied.

Edward just shrugged his shoulders. "No problem, I ain't got a life to disturb." With that, the two officers headed for the Insignia.

"What do you think, Will? Is he lying or sincere?"

Frashier got in beside Day and shrugged his shoulders. "I get the impression he is hiding something. We need to find out what that is." Day nodded and typed in the address Edward had given them into her satellite navigation system, and was directed to the outskirts of the town.

When she arrived, she saw the road was closed, and a sign that said 'Hastings Row' had been ripped from the ground and lay on its side next to the closed sign. The two officers got out and headed beyond the sign to a wooden fence that had been erected around a large housing development. A large metal chain and lock stopped them from going any further.

Day noticed a board with plans on it. She beckoned Frashier over, and they both read it.

The new Hastings Estate.
Out with the old, and in with the new.

They both looked through the fence at the new homes, and several old ones that had a bulldozer parked nearby, ready to bring them to the ground. A young, bearded security guard walked towards them.

"I'm sorry, but I am afraid the site is closed, and the show homes aren't open until the morning."

Day took out her badge and asked, "When was this Hastings Row?"

The guard replied almost sarcastically, "It will always be Hastings Row, Officer. The old homes were part of a housing association estate until about a year ago when the area was brought by a local developer while they got planning permission. They were filled with homeless people, squatters mostly. They were moved on, and then the place began to be bulldozed."

"I know it's a bit of a long shot, but has number sixty-eight been knocked down yet?"

The guard looked at the remaining houses and pointed to a house that still looked like it was lived in. "That's number sixty-eight!"

Frashier asked, "Could we have a look around it, please?" The guard produced a set of keys from his pocket and opened the lock, allowing them in. He escorted them to the property.

Day was the first to enter, noting a distinct smell of human waste. The guard noticed her hold her nose and remarked, "This was the last home to be vacated by the squatters. I'm afraid they left it in an appalling state. It will be gone tomorrow."

Frashier held his nose and asked, "Could you let us get on with our work, Mr…?"

"James, Joe James. I work on the security side of Gold Developments."

Both officers looked at the guard. "Gold Developments? Is that a subsidy of Gold Security?"

"Yeah, they've been after this land for years. When Rachael and her partner acquired the land, they created Gold Developments."

Day saw some post and read the name, while Frashier asked, "Who is her partner?"

The guard answered quickly, "Nigel Pugh."

Day held up an envelope for Frashier to see, opening the letter. It was dated a month ago. She looked at the guard. "Does the post still deliver here?"

The guard responded with mild humour, "Not unless they climb the fence."

The two officers collected all the mail from the mat, and after taking a look around the place, they left.

After watching the two officers depart the site and head towards the Vauxhall, Joe picked up the phone. "Hi, it's Joe, up at Hastings Estate."

The male voice on the other end abruptly spoke, "What's up?"

"The police have been snooping around the old Pugh house. Took several letters and pictures of the place."

"That is of no concern. The house will be gone in the morning."

Joe nodded. "Just thought I would give you a heads up."

"Thank you, Joe. It is much appreciated." Satisfied at a job well done, Joe returned to his security hut to wait out the rest of his shift.

When Angels Feast

By
Kevin Bailey

CHAPTER FIFTEEN

When the two officers got into the car, Day glanced over at Frashier. "Seems a little suspicious the house belonging to Nigel Pugh is still standing when all the others have all gone?"

He nodded. "It is even more suspicious a letter post-dated a week ago has been delivered to a new housing development, and is addressed to Nigel Pugh, CEO of Gold Developments." He showed her the letter he had opened.

"I think we had better get back to the station and find this Nigel Pugh?" Frashier agreed with his colleague.

Once back at the station, Day headed for Records, and sat down at one of the many computer systems in the large oval room. She typed in 'Nigel Pugh,' and a file and picture of the man appeared on the screen. It also said, 'additional information concerning file.'

After about an hour reading all the information, she was ready to report her findings, and headed towards Eliote's office, knocking on his imposing door.

"Come in." Permission given to enter the boss's lair, Day opened the door and walked over to Eliote's desk.

"I have hit a little snag concerning Mr. Pugh, Gov. There is a discrepancy in the files."

Eliote beckoned her to a chair and placed the piece of paper he was reading down. "Okay, give me what you've got."

Day flicked the cover of the file back, and began to read him the information. "I have found two records that fit our Nigel Pugh."

"Two?"

"The first is this one." She handed him a photo of a black-haired, suave, sophisticated man. He was smiling at the photographer, and Eliote thought the man looked like a younger version of the English actor, Nigel Havers. "His name is Nigel Edward Pugh, date of birth: seventeenth of June 1967." She turned a page. "Born in Greece to an English father and a Greek woman, raised in Worcester. His known addresses in the town are 68 Hastings Row, Chelmesbury, and 20 Hectors Close."

Eliote stated, "If you have a record on Nigel, then that must mean we have something on him."

She began nodding profusely, and showed him the list of convictions. "As you can see." She pulled away the document. "I'll give you a brief outlook: raped an eighteen-year-old girl at knife point after a party in '87, armed robbery of a jewel shop in Glayton in '91, beat up a copper in '99…" She smiled up at him. "You get the picture."

"What about his current whereabouts?"

Day tapped the edge of the file against her hand. "Well, that's really where this story ends. According to this, he was reported missing in 2002, by his business partner…"

Eliote groaned. "…don't tell me…Rachael?"

"Strange thing is, Gov, according to the records, she was the eighteen-year-old who was raped by him."

He rubbed his chin. "Never heard of that before, a rape victim working alongside her rapist." Day passed over the file for him to see. "That's strange." Scanning the information, she just gave him for his own peace of mind, Eliote passed it back.

"What's even stranger is the next part." She turned a page and recounted the info, "I have found another file." She handed him another photo, and apart from an older look, the two men were very familiar.

"Well, my untrained eye says these are the same man."

Day immediately agreed, "This one," she pointed to the older image, "is of Nigel Anthony Edward Pugh, also born on seventeenth of June 1967, to parents Anthony Pugh of Hastings Row. It doesn't register the mother. This man has no convictions."

Eliote scratched his head. "Could they be the same person?"

She shrugged her shoulders. "I don't know Gov, but I will, of course, have to do some digging into that. At the moment, I have more info for you…" He beckoned her to continue. "This other Nigel is also registered on the files as the managing director of Gold Security and partner in Gold Developments." She turned the page. "I decided to go on the Land Registry website and after looking through some files, I am reporting Edward is lying to us. The house where he lives in Hectors Close, does not belong to him, or his mother. It belonged to Anthony Pugh, Nigel's father. The last mortgage payment was made in February from an account in the name of Gold Security."

"So, why would he lie to us about that?"

She merely shrugged her shoulders. "I don't know, but maybe we should ask him."

"I think you should." Day passed him the file, and he gave her an order, "Find Frashier, and the two of you go and bring in Edward Pierce for questioning."

Day looked at her watch. "It is two-o-clock in the morning, Gov."

He smirked and rolled his eyes sarcastically. "Is it really? I thought it was eleven." Day smiled, and left the office to find Frashier.

Eliote watched her go. He was going to miss her drive and determination. After cursing himself thoroughly, he picked up his mobile and rang the Doctor.

"Chief Inspector, what a delight," Strong said in his usual tones.

Eliote returned the greeting, and then asked, "Have you got any findings on the male skeleton found near the Millennium Green, Doctor?"

Strong thought for a few seconds, obviously doing it to annoy Eliote. Finally, he responded, "At the moment, I can't answer that question. Unlike the female, the male bones are in a poor state."

Eliote was indeed, annoyed at this revelation. "Okay, what of the skeleton found at Gold Security? What about taking an x-ray and sending it to several of the local dentists? See if any of them can identify the teeth?"

He heard Strong move paper. "It's possible," Strong said, clearly thinking out loud. "I did notice the teeth do show signs work has been carried out on them."

Eliote looked over at the picture of his family smiling at him. "Do it, Strong."

"I will do, unless you and your department don't find me any more skeletons," came the sarky retort.

Eliote chuckled, irritation forgotten momentarily. "You love it really."

Strong yawned. "Not as much as I love sleeping."

Eliote looked at his watch. Day had been right; it was late. "Blimey, is that the time?"

"If its twenty to three in the morning, then, yes, that is the time."

Eliote closed the file and turned off his desk light. "If you're finished, Doctor, you may call it a night."

"I have a small team coming in to take over at five. Penny is leading them so I can go and get some sleep. Unless in the next two hours, you find me more bodies…"

"You never know what the future may hold. I most defiantly didn't."

Strong let out another yawn. "Sorry, I wasn't yawn…"

"Oh for heaven's sake Go, and get some sleep, Richard, so you are fresh-eyed to look at the bones more closely."

"Got another two hours, then I can go sleep." His words were slow and careful, trying to disguise his obvious sleep deprivation.

Eliote smiled. "See you tomorrow." He then hung up, and headed for his Saab.

***

Day and Frashier arrived at Hectors Close, and the female detective approached the front door and rang the bell. When she didn't hear anything from inside, she banged hard on the door. "Mr. Pierce, it's the police, open up please!" On this request, she saw lights go on in the house. Slowly a figure walked up a corridor and opened the door.

Edward was wearing a pair of pyjamas and a dressing gown. He yawned heavily, and, with tired eyes, remarked, "What do you want at three in the morning? Can't you let a man sleep?"

Day looked seriously at him. "Mr. Pierce, I would like you to accompany us down to the station."

Edward looked at her and laughed. "You're joking, right?"

Day certainly was not joking. "Please, or I will arrest you. Either way, you are coming down the station."

The smile disappeared from his face. "Can I at least go and put some proper clothes on?"

She nodded, and they walked into the house.

When Edward was ready, he was taken out to the Insignia. The three of them noticed that a group of about four residents had gathered to see what was going on, and he shouted over, "It's bloody police harassment!" He turned, and after locking the front door, jumped into the back seat of her Vauxhall. Frashier sat next to him, and Day jumped into the driver's seat and drove away.

***

Eliote returned to the Priory, once again finding it in darkness, except for a light on behind the curtains in the dining room. He didn't notice the small car parked next to Henry's old car. He parked his car in his usual space and headed into the house. He heard talking coming from the dining room, and when he opened the door, he found Charlotte and Henry speaking in depth. They both looked up at Eliote when he came into the room.

"Am I disturbing you both?"

Henry stood up slowly and swayed towards him. "Not at all," he stuttered. "We went to the local pictures, and thought we would have a few drinks afterwards…"

Charlotte piped up. "…Well, I thought he needed cheering up, Simon, so I took him out."

Eliote smiled at her. "I was going to ring you tomorrow to see if you were alright. I haven't seen you since the bodies were recovered next to the Millennium Green."

Charlotte stood up and nearly fell over. "I am alright, just needed a rest." She started to laugh, and her laugh was infectious.

Eliote approached the drink's cabinet and grabbed a bottle of red wine. "I might join you for a glass."

Henry handed him a bottle that was already opened, and he grabbed a glass and poured himself a large helping, before sitting down on one of the chairs. "What shall we toast to?"

Henry poured Charlotte another glass, and then one for himself. "What about 'family'?" he said, looking at Eliote.

"Family it is then, Henry." He raised his glass to the others, and took a long drink of the smooth, red wine.

***

After the evening she'd had, Day gratefully opened the front door to her apartment in Glayton. Throwing her coat and bag on a chair, she let out a big yawn. All she wanted was a cuppa and then bed, so she headed for the kitchen. Yawning again, she switched the kettle on, and was about to get a cup from the draining board, when the downstairs buzzer for her flat rang. "Who the hell is that at this time?" she said, and headed out of the flat. She moved down the stairs to the main door, looking through the peephole. On seeing who it was, she quickly opened the door. "Will, are you all right?"

The detective helplessly shook his head, finally letting more tears fall. "I can't lie anymore, Miranda, not to you anyway."

She frowned worryingly. "About what?"

"About the fact that Eve Boyd was my daughter!"

Miranda Day stood on the doorstep for several seconds, unable to speak. She was frozen to the spot, shocked to the core at Frashier's confession. She took several deep breaths, and then softly, but bluntly, spoke, "She's what?"

Frashier stood crying, but relieved he had finally told someone of the burden he had been carrying. "She was my daughter!"

Day spotted an upstairs curtain twitch from a house across the street. "You'd better come in, Will." She beckoned him in, and he climbed the stairs and entered Day's apartment.

He walked into the spacious, but minimalistic, sitting room and slumped into a leather chair, his head in his hands. She handed him a pack of tissues, and he thanked her. Moving to one of the cupboards, Day pulled out a bottle of Cinzano and some lemonade, pouring two large glasses and handed him one. "I don't have any whiskey. All I've got is this."

Frashier accepted the glass and took a big gulp of it. "I'm not worried, Miranda. A drink is a drink."

She walked to the sofa opposite, sat down, and took a mouthful of the drink. "I think you should tell Eliote about this, Will."

He looked up from his drink and glared at her. "Why should I tell that wanker?"

Day responded matter-of-factly, "You are personally involved in the case. It could cloud your judgement!"

Frashier snapped, "Don't you think I don't already know that? Especially as my judgement is already clouded! Look at the way I am treating Pickington, for what?" He clenched his free hand into a fist. "For doing his job properly, and asking questions of me?"

Day shrugged her shoulders. "He's big enough to handle himself," she said taking another mouthful.

"Well, what about Jane's case? If it were any other case, I would have handed it over to uniform by now, and moved on, but how can I?" He wiped away fresh tears with the back of his hand, ignoring the tissues.

"That is why you must tell Eliote…"

Frashier's head jolted up. "How can I? The woman I loved, more than anything else, is dead, alongside a daughter I have never met, but loved all her life." An expression of determination crossed his face. "I still have a few answers to find. What was she running from? Did something, or someone, frightened her?"

Day regarded him quite seriously. "If you continue with this investigation, Will, and the truth comes out, Eliote may seriously suspect she was running from you!"

"Don't be daft, Miranda. I would never have hurt anyone, you know that."

"I know that, but put yourself in his position. It does look very suspicious."

"I see your point," he said, examining the liquid in his glass. "I just want to finish this off, before I tell him."

"Okay." She shifted forward in her chair. "Could she have been running from her husband, Alex?"

"I don't think so." He downed the remainder of his drink. "Everyone I have spoken to has told me she left him two weeks before she died, and besides," he said, placing the glass on the side table, "his mother informed me she was going somewhere not even Alex knew about. A place he wouldn't find her. The only clue was the number for a nursing home."

"What would she be ringing a nursing home for?" She headed for the cupboard and made two more glasses of Cinzano and lemonade.

"It's daft, isn't it?"

Day nodded and sat back down. "Could she have relatives at the nursing home?"

Frashier shook his head. "That doesn't seem the case. Her mother said she worked there years ago."

Day rested the glass on her chest, pressing her cheek to the rim. "Will, I won't tell Eliote yet." She emphasized the final word carefully. "Your next job is to visit this nursing home, and find the connection. Then, you must speak to Eliote."

"Thank you Miranda." He took a good couple of mouthfuls of his drink, and returned the glass to the table. "Would it be alright if I stayed on your sofa?"

Day contemplated the nearly empty glass. "Well you're in no fit state to drive." She stood up. "Fill our glasses again while I get you a blanket." With some resignation, Day went to the linen closet. When she returned, Frashier was passed out cold. Tucking the blanket around him, she murmured softly, "What have you gotten yourself into?" Shaking her head, she turned off the light and made her way to her own bed.

WHEN ANGELS FEAST

By
Kevin Bailey

CHAPTER SIXTEEN

The next morning, Simon Eliote drove his Saab into the car park at the station. He was the happiest he had been for months. The evening with Henry and Charlotte had been fun, and they had arranged to do it again. He parked his car in his space, and got out and headed to the main entrance. In the reception area, he found Rachael and a smartly-dressed woman, whom Eliote assumed was her solicitor, waiting.

She glared at him as he passed, and he heard her say, "When are they going to see me? I have a mess to deal with."

The solicitor touched her hand. "Calm down, Rachael. They will get to us shortly."

Eliote smiled to himself, typed in his code, and headed for the CID unit. He approached his office, and after putting his coat and briefcase on his desk, he headed out into his domain.
When he looked around, he saw a few officers sitting on sofas, reading files alongside DS Denver Delaney. Periodically, he jotted down relevant information. Delaney acknowledged the Chief Inspector and continued with his work.

From another part of the department, he heard DCs Pickington and Dawes talking on the phones to witnesses from the fire. He thought to himself, 'It's so good when the department is doing what it should be, and everyone is busy,' but as he looked over at Day's desk and Frashier's office, he started to feel a little miffed. Both were empty.

He stormed back to his office and grabbed his mobile phone, wondering who to ring first. He scrolled down his contacts list until he found Day's number. It rang for several seconds, and then connected. He heard the sound of the phone hitting the floor, and someone trying to grab it. Day's groggy voice filled the void.

"Hello?"

Eliote sounded concerned. "Are you alright, Day?"

There was a pause. "Yeah, Gov, I'm fine why?"

He looked at his watch. "I was just wondering, as it is now nine-thirty, and you and Frashier have people to interview." He heard a commotion, as if someone had fallen out of bed, and a lot of swearing.

Eliote smiled and asked again, "You okay, Day?"

"I'm sorry, Gov," she stuttered. "I'll be there as soon as possible." The phone went dead. He smirked slightly, remembering times he had been late.

He scrolled down through the contacts again, and rang his number two. Even though the voice was also muddled, Frashier answered quickly and bluntly, "Gov."

"I need a report on the shooting case. How are you getting on with that?"

"I have a few leads which I am following up on." Eliote didn't know it, but Frashier was lying through his teeth.

"Have you handed over the 'Jane Boyd' case to uniform, as I asked?"

There was a pause, and Eliote heard a deep sigh. "Not yet, Gov. I have been a little busy."

Eliote looked out at the department, held his breath for a second to calm himself down, and then replied, "Not to worry, Inspector. As you're busy, I'll deal with it." He heard Frashier try to protest, but Eliote just hung up, and headed out to find Pickington, who had finished his own phone call. "Constable?"

The bearded officer nearly jumped out of his skin. "Yes, Gov?"

"I want all the information on the 'Jane Boyd' case on my desk in," he thought about it, and looked at his watch, "thirty minutes."

Pickington nodded. "Yes, Gov."

Eliote turned and walked away, heading back to his office. The constable looked over at Dawes, who, even though she had been on the phone, heard the conversation. "What do I do now, Dawes?"

She shrugged her shoulders. "You're just gonna have to do as you are ordered." She picked up her mobile. "And I'll let Frashier know."

Pickington stood and headed for Frashier's office, to gather the files. Exactly thirty minutes later, Pickington was stood in Eliote's office, like a small school boy awaiting detention.

"Is this it?" Eliote demanded.

The constable stood still, his head bowed. "Yes, Gov. Inspector Frashier hadn't written up his notes on the case, so what you see is all of it."

"Where are your notes, Constable?" Eliote flicked through the pages of the case file. "You did work alongside the inspector, didn't you?"

"Not on this case, Gov. On the shooting in the high street."

Eliote glared at him. "I'm sorry, are you saying he worked on his own?"

Pickington nodded. "Yes, Gov!"

Eliote slammed his fist on the table, making Pickington jump. "This is just not…" Before he could finish his thought, there was a knock on the door. "Come in!"

Frashier opened the door and walked to stand next to Pickington, handing over some files.
"Here we go, Gov, the files for uniform."

Eliote took them from the inspector, surprised by his amicable nature. "Thank you, Inspector." He glanced over at Pickington. "You are dismissed, Constable." The officer nodded and quickly left the room, leaving the two senior officers to their meeting.

Eliote pretended to read the files, turning pages every so often. This was obviously annoying Frashier, who, Eliote noted, was twitching.

"Is everything okay with the files, Gov?"

Eliote just nodded, and every so often, would say, "Hmm" and "Ah." This seemed to have the positive effect Eliote was after, as he glanced up and saw Frashier pacing the room. He decided to put him out of his misery. "I think everything is in order, Inspector." Eliote threw the file into his out tray, regarding Frashier angrily. "I want to ask you one thing, Inspector."

Frashier stopped pacing and looked at the cold, green eyes. "Yes, Gov?"

"I want to know why you visited Mrs. Emilia Lock."

Frashier peered over his shoulder, through the office window at CID. "So, Dawes and Pickington talked?" he said, giving them an evil stare.

"I AM THE HEAD OF THIS DEPARTMENT!" Eliote screamed at the Inspector, making Frashier turn quickly. "I hear everything, and I know what is going on, even if you think I don't, and if you go and visit relatives, I suggest you take someone with you, as support."

Frashier stood tall. "I went to Mrs. Lock to inform her of our findings," he lied, and Eliote knew he was lying.

"Our findings…and what are they?" He looked over at the files in his tray. "Those? If those are our findings, then I wouldn't take them to a court of law. The case would be thrown out!"

Frashier bowed his head. "Can I speak openly, Gov?"

"Don't you always?"

Frashier balked. "I felt, and still do, that there is more to this case than meets the eye, and it warrants a CID officer to deal with it!"

Eliote sat back in his chair. "You do, do you?"

"I do, Gov. Someone scared her enough for her to take the children out into the cold. There is also something else." He bent over the desk and pulled out one of the files. "There was a substance found in all three bodies. Strong identified it as Zilpaterol Hydrochloride. Why would they have an American weight gaining drug used for cattle in their blood? It just doesn't make sense."

Eliote could sense there was more to it, and could see the pain emanate from his number two's eyes. With reluctance, he stood and paced to the window, back to Frashier. "Right then, Inspector, I'll give you two days." Eliote turned and looked at the calendar on his desk, and then at Frashier. "Today is Monday. We will reconvene on Wednesday, and at that time, the files go to uniform, whether you're finished or not." He glared at Frashier. "Do I make myself clear?"

"Crystal, Gov."

Eliote smiled slyly, remembering he had heard those words before. "Okay then, until Wednesday."

Frashier turned and left the office. Eliote followed after a few minutes of silent thought.

"Gov, have you got a minute?" DS Wright said, as she returned from the local dentist's. He nodded, and they returned to his office.

Once inside, Eliote asked, "What have you found out Sergeant?"

She handed him a piece of paper, and he read it out loud, "'I can confirm after looking at the x-ray, the work carried out on the teeth was done by myself about twenty years ago, not long after I came to the area. The name of the patient is Nigel Pugh. Signed T.A.M Bennett.'" Eliote smiled. "Good work, Sergeant." Wright walked out of the office, just as Day walked in, looking very dishevelled.

"Sorry for being late, Gov. I had a rough night."

"Not to worry." Eliote passed her the piece of paper Wright had just given him, and after reading it, she looked at him.

"That's a little bit of luck, Gov."

"It is. So it's time to use that luck on our guests, Day." She nodded. "Who do we pick first?"

Edward Pierce was sat in a cell, staring at the wall, wondering why he was in custody, and when was he going to be interviewed. He walked to the bench, and sat down, returning his gaze to the floor. He looked up at the door as he heard a key turning in the lock, and Day walked in. She requested he accompany her to an interview room, where Eliote was waiting.

"Sit down, please, Mr. Pierce." Edward did as Eliote asked. Day sat down next to her superior, who put on his glasses and peered over at Edward. "Can I ask why you gave us a false address for a Mr. Nigel Pugh?"

Edward looked at the detective, hatred in his eyes as the name was mentioned. "I didn't. That's where the bastard lives."

Day showed Edward the photo of the estate. "I personally visited the address you gave me, and that's what is left of the estate. It hasn't been lived in for years, and now, it is being redeveloped."

Eliote tented his fingers. "So, why lie to us?"

"I AM NOT LYING!" he screamed at the two detectives.

"Yes, you are," Eliote snapped, ignoring the outburst. "And I want to know why?"

Edward stood up and approached the door and his head drooped. "I hate that man more than anyone else! He killed my wife." Along with the tears in his eyes, there was a severe sense of malice in his voice. "I would have loved to have killed him."

Day raised an eyebrow. "So, did you kill him?"

"No, last I heard he was swanning around the globe."

Eliote pulled out a photo of the skeleton that had been unearthed at Gold Security and showed it to him. Edward walked back to the table, and after sitting down, glanced at the photo. "What is this?"

Eliote tapped the photograph. "This skeleton was found underneath the offices of Gold Security. We have conclusively identified the man as Nigel Pugh."

Edward seemed to cheer up. "Really? Nigel Pugh? Oh fantastic! My dream has come true!" he said, laughing.

"We believe the body has been in the ground for about thirteen years." Eliote placed the photo back into the file, and pulled out the sheet Day had gathered from the Land Registry. "When we checked up on where Nigel lived, it said he lived at 20 Hectors Close." Eliote pointed at Edward. "Your house."

The revelation of this information wiped the smile clean off Edward's face. "But that can't be, I, I, I would never have lived in a house that belonged to him!" he spat.

"But you work for Gold Security?" Day remarked.

"Rachael is a good employer."

Eliote showed Edward the manuscript Day had retrieved from the computer. "Nigel Pugh was a partner in the business…"

Edward butted in, and looked straight at Eliote. "…Never, I would never have worked for that man!"

Eliote changed his tactics. "Why did you think he killed your wife, Mr. Pierce?"

Edward revealed some information to the officers he had kept hidden for some time. "The day she was murdered, my son found Pugh outside our house. He was acting all weird. He told the police he was coming to find me."

"Why was he coming to find you?" Day asked.

Edward shrugged his shoulders. "To ask if I wanted a job, I suppose. The funny thing is, when you lot asked if he had ever been to the 'Castle' pub, he told them he had never set foot anywhere near there, but that's where all us security guards used to drink, and that's how I met him."

"I know you hate him, but what was he like?" Day pushed for more information.

"He was one of those people who got what he wanted, and didn't care what the effects of his ambitions cost him."

"Did he want your wife?" Day's question was daring, but pertinent. Eliote watched him tense up and glare at Day.

"He tried, but she always rebuffed him. Said it was because she was married."

Eliote picked up another file and placed it on the table. After opening it, he looked up. "If Mr. Pugh did indeed kill your wife, why did she meet him on the night in question?"

Edward gaped incredulously at the detective. "She never did! You lie!"

Eliote took out a piece of paper. "This is a signed statement from one Elizabeth Berry, your wife's best friend. Do you know her?"

"Yes, I know her well. They were like ruddy sisters, always together."

Eliote read the statement. "She says your wife, May, was seeing Nigel behind your back." Eliote could see him began to shake. "They had been seeing each other for months."

Edward banged his fists down on the table. "You're lying; she was the most…"

Eliote continued, disregarding the suspect's behaviour. "…It also says May felt you suspected, especially after she'd had a termination. Her excuse to you was, and she quotes this, 'You couldn't afford another child.' How did that make you feel?" Eliote stared at Edward, and could tell he was about to explode at any moment, but he did the opposite, and burst into tears.

"I wanted another child, but she was adamant! I held her hand at the clinic, cried when they did the procedure, and on the way back, she was silent. I knew the child couldn't be mine. I'd had an accident, and was told I'd be unable to father another child."

Eliote almost felt sorry for the man's pain. He nodded to Day. "Okay, Mr. Pierce, we will take a break and return later." Day stood up and pressed a buzzer on the wall. A constable came in and escorted the broken man back to the holding area.

When they had gone, she looked over at Eliote, who was looking at the door. "What do you think, Gov?"

He shook his head. "I don't know," he paused. "Let's give him a break, and then get him back, really push him. He knows more than he's letting on." Eliote tidied up the files, and then stood up. "Let's go and talk to Rachael. She's probably climbing the walls about now."

WHEN ANGELS FEAST

By
Kevin Bailey

CHAPTER SEVENTEEN

Loughton on Green

Pamela Griffiths was just getting up, when a smell caught her attention. "Oh, those ruddy drains again." She got out of bed and walked to the bathroom, expecting to see the toilet bowl full of water. To her delight, it was as clean as she had left it.

When she walked into the corridor, the smell was worse. After opening several windows around the bungalow, the smell seemed to disperse. Happy that whatever it was had gone, she closed the windows, but her happiness soon dissipated, for the foul smell was back.

She decided to ring her son, and soon, Trevor was exploring the origin of the foul smell. "Seems to be coming from the basement. Maybe an animal has died down there, and we didn't know about it when we were tiding up." The two of them ventured into the cellar and examined all the small room for anything, but all they found were boxes of Pamela's junk.

"Trev, where do you think that smell is coming from?"

He pointed to a wall. "A drain may have burst, and it's seeped into the house."

She sighed. "I was starting to love this place." She walked to the wall, and the smell was excruciatingly bad. "I'll have to get someone in."

The two family members walked up the stairs and went into the front room. He explained they would have to dig up the floor boards. "Couldn't you do it? It'd be cheaper." Heading back to his car, Trevor removed a long metal tool box. He brought it in to the house and placed it on the floor. Withdrawing a crowbar, he walked to the middle and began to pry up the floorboards.

***

Eliote and Day walked into the interview room to find Rachael and her solicitor looking angry. Both gave them an evil stare, and even before the two detectives had sat down, Rachael's solicitor scowled at him. "I must protest at the way my client was asked in, and then left for hours to be interviewed."

Eliote sat down. "I apologise for the wait." He put on his best, sugar-coated professional voice. "We had to interview another suspect…"

The solicitor snapped back, "…oh, so my client is a suspect?"

Day looked at her. "At the moment, everyone is a suspect."

Eliote looked over at her and nodded. "Shall we begin?" and watched as Day placed a CD in the recorder.

Rachael regarded Eliote carefully. "What do you want, Chief Inspector?"

Eliote looked at her through his glasses. "I just want honest answers to my questions, Miss Walker."

She sort of nodded, as if not really interested in being there. "I'll do my best."

The two officers both glanced down at their files, and Day placed a photo of the remains of Nigel Pugh in front of her.

"What's this?" Rachael asked.

"After the fire, investigators found this body buried in a floor in the basement of your business..." Eliote clarified the image for her.

"...So?" she said, matter-of-factly. "The building is over forty years old, and there have been several companies who have occupied the site. Many of them have had dark secrets, which have been exposed over the years." Sarcasm dripped from her tone. "Why haven't you interviewed any of them?" Her solicitor tried to stop her from saying too much, but Rachael raised her hand to stop her. "I haven't got anything to hide."

Eliote took the photo and glumly said, "We believe this body is that of one of your partners." He took out the report Day had gathered. "A Nigel Pugh."

Rachael visibly tensed. "No, it can't be! I only spoke to Nigel last week!"

Eliote continued, "I am afraid it is."

Rachael just sat there, shaking her head. It was Racheal's solicitor who responded, "My client has no reason to lie to you, Chief Inspector. If she says she spoke to Nigel last week, then she did."

Eliote took out the statement from the dentist and spoke towards the tape deck, "I am showing Rachael the dental record confirming the identity of Mr. Nigel Pugh."

After reading the statement, Rachael burst into tears. "I don't believe it."

Eliote handed her some tissues. "We will come back to that later." He withdrew more reports from the file. "The investigator, on the cause of the fire, believed it was arson. Can you tell me who would want to set the place on fire?"

Rachael shrugged her shoulders. "Loads of people hated us!" she snapped. "Rival companies whom we had taken business off, previous partners, the list is endless."

"Why didn't you mention, when we last spoke, that Nicolas Waite is a partner…?"

"…Was a partner!" She glanced at her solicitor. "He had once been my lover," she looked over at Day, "as you already knew." Day nodded, verifying the fact. "He had come into money, a lottery win or something, I never asked, so invested the money in the business, but then he changed. He became a drunk, wanting his money back, so I let him have it." She blew her nose. "We haven't spoken since then."

"Why didn't you tell us this before?" Day demanded.

"I thought you would put two and two together, and, as usual with you lot, get a hundred."

Eliote looked at her. "I am now at two hundred." He smirked. "You see, from our perspective, it points the finger of blame at you." Rachael was about to say something when Eliote brought out the gun. "Do you recognise this weapon?"

"Of course not, why would I?"

Eliote lowered the gun and placed it in front of her. "This gun belonged to Edward Pierce. A similar gun we located at Andows, but records confirm this was also brought by Edward in America. Ballistics have identified this as the gun that killed Nigel and Nicolas." He fibbed slightly, seeing where it would take the investigation.

She examined the gun with her eyes and shook her head. "This is the gun that killed Nigel and Nicky, my god."

"Did you buy this gun off Edward?" Eliote probed deeper.

She shook her head profusely. "I have never bought a gun. I don't like them. Why do you ask?" she queried, slyly.

"I ask, Miss Walker, because this gun was found in your business's safe after the fire. You must have known about it, and I want to know who brought it?"

The solicitor was about to protest, but Rachael stopped her again and answered, "I have no idea who brought it. It must have been one of the other partners." She laughed. "Nigel, most likely. He was always fascinated by them. Sometimes, he would get his phone and pretend he was James Bond." She paused and enquired, "You said it was found in my safe? Well, I have never seen a gun in there, and I should know. I go in there all the time."

"Okay then, can you think of anyone else who uses the safe?"

Rachael nodded. "Loads of people use the safe. My receptionist, security guards, oh, and of course, Mary."

"Mary?" Day enquired.

"My secretary, Mary Gittings…"

Day piped up. "…Mary Gittings, the fiancée of Nicolas Waite?"

Rachael smiled slyly and nodded. "Yes, funny isn't it? The future wife of my lover working with me. They had met while he was still a partner in the business. I hated seeing them together, but when he left, I kept his new love on." She snubbed Eliote's glances and remarked, "She is a good secretary, but she had no clue about us, even though we flirted like mad." She remembered some examples.

"After me and him would meet for lunch in a hotel room, I would come back to the office and laugh, knowing what I had done with her fiancé, as she was typing outside the door." She looked at the wall and smirked, "There was another time he arranged to meet me after work. We ended up making love on the desk. The next day, I watched, laughing inside, as she sat on the edge of the same desk, and placed her hand on the spot where he took me. She asked what I wanted her to do that day. Even now, it makes me laugh." Both officers realised what a cruel woman she was. "I think it was blind intolerance to the fact she thought he loved her, but he didn't. He loved me, and if it hadn't been for Mary getting pregnant, we would be together now." She remembered the happy times.

Eliote brought her back to reality. "Can I ask why you worked with a man who raped you when you were eighteen?"

Rachael scowled. "I forgave Nigel a long time ago. The night in question, we were at a party, and he was drunk and," she looked over at Day who was looking strangely at her, "I know that is no excuse for what he did, but he paid for his crime, and my family and I punish him every day of his life for what he did."

Eliote glanced at her. "You still haven't answered my question, Miss Walker, and I would also like to know what you are punishing him with."

She seemed to go distant, as if remembering the past hurt her somewhat. "My father and Nigel created Walker and Pugh Security Services, and I came into the fold because I hadn't obtained the qualifications to be a vet. At first, it was strange, but it just worked after a while." She focussed on Eliote. "When we had the encounter, my father was devastated. They had been friends, and so he stripped him of his partnership. When he came out of prison, he was met at the gate by my father, and his punishment was that he had to work with me every day, and he couldn't quit. I became his boss."

Eliote was flabbergasted. "A bit of a strange arrangement?" To cover up his disbelief, he stood and stretched his legs.

"It was. Nigel agreed to the punishment, and with his time away," she said, making an air quote with her hands, "he has been involved in the dealings and creation of both Gold Security and its sister company, Gold Developments, and is one of my top advisors."

"I'm guessing you knew about his other times in prison?"

She nodded. "I knew. Giles Edwards came to me, and asked if there was still a place for him at Walker Security Services. I remembered the punishment, and allowed him back with open arms, it was then that we formed Gold."

Eliote walked to the door and looked back. "When was the last time you saw Nigel?"

"I told you I spoke to him a week ago."

He returned to the desk. "I didn't ask you when you spoke to him. I said, saw him."

She shrugged her shoulders. "Don't know. We both lead different lives. I have a conference call with him every Friday."

"Do you have a number we can contact him?" Day asked her.

"No, he rings me."

Eliote looked down at the photo of the skeleton. "If you're speaking to Nigel, then I think we'd better find a way of contacting him, especially as according to our enquiry, he was buried in your basement."

Day glanced up at Rachael. "There must be a number for him. In case of an emergency?"

Rachael shook her head. "There was one, but with Nigel's travelling around the world on his trips, we never used it." Day took out a notepad and asked for the number. Rachael took out her phone and dictated it to her. "Whether it works or not is another thing."

Eliote smiled and thanked her for her help. "Okay, Miss Walker, you can go for now, but we may still want to talk with you."

Rachael and her solicitor stood up, and, without saying a word, walked out.

Day watched them go and looked over at her boss. "What's next, Gov?"

Eliote tidied the files away, and then the two of them left the room. "The most important thing is to try and find out who has been impersonating Nigel Pugh. I mean, there can't be two of them." She nodded. "So, try the number!"

"What if it doesn't connect, or there is no answer?"

Eliote stopped at the entrance to CID. "Then, get onto the network supplier and get the relevant information, name of account holder, address…"

Day opened the door. "The usual then?"

Eliote tipped his head to the side. "The usual."

***

Back in Loughton, Mrs. Griffiths had watched Trevor dismantle the front room, but what they discovered shocked them both. They seemed to be on another floor, hidden about twenty centimetres beneath the one they had ripped up, but on this floor, there was a trap door. Trevor approached this new opening and lifted it by a catch. The smell that greeted him was beyond anything he had smelt before, and they both held their noses and looked down into the space.

"It's a secret room, hidden beneath my bungalow!" She sounded shocked. Trevor shone his torch in and around the room. He noticed a doorway leading into a far off room, and could see a mass of liquid oozing from beneath a door. Only, it wasn't actually liquid. The mass was moving; a throbbing hoard of maggots.

Trevor turned a little white and looked at his mother. "I think we should get someone out to investigate this, Ma."

She squinted in the darkness. "What, like a plumber?"

Trevor swallowed back the rising bile in his throat. "I was thinking more like the police!"

WHEN ANGELS FEAST

By
Kevin Bailey

CHAPTER EIGHTEEN

Sometime later, PC Raymond Perkins and Sergeant Nigella Grant arrived in their Vauxhall Insignia. They had been in town investigating a disturbance of the peace, and had been re-routed to Loughton.

Trevor and Mrs. Griffiths met them on the front step and escorted them into the home. "So, Mr. Griffith," PC Perkins enquired. "You told Operations you had discovered a hidden room full of maggots?"

Trevor nodded and when they entered the room with the false floor in, the smell hit them as well. PC Grant looked down into the hole, and when Trevor handed her the torch, she too scanned the area, and was directed to the doorway.

"Have you a ladder?"

Trevor shook his head, and it was Mrs Griffiths who replied, "I think Emelia next door has one."

Perkins was escorted next door, and moments later, Sergeant Grant was descending into the hidden room. The three observers watched as she carefully made her way to the door, making sure she didn't get hurt. When she arrived, she opened the door slowly, and the smell became worse. She placed her hand over her mouth and nose, and entered the room.

What she discovered sickened her, and she came quickly back to the ladder. Her face had no colour in it, and she looked horrified. When PC Grant helped her reach the top, she quickly asked where the bathroom was. She ran there, and as soon as she reached the bowl, she was violently sick.

PC Perkins, concerned for his colleague headed to her, and she had her head in the toilet. "You okay?"

Grant shook her head. "You'd better get on to CID and the SOCOs. Get them here." She turned, and was sick again. After recovering, she finished her ordeal and gazed sickly up at the worried Perkins. "Then you can move the residents out and seal off the area. This is now a crime scene."

"What did ya find done there?"

The image came into her mind. "What I found isn't for the faint-hearted. So just do as I tell you, Constable," she gagged again. He backed from the room, and left her alone.

***

Eliote and Day returned to the interview room where Edward was waiting. "Mr. Pierce, you said when your son saw Nigel Pugh, he was acting all weird like? What did you mean by that?"

Edward looked up at him. "Well, my son said he was looking white, and kept saying how he was a friend of the Chief Constable. I was told by your lot he was given an alibi by the said Chief Constable's daughter."

Eliote pulled out the second gun, and placed it in front of Edward. "The gun you sold to Andows? Is this the one?" He pointed at the gun on the table.

Edward looked down, and after examining the barrel, he nodded. "Yep, that's the one." He pointed to two symbols above the grip. "It still carries my name on the casing."

"You're sure that that's the gun you sold to Andows?" Eliote queried. Edward was positive. Eliote took out the image of the gun they had been shown in the gun merchant and showed it to Edward. "So, what is this, then?"

Edward looked at the image and bowed his head. "Ah."

Eliote glanced down at the image. "Is that all you have to say?" Edward nodded. "We located this Berretta in Andows, and the female assistant said you sold it to them."

Edward stood up once more and walked to the door, Day asked after him, "We searched your army records, and it mentions nothing of either Berretta. Can you explain that?"

Edward kept looking at the door. "I brought them illegally." He turned back. "When I was in America."

Eliote remarked. "What, both?"

He turned and glanced over at Eliote. "One was for me, and the other was a gift for my boy." He walked back to the table and pointed to the image. "That is why this one is rusty. He used to play with it all the time." Eliote seemed shocked. A friend of his, who was a rifle instructor, had always said a gun loaded, or not, was not a toy, and it irked her when children were allowed to play with them.

Still reeling from this announcement Edward continued trying to relieve the two detectives. "It was never loaded. I ain't that daft. Besides, I had the firing pin removed." He became saddened. "But when May died, I got rid of them both."

"Who brought the second gun, Mr. Pierce?" Eliote demanded. Edward just sat there opposite, remembering his wife. "WHO BROUGHT IT?" Eliote shouted. This made both Edward and Day jump.

"I sold it to the business."

Day, still a little shaking from Eliote's outburst, demanded, "Who in the business brought it?"

Edward looked disturbed. "It was Nigel. I sold it to Nigel."

Eliote examined the gun. "You sold a gun to a man you hated?"

"Yes," he said, defiantly.

"Explain it to us," Eliote ordered.

"I was in need of some money to pay the rent. So I asked around if anyone would like it, and he was the only one." He smiled slyly. "Bought it from me for a couple of grand."

Eliote pulled out the ballistics report. "This gun killed Nigel and Nicolas."

Edward held up his hands in defence. "I didn't kill either! I was in hospital when Nicky was killed."

"Yes, we know, but you would have had access to the gun."

Edward's brow wrinkled. "How?"

"This one," he pointed at the berretta in the bag, "was in the safe, and was used to kill Nigel."

Edward looked coldly at Eliote. "I DID NOT KILL HIM," he said, gritting his teeth. "When she died, I was heartbroken. I didn't go to work. I didn't go out. My children were taken from me, put up for fostering, I couldn't even look after myself," he paused, remembering difficult times, then he continued, "I went back to work three years later. Rachael had been looking through records, and had found out I had done some royal protection, so asked me back when Prince Charles came to Chelmesbury to open the new market. I went to the doctor's, and was proclaimed fit for work."

Eliote wrote down all his notes and looked at Edward. "Ok, I am releasing you from custody, but I may need you to come back for questioning at a later date." Edward nodded, and Eliote looked at Day. "Sergeant, escort Mr. Pierce out." They both left the room. Eliote watched them, and then, after turning off the recorder, he headed out to CID.

Thinking about all the cases, he was distracted by a phone ringing on a desk he was passing. He looked around and saw officers on phones. He placed the files on the desk, and picked up the phone. "CID, DCI Eliote." It was Constable Perkins. After he had informed the Chief Inspector of the discovery in Loughton, Eliote said, "I'll get Strong, and we'll be on our way." He hung up and headed for Day.

Soon, the detective, Doctor Strong, and a van full of officers arrived at the bungalow in Loughton. SOCOs got straight to work pulling up the remainder of the floor boards, checking each one for evidence. Eliote and the Doctor got suited up and both entered the cellar. They could see the doorway, and the maggots had vanished back into the room.

Strong took out a torch and scanned the first room. He pointed at a set of steps which were hidden behind some book cases. Eliote went to investigate, and when he arrived at the top of the stairs, he tried to push the door open, but something was stopping it. He took out his phone and rang Penny, who was working with the SOCOs.

"Hi, Penny. I need you to go to the other side of the bungalow, and I'll bang on this door. See if you can hear me." She acknowledged, and Eliote found a hard object and began banging on the door.

Minutes later, he heard something being scraped above his head, and the door began to creak open. The smiling face of Penny Hardcastle was looking at him. "Welcome to the dungeon," he sarcastically said, and with the light now emanating into the dark, he spotted a light switch and pressed it.

He really wished he hadn't, as both he, Strong, and Penny got a glimpse of the place, and 'dungeon' wasn't the word he should have used. It was more like a torture chamber, with chains attached to the walls, hooks and a bed in one corner. When Penny took out a florescent torch and scanned the area, they could all see sprays of blood. It reminded Eliote of someone putting a brush in paint and flicking it across the walls. He looked over at Strong, who was examining the hooks, and watched as he used tweezers to put chunks of meat into evidence bags, while Penny was taking swabs off the walls.

Eliote went up the steps, allowing the two doctors to do their jobs. He headed for Trevor and Mrs. Griffiths, who were both being looked after by a neighbour. Eliote removed the protective overalls and headed for them. Both were sat at a table in an identical bungalow. He introduced himself, and then asked, "How long have you lived in the bungalow?"

Mrs. Griffiths answered, "Not long, a couple of months."

Eliote nodded and wrote the info down in his tatty notebook. "Do you know who owned the property before?"

It was the owner of the other property who answered, "Her name was Mrs. Sylvia Southwick."

Eliote glanced over at the women, holding a cup of tea. "And you are?"

She approached him and answered, "Mrs. Emilia Lock. I've lived here with my family for about thirty years."

Eliote eyed her up and down. "I thought this village was a place for…"

Delicately raising an eyebrow, she peered over at him. "…The elderly to come to die, by any chance?" She smiled. "Shame on you, Chief Inspector."

He started to stutter. "I, I, I meant no offence."

Emilia sort of laughed. "None taken. You are sort of right. It has become what you said, but it was once a thriving family area. My husband and I brought my daughter, Jane, up here."

Eliote looked at her, and the two names came into his head. "Your Jane Boyd's mother?" She nodded. "I am so sorry!"

She shrugged her shoulders. "Thank you, but hey, our William will find out the truth. I've known him since he was a child."

Eliote looked confused. "Our William?"

"Yes, Detective Inspector William Frashier. He and Jane were best friends."

Anger crossed Eliote's face at Frashier's deception. "He never told me that!"

Emilia placed her hand against her mouth. "I hope I haven't got him into trouble?"

Eliote didn't answer her question, but asked one in return, "You said a Mrs. Sylvia Southwick owned the property? How can I get hold of her?"

Even though she felt a sense of guilt that she had obviously got Frashier into trouble, Emilia replied, "Unfortunately, she is dead. She died about a year ago, and since then, it has been rented out."

Eliote looked over at Mrs. Griffiths. "Do you rent the property?"

The elderly lady shook her head. "No, I sold my big house in Glayton and came here for a quieter life. Some chance of that," she said sarcastically.

Eliote addressed Emilia again. "Do you know if Mrs. Southwick had any next of kin?"

"No. When she died, the property was handed over to her solicitor," she paused, "I have no clue who…"

Mrs. Griffiths spoke up. "…Heath, Marlow and Morris, up on the high street." Eliote wrote the information down, and she continued, "I dealt with them through the estate agent, Bishop and Brown's." Eliote scribbled the name down.

"I have the itinerary for the place somewhere." Emilia informed him. "I was going to have a look around, as it is larger than mine, but when I saw the asking price, I decided to stay where I was." She approached a drawer and pulled out the documents on the property, handing it to the detective, who read from the itinerary.

> *'Bishop and Brown are proud to introduce to you, this stunning bungalow set in the picturesque village of Loughton on Green in Shropshire.*
>
> *It is an ideal spot for an older couple, who are looking for a quieter life. The property, unfortunately, is in need of some renovations.'*

Eliote asked Emilia if he could keep it. She nodded, and he placed it underneath his notebook. "Did you see any of the tenants?" he asked her.

"There was only one I think, and she didn't stay long." She tried to remember the name. "Terry, I think," she nodded, "Yes, that was her name. Terry Hawkins." She continued to recollect. "Stayed for a few months, lots of noise and drilling going on, and then there was peace again. A few people would turn up at night, and then you would see her planting flowers in the garden at night."

Eliote was about to ask another question when there was a knock at the door, and Constable Perkins entered the kitchen and approached Eliote.

"Sorry to disturb you, sir, but Doctor Strong has sent for you." He looked seriously at him and informed him, "He is about to go through the door into the back room. Thought you'd like to be there." Eliote bid the ladies goodbye and followed after Perkins.

On the way back, Eliote took out his mobile and rang Day. "Day, I need you and Frashier to get to Heath, Marlow, and Morris solicitors. Check up on a Mrs. Sylvia Southwick, her will, and everything."

"Got it."

"Then get on to Bishop and Brown's Estate Agent. Get some details on a female by the name of Terry Hawkins, full background check."

"We will be on our way, Gov."

"Thank you." Eliote put his mobile phone away, still slightly seething at Frashier's betrayal and contemplating how he would deal with the situation. Ducking under the crime scene tape, he put those thoughts aside and headed back into the bungalow.

After putting on some more protective clothes, he descended down the steps and found Strong waiting for him. "Shall we?" the doctor asked, beckoning him towards the door.

"As usual. After you, Doctor!" The two men put on protective masks and goggles and walked slowly into the other room. Strong turned and headed for two large freezers, stepping over thousands of maggots on the floor.

"Lovely," he muffled over to Eliote and pointed to the floor. Eliote nodded and looked up to an extension lead casing on the wall, two plugs were attached, but the wire connecting the socket to the plug was missing.

"I think we have found the reason the freezers are off," he said behind his mask. Strong nodded and approached the first freezer and opened it.

Even with the mask, the smell was unbearable, but Strong persisted and examined the contents. Most were green, flies swarmed around the decaying meat, laying the maggot larvae onto the mouldy flesh.

"What do you reckon was in there, Doctor?" Eliote asked looking down into the nearly full chest freezer.

Strong looked at the contents. "A few dozen frozen chickens, a little bit of lamb, and a few sausages. Nothing unusually in here."

Eliote agreed. "If this turns out to be nothing, Brightly is gonna have my hide for using all her precious resources…"

Strong stopped him. "…But this is interesting."

Eliote looked down, and saw what could best be described as a mouldy piece of rump steak.

"That would have been a corking piece." He felt his stomach grumble, Strong looked back at him.

"I have a hunch that this isn't animal." He grabbed the steak, and after wiping away a handful of maggots, he felt it. "The composition is wrong."

Eliote looked at the meat, and then at Strong. "If it's not animal, that can only mean one thing…"

Strong nodded. "Human, I'll bet my entire month's salary on it!"

WHEN ANGELS FEAST
By
Kevin Bailey

CHAPTER NINETEEN

Inspector Frashier drove his BMW into a parking space. As he got out, he stared up at the very imposing building and a chill went down his spine. He had found out that before it had become a nursing home, it had once been the local mental institution, and prior to that, a work house.

He approached the front door and rang the bell, one of the two large oak doors opened, and a male attendant asked, "Can I help you?"

Frashier took out his warrant card and showed it to him. "I am looking for Mrs. Gladys Cook, the Home Manager."

The attendant escorted the detective to a waiting room. "I'll go and get her for you."

Frashier smiled and looked around the smart waiting room, posters on the wall showed elderly people enjoying sports, food, travelling, and other pursuits they could get from Brooklings Homes.

"I see you're admiring our company's posters, Inspector. Maybe you have an elderly relative you wish to house?" Frashier turned and saw a woman who reminded him of Hattie Jacques from the *Carry On* films. He half-expected to hear Sid James laugh at any moment.

"No, I haven't. My mother and father died a long time ago." He changed the subject. "I didn't know you did all these things?"

"Oh yes. We try and keep our residents as active as possible. It makes them feel better." Mrs. Cook escorted him to her office, passing indoor tennis courts and a billiards room, where two men were deep in a game.

"I can see a lot of activities. Maybe one day, I'll come here."

She smiled. "You never know. Have you the money to pay a thousand pounds a month?"

Frashier stopped and gawked at her. "A grand a month to stay here? How many residents have you got?"

She did a rough calculation in her mind. "About one hundred and twenty-six, sorry, twenty-five. We lost Mrs. Green a couple of days ago."

Frashier was in awe of the size of the place. The pair arrived at a well-presented office. "Come in, and please sit down."

He sat down on a comfy chair and looked at Mrs. Cook. "I am here about Jane Lock."

Her facial expression dropped. "Yes, Jane was a good worker. She would treat the residents with humanity and respect. When she left, we lost a good one." She tapped a finger to her chin. "Did try and keep her, promised her the world, but she was adamant she wanted to go to college and then, university. I could not stop her."

Frashier nodded. "She was like that."

Mrs. Cook smiled softly. "You knew her?"

"Yes, we went to primary school together. She knew what she wanted, and usually got it." There was silence for a few seconds.

"So," Mrs. Cook asked, "what can I do for you?"

Frashier put on his policeman's face. "According to her mother…"

Mrs. Cook abruptly spoke up at the mention of Jane's mother. "…How is Em holding up?"

Frashier smiled. "She is fine." Mrs. Cook apologised for interrupting him, and he continued, "A few days before she died, she rang here and spoke to someone. I was wondering if anyone here knew her?"

"I'm sure there are a few who were here when she worked here." She took out a black notebook, and Frashier saw hundreds of names. She scanned them, and as she did she remarked, "No…" This continued over several pages, then she found a few names. "Yes, here we go." Frashier took out his notebook and began writing down the names she said, "Heidi Gower, Dean Hamden, Elizabeth Jones, Michelle Clarkson…" Mrs. Cook riddled off a few more names, "Karen Bates, Mike Rowe, Thomas Little." She came to the last page, "Oh, yes, Georgina Green." She looked up at him. "Does that help you?"

"I would like to speak to these people. Could you make it possible?"

"Of course." She stood up and disappeared into the place, leaving Frashier alone in the office.

***

Back in Loughton, Strong had thoroughly examined the first freezer. He turned his attention to the second one. As he examined the contents, Strong placed each piece of suspected meat into evidence bags. He had little doubt they weren't human.

"Wouldn't catch me with my hands in there!" Eliote said, feeling a little squeamish as he watched the good doctor rummaging around examining the green meat. He could see the maggots wriggling, almost dancing, ecstatic at being able to get to places they hadn't before.

Suddenly, Strong felt something hard in between the gruesome chunks, and slowly pulled the objects out to reveal a hand and a skull. Eliote saw raven black hair was stuck together, hiding cut marks, and maggots emanated from the incision, as well as the eyes and ears. The hand was ridged.

"Yes, that answers it, its human alright," Strong said, pointing to the skull with the hand. Eliote felt a little nauseous and turned away from the freezer, heading out of the room. He found Penny examining the bed.

"What have you found, Penny?" he said, taking deep breaths and removing the goggles.

"Bodily fluids, semen and urine, also blood," she paused and could see that the colour had gone from Eliote's face. "What did Strong find in there?"

A voice bellowed from the other room. "Mouldy human flesh, Penny, and its affecting our great detective."

Eliote glared at the other room. "No, it's not. I just needed some air. The smell is revolting."

There was a muffled laugh coming from the other room. "It's not affecting me," Strong said sarcastically.

"Well, you're used to it," Penny snapped. Eliote slightly smiled and walked out of the cellar, heading back to Emilia's place.

"Mrs. Griffiths, Mr. Griffiths," Eliote said, as he walked into the property. "When you've been doing any work in the house or garden, have you come across anything unusual?"

Trevor looked up at him. "Why do you ask that?"

"I have to ask, Mr. Griffiths." Eliote glanced at the elderly lady, and she shook her head.

"I can't say I have?" Eliote pushed her a little, and she remarked, "I was doing some planting in one of the flower beds, and found what I thought was animal bone." She froze. "It wasn't, was it?"

The detective looked at Emilia. "You said this Terry Hawkins would come out at night and plant flowers. That's a bit unusual, wouldn't you say?"

Emilia nodded. "As I said, Chief Inspector."

Eliote looked over at Mrs. Griffiths, and she was sat in shock. "I'm afraid you will not be allowed into the property, or grounds, until we have finished."

"I don't think I will ever go back in there," she said, adamantly.

"Is there anywhere you can stay?"

Trevor nodded and answered. "Me and the missus can look after her."

Mrs. Griffiths looked up at Eliote and seriously asked, "You have found human remains, haven't you?"

He bowed his head and nodded. "Yes, we have," he paused and looked seriously at her. "I need your permission to dig up the garden."

"Do what you must, Chief Inspector."

"Thank you." Eliote watched as Trevor took the lady away, and followed them out. "Potter, can you escort Mrs. Griffiths and her son to their car, please."

The blond officer nodded, and the three of them left the scene. Eliote sought out DS Wright. "Sergeant, get on to the university, and get the geophysics down here. I want a sweep of garden." She nodded, and he headed back to the house.

As he neared the house, Eliote saw a grey Vauxhall Insignia drive up the road and park next to his Saab. Day got out and headed for his location. "What did you find out, Sergeant?"

"I went to the solicitors and spoke with Mr. David Morris. He has been dealing with Mrs. Southwick's estate, and according to him, the will said the land she owned in Whatling Street…"

Eliote swiftly held up a hand. "…She owned land near Gold Security?"

Day inclined her head. "She owned all the land surrounding Whatling Street, Gov. Her husband was a farmer by trade, and where Gold Security is located, was the exact location of their farm."

Eliote rubbed his chin. "Mm, there will be no real connection between the cases, but it is interesting."

Day crossed her arms. "There's more, Gov. It seems Mrs. Southwick was a philanthropist, because the will says the land was to be given to the county for cheap homes to be built. All the businesses in the area have been told to move. But get this." She took out her iPad and touched the screen. A newspaper article, containing a picture, came up of several people stood next to the Whatling Street sign. He read the story.

'Business Owners Fuming as Council Informs Them to Close up Shop'

Local businesses along Whatling Street, which employ thousands of Chelmesbury workers, have been given notice to vacate businesses as the land is being turned into affordable homes.

Councillor Elaine Martin has told the paper the reason behind the foreclosures is because of a will that belongs to the owner of the land.

Mrs. Sylvia Southwick, previously residing in the Loughton on Green area, wants the land turned into homes for the poor.

Nigel Pugh...

He stopped reading and looked at her. "When was this article written?"

"About a month ago." She pointed at the picture. "This man is supposedly Nigel Pugh."

He shot her a strange look. "Supposedly?"

"Yep! But I know him as Johnny Gittings!"

***

Frashier sat waiting for the first name on the list to arrive. He had set up his phone as a recording device, and his notebook was open on a clean page. There was a knock at the door, and Gladys walked in with a grey-haired, elderly lady. At first, he thought it was a resident, but she was introduced as Heidi Gower, the assistant manager of the home.

"Mrs. Gower, I am investigating the death of Jane Boyd." She seemed to screw her face up in puzzlement at the name so Frashier enlightened her. "You would have known her as Jane Lock."

The lady smiled warmly. "Janie Lock, was a wonderful carer, full of promise. Could have easily been the manager, if she'd put her mind to it."

"Why do you say that?"

"Jane was a leader, even used to boss me about. She had this aura about her."

"Before she died, she rang here. Did you speak with her?"

"I'm usually in the kitchen; dealing with the cook and his assistants. My line is internal calls only."

"If you can think of anything, let me know." The conversation was brief, and to the point. Frashier knew he had to get through several interviews, so it was appropriate.

The lady smiled and nodded, and then left the room. Frashier saved the recording and prepared for the next, he didn't have to wait long.

Dean Hamden was a black-haired, middle aged man. He reminded Frashier of Mr. Bean. "Please sit down, Mr. Hamden."

Dean did as was instructed and sat opposite Frashier. "So, you are here about Jane?" he said, with a Scottish accent. Frashier indicated in the affirmative. "Aye, I knew her. She was one of a kind. Hardworking, caring, but not just to the residents. I'd been going through a turbulent time in my life. My mother had died." He lowered his eyes in sorrow. "She looked out for me, kept me sane."

"So you liked her then?" Frashier asked.

"Oh, aye, I liked her alright. I asked her out for a drink once." He sighed heavily. "She kissed me on the cheek, and said that she was attached to someone, but thanks for asking. I was a little dejected, but when I saw that little…" He was about to say something nasty, but stopped himself. "…when I saw Alex, I thought, 'She is in safe hands.' I didn't feel so bad."

"I asked Mrs. Gower the same question as I am about to ask you." Dean sat up in the chair. "Before Jane died, she rang the number for this place." He looked around the office. "Did she ring you?"

He shook his head. "I wish she had. I would have done anything for her."

Frashier smiled. "Okay, Mr. Hamden, you are free to go."

Dean stood up and approached the door. He looked back. "You knew her too, didn't ya?"

Frashier looked up and nodded. "Yes."

Dean smiled. "I thought I recognised you. I bumped into you three in the street. You all seemed happy." It was Frashier's time to feel sorrow as Dean left the room.

The next five people said similar things to Dean and Heidi. They all praised Jane, and were shocked at the news of her death.

Finally, there came a knock at the door, and a middle-aged woman came in and looked at Frashier. She reminded him of a cross between Morticia Addams and Nicola Sturgeon of the SNP. In his mind, he heard the Addams Family theme as she almost glided across the room.

"Mrs. Green?" he asked. She nodded and sat down. "I am investigating the death of Jane Lock."

"How may I help you, Inspector Frashier?" She crossed her hands in her lap.

He looked surprised. "You know my name?"

She once again nodded. "I saw you at Jane's funeral. You were sat talking to Greg."

"I was." He thought back to that terrible day, and fought back the tears. "So," he said coughing. "You knew Jane well, then?"

"Not as well as you did," she said aggressively, almost confronting him.

"I don't understand?"

Mrs. Green gave a sly smile. "Jane told me about you and her. The fact that you loved her, and she could never feel the same about you." She looked deep into his eyes. "About Eve!"

Frashier stared into her dark eyes, and could see something that scared him. "You know about Eve?"

"Do not panic, Inspector. I am not gonna go around and tell everyone about your dark secret. Mind you," she sat back in the chair. "It could look bad for your career."

"Are you threatening me, Mrs. Green?"

"Hell no." Her demeanour changed. "I just can't get used to the fact that Janie has gone. I am sorry for the way I spoke. It was stupid of me. You must be feeling it too." Frashier again looked confused. "About the loss?"

"Oh, yes." He wasn't convinced she was as saddened as he was. Those eyes seemed to be watching his every move. "I have asked the others the same question. Before she died, she rang…"

Mrs. Green abruptly cut him off. "...She rang me, and asked if she could stay at mine for a few days."

Frashier wrote this down. "When was the last time you saw her?"

She looked at the window and replied, "She rang and I picked her up. She and the two children stayed at mine for a couple of days, but then her husband rang her, and said he was coming to see her. She grabbed some of her stuff and left quickly. She didn't tell me where she was going."

Frashier studied her, but she seemed to have raised some form of barrier in which he couldn't see through. "So, you have no idea where she was going?"

She shook her head. "None." She looked him straight in the eye. "I thought she might have contacted you?"

Frashier tried not to bite. "Do you have any of her belongings?"

Mrs. Green gave a wry smile. "Unfortunately, nope. She only came with the bare essentials."

Frashier forced a smile. "Okay, Mrs. Green, we will be in contact." She rose and almost glided back to the door, leaving him. Seconds later, Mrs. Cook returned and found Frashier picking up his belongings. "What is the story of Georgina Green?"

Mrs. Cook looked at the door and replied, "She is a strange woman. Keeps herself to herself, but the residents love her," She turned her head back to the detective. "Is there anything else I can do for you, Inspector?" Frashier had no more questions. Mrs. Cook graciously guided him out of the facility. Neither noticed a figure watching them from above.

From an upstairs window, Georgina watched him leave and smiled. "Goodbye, Inspector," she said with animosity, and turned and walked to a door. Opening it, she piped up, "Hello, Hilda! It's time for your bath!" The portal squeaked closed.

WHEN ANGELS FEAST

By
Kevin Bailey

CHAPTER TWENTY

"I want you to go and pick up Johnny Gittings. We need to have a little chat with him." Day nodded, jumped back into her car, and vanished in a cloud of dust, leaving Eliote to return to the bungalow.

Strong had finished in both freezers, and had assembled many evidence bags, which were being taken away by his team. Eliote walked up to him. "How many people do you think were in there?"

The doctor looked at the bags. "A rough guess, I'd say about four, but I'll know more when we get back to the lab."

Eliote looked at the bags. He could just see a couple of skulls, a few fingers, and several complete hands. "I shudder to think what was going on in here, Doctor." He perused the small room. "To think that a place like this is here on our own doorstep."

The doctor nodded. "It feels like Cromwell Street. I dread to dig up the floor. I just don't know what we'll find."

Just then, there was a cough at the door, and Penny appeared in the doorway. "Chief Inspector, geophysics is outside."

Both he and Strong went out of the cellar and approached a Land Rover, where a skinny, grey-haired, bearded man was waiting for him. "Ah, Doctor Strong. It's been a while."

Strong nodded. "It has indeed, Ade." Strong motioned to Eliote. "Chief Inspector Simon Eliote, this is Professor Adrian Knight, head of Geophysical Studies at the University of Chelmesbury." The two men shook hands.

The professor rubbed his hands together. "So, where do you want us to start, Chief Inspector?"

Eliote looked at the bungalow. "Start in the basement, and work out into the garden and surrounding areas."

Professor Knight took a cursory glance around the location. "What about time frame?"

"As long as it takes, but, can I remind you, this is a murder investigation."

"So ASAP, then?"

Eliote nodded, and watched as the three members of the geophysical team got to work. They pulled out what looked like a child's push-along cart, and something that reminded Eliote of a Zimmer frame. The bearded man looked over at them and touched the push-along cart. It had a sticker on it saying, 'radar one.'

"We will probably use ground penetrating radar. It gives us a better view of the ground." He paused. "We use it on archaeological digs to search for pits, graves, and deeper wall foundations. My colleague," he pointed to another bearded man, "will use the other equipment to geophis the garden. His task will be to see if there is disturbed ground, which could identify large pits and graves in the garden."

Eliote nodded, he'd been a big fan of Channel Four's *Time Team*, and knew roughly what he was talking about. "Whatever you find could be important, Professor." The bearded man nodded, and Eliote looked over at Strong, "Did Penny finish her analysis on the Berettas?"

Strong shook his head. "She's been a little preoccupied."

"Of course, but I'm going to need it as soon as possible."

Strong sighed. "Is that an order?"

Eliote looked over and smirked. "No, it's a sort of request."

Strong smiled. "Okay, I'll get her on to it right now, but you owe me one."

"Of course." Eliote walked back to his car and headed towards the station.

***

Penny stood up against a bench, and was examining the rusty Beretta. She started by taking it apart, and after a while, it was in pieces. She examined every inch of the parts. Something wasn't right. She picked up the evidence sheet, and with her finger, scanned through the writing. She glanced over at a large grey box. Rummaging through the contents, she came across the second pistol. Opening the bag, she took out the second Beretta, and carefully dismantled it, so both pistols were side-by-side.

The problem stood out like a sore thumb. The firing pin was missing from the pistol that was found in the safe, but was clearly intact from the rusty gun. "I thought this one was…" She stopped and took out a magnifying glass, as she had spotted something on the firing pin. She looked at it in more detail, and discovered what could only be described as the top of a fingerprint.

Obviously, it had been cleaned, but not thoroughly enough. She walked the mechanism to a scanner and took a photo. Clicking over to the database, she checked to see if there was a match. It came back inconclusive. She thought for a few moments, and then picked up the phone and dialled a number. "Hi Heather, its Penny Hardcastle. Can I come and test a pistol on the range?" She heard her reply. "Thanks."

***

Johnny was at his office, looking at the accounts, when there was a knock at the door and his secretary walked in. "Sorry to bother you, Mr. Gittings, but the police would like to have a word with you."

Johnny looked down at the accounts and replied sarcastically, "Tell them I'm not here."

Just then, Pickington walked into the room. "I'm sorry, but that will not happen, Mr. Gittings."

Johnny looked up and saw the detective looking at him. Potter stood outside the door, and both looked imposing. "Ah, okay. Susan, reschedule my appointments for the rest of the day." He grabbed his coat from behind the door and looked at Pickington. "I am all yours, officers." They swiftly removed him from the premises.

***

Simon returned to his office, and was just preparing for his interview, when the phone on his desk rang. "Eliote."

It was Penny. "Can you come down to the range? It's urgent."

Eliote was a little flustered. "Penny, I am preparing for an interview. Can it wait?"

She was adamant. "I think you need to see something!"

He relented. "Okay, I'm on my way."

The gun range was in the older part of the station, and was a good minute's walk from CID, along the maze of corridors that made up the complex. When he walked into the range, he could smell the gun oil and powder. To some, it was quite nauseating, but when he had been in London, he'd spent many hours in ranges. However, since he had been forced to shoot the man at the shopping centre, he had not ventured anywhere near them.

"So, what was so important that I was called from my preparations?"

Penny apologised, and walked with him to a table, where an officer in a baseball hat and holding goggles was waiting. "Chief Inspector, this is Constable Heather Hatling." The two officers exchanged greetings. "And I believe you recognise these two pistols." Eliote nodded, and Penny turned and looked at Constable Hatling. "Well, would you do the honours?" She handed Eliote a pair of ear protectors.

Eliote watched the capped officer load a clip into the first Beretta and enquired, "Now, that is the one we found in the safe."

Penny nodded, and as Constable Hatling lined up the pistol, aiming it at the target, she turned off the safety. Simon waited for the gun to go off, but was disappointed when there was just a click and nothing else. "What just happened?"

Penny indicated for him to wait a moment. "Now, for the other." He watched the female firearms officer take out the clip from the first pistol and insert it into the butt of the rusty weapon.

"I'd advise you to step back a little," she requested. "I cannot say what may happen, Sir." Eliote and Penny did as instructed. She turned off the safety, and pulled the trigger. This time, it went off with so much force it pushed her back slightly. She then proceeded to squeeze the trigger again and again until the gun was empty.

Eliote was both shocked and angry. "I was told that the rusty one didn't work. The firing pin had been removed."

Penny and Heather looked at him. "I'm sorry to say, sir, but this weapon is armed, and very dangerous to both victim and user. The rust may make the gun explode."

Eliote looked down at the other gun. "And this one is useless."

Heather nodded. "Without the firing pin, it's as useless as a child's play toy."

Eliote turned, and Penny reported the other find. "I found a partial fingerprint on the pin. I think it has been swapped from the other Beretta."

"Enough to identify the person who switched the pins?"

"My findings were inconclusive." Penny sighed.

"Okay thank you, Penny, Constable Hatling." Eliote stormed off.

Instead of heading to CID, he headed for his car and drove quickly towards Andows. On the way, he rang Day, and then Pickington, asking for them both to have Johnny fingerprinted, and the info sent to Penny to analyse. He approached the shop and pulled up outside. He got out and headed for the front. The same attendant he'd met earlier came to meet him.

"Can I help you, sir?"

Eliote took out his wallet and showed who he was. "I need to ask you some questions about the rusty Beretta." She looked unhappy. "Is there a problem, or do I have to take you to the station? Whichever way, I want the truth."

"It was borrowed for a couple of weeks."

Eliote glared at her. "When, and by whom?"

"Just before that lad was shot in the high street."

Eliote, slightly annoyed, remarked, "Nicky Waite?"

The clerk bowed her head in shame. "Yes, I went to school with him. His death was so sad."

"So, it was borrowed by whom?" She was reluctant to say the name, but Eliote demanded, "BY WHOM?"

***

Johnny Gittings walked into the holding cell. Inspecting the room, he looked back at Pickington, and said sarcastically, "No three-star service then, Constable?" Pickington ignored him. He went to close the door, and there was another sarcastic remarked, which bellowed down the cell block. "Can I have breakfast at seven, please?" The door closed. Gittings sat down on the metal bench and began to laugh.

***

Eliote returned to the station, and was about to head from his office to the interview room, when Frashier approached him with his report. "I have done as much as I can, Gov. So, here we go. Do what you must do."

Eliote walked to the door and closed it, returning to his desk. "I want to know, Inspector," he glanced up at the detective, "why have you taken it upon yourself to investigate the Jane Boyd death?"

Frashier looked at the floor. "Cause it's my job." he said defiantly.

Eliote's attitude changed. "I know about your personal attachment to Jane, Inspector."

Frashier glared at him. "Someone's talked, haven't they?" He cursed under his breath. "It was Pickington, wasn't it?"

The men stood toe-to-toe. "No one told me anything. I wouldn't be a very good detective, if I didn't do a little detecting work of my own. You see, I've been watching and listening. You might think I've not been observant, but I have. I've watched as you slinked off to investigate the case, leaving the team to the other cases."

Frashier glared at Eliote. "And you haven't? You've been so preoccupied with your own inner demons, you didn't see a good detective slip through your grasp. Day deserves better than this place!"

"Oh, so it's like that, is it? You can't handle criticism, so you go on the offensive. Let me tell you about my inner demons, shall I?" Frashier sighed, crossing his arms in indignation, as Eliote spoke, "Three years ago, this week, I lost the only family I had. They were ripped away from me, killed in a fatal car crash. I have been trying, and failing, to deal with that, plus attempting to hold this bloody team together. Those are my inner demons you are so kindly referencing." He pointed at the detective. "What are yours?"

For the first time since Eliote had come to Chelmesbury, Frashier showed his emotions, tears trickling down his face. When he raised his head, his eyes were red. "One of those dead girls…Eve…was my daughter!"

When Angels Feast

By
Kevin Bailey

CHAPTER TWENTY-ONE

The room had been silent for several minutes; the only sound came from beyond the door. Eliote looked at his dishevelled colleague. All along, he had been acting with self-pity, thinking only he could feel pain. Now he realised how bad a person he had become. "I am so sorry for your loss, Inspector, I really am."

Frashier sighed. "She never knew me as her Dad, so I can't understand why I feel like this?"

Eliote warmly smiled. "It's a father thing, Will." Frashier sat down and burst into tears. Eliote stood and placed his hand on Frashier's shoulder, handing him a pack of tissues. "I am told the pain gets better in time, but for me, the pain has never gone away. For you, my friend, it's going to hurt like hell."

"I would like to ask for some compassionate leave, Gov."

Eliote nodded. "I understand, Will. I'll give you as much time as you need."

Frashier stood up and looked at him, a slight smile on his face. "Thanks, Gov." He quickly vacated the office.

Shortly after his departure, Day poked her head in the door. "Is everything okay, Gov? I just saw Inspector Frashier leaving, and it looked like he had been crying." Eliote asked her to close the door, which she did. "So?"

"He has asked for some compassionate leave, and I have granted him his request."

Day nodded. "So, my transfer is on hold then?"

With everything going on, he had forgotten about the transfer request. "I'm sorry, Day. I now need you more than ever."

She cursed under her breath. "Right, Gov. I'll be going nowhere," she said the last sentence softly, so he could not hear her and left. Eliote was about to head to Brightly's office, with the latest report, when his phone rang.

"Eliote!"

It was Potter. "Gov, geophysics have discovered what they believe are more bodies at the bungalow. The Doctor is asking what you wish them to do."

"Okay, Potter, tell the Doctor I am on my way." Eliote grabbed his jacket and headed out of the door.

As he was just about to get to his Saab, Sergeant Delaney collared him. "Sorry to bother you, Gov, but we have a breakthrough. Seems a detective working on the original golf course case was checking a missing person's file when he made a match."

Eliote was intrigued. "Did he check on the information?"

"No, according to sources, he was reassigned to another case." Delaney read his notes. "The Christmas Day Murders."

Eliote shrugged his shoulders. "Never heard of the investigation."

Delaney seemed to be in deep thought. "Cold case number 02589, I think." He looked at Eliote. "For eighteen years, a victim was found in, or around, the towns of Glayton and Chelmesbury. No killer was ever found, but the investigation was on-going. When the killing stopped, it was passed to us."

Eliote walked with the officer back into CID. "What happened to this missing person's case which is connected to the body found on the golf course?"

Delaney approached the area he had been assigned. "It became just another case passed to us. It was filed away in case of any new leads." He handed Eliote the large box file.

"And this is it?"

Delaney nodded. "According to the report, the detective believed her name was Candy Sutton." He handed Eliote the file, and he read the information.

> *Candy Sutton, born April 9th 1965 in Tennessee, USA. Reported missing by staff at her Youth Hostel in Glayton in 1996. Body never found.*

"Have you got onto the police database? They may have more on this case."

Delaney nodded and handed him a printed out copy of the information.

The first thing he saw was a picture of a very attractive, blonde woman, who was smiling at the camera. "I see from the file that no suspect was ever arrested."

"There were several suspects." Delaney turned the page in his notebook. "The prime suspect in the disappearance was Anthony Green, who was questioned thoroughly, but was never charged with the crime. According to the lead detective, there just wasn't enough evidence against him."

Eliote became intrigued. "Okay, what have we got on this Anthony Green?"

"Not much really except that he no longer resides in this county," Delaney replied. He looked at a piece of paper in his hand. "His last known address on the electoral register had him residing at 28 Hectors Close, Chelmesbury."

Eliote looked at the image of Candy, and asked bluntly, "Any additional information on Green, or is that it?"

"Police Scotland want to question him about the disappearance of three women and one man in Edinburgh, but attempts at finding him failed. He didn't resurface again until 2010, when he was spotted in Texas, at an airport. His name alerted the American police to an arrest warrant issued by Interpol."

"If you've got a file on it, it means that there is more information to follow."

"Yes, whilst being arrested, he proceeded to stab the police officer to death." He looked up at Eliote. "You know what the American police are like. He's killed one of their own, so they will want the ultimate punishment."

"Where is he now?" Eliote said, reading the police file. "I see, he's on death row, awaiting sentencing." He read a statement from a solicitor and remarked, "Am I reading this properly that the governor of Texas wants him dead straight away, due to public outcry, but his solicitor keeps appealing the conviction with the supreme court due to police brutality?"

Delaney nodded and showed Eliote a picture of the accused. He looked as if he had been in the ring with Mike Tyson. He then showed him the evidence that Green's solicitor had produced. It was an image of a man whom Eliote realised was Green in a Hannibal Lector-type mask with a board containing several numbers.

"What's all this about?" Eliote said, holding up the picture.

"Seems that the victims in Edinburgh had been cut up like animals at a slaughter house, and then eaten. It seems as if it was some sick joke by the officers at the penitentiary," Delaney replied.

Eliote could understand why the appeals were being held, if this was the way he was treated.

He read down the lists of crimes Green had committed on his suspected victims, and it was appalling brutality against human beings. The victims were treated like animals. As he read through the records, he noticed, at the beginning, Green's crimes were petty, with a little time in prison. He'd stopped for several years, and was going straight, but then his supposed first victim, Stacy Holder's, full body was never found. Subsequent parts were washed up in the Tyne with cut marks on the flesh.

"So, you're telling me," Eliote commented on the file, "that all these crimes weren't brought to justice, because not enough evidence arose against him, and he simply slipped the net?"

"Yes, it seems without the proof they needed, they could only say he was a suspect."

Eliote was shocked at this conclusion. "Surely, as a suspect, they would have been keeping a track on him?" Delaney read his notes, but there was no mention of that fact. Eliote cursed under his breath, and then looked at Delaney. "Get on to Police Scotland, and have them send the case notes. I want you and your small team to go through it with a fine tooth comb. I am going to visit the superintendent and see if she can request an interview with Anthony Green." Eliote walked away, picking up a phone and making a call.

When he was finished, Eliote walked around a corridor and bumped into Day. "Ah, Sergeant, you don't fancy a trip to America to interview a suspect?"

She was reluctant. "Sorry, Gov, but my passport expired last year. I do know Frashier still has a valid passport."

Eliote cursed. "But he's on compassionate leave. I'll have to find someone else."

Day stopped him. "Frashier is like you, Gov. He needs to be busy, and, if you value my opinion, please send him to do it."

"Get all the information he'll need ready for him, while I go and okay it with the evil queen of statistics." Day sniggered and left.

***

After Eliote had consulted Brightly about his request, she had asked whether a video call would be more appropriate. Without giving her too much information, he had informed her that he felt a face-to-face meeting would be more beneficial to the case and that he wanted Frashier to go as he was best suited to the job.

As he drove the Black Saab onto the empty market square, Eliote felt a slight sense of guilt at lying to Brightly, but as he parked outside Frashier's apartment the guilt passed. Getting out, he zipped up his coat and walked to an insignificant blue door. Peering at a list of residents, he spotted, 'W FRASHIER,' and pressed the buzzer next to the name, waiting patiently. Looking towards the shadowy castle which was lit by the fading night sky, he wondered if the inspector was home.

Across the way, in the old supermarket car park, Frashier was getting out of his car. After grabbing some food shopping from the boot, he walked towards his home. As he walked between the empty market stalls, he heard his name.

"Ah, Frashier, there you are! I was beginning to think you had left the country!"

Frashier replied quietly under his breath, "Wish I had." He approached the blue door and opened it. Both men entered a hallway. There was a musty, oldness about the place which reminded Eliote of the smell you get when you enter a stately home. After the two men had climbed the two flights of stairs, they entered the relatively clean flat.

Eliote walked into the spacious, white-walled front room and sat down on the only piece of furniture in the room; a corner suite. "Lived here long, Inspector?"

From a fair-sized, spotless kitchen, Frashier replied, "About ten years." He changed the subject. "Can I get you a coffee, tea, or I'm sure I could find some alcohol."

"Tea please, two sugars and a little milk," Eliote replied. While he waited, Eliote examined the room. It wasn't the type of place he'd imagined Frashier living in. "Nice place," he remarked as Frashier walked in carrying two mugs. He handed him one, and sat down opposite.

"Why are you here?" Frashier asked, getting straight to the point. Eliote was silent for a while, and Frashier glared at him. "Gov."

"What!" Eliote stumbled. "What, oh yeah, I need a favour."

Frashier almost laughed. "You must be joking. You want a favour?"

Eliote stood up and nodded. "Well it's more of a request really, I need you to go and interview a suspect about a cold case. I know we haven't always seen eye-to-eye, Will, and that you are on compassionate leave, but with all the cases going on, you're the only spare superior officer I have."

"Surely there are others, Gov," Frashier said reluctantly. "With the way I have been feeling, I just want to go and bury my head in the sand, and…"

"…sulk."

Frashier felt like giving Eliote a piece of his mind, but refrained from doing so. "I can't, Gov."

Eliote knew what must be done. "Look, Inspector…Will, I need you to do this, as there is no one else," he lied.

Frashier was quiet for a while, before finally giving his answer. "Okay, I'll go and get some stuff, and then I'll head for…" he paused, "…where am I going, Gov?"

"The suspect's name is Anthony Green." Frashier fumbled for a notepad, and wrote down the name. Eliote continued, "He is being held at a prison in Texas."

Frashier's pencil skidded across the paper. "Texas?" Eliote acknowledged the destination, and Frashier answered sombrely, "Okay, Gov. I'll get to the airport and head for Texas."

"I'll have some information on the cases sent to you via email. You can read up on the long plane journey over. The Superintendent is liaising with the American police, arranging to have someone meet you when you arrive." Frashier nodded, and Eliote continued, "So get some sleep, as you're booked on the 0815 flight in the morning. I'll get someone to get you to the airport!"

Frashier escorted his boss down the stairs and after saying, 'goodbye,' he closed the door and remarked under his breath, 'Prick!'

***

Eliote walked back towards his Saab, and after looking at Frashier's apartment, he headed for Loughton. When he arrived, Potter was stood next to two squad cars which were acting as a gate, police tape between them. He parked up and headed for the tape.

"Evening, Gov," Potter said, and directed him to the Land Rover parked next to the house.

Professor Adrian Knight was looking through tainted oblong glasses at a screen. Strong sat next to him in the back of the vehicle, and the professor was pointing to parts of data. Eliote stood next to Strong and looked at the lines on the screen. "So you discovered something?"

The professor looked excited. "Oh, we found something all right. Most are probably medieval pits, but," he pointed at something, "this could be interesting for you. These appear to be grave cuts."

Eliote looked at Strong. "What do you want to do?"

The doctor rubbed his chin. "We have to dig up this pristine lawn, and see what's there!"

Eliote agreed and looked at the Professor. "Hang on. Before we do that, what did you find in the basement?"

The professor pressed a key and showed Eliote what he had found. He pointed to a black blob on the screen. "These blobs are similar to what we found in the survey in the garden. If you dig there first, then we can surmise that these are the same."

Eliote looked at the Doctor. "Are you ready?"

Doctor Strong glanced to a minibus and at a group of SOCOs waiting. "Oh, I'm ready." He signalled the occupants, who began to exit the minibus. He walked to them and directed them into the cellar, and began organizing the teams to locations planned with geophysics. They began by hand-removing the concrete to get down to the earth below.

***

As the digging began, Frashier walked towards the airport lounge and prepared to board a plane for America. Frashier hated flying, he always had, but with the chance to go to America and interview a killer on death row, how could he refuse and it would take his mind away from his pain, even for a little while.

After walking down the terminal, he found his gate. Grabbing a coffee, he waited for it to open. He looked at his watch, it read, '7:46am.' "Ages yet," he said to himself, and was about to begin reading through the emails, when his mobile went off. He saw it was Strong.

"Evening, Richard." Strong sounded tired, and he could hear the sounds of digging in the background. "Where are you?"

"Loughton on Green, digging up a basement." His manner changed. "I heard that you asked Eliote for compassionate leave. I just wondered if you wanted to meet up and talk about it?"

Frashier watched as the lounge filled up with passengers and suitcases. "I'm a little…"

Strong butted in, nearly stuttering. "…Of course you want to be alone at a time like this?" Suddenly over the tannoy came a request for boarding of another flight. "Where are you Will?"

"I'm at Birmingham International, preparing to board a flight to America, to interview a suspect by the name of Anthony Green."

***

Strong looked over at Eliote, who was talking to Potter. "I wasn't told you were leaving the country."

He heard Frashier sarcastically say, "I'll miss you too, Richard."

Strong smiled and then looked at the earth. "Well, thanks for leaving me to dig up what appear to be more bodies in the basement." He heard Frashier laugh.

"I'm sure you'll cope, you always do." Strong was distracted by one of the SOCOs lifting up an object. It looked like a human jawbone, muscles and bits of flesh still attached. "I've got to go; we have found something. Safe journey, old friend."

***

"Cheers old buddy," Frashier said, as he saw that his gate was preparing to open. "I've got to go too, they're about to open the gate and allow us on to the plane."

"Thanks for leaving me with that cantankerous head of ours," Strong sarcastically replied.

Frashier smiled. "I'll be back as soon as I can. Keep it together until then."

"I'll try," and then he hung up.

Frashier grabbed his belongings and headed with the crowd of people towards a desk. After giving his boarding pass to the attendant, he walked through a glass door and down the umbilical, approaching the aircraft.

A pretty stewardess was waiting. "Good evening, sir! Welcome onboard. May I see your pass?"

Frashier showed her his pass, and she directed him to his seat. He placed his carry bag in the overhead rack and sat down. He pulled down the foldaway table and placed his iPad on to its surface, scanning the email Eliote had sent.

Behind him, he heard a sweet, beautiful voice. "Excuse me, I have the window seat."

Frashier turned and looked up, and saw a beautiful young women looking at him. She was about five feet in height with flowing blonde hair and crystal blue eyes. He was almost tongue-tied. Frashier apologised, "Oh, please forgive me. I don't like planes."

She smiled. "I'm not keen either." Frashier took his belongings and allowed her to sit in the window. She extended her hand and introduced herself, "As we are going to be neighbours for the long journey to The States, my name is Jeanette Hastings. I am a teacher from Shropshire, going to see some of my family who emigrated."

Frashier took the soft hand and shook it. "What part of Shropshire are you from, Miss Hastings?"

"Oh, please, only my students call me Miss Hastings. It's Jeanette, and I live in Glayton."

He was surprised. "Well, I am Detective Inspector William Frashier from Chelmesbury CID. I am on my way to The States to interview a felon."

She didn't seem as surprised as he was. "I could tell you were a copper!"

"Was it my questions or can you sense things?"

Jeanette shook her head with a small curve of her lips. "I saw the DI Frashier name at the top of the email on your iPad."

"You're very observant?" He chuckled at the joke.

She placed her phone on the table in front of her. "In my profession, I have to be." Frashier grinned. From that moment on, he had a companion, and he was the happiest he had been for weeks.

***

As the plane soured across the sky towards America, a brand new white Mercedes SLK pulled into the visitor space at Chelmesbury Police station. A smartly dressed man got out and approached the entrance, walking casually to the reception desk.

The officer behind the glass approached and spoke to the stranger. "Good evening, Sir. How may I be of service?"

"I would like to speak to the head of CID. It concerns a case he is investigating."

"And who are you, Sir?" the officer asked.

The man brushed a hand over his suit. "I am Nigel Pugh, and I understand he has been looking for me."

WHEN ANGELS FEAST

By
Kevin Bailey

CHAPTER TWENTY-TWO

Eliote was instructing some of the CID officers who had come to take over the night shift, when his phone rang. "Eliote."

It was Pickington. "Sorry to bother you so late, Gov, but you'll never believe who is in a holding cell."

Eliote had no clue. "Kylie Minogue?"

Pickington scoffed. "No, Gov. A man who claims to be Nigel Pugh."

Eliote hung up, jumped into his Saab, and drove frantically back to the station. When he arrived, he found Constable Pickington down a corridor. Both men walked to a room with a blacked out window which looked into the holding cell.

"It can't be?" Both officers looked from the man to the picture they had on file. After yawning, Eliote ordered Pickington to place the man into an interview room, and get Day. Pickington disappeared. Eliote watched the man. If he was definitely Nigel Pugh, that left Eliote with a dilemma. Who was the body in the basement? The plot thickened.

***

Sergeant Day was sat in an outside smoking area, drinking a cup of tea, when she spotted Pickington looking at her. "What's up Phil?"

He grabbed a cigarette from the pack on the table. Lighting it, he responded, "The Gov wants you in Interview Room Two."

She drank some more of the tea, and didn't seem to be rushing, instead lit a cigarette and then announced "He can interview Johnny on his own. I'm fed up with being at his beck and call."

Pickington took another drag. "He ain't interviewing Johnny. It is a guy called Nigel Pugh."

For a second or two, the name didn't compute. "Wait, did you just say 'Nigel Pugh'?"

"Yes." Pickington said, flicking some ash into a pot.

Day put out her cigarette and headed quickly to the interview room. Eliote was waiting for her.

"Shall we do this, Sergeant?" She nodded, and they entered.

"Sorry to have kept you, sir," Eliote said as he walked in.

Nigel smiled. "Don't mention it."

Eliote and Day sat down, and looked over at the smartly-dressed man. "Before we begin, I would like to ask you for some identification. It's just a precautionary procedure, you understand?"

The man nodded and took out his wallet, producing a photo card driver's licence and several debit cards. He took out his passport and handed them all to Eliote and Day. "Thank you, Mr. Pugh," Eliote said, looking at the proof. Satisfied, he handed them back to Nigel. "I'm sorry for asking, but a skeleton was found in the basement of Gold Security, and DNA confirmed that it was you!"

"Well, as you can see, I am alive." Eliote scratched his head.

"I can see that. This makes it interesting for us. The DNA was conclusive it was you."

Nigel smiled. "Well, it must be wrong," he said bluntly.

Eliote and Day just looked at each other in amazement. Could Strong have been so wrong? Eliote turned and looked at the man. "Okay, Mr. Pugh, where have you been hiding?"

The man glared at Eliote. "Hiding? I have been travelling, representing the company all over the world. I contact the office as, and when, I need to. Or if Rachael needs a conference call."

"When was the last time you had a 'conference call'?"

Nigel sat forward and replied, "Last week, I think. There was some flap on about the land and a will."

Eliote took out the article and showed it to Nigel. "I'm guessing it was because of this?"

Nigel nodded, and read the title.

'Business Owners Fuming as Council Informs Them to Close up Shop'

"Yes, this is it. I told her it was in the best interest she dealt with it, and I carried on with my business." Eliote took the article and read it out loud,

> "*Nigel Pugh and other owners are trying to prevent their businesses from being shut down. Mr. Pugh, currently residing in Glayton, told the paper, "We are taking this to the highest level of government. We employ thousands of workers who will become statistics. We do not want that, etc. etc."*

Nigel seemed to become uptight and stuttered, "Yes, yes, yes, I remember I did say that." His attitude changed again. "I would, of course, hate for my hard working and loyal workers to be laid off."

"But aren't you trying to buy somewhere else?" Day commented as she rummaged through the many sheets of paper in the folder. "In Docklands Green, Glayton?"

Nigel nodded. "Yes, but that site will be a smaller venture, and so, of course, there will be a few redundancies."

Day pointed at the photo. "Do you know who this is?"

Nigel examined the photo. "That's Johnny Gittings, an old friend and associate."

"It says that he is you. Can you please explain that?"

Nigel sat back and looked a little smug. "I couldn't get back for the picture, as I was in Hong Kong at a security show. Johnny said he would stand in for me. All I had to do was give a brief statement."

Day wasn't convinced, and neither was Eliote. "You said you've come back from Hong Kong. Can you give us some information about where you stayed?"

"Of course I can, I stayed at the Cosmopolitan Hotel in one of the recently renovated rooms," Nigel answered quickly. He closed his eyes and leaned back. "From my room, I would watch the vibrant city quiet down." He smiled. "It was so magical."

Eliote asked another question. "Where was the conference held?"

"At the Hong Kong Convention and Exhibition Centre," Nigel responded abruptly. He looked straight into Eliote's green eyes. "A great venue."

Day wrote the information down. "Okay, Mr. Pugh, thank you for coming in."

Nigel straightened himself up. "Not at all. Anything to help the police and their enquiries."

Eliote looked over at Day, and ordered, "Sergeant, can you take Mr. Pugh to have his fingerprints done?"

Nigel stopped them. "My fingerprints, why do you need them?" he said nervously.

Eliote turned and confidently replied, "It's just a precaution to eliminate you from our…"

"…It's just not good enough, Chief Inspector. I have come here voluntarily, and this is how I am treated?" He stood up, and Eliote could see he was angry.

"Please calm down, Mr. Pugh."

Nigel glared at him. "Calm down? I feel like a bloody criminal!"

"Have you got something to hide from me, Mr. Pugh?" Eliote responded with calm and clarity.

Nigel froze and shook his head. "No, I am just appalled. I have a good mind to report you to the IPCC."

Day went to say something, but Eliote stopped her. "You do what is right for you, Mr. Pugh, but remember this. I could arrest you, if I feel that you are holding something from me."

Nigel barked, "On what grounds?"

"Well, let's start with perverting the course of justice," Eliote snapped back. "You see, I do not believe that a pathologist, who has been doing his job for years, got a DNA sample wrong. The DNA analysis, and a written statement from a dentist, has clearly showed that this person," he produced the photo of the skeleton and waved it in Nigel's face, "WAS Nigel Pugh, and until I get to the bottom of that problem, I will assume that something is wrong with you!"

Nigel folded his arms together. "Then, I am going to need my solicitor present."

Eliote stood up and looked at him. "That's your right." He walked to a wall and pressed a buzzer.

An officer walked in. "Yes, Gov?"

"Constable Owens, can you escort Mr. Pugh to a holding cell, and contact his solicitor?" The constable nodded, and as he was taking Mr. Pugh away, Eliote remarked, "Oh, and Owens?"

"Yes, Gov?"

"Do his fingerprints while you're at it." Nigel was about to protest, but Eliote waved them away. Nigel began muttering to the constable, and looking angrily back at the detectives, as he was escorted down the corridor.

Eliote looked over at Day and yawned. "We will reconvene in the morning," he said, rubbing sleep from his eyes. "Give our guests a night to think about their stories."

"It seems strange to me, Gov. We were looking for a man who no one has seen for years, and he turns up unannounced."

"I agree. I think we should get Rachael back in, don't you?"

"What about Edward?"

"Get him in as well. Tell you what, let's get all of them in. Play one against the other, so to speak." Day smiled and stretched. Eliote ordered her to go home. "Tomorrow will be a busy day, Sergeant." She nodded, and they went their separate ways.

***

The Boeing 737 touched down at Houston's Bush Intercontinental Airport in Texas, but for Frashier and Jeanette, the flight had gone quickly, too quick for the both of them. Frashier had never laughed so much. She had kept him in stitches, telling him tales of life spent with her mother in America and her dear father in Glayton. Only as they prepared to leave the plane, did he think of Eve or Jane.

"You lost someone didn't you?" she asked, gazing at him.

Frashier stood up and grabbed his belongings from the overhead lockers. "I did." He said sadly, grabbing his flight bag. "But I have to move on!"

"Well, I'll give you my number. If you get a free moment, give me a call."

"I will." He took her hand and kissed it. "Thank you for a great time. I haven't laughed so much in a long time."

"I don't think everyone liked it," she said, peering back at a snooty-looking woman who was giving her an evil stare.

"She's just jealous." Jeanette smiled.

"Yeah, she looks lonely." The woman raised her nose to them and walked down the aisle to the door. They both laughed, and after grabbing their belongings, they made their way off the plane and headed to the main terminal.

Jeanette turned and kissed him on the cheek.

"What was that for?" he asked.

"When I fell asleep, you were the perfect gentleman." He smiled warmly and remembered when she had fallen asleep on his shoulder, he had got the attention of the flight attendant. They placed a blanket over her, and she had stayed there whilst he had read through the files.

"Don't mention it, what are friends for?"

Arm-in-arm, the two new friends walked to arrivals, and went through customs. After about thirty minutes, which seemed longer, they exited the airport, and Will gave Jeanette his hotel number and his room. She smiled, and said that she would be back in the neighbourhood sometime in the week. She leant forward and kissed him again on the cheek, and then headed for a Greyhound bus parked in a bay. After watching her leave, he walked to a waiting area, but didn't wait long.

A grey Ford salon approached the pickup area. A tall man in a long raincoat got out, and approached Frashier. He spoke in an American accent. "Mister William Frashier?" Will nodded and got up. "Hi, I am Detective Daniel Markovitch, the man who brought Anthony Green to justice." He made the introduction proudly. Frashier looked at the American detective. He reminded Frashier of the TV detective, Colombo, the streaky black hair the long raincoat, the striped suit underneath. He half-expected to see a basset hound in the back seat, but to his dismay, there wasn't.

Markovitch turned and beckoned him to the car. There, Frashier was introduced to the driver, and they drove away from the airport, and headed for the prison. Once on the freeway, Frashier looked at Markovitch and asked, "What is Green like?"

The detective turned and looked at his British counterpart. "Green is what I would call a retard. Mentally, he has the mind of a genius, according to his school records, which we acquired from you Brits. He had A-pluses in all his exams, went to college and then university to study medicine, but for some reason, he left his studies and began a life of crime." He paused as the driver veered. "Green sees people like we see animals, food for his twisted mind."

Frashier looked at the detective. "Is he a cannibal?"

"He is always telling anyone who speaks to him that all humans are food." Markovitch paused and looked straight at Frashier. "And they taste like pork. When anyone goes into his cell, they are escorted by several guards, in case he attacks."

Frashier didn't like the sound of that. "If he's that bad, how will I interview him?"

Markovitch smiled. "You Brits have no guts. No wonder terrorists come and use your country like a hotel." He looked at the driver, and they both laughed. "Do not worry yourself 'Inspector,' you will be safe," he said, looking back at the long road ahead. "We have created a special room where he can talk to you."

Frashier was relieved. Memories flooded back of his time with Alex and Jane at her parents' house, watching the movie *Silence of the Lambs*.

Frashier sat back in the seat, both angry at Malkovich's comments and happy, as he didn't want to be in a room with a cannibal. He watched the houses disappear to be replaced with deserts. His thoughts turned back to Jeanette, and he wished he was with her now. He looked down at the sweat patches on his shirt. "Will I be able to stop at my hotel to freshen up, before we get to the Penitentiary?"

Markovitch shook his head. "I am afraid that will not be possible. We are running to a tight schedule." He looked at the road ahead. "They're probably preparing the prisoner right now."

As they travelled the long desert freeway towards their destination, Frashier asked more questions. "So, how was he caught?"

Markovitch seemed to smile as he informed Frashier of the capture. "Well, we had been alerted to him by Interpol. Police in Edinburgh had wanted to talk to him about some deaths, when he was stopped at the airport. He asked if before they went anywhere, he could go to the bathroom. Once inside, he jumped and killed the officer, like some rabid dog, and escaped through an open window onto the runway." Frashier imagined it almost like a Hollywood movie. "After a stand-off at a motel, where he was holding a few hostages, a few of us broke into the hotel and arrested him. He had threatened to kill and eat them, if he didn't get his own way."

Frashier was surprised. "It's a bit strange to me he has been arrested for the murder of a police officer, but not for the people he supposedly killed in Edinburgh."

Markovitch shrugged his shoulders. "Not strange to me." He pointed and tapped his head. "He is retarded, like I said." He turned and looked over at Frashier. "He should have been killed in your country for his crimes, but at least we have the pleasure of doing it for you." Frashier just gulped as Markovitch looked ahead and pointed, "That's where we're going to." Frashier turned and could see a grey stone building, which seemed to rise out of the desert like a mirage.

"Welcome to Hell," the driver announced.

As they turned off the state highway, the British detective got his first proper look at the imposing prison fortress. The outer wall of the penitentiary was approximately twenty-five feet high, with rolls of barbed wire across the top, more razor wire above that. Around the perimeter were watch towers, and officers stood next to large searchlights, armed with machine guns which were aimed at the jail complex.

The guards watched the car turn into the main entrance, and Frashier felt like he was being brought to this jail as a prisoner. It wasn't a feeling he liked. Markovitch got out when the car came to a stop and approached a guard at the entrance and showed his badge.

The guard examined it and then looked at a clipboard. He moved his finger down the list of names until he found the officer. Happy that everything was above board, he walked with Markovitch to the car and looked in through the window.

"Detective Inspector Frashier?" Frashier nodded. "Can I see your identification please, Sir?" Taking out his wallet, he opened it to show the guard his warrant card. "Thank you, sir."

The guard walked back to the entrance, and the gates opened. Markovitch got back into the car, and the driver drove the car through. The gates closed behind them. Frashier was glad for air conditioning as it took what felt like several minutes for the second gate to open, and the car manoeuvred into the inner sanctum.

The car stopped in a space, and Frashier got out. He could feel why the driver had called this place hell. The heat from the sun was excruciating. He looked out of the gate at the desert, seeing why they had built this place here. He took off his jacket and threw it over his shoulder, and followed Markovitch and the other detective into the inner buildings.

After walking through some steel doors and the x-ray machine, they were greeted by a man in a white coat. "I am Doctor Josef Guanine. I am in charge of the 'special' patients." He raised his large eyebrows as he said 'special.' Doctor Guanine addressed Markovitch. "I'll escort Mr. Frashier to the meeting with Green." Frashier looked at the doctor. He was about 5ft11 with round spectacles and a large bulbous nose. Even though he was smaller than Frashier, he seemed to be looking down at him from behind the glasses, with the coldest eyes Frashier had seen on any man.

Frashier felt a shiver go up his spine, and he felt like someone had walked over his grave. Markovitch nodded and looked at Frashier.

"We will be outside to take you to your hotel."

"This way, Mr. Frashier." Frashier followed him up a long green corridor and around a corner. In front of them was a large, grey door. Doctor Guanine took out a key and opened the door. Frashier walked into a large stone room. A glass screen had been set up to divide the room in half. It was about five inches thick, and it contained a microphone, He scanned the room and saw large speakers attached in the corners.

On the other side of the room was another large door, and he could see shackles were attached to the wall opposite with long chains. He also spotted more speakers attached to the corners.

Frashier approached a black chair, and placed all his belongings on to a table nearby and waited.

After a short period, which to Frashier seemed like ages, the other door opened and four men emerged through it. All of the men had armed themselves with batons, and every so often were pushing an orange-suited man in the middle. When they got to the shackles, one of the men fitted them around the prisoner, and then they left.

Frashier was now face-to-face with Anthony Green. "Mr. Green."

The man nodded and spoke back with a sleazy American accent. "Yeah."

Frashier pulled out his badge, and showed his warrant card to Green. "I am Detective Inspector William Frashier…"

"…Now, when my solicitor told me that a police detective from the county of Shropshire was coming all this way to Texas to see little old me, I wondered why?" He laughed. Frashier looked at the man. He was about six feet tall, with streaky brown hair and a rounded face. His green eyes seemed to be at the back of his large eye sockets, which made his face seem strange.

"We are investigating the discovery of a skeleton found at a local golf course." Green raised an eyebrow. "Beneath a stone," he paused to look at Green, "we found your initials on a note." He turned and showed him blown up photos of the grave and the note. Green just shrugged his shoulders, and replied with contempt,

"I do not know what you are talking about. I used to live in Chelmesbury, but I left there when I was a lad."

Frashier looked into the cold eyes. "Oh, come on, Mr. Green. I have come all this way to see you. At least you could give me something."

Green lay back against the wall. "I do not know what you are talking about…"

"…I think you are lying."

Green ran to the screen, the only thing stopping him from smashing through was the chains. He looked menacing, and screamed at Frashier, "And I think you would do nicely on a barbeque!" He returned to the wall, "I have nothing further to say, Detective Inspector Frashier from good old Shropshire." Frashier grabbed his belongings, and was about to leave, when Green remarked, "How is Chelmesbury? Still peaceful as ever?"

Frashier decided not to answer, and left.

Green watched him go, saddened the Shropshire detective had gone. Maybe he would be nicer to him, if he came back.

As he waited for the brutal guards to return, his thoughts turned to the peace and quiet of the River Teme that ran through the town, remembering as a child punting up and down the river seeing the castle on the hill. The realization hit him that he was never going to see his homeland again. A tear trickled down his chin, and he wiped it away.

'I don't want the vile guards to have any excuse,' he said to himself, and the feeling of trepidation came to him as he heard the key in the lock.

WHEN ANGELS FEAST
By
Kevin Bailey

CHAPTER TWENTY-THREE

Frashier was taken back to his hotel. Markovitch patted him on the back as they climbed the steps to the hotel entrance. "Don't look so down, buddy. That's more than anyone else has got out of him." He opened the entrance door, and both men walked into the foyer. "We still don't know why he attacked that officer."

Frashier sort of smiled. "Ok, I am gonna go to my room, and then I am getting in contact with my station." Markovitch walked with him to the reception desk, and left him alone. The brunette receptionist smiled at him, and spoke with a posh English accent, which surprised him.
"Good afternoon, Sir. Welcome to the Endeavour Hotel. Can I help you?"

Frashier put down his luggage and responded, "Ah, good afternoon. I am William Frashier. You have a reservation for me?" The receptionist typed in his name, and the screen changed to show his details.

"Ah, there you are." She looked at him and smiled. "You are in room 448 on the fifth floor. I'll get a porter to come for your bags." She rang a bell and handed him the register. He signed his name. "Thank you!" She gave him a keycard, just as the Porter came, and he was escorted to his room.

When he arrived, he unlocked the room, and the porter carried his luggage into the room. Frashier gave the young man a tip, and after he had gone, the detective sat on the bed and looked around. It was a pleasant light blue coloured room with matching blue fixtures and fittings.

Frashier turned and looked at the phone beside the comfortable bed. He picked up the receiver, and the receptionist spoke to him, "Reception?"

"Hi, this is Mr. Frashier, room 448. I need to make a long distance phone call to England. How do I do that?" The receptionist asked for the number, and she made the call, forwarding it to his room. It rang a few times, and then he heard the distinctive tones of Eliote.

"CID."

He looked at his watch. "Good morning, Gov."

Frashier could tell from the tone of Eliote's voice that he was happy to hear from him. "Ah, how is it in sunny Texas?"

"It's wonderful," Frashier lied.

He heard Eliote laugh. "I bet it is," There was a pause. "What can I do for you, Inspector?"
"I have made contact with Green, and he is a slimy bastard. If I am to get him to confess to the crimes, I am going to need more than what I came with. I am also going to need some pictures of Shropshire, Chelmesbury, and especially Glayton."

"Shropshire?" Eliote asked.

"Yes, as I was leaving, he asked about Shropshire."

"Make him homesick, might open him up a little."

Frashier nodded. "My thoughts exactly. Also a few pictures of his house to get him feeling low."

Eliote agreed and informed him, "I am doing some interviews today, and I'm going to pop around to 28 Hectors Close…"

"Hectors Close? I'll make sure Green knows about it."

"Good hunting, Inspector," Frashier hung up and walked into the matching coloured bathroom. After a shower, he went down in search of lunch.

***

Eliote walked up to Dawes, and ordered her to get together the appropriate information, and send it to Frashier. He approached his office and contacted Strong.

Doctor Strong's team had been working most of the night on the basement, and were astounded at what they had found. When the chief pathologist saw it, he was shocked. Penny gave Strong a run down. "We think there are up to six people buried here, from the skulls to fibulas." She indicated to a long bone on the tray. "All of them show signs of butchery."

Strong looked at the lit-up holes. "Not a nice place to visit?"

"No. Whatever went on here wasn't nice, almost a torture chamber."

Strong was about to walk to a hole where one of his team was scrapping away a layer, when he heard his phone ringing. He walked to his leather bag and took out the iPhone, answering using loud speaker.

"Welcome to the dungeon, how may I be of service?" He heard the voice of Eliote, and for the first time since he had known him, it was sort of friendly.

***

"Good morning, Dungeon Master. What have you to report?"

Strong responded in his usual way, "At present, we have found what appears to be six bodies buried in the basement. My team is, of course, beginning to excavate more of the pits that were discovered on the geophysical scans."

"When do you begin in the garden?"

He heard Strong sigh. "Hopefully later today. I have my daughter coming with a team to help, and she will begin out there, while I work in here."

"There may be another site," Eliote reluctantly said. Strong was silent. "Are you still there?" He looked at the receiver, and saw it was still connected, "Strong?"

"I'm still here." He let out a long breath. "Another site?" Eliote knew the Doctor probably wasn't happy at this news.

"If the person who Frashier is interviewing turns out to be the killer, he used to live at a home in Hectors Close, so I may need a team to investigate there."

Strong seemed a little angry. "I have scrounged and begged for the large team I have, and now you are telling me, I may have to split it?"

At that moment, Day walked in with an empty cup and made a gesture. Eliote nodded and, then he returned to the call. "Yes, unfortunately!"

Strong was blunt. "So be it." The phone call abruptly ended, and Eliote returned the receiver, heading out into CID. He found Day carrying his tea. He took it from her, and after taking a few sips, he looked at her.

"Strong isn't happy."

"When is he happy?" she responded.

He smiled and sat on the edge of the desk to drink the remainder of his drink. "I just told him that there may be another site." Day cradled the mug in her hands, confusion crossing her features until Eliote explained, "28 Hectors Close. If Green is the killer, then I want his home searched."

"That's gonna take a lot of manpower. Will the gaffer upstairs allow it?"

He looked over to the door. "I have to report in later, so I'll tell her then." He smiled warmly at her, finishing his drink and heading for his office, but was stopped by DS Wright.

"Gov, we may have found something on the CCTV footage from Whatling Street."

Eliote looked over at Day, and they both followed the female detective to a small room, where Constable Dawes had set up a large TV. "Let's see it then!"

On the screen, Eliote could see trucks and vans driving quickly up and down the road, delivering their wares. Day looked at Dawes. "What time did the fire start?"

The officer looked at her notes and replied, "According to the security guard, he thinks it started around eight. He said in his statement," she flicked through her notes and then read from them, "'I passed the building at about five-thirty, and there was still a lot of movement in the building.'"

Eliote commented, "Probably the last few leavers, preparing for the next day's shifts."

The other officers nodded and then Wright continued still reading from the statement, "'I passed the site at about seven-forty-five, it was in complete darkness, except the security lights.'"

Eliote looked at Wright. "Fast forward to five-thirty." She nodded, and they watched as the security van drove slowly past. "That fits with the guard's statement." Eliote spotted a silver, Bentley Continental pull up at the main gate, a well-dressed man got out. He grabbed a briefcase and headed for the main reception area, and was allowed in by a woman, who then left the site.

Day examined the image and rubbed her chin. "Wright, check-up on the car, all details!"

"Yes, ma'am." She approached a computer terminal and typed in the reg. The information came up on the screen, and she turned and reported, "Car belongs to…"

Day said the name before she did. "…Alex Boyd, I thought I recognised him."

Eliote looked from Day to Wright, who nodded in agreement. "That's who the car is registered to. Mr. Boyd lives locally."

Day nodded and looked at Eliote. "Mr. Boyd is Jane Boyd's husband." Eliote seemed lost, so Day clarified, "The woman whose body was found in the ditch."

"Right." Eliote studied the car on the screen, pondering aloud, "What is the connection?" He puzzled over it for a few seconds and then ordered, "Fast-forward until the car leaves." Wright pressed the scan button, and the image sped up. Suddenly, Eliote demanded, "Stop!" She pressed play, and they spotted a cream-coloured Jaguar XJS.

Wright turned and informed the two detectives. "A car matching that description was seen driving quickly away from the high street, the morning Nicky Waite was shot."

"Slow play, Constable, and do a check on it," Day ordered.

"I can't see the registration, ma'am. It's as if the driver is keeping the registration plate covered. They seem to know exactly where the cameras are located."

"There cannot be that many XJS's in Chelmesbury?" Day inquired. Wright typed in the make, and about two hundred cars and addresses came up. "I want you to cross reference every one of those owners with all the people connected with Gold Security or any of its affiliates."

She did as was instructed and two hundred became zero. "Dead end, Gov," she informed the two detectives. Eliote cursed under his breath, and returned to the image.

The XJS kept driving up and down the road, until finally, it parked up just down from the site. A man in a hoody got out, and began to snoop around the site. They watched as he approached the boot of his car and grabbed several boxes, returned to the buildings and disappeared into the shadows.

They watched as the time ticked by. Several cars and vans went past, and twelve minutes later the hooded man emerged empty-handed, jumped into the car, and drove off.

The time elapsed, and at 6:45, Alex and a woman, who they all identified as Rachael Walker, emerged dishevelled from the main reception area. After giving each other a peck on the lips, jumped into their appropriate cars, and went separate ways from the site.

7:00 came along, and the security guard drove past again slowly.

"The guard was bang on," Wright said, triumphantly holding up the statement.

Eliote nodded. About two minutes later, the XJS was back, and they all saw him park and head to a walkway that ran down the side of the building. When he returned, they could all see the flickering of flames coming from the back of the building, and the tape finished as the car drove away. Eliote gazed at the dark screen, pondering his next move.

"We have to identify that car. If we do, we have found the arsonist, and most defiantly a murderer."

"You think so, Gov?" Day looked over at him.

"I do." He peered over at Wright and Dawes. "I want you two to keep going over the recording, frame-by-frame, if you have to. We have to identify that car." Wright nodded, and Day and Eliote left the room.

"What now, Gov?" Day asked as they walked to her desk.

Like a great chess player, he pondered. "I better go and check up on Strong, make peace with him."

"What do you want me to do?" she asked.

"This 'Nigel Pugh'…check everything he has said to us. I want to know where he's been, and what work he has done for Gold Security. Then let's get Rachael brought back in?"

"We have only just released her from custody, are you sure?"

"Yes," he said bluntly. "And let's get this Alex Boyd in as well. See what he has to say." Eliote left Day to complete the tasks, while he went to face the music with 'the Gaffer.'

WHEN ANGELS FEAST

By
Kevin Bailey

CHAPTER TWENTY-FOUR

Back at Loughton, the team was busy. Penny had not spoken to the Doctor for hours. She had left him to calm down, and now, she went to report on her findings. "Strong?"

He looked up from his hole and smiled. "Yes Penny!"

"We have finished work in the basement. All remains have been catalogued, and are ready to be taken to the lab."

"Thank you." He stood up and stretched his legs. "After the remains have gone, shut down the basement and begin on some of the magnetometer blobs. Dig and find out if they are human or animal remains, as this one is." Penny gave a curt nod. As she was moving to head back to the site, she saw Eliote's Saab pull up. The detective got out carrying a brown file.

"Afternoon, doctors."

Strong ignored him and continued with his animal. Penny leaned forward and spoke directly at him. "He's still in a pig with you about splitting his team."

They both heard a heavy sigh, and Strong responded, "I'm not in a pig."

Penny and Eliote smiled, and she left the two friends to it. "If you're not in a pig, what are you in?"

Strong didn't look up as he replied, "A bloody huge dog's grave." They both laughed. Eliote stood next to the grave and showed him the photo of the skeleton which was found at Gold Security. "Why are you showing me this?"

"Are you absolutely convinced this is Nigel Pugh?"

The doctor took offence and began making obscenities, walking around waving his hands in the air. "Why the fucking hell are you asking me that? The DNA confirmed that he," he pointed at the picture, "was the aforementioned 'Nigel Pugh.' DNA never lies, Chief Inspector."

Eliote stepped back, he felt like the doctor was going to hit him. "How have we got DNA for Nigel?"

"If memory serves me correctly, he was the suspect in the murder of Mrs. Pierce as well as the rape of Racheal Walker. Procedures dictate DNA samples of all suspects are taken."

Eliote pulled out the picture of the man in custody and showed it to Strong. "If Nigel Pugh was buried in the basement, then who is this?"

Strong shrugged his shoulder, examining the face of the man in the photograph. "Well they have the same cheek bones and facial features. They could be doubles, of course. What about DNA?"

Eliote produced the record. "According to DNA, he is Nigel Pugh. Fingerprints are a little strange though. They are inconclusive."

Strong sat on the edge of the grave and pondered, "They could be identical twins."

Eliote kicked himself for not realizing that fact. "Of course, but I always thought they had the same fingerprints?"

Strong smiled. "Oh, my dear Chief Inspector, what are identical twins?"

"Well, they come from the same egg!"

Strong quickly replied, as if reading from a text book, "Monozygotic." Eliote shrugged his shoulders. Human biology had not been a favoured subject of his. Strong climbed out of the grave, and commenced explaining to Eliote the intricacies of monozygotic twins. "Which, in layman's terms, means they develop when a single fertilized egg splits in two, creating two embryos. The fingerprints are not a genetic characteristic. They are part of a phenotype, which mean they are determined by the interaction of an individual's genes and the intrauterine environment."

"Right, I get it," he pretended, trying to look convincing.

"Identical twins' fingerprints will tend to be similar, but there will be subtle differences, making even their fingerprints unique to the twin." Eliote patted him on the back and headed back to the Saab, driving off quickly.

When Eliote arrived back at the station, he demanded that Nigel be brought into Interview Room One, where he was waiting for him. "Ah, sit down, Mr. Pugh."

"I must protest at my treatment," Nigel was a bit more distressed than he had been earlier. His suit was quite wrinkled.

Eliote wrote down the complaint. "It's been noted, Mr. Pugh." He placed his pen down and looked straight into the man's eyes, which made him feel slightly intimidated. "When did you discover that you had an identical twin brother?"

The man protested again. "I do not know what you are talking about. I am an only child."

Eliote looked at the fingerprints on the file in front of him. Pressing his index fingers to his lips, he related the new information to the suspect. "I found out something today, Mr. Pugh, something interesting about human biology. Fascinating subject!"

"What has that to do with me?"

Eliote leaned back in the chair. "What do you know about fingerprints?"

The man looked at his own fingers. "What, apart from the fact we all have them, nothing else, why?"

"Oh, so you didn't know we all have unique fingerprints? Even identical twins have unique prints." Eliote laid out both sets of fingerprints in front of Mr. Pugh. "So, I ask again, when did you know?"

"I'm not saying another word until I have a solicitor present," Mr. Pugh gave Eliote a slimy smile.

"As I explained before, that is your right. I'll get you your solicitor, and then we will begin again. This time, I'll want answers." Eliote left the interview room, returning to Day, who was waiting outside impatiently.

"Gov, did he say anything?"

"Only that he wants a solicitor, so can you arrange one for him?" Day nodded, and informed him Rachael and her solicitor were in Interview Room Three.

The two detectives walked in casually and sat down at the table. Eliote began, "Rachael, I need to ask, did you kill your partner

Nigel Pugh?" He directed her attention to the picture which he had placed in front of her.

Both scrutinized the image, but it was only Rachael's solicitor who responded to the accusation. "I object to the way my client has been dragged in here again to answer a question like that! Where is your proof?"

Eliote casually read from the file. "When you were raped by…"

"…My client suffered mental and physical torture from that rape, Chief Inspector! She does not want to relive it," the solicitor protested.

Eliote raised his hand to apologise. "Please do not think I don't care. Your client, as you call her, has my deepest sympathy, but I have a murder investigation to deal with, and she may be the key to solving that case." The solicitor conceded, and Eliote was able to move on with his questioning. "Thank you, Miss Walker." He shifted his gaze to Rachael, probing further. "How did you feel towards Nigel afterwards?"

"I hated him for what he had done to me. He just laughed as he 'gave me one,' as he called it." She bowed her head, "I wished I'd known about that gun. I would have killed him."

Eliote turned a page in the file. "Your father allowed him to stay on as a silent partner, which must have hurt?"

"You have no idea," she said with anger. "When my father died, he got all the shares in the business. I had to work for him, the man who had raped me. I was excluded from business meetings, kept in the dark about contracts, and not told of any new members of staff appointed. Then, he decided to travel around the world making business deals."

"Bit lucky hey, wanting to travel?" Day slyly remarked.

Rachael glared at Day and continued, "Before he went, we created Gold Security, and he made me the chairman, to begin a building process to help the business grow and prepare it for greater things."

Eliote could see the passion in her eyes. "And now that Nigel's back, what now?" He folded his hands on the table top. "He will no doubt want to stop being a silent partner, he may even want to take over as the new chairman."

"He has come back to show you that he isn't dead," Rachael stated emphatically.

Eliote smiled. "I'm so glad you brought that up!" He flicked through the pages of the file until he found what he was looking for. Leaning forward, Eliote revealed a soon to be shocking bit of information. "The tests on this body confirmed that this," he pointed at the skeleton photo, "is Nigel Pugh. So the man who came to prove Nigel wasn't dead must be an identical twin brother."

"Where is your proof, Chief Inspector?" she snapped back.

Eliote didn't answer her, instead asked, "Did you know that identical twins don't have the same fingerprints? I was fascinated by that fact. Both twins have a unique print, identifying which is which." He pressed his forefinger down on the second photograph. "This is not Nigel Pugh. You, yourself, are the proof."

Rachael appeared puzzled. "I don't follow you."

"When you were raped, Nigel and a few others had their fingerprints taken." Day placed the pages on the table in front of the two people. "None of these match this man's," Eliote pointed to the picture of the man claiming to be Nigel Pugh, "fingerprints. So, I ask again, did you kill Nigel Pugh?"

Rachael leaned over to her solicitor and whispered to her. The solicitor glanced over at the detectives. "My client would like a break for guidance on her next course of action."

"I thought she might." Eliote faced Day. "We will have a break for one hour." The solicitor nodded in agreement, and the two detectives got up and left.

As Eliote and Day returned to CID, Pickington approached, and informed them Alex Boyd was in the smaller Interview Room Two. "Do you want to speak to him Gov?"

Eliote looked at the constable. "Not until we have finished with Rachael. Let's see what she has to say first."

Day glanced at the interview rooms. "What about Mr. Boyd?"

"Let's leave him to stew for a while, shall we?" Eliote grinned, and left the two detectives. As he approached his office, Eliote was stopped by another officer.

"Sorry to bother you, Gov, but I sent the fingerprints to other forces, and this crime sheet just came in from Scotland Yard."

"Why did you do…" Eliote stopped talking when he saw the information. "Thank you, Constable." He patted the officer on the back and headed to Interview Room One. Upon entering, Eliote intentionally slammed the door, watching the suspect jump up in his seat.

"Now what, and where's my solicitor?"

Eliote smugly sat down in front of him and looked at the crime sheet. "Do you know what this is?" He waved the sheet under the man's noise.

"Should I?"

"This is the key to unlocking this mystery. You see, one of my detectives used their initiative and sent your fingerprints to other forces in the UK." The man became stiff, and began rubbing his hands together, as if knowing what was coming. "We got this back from Scotland Yard. Shall I read it?" The suspected Nigel Pugh didn't answer. "I'll take your silence as a yes." Eliote placed the sheet in front of him. "This proves that you are not Nigel Pugh, but Edward Grant."

The man held his head in his hands. "Those damn fingerprints!" He banged his fists on the table.

"It says here you were sent to prison for burglary in London, and then, when you got out, you were charged with attempted murder. The case was subsequently dropped." Eliote slid the sheet back with a finger. "The genes must run in the family."

Edward didn't say anything. He stood and walked to the wall. "I was a drug addict, I needed my fix, so I broke into a very posh London house. I didn't realise it belonged to a superintendent in the Met." He glared at Eliote for revealing his hidden dark secret. "I was placing the jewellery in my hold-all when the owner of the house came home with his friends, and I was arrested and charged."

Eliote looked at the man. Years seemed to have been removed from his face as he explained himself. "And the attempted murder charge?"

"The drug dealer I used was shopped to the police by another addict, and so I beat the crap out of him." Edward Grant returned to the table and sat down. "The case was dropped because he'd been placed to give you lot eyes on the street, a spy. They didn't want their operation to be compromised, so I was hushed up and moved away, a new life in the country."

"So did you kill Nigel?"

"No, I didn't," he stated. "I never even knew he existed. I had been adopted as a baby, but my new family hit hard times, and when I turned sixteen I was abandoned, so I lived on the streets, in shelters, but doorways mostly, until I was arrested for petty crimes and sent down for a year. When I came out, I was found a job cleaning in a factory. It was boring but I was paid, and was able to afford a small bedsit." Edward almost was ashamed to admit the next part of his story. "Then, I got hooked on drugs, lost my job, my home, and I was back on the streets again."

Eliote did feel some sympathy for the man. "When did you first find out about your brother?"

"Giles, my probation officer…"

"Is that Giles Edwards?" Eliote asked, raising an eyebrow.

"Yes, he brought me to Gold Security, and there on the wall in the main foyer was a large picture of the company members, and I saw myself." He shifted his gaze upward, remembering the moment.

"That must have been very strange, seeing someone who looked exactly like yourself."

"I just couldn't believe it."

Eliote asked, "How did Nigel take it?"

"He was the same. We both felt we were looking in a mirror that showed its user what could have been. You see, he had not been told he had a brother either. He thought as I did, we were just two people who looked the same."

"And then what?"

"He paid for tests, and it confirmed that I was his identical twin. We approached his dad, and he confirmed it." Edward smiled. "I had a family again, and I was brought on board, even given some shares in the business."

Eliote looked at the happy man "So why are you impersonating him?"

Edward just looked up. "That's been my job for years, Chief Inspector. When it came to appearances, I would turn up at conferences, instead of Nigel, do my act, and leave."

"When was the last time you saw him?"

Edward started to go stiff again, and stuttered when he answered. "I think we were at Dad's, and we were having a family meal, which turned sour."

"Sour?"

"Dad was saying he wished Nigel was the one who had been put up for adoption, instead of me. There was a big hoo-ha, and he left in a huff. That was the last time I saw him alive."

"I am glad that the mystery of Nigel Pugh is sorted, but what I want to know is how did he end up buried in a basement? My gut feeling is you know."

"Okay," he bowed his head, "you're right. I buried him there."

"Why?"

"He had everything, I had nothing. So I became him full time. I allowed Rachael to run the business. Nigel had been horrid towards her, and so, I gave her what should have been hers."

"You loved her, didn't you? That's why you killed your brother?"

Edward glared at Eliote. "I did not kill my brother, and I think you've misunderstood me. You see, I'm gay."

Eliote pushed his hand through his hair, and realised he was no further in identifying the murderer than he was before. "Okay how did he die?"

Edward just shrugged his shoulders. "I don't know. I just buried him."

Frustrated, Eliote paced to the door, turning his head back angrily. "You must have seen something on the body to identify how he died!"

Edward shook his head. "Sorry, I didn't. All I knew was that he was dead!"

WHEN ANGELS FEAST

By
Kevin Bailey

CHAPTER TWENTY-FIVE

Eliote stormed from one interview room into the other, and found Day waiting for him. Seated at the table was a solemn looking Rachael and her stern female solicitor. "Miss Walker," he said, before either had time to say a word. "Do you know an Edward Grant?"

"Yes, he is Nigel's brother."

"Well," he said, sitting down and frowning, "he's next door, and has just informed me of his story. Whether I believe him or not is another thing, but then, you knew he was here, didn't you?"

"Yes, I asked him to come, to keep up the charade of Nigel being alive. He jumped on a plane and when he arrived in the UK, he came straight to my apartment, and I informed him on what to say."

Eliote watched Day write this information down. "Okay, I'll ask you once again, Miss Walker, did you kill Nigel Pugh?"

She burst into tears and screamed, "NO, I DIDN'T KILL HIM!" She was handed a tissue from her solicitor, and continued, "I didn't. He was already dead."

"Edward says he buried the body, is that true?" Eliote asked, and she nodded.

"We all helped bury him."

Day looked puzzled. "We, who else was there?"

"Myself, Teddy…"

"…Teddy?" Day interrupted for clarification.

Rachael leaned forward him her chair and responded, "That's what we called Edward. He hated his name, because it was the name his adoptive parents had chosen for him. So, he became known to us as Teddy." Day was happy with this information, and gestured for her to continue. "And then, of course, Nicky."

"How did he die?" Day enquired, and Rachael answered very quickly.

"Nicky said he had a hole in his chest that looked like a gunshot wound, so he would have died immediately."

"Who discovered the body?" Eliote queried.

Rachael touched her chest. "I did, it was a Saturday morning, and I had come in to sort some deal out…"

Eliote stopped her. "…You said before you were excluded from any of the day-to-day running of the place?"

"I was, but this deal was beneficial to our future. Nigel demanded that I pretend that everything was happy, and we were partners. When I arrived, all the lights were on, and the alarms were all switched off. I searched the offices, and there he was, slumped in his chair." Rachael crumpled the tissue in her hand, tearing it. "I panicked and rang the two people I trusted." She counted them on her hand. "Nicky, he was in bed with 'her,' but hearing the panic in my voice. He came straight around, and then Teddy. It was then we came up with a plan. With Nigel dead, the business would be put into liquidation, and it would be the shareholders who would get all the money, not me. With Nigel still alive, I could buy out the shareholders with the substantial amount my father left me. I could then do what I wanted."

Eliote was appalled. "So, this is about greed…"

"No, it's about keeping my family's business going, when others have gone. It's about keeping people like Johnny Gittings from getting my company."

Eliote stood up to stretch his legs and then enquired, "What has he got to do with it?"

"When my father died, Nigel got the business. What I didn't realise was he then handed shares out to a few people. Teddy got some, and so did Johnny. I was furious, and tried to buy him out, but he turned the tables, and tried to buy me out. Of course, I refused, and have been fighting him ever since. To top it all off, along came that bloody will."

"So," Eliote turned over the pages of the file, "where does Alex Boyd fit into all this?" Rachael seemed to perk up at the mention of his name.

"We know he was there on the night of the fire," Day said, showing her the image from the video.

"We made a deal. Alex is buying up the land to redevelop it into a plumbing college and a new headquarters building for his business."

Eliote stopped her briefly before she could go on. "But surely the land is worthless. The will states the land be turned into affordable homes, no businesses."

"He doesn't know about the will. I was hoping the deal would go through before he found out. Now the deal is done, I am a rich woman."

Eliote was disgusted by her callous behaviour. A man was dead, and all she seemed to care about was money. "Well," he said, triumphantly, "you'll be a rich women sorting out deals in prison." Both Rachael and her solicitor went to protest, but he silenced both of them, "Rachael Walker, I am charging you with perverting the course of justice, not registering a death, and aiding and abetting in a criminal offence." He read the rest of her rights, and then she was taken away.

Outside, Day watched her being escorted to a cell. She remarked to Eliote, "She really was a greedy cow, Gov!"

Eliote squinted down the hall to Interview Room Two. "Come on, Sergeant. Let's see what Mr. Boyd has to say on the matter, shall we?"

Interview Room Two was much smaller than the others. It had been a design flaw, but Superintendent Brightly had kept it, and the officers used its cramp appearance to make suspects feel a little claustrophobic.

Alex was talking to a female in a grey wool suit, whom Day recognised as Barrister Kate Bellows. The two pairs eyeballed each other and as soon as Eliote sat down. The barrister spoke directly to Day on behalf of her client. "Detective Sergeant Day, I want my client released. He has been treated in a distasteful way, especially as he is still mourning his deceased family."

"Sergeant Day is not leading this interview, I am, Miss...?" Eliote answered making her turn and look at him.

She turned her nose up at him. "Barrister Kate Bellows, and you are?"

"Detective Chief Inspector Simon Eliote."

"Your Lady Mardon's nephew aren't you?" she responded quickly, almost before he had finished saying his name. "Yes, I've heard about you."

"All good, I hope?" Eliote immediately pegged her as a snob.

"Huh, we shall see."

Eliote looked over at Alex. "Mr. Boyd," Eliote opened the file in front of him and began. "On the night of the suspected arson attack on Gold Security, your car, a silver Bentley Continental," he read out the registration, "was seen parked in the car park outside the building. Can I ask why you where there?"

Miss Bellows piped up. "My client's business is of no concern to the police."

"On the contrary, Barrister, your client could be charged with fraud." Eliote stared down Miss Bellows, as Alex finally spoke and seemed shocked at Eliote's words.

"Fraud?" He looked at his solicitor, who was shaking her head, trying to stop him from saying anything else. "I was finalizing a deal, if you must know, with Rachael and her partner, Nigel Pugh."

Eliote raised an eyebrow. "Nigel Pugh?"

"Spoke to him on the phone. We all agreed a price for the land of six point two million." He drew in a shaky breath. "We signed some documents, and after Nigel hung up, me and Rachael finalized the deal, there and then, on the desk." The memory excited him.

Eliote turned over the page and brought him out of his daydream. "I am sorry to be the bearer of bad news, but I think the deal may be off…"

Alex was clearly puzzled and snapped, "…What do you mean it's off? We cemented the deal."

Eliote took out the photo of Nigel and showed it to him.

"What's this?" he demanded.

"Those are the remains of Nigel Pugh…"

"…No, it can't be I, I, I," he stuttered. "I spoke to him on the phone, and he agreed to the sale!"

Eliote showed him a picture of Teddy. "You spoke to this man, Nigel's identical twin brother." He replaced the photo into the file. "It was a scam." He took out a copy of the article about the will, and passed it to the two people sat opposite him. "As you can see, the land is being sold for peanuts, and I mean, peanuts!" He gave them a few moments so they could read the article. "All the buildings are being demolished. This is to make way for affordable housing on the site, as instructed by this." He placed a copy of a will onto the table in front of Boyd. "The Last Will and Testament of Mrs. Sylvia Southwick…"

"…but we had a deal!" he said, almost sobbing. "It was signed and sealed, the money was even transferred to their account."

Eliote looked over at Miss Bellows who was glaring at him. "I think, Mr. Boyd, that you should speak to your legal representative."

Alex bowed his head in shame. "I had no legal advice." He addressed the two detectives, dark circles having formed under his eyes in a matter of minutes. "I've been desperate for that land ever since I came back. I have a vision of creating a plumbing and heating college on the site, plus I was moving my HQ from London to a state of the art building here in Chelmesbury."

Eliote examined the broken man and then changed tact. "When you were sealing the deal, as you call it, did you see anything out of place or unusual?"

"I was indisposed." He huffed. "My mind was on the job at hand."

"Mr. Boyd," Day said, making them both look at him. "Did you have anything to do with the fire?"

Alex glowered at her and so did Miss Bellows, who nearly hollered, "WHAT IS THAT SUPPOSED TO MEAN, SERGEANT?"

Eliote stood up to the barrister. "You can see it from our side, Barrister," he said, pointing at her client. "In his own words, he is desperate for the land. I've seen it before. Get someone to set fire to the buildings, it reduces the asking price."

Miss Bellows went to reply, but Alex stopped her. He scowled at Eliote. "I am the innocent party here, Chief Inspector. I have done nothing wrong, except treat Rachael with respect. I offered a helluva lot more than what the land was worth. They would have been a lot better off with me."

Eliote looked at the man and didn't know whether to feel sorry for him or laugh at his stupidity. Day brought him out of his thoughts by asking, "If you're the innocent party, what about all the employees? They are getting nothing from this deal, except a pat on the back. Well done, oh, but sorry, old boy, you've not got a job anymore,"

Alex looked coldly at her. "What concern is that for me? The company is not closing. It is simply moving to another site in town. Rachael did disclose that to me,"

"Not the only thing she disclosed," Day muttered under her breath.

Miss Bellows heard her comment. "How dare you insult my client?" She addressed Eliote, "Are we done?"

"We will keep him in custody," Eliote began. Miss Bellows was about to protest, but he ignored her. "UNTIL," he snapped. "We have corroborated his story."

Miss Bellows turned her nose up at him again. "How long will that take?"

Eliote smiled over at Day. "It shouldn't take us long." They gathered their belongings and walked out of the room.

Once outside, Day faced Eliote. "I apologise for my outburst at the end, Gov."

"I accept, but next time, keep it to yourself." Refocusing on the business at hand, the wheels in Eliote's head were turning. "Let's go and get something to eat, and then, I want to interview Johnny Gittings. We've kept him long enough." The two detectives headed towards the canteen.

***

Frashier made his way back to the specialized holding area. After a few steadying breaths, he entered back into hell, ignoring the man in chains.

"So," Green said, greasily. "You've returned. How quaint."

Frashier stayed silent, which seemed to aggravate the prisoner. The detective just carried on placing loads of pictures of Shropshire all around the walls of the room, so Green could see them.

When he had finished, he returned to the table and opened the file, redirecting his gaze to the chained man. "Shall we begin?"

Green lifted his hands, which made the chains clank together. "I ain't going anywhere for a while. Are you?

Frashier gave a wry smile and stood facing him. "My team in Shropshire have found two freezers full of decaying human flesh." Frashier looked around the room at the pictures and then carefully observed the prisoner, staring forlornly at the images.

Green looked coldly at him. "It would seem you have found what used to be my medicine, Inspector."

Frashier raised an eyebrow. "Your medicine?"

Green walked as far as the chains would allow and stared intensely at him. "You give me the pictures for my cell, and I'll tell you what you want to know."

"Of course," Frashier said, examining the smiling Green. He realised how shallow the man in chains actually was, thinking to himself, 'How could this man be a cold hearted killer, when he was so easily bribed by a few photos?' "I'll pass them on to the guards for you."

Green seemed to become saddened again. "I will not get them, Inspector,"

Frashier approached the window. "I'll make sure you do; you have my word!"

Green seemed to smile at this. "Thank you, Inspector Frashier."

The detective returned to the table and then asked, "So why did you become a cannibal?"

Green licked his lips, and replied calmly, "Have you not ever wondered what human flesh tastes like?"

Frashier shook his head. "Can't say that I have."

Green looked charged, almost erotic "Well I did." He hesitated, as if remembering the person he had once been. "When I was young, I was a weak and feeble man. I couldn't even hurt a fly, but then, I discovered the cure…"

"…Your medicine?"

He answered quickly, "Oh, I can taste it now."

Frashier watched as the man seemed to writhe with ecstasy. He brought him out of his thoughts by clicking his fingers.

"Why did you call it your medicine?"

"Because when I was feeling down, I would have some and it would cheer me up." He once again approached the window and licked his lips. "I could do with some right now."

Frashier felt the hairs on the back of his neck stand up and he quickly replied, "Unfortunately, the flesh in the freezer was taken away." Green returned to the wall and sulked. "What were you doing when you nearly got caught in Scotland?"

Green was silent for a while and then responded, "I was looking for more stock!"

Frashier looked at the image of the skeleton found at the golf course. "Was the woman found under a stone at Chelmesbury Golf Course your stock?" Frashier saw Green looking a little confused by this question, and was obviously trying to find the right words to answer.

After a while, Green began smiling and calmly said, "Yes, she was my first. She tasted so damn good." He looked at the images of Shropshire. "Our parents are always saying things that taste bad are good for you, but she tasted so damned good."

"What was her name?" Frashier said, glancing down at the name in front of him. He was testing Green.

"As your file probably says Inspector, her name was Alex," Green replied with a wicked laugh. "A beautiful name for a beautiful, and tasty, woman." He raised his eyebrows. "Don't you think, Inspector?"

"I wouldn't know. I haven't seen a picture of her," Frashier answered back.

"When I close my eyes, she is looking in shock as I slit her throat." Green was clearly reminiscing now. "The sound of her gagging is still as exciting as it was the day I killed her."

Frashier could see how excited Green was becoming, and once again, brought him out of his daydream. "Tell me about her?"

Green slumped against the wall. "She was an American traveller. I'd met her at a party, and we had got on like a house on fire…"

WHEN ANGELS FEAST

By
Kevin Bailey

CHAPTER TWENTY-SIX

1996

The residents of Chelmesbury had been celebrating the New Year in style. Everywhere you went there were street gatherings, and every club and public house in the town had some sort of party.

It was in the Black Falcon pub that the younger Anthony Green stood against the bar and glanced around at the happy and cheerful people in the room, when he spotted a white, blonde woman at a table on her own. Feeling a little adventurous, due to the drink, he approached her, and she smiled.

"I was wondering when you were going to notice me sitting here on my own. I was going to give you a little longer, and if you hadn't made your move, I was going to come over. I have been looking at you all night."

Green smiled. She was beautiful, and her skin like silk. "Well," he said. "I am Anthony Green, and you are?"

"My name is Sutton, Alex Sutton."

He smiled warmly. "And what brings you to Shropshire, Miss Sutton?"

"I am visiting from Tennessee. My parents died, and left me some money to go travelling. So, here I am."

He stuttered a reply. "I am glad." Alex gave him a peculiar look. "No, no, not that your parents died, of course." He got all tongue-tied. "Oh, you know what I mean." She smiled and so did he.

The two stayed talking until they were kicked out of the pub in the early hours of the morning. Green walked her back to her bedsit, and, being the perfect gentleman, he watched as she sadly climbed the steps and disappeared inside the building.

When he returned to his home, he was greeted by his step-mother, who was waiting for him. "What time do you call this? You are a naughty boy, Tony!"

Anthony looked at her and snapped, "I am not a child anymore, and I will be home when I want." He walked to the stairs, and then turned back to face her. "Anyway, you are not my real mother." This line seemed to hurt her, and she gave him an evil stare, which he didn't see. Instead, he went up to his room and slammed the door behind him.

A little time later, he heard his father come to bed, and then the sounds of his step-mother moaning as she was having intercourse with his father. He turned off the David Bowie CD and lay down on his bed, imagining he was having intercourse with his stepmother. He undid his trousers and masturbated to her screams and moans...

Frashier felt a little sick at what he had heard so far. Green's arousal was again evident as he recounted the memories, and Frashier did his best to ignore it.

"So, what happened then?" the detective asked.

Green laughed at him. "A little prudish are we, Inspector?"

Frashier stayed calm, trying not to let this man into his head. "Just continue."

Green carried on reminiscing, "Well, I went around to Alex's bedsit the next morning, and we went for a long walk," he said, with a large smile on his face…

> *Anthony and Alex walked around the town, hand-in-hand. They laughed and joked like other happy couples, and then they decided to walk around the municipal golf course.*
> *When they became tired, they sat down in some undergrowth and talked some more. Unexpectedly, Alex bent over and kissed him. He pulled away and looked into her longing eyes.*
>
> *"What was that for?"*
>
> *She smiled warmly at him. "You have been so kind to me. I have to be honest. I lied to you a bit. I am dying of cancer, and I wanted to explore the world."*
>
> *She smiled at him, but he seemed cold. "Dying?"*
>
> *She didn't expect him to be angry. "Yes, I have about three months to live, and my family paid for me to go and have one hellava trip, so I came here." She bent over, and they kissed once more, but this time, it was more passionate. Before long, he was no longer thinking of making love to his mother. Now, he was making real love to another woman, and was enjoying every moment.*

Frashier looked at the man in front of him. "How did that make you feel?"

"Are you trying to be a psychologist, like Doctor Guanine?"

Frashier shook his head and replied, "I just want the truth."

Green looked at him, evilness emanating from every pour. It was the look of a man who had killed many victims. "I'm not sure you can handle the truth."

Frashier looked back at him, and Green could see some small spark in his eyes. "You're not like the other coppers. There is something evil in your eyes."

Frashier was taken aback. "I am not evil."

Green approached the glass, scaring Frashier. "Do you ever feel like killing somebody? You get this intense feeling of pleasure when you see you are really an ANGEL OF DEATH!" he shouted.

"NO," Frashier said, shouting back.

Green became insistent. "You cannot hide it from me, Inspector. I see murderers, rapists, all kinds of scum in here, every day I have been incarcerated in this god-forsaken place. You can smell it in the air." He pointed at the inspector. "And I can see it in your eyes. You would love to come in here and kill me. It's all there, hidden deep within your eyes." Frashier seemed shocked at this outburst, but then, Green changed the subject, went back, and rested against the wall. "I was once like that; always wondering what it would feel like to kill somebody, maybe even try their flesh, and so I did..."

> Green looked at what he had done, and suddenly, he felt guilt for the one he loved. The feeling appalled him. As Alex lay on the ground, happy and pleasured, her eyes closed, he placed his hands around her neck. She tried to kick and punch out at him. He continued to squeeze until she stopped.

He waited a little longer, until he was certain she was dead. Taking out his penknife and cutting out a large chunk of her flesh, he placed it in a bag, and he went back onto the course.

"...So, you killed her because you felt guilty. How many times have I heard that excuse?" Frashier said bluntly.

Green came quickly to the glass and bared his teeth like some crazed animal. "You know nothing, Inspector. You sit behind glass and that badge you wear. I have seen the world," he said, returning to the wall. "I enjoyed its benefits. Doesn't mean I don't feel guilt."

Frashier looked at the sombre man. "Okay, I apologise for my outburst. Please continue." For a moment or two, Frashier was worried Green was going to stay silent, but was relieved when he began revealing what happened after Alex had been killed.

"I began snooping around the course, keeping myself hidden in the outgrowth, and then I spotted some grounds men had left their tools against their trailer, while they had gone for a break." He became silent, as if remembering what had happened. "I first made sure there was no one on the green who would see me run off with equipment. I darted across the green and grabbed a shovel. I returned to the spot where I had just killed Alex. On the way, I found a deep, dark thicket, which was surrounded by trees."

Frashier stopped him in his tracks by pulling out from his files a picture of the burial site. "This place?"

"It hasn't changed much, has it?" Frashier shook his head, and Green continued, "It was secluded and quiet. I was there for a good thirty minutes, and no one knew I was there. Even though golfers passed my location several times"

Frashier then enquired, "What about Alex? Wasn't she visible to them?"

"We had found a large covering of trees and shrubs, to do the wicked deed. I did panic someone would lose their ball and find her, but they didn't. So I begin the mundane job of digging her grave..."

After a while, he had finished the hole, and went back for the body. Using his last ounce of strength, he lifted her corpse and carried it to the thicket, dropping her into the dark. With shaking hands, he took out a piece of paper and wrote a note to whoever would find the body, and then buried it with her.

Looking around, he saw a large stone. Using the penknife, he carved a message and placed it on the grave. It would become a marker for him to find again.

After tiding up, he ran home. Finding no-one was in, he went into the kitchen, took out a large frying pan, and cooked the piece of flesh. The feelings inside of him made him feel strong and happy as he gorged on the meat of his victim.

He heard the front door open. Quickly he finished off the remaining piece and began washing up. His father approached the kitchen and smelt the air. "Nice smell in the air, son. You been cooking?"

Green nodded and rubbed his tummy. "I feel like I have been looking for something for years, and after eating that meat, I feel alive," he said, placing the pan onto the draining board.

"That good, aye?" His father turned. After getting changed, he headed back out into the hall and approached the front door. He shouted back at his son, "Tell your stepmom, I'll be back later," he stuttered. "I, I, I'm going down the pub with me, me, my mates from work." His father was unaware of anything amiss.

"Okay, Dad," he said, standing against the sink and savoured what he had tasted...

"That was the last time I saw him alive. According to the note, he left my stepmother. He ran off with his secretary. She was devastated, and just sat in her room for days, crying."

A little part of Frashier was starting to feel sorry for Green, even though he was a cannibal and an evil twisted killer. Frashier had been through the same. His father had been a brash, business tycoon, and had run away with his secretary. With the shame of the failed marriage, his Italian mother committed suicide. He had never forgotten the moment he had walked into his home and found her hanging. His mother's Italian family had sent him money, and he was cared for by a loving foster family until he grew up. He had become a police officer to try and get over that incident.

Frashier looked up at Green, and saw the man looking at him. "Remembering something hidden deep within your subconscious, Inspector?"

"No," he lied. "So, what happened after that?"

Green began smiling widely. "When I went up the stairs and saw my stepmother naked on the bed, crying into her pillow. I began to feel aroused, and she turned and noticed. I went bright red and moved to head back to my room, when she stopped me, took my hand, led me back into the bedroom. She took off my clothes, laid me down on the bed, and made love to me."

Frashier could clearly see that Green was aroused again, and a beaming smile appeared on the monster's face. He looked at Frashier and continued, "Then, after spending hours making love, we lay cuddled up to each other, our flesh touching, and it felt so good," he paused and glanced at Frashier. "But, my dear Inspector, the feelings weren't as good as my taste for human flesh…"

> *Green, looked over at his stepmother. She was asleep, her breasts visible under the sheet. He wanted to caress them, but he had a job to do. Quietly, trying so hard not to wake her, he got up, put on his clothes, which seemed to be scattered*

around the room, walked out of the door, and down the stairs. He grabbed his wallet and cards. After writing a note to his stepmother, he left the house and headed for his small fiesta, glancing up at his stepmother's room. He started the car and drove it quickly away.

Mrs. Green woke, and realised that she was alone. 'Had the last hours been a dream?' she wondered. She decided to find out. Getting up, she headed for Anthony's room and was shocked to discover it clean and tidy. She grabbed her dressing gown and went to the bannister. She shouted down the stairs.

"Tony, are you still here?" But the house was quiet. She moved to the kitchen, and that's when she saw the note on the table. She picked it up, and it was Anthony's writing. She began nervously to read it:

My Beloved,

I have never told you this, but I am so in love with you, always have and always will. I say this with all my heart and soul.

What we did today, I have dreamed of since I found out what sex was. This may come as a shock to you, but I used to sit awake at night and listen to you and dad having sex and imagine it was me there and not him.

So, when you read this, I will be gone, but not forever. I have many things to do before we meet again, but for now, I'll see you around.

*Your lover,
Anthony*

Mrs. Green read the note and went back up the stairs. She looked in the mirror and saw the woman she should be. Changing into clothes, she went out.

Frashier looked at Green. "Did you really love your step-mom?" Green nodded.

"I had hated her as a child. She had come to live with Dad months after Mum had died, but then, I grew to like her. She could, of course, be bossy, but she never hit me."

Frashier yawned and then apologised. "Please continue."

Green lay back against the wall. "I started to fancy and fantazise about her, especially after the day I walked in on her having a bath. She didn't seem to mind me being there, and we talked as she soaped herself." Green had a smile on his face, as once again he was enjoying the memory.

His happiness was disturbed by a knock at the door, and in walked Markovitch and a few guards. Green glared at one of them and hissed like something from a pantomime.

"Sorry to interrupt Inspector, but it's time for Green," he glared into the other room, "to go back to his cell."

Frashier looked over at the prisoner. "Can I ask him one last question for today?"

"Sure, fire away." The other guards left and re-entered the other room.

Frashier asked his question as they undid the chains. "Where does your stepmother live?"

Green answered quickly. "I think it was number 103 Becton Green Lane. She is a care worker, and she had to leave my home, when my father went missing," he said, smiling. Frashier wrote this information down as well as commenting he would ask Green about his father later. He then looked up, and in earshot of Green, he spoke to the American detective. "These photos," he said, pointing at all the images of Shropshire. "Can they be given to Green for his cell?"

Markovitch nodded. "I'll see what can be arranged." Both men looked over as Green was being prepared to be led away.

"Enjoying the view, Detective Markovitch?" Green said, smiling trying to provoke him. "I thought you Americans liked this sort of thing." He held up his hands to reveal the chains.

"When I look at you, Green," he said, voice dripping with disdain and disgust, "the only thought I have, is seeing you on that table, when they put you to sleep for what you did!"

Green smiled, his tactic had worked. "Touché, Detective. The only thing I can think which could involve you, is you being dead, placed on a table with a knife and fork. Perhaps a little salt and pepper and an endless supply of gravy." He licked his lips and remarked, "Yummy!"

The American came up to the glass and glared coldly at Green. It was his turn to be the intimidator. "I am so looking forward to the day the governor gives the word, and they inject you. I'll be there with the parents of that officer you killed."

"My heart bleeds for them," Green said sarcastically, and then he smiled at Frashier. "Don't forget my pictures, Inspector."

"I won't forget, Mr. Green."

Markovitch glared at Green. "Yes, because I'm coming to ram them down your throat!" The two men glowered at each other.

Frashier tapped Markovitch on the shoulder. "It's what he wants." The detective turned and looked at his counterpart. "He ain't worth it!"

Green scowled over at him. "Spoilsport."

Frashier scrutinized Green, and he saw that evil side emerge. Like a naughty child, he bowed his head, and was taking away. "You'll make sure he gets these?"

Markovitch nodded. "Oh, I'll make sure he does, you have my word." He helped Frashier take them down.

WHEN ANGELS FEAST
By
Kevin Bailey

CHAPTER TWENTY-SEVEN

After an hour, Green returned to his cell. When he entered, he found all his belongings were scattered across the floor, and he noticed that all the pictures had been cut up and thrown into the toilet bowl. As he was pushed in, he turned and looked at the guard he hated, evilness in his eyes.

"Why have you done this?" he demanded.

The guard just laughed. "For the family who you destroyed." He sneered. "They like you don't have a future."

Green lunged for him. "YOU BASTARD!!" But he wished he had kept his mouth shut as the other guard rammed his baton into his stomach and across his chest. Green doubled up in pain.

Laughing slightly, the guard looked at his comrade. "Keep a look out and wait for me by the door."

The black guard shook his head. "This is wrong, man, and you know it."

The guard holding the baton against Green turned and glared at the other guard. "I am your supervisor, and you will do as I say, so go to the door and keep a look out."

The black guard said a few expletives. "I don't want anything to do with this." He stormed out of the room, leaving his comrade in shock.

Green looked up from the floor, a slight smile on his face. "You and your boyfriend having issues?" he mocked and had a baton thrust near his face.

"One more word from you, Green, and you'll wish you were dead. Now tidy up this mess." The guard turned and hurriedly walked out of the cell, slamming the door shut behind him.

Green lay on the floor and caught his breath. Blood trickled onto his orange jumpsuit from an open wound on his side, and his ribs hurt. Sobbing painfully and uncontrollably, he sat up and crawled to the toilet. With his hands shaking in pain, he retrieved the cut up pictures and watched the soggy paper disintegrate in his hands.

***

Frashier returned to his hotel. After ordering an evening meal, he went up to his room and grabbed the book he had brought with him on the trip. It had been written by Lewin Richards, a Shropshire author whose previous books had been turned into a multi-million-pound film franchise.
The Soldiers of Truth was the ninth book in the series. As he read the novel, he escaped the real world, and became Intelligence Agent Martin Starkey. Just as he was really getting into the story, the phone beside his bed rang, and he put down the book and answered, "Hello?"

It was Jeanette. The sound of her voice made him forget about the book, and he felt alive and refreshed. "Hi, would you like to go out for a drink? My family are doing my head in." Frashier looked over at the book, remaining quiet. "That is, unless you have other plans?" she queried sweetly.

"I have no plans."

This seemed to make her happier too. "Okay then, I'll just change, and then I'll be on my way to your hotel."

Frashier smiled. "Sure, I'll meet you in the hotel lobby in an hours' time."

"Ok, it's a date then," Jeanette answered back. The line went dead, and he ran into the bathroom for a shower.

***

As Simon and his team of officers arrived at Green's old house, a mini-bus full of SOCOs, led by Strong's daughter, Felicity Owen, or Flick as she was affectionately known, arrived. The auburn-haired pathologist got out and approached him. "Ah, Chief Inspector! It's pleasurable to see you again."

Eliote smiled. "Likewise, Flick."

She rubbed her hands together. "So, where do you want us to start?" Eliote motioned for her to stay with her SOCOs, as he hadn't contacted the owner yet. She acknowledged, and both he and Day approached the front door and rang the bell.

The door creaked open, and a forty-year-old man stood looking at Eliote and the vehicles behind him. "Can I help you?"

Eliote took out his warrant card. "Hello there. I am DCI Simon Eliote, and this is DS Miranda Day. Am I correct that you are the owner of the house?"

"I am. My name's Oliver Broome."

Eliote shook hands with him. "May we come in, Mr. Broome?"

The man escorted them into a tidy and well-presented home. "So, what is this all about? Why are all those officers outside my home?" he said, peering out of the window.

"I know that this will come as a shock, but the previous owner was…"

The man stopped him. "Anthony Green."

"You've heard of him?"

Mr. Broome went to a unit, and pulled out several newspaper cuttings, passing them to Eliote. "I knew the lad. He was in the same year as me. I was shocked when I found out he was a serial killer. At school, he was one of the 'in-crowd,' so to speak."

"Well, as you are aware, he is on death row for killing a police officer in the United States, but he is also the prime suspect in a series of murders committed in Chelmesbury. Most of the bodies have never been found."

Mr. Broome frowned and looked out of the window, into the garden. "You think there are bodies out there, don't you?"

Eliote nodded. "I won't lie to you, Mr. Broome, but yes, I do believe the remains of several victims lie in the boundaries of your home. I am here to ask for your permission to dig up your front and back garden and the cellar."

Broome thought about it for a while. "Do I have a choice?"

Eliote nodded. "Of course you do…" Before he could answer, Eliote continued on, "However, I could get a warrant, and then you would have to allow us."

Broome resigned to defeat. "Well then, as my hands are tied, you'd better get started."

Eliote thanked him for his cooperation. "Before we start, have you ever found any bones in the garden?"

"Yes, when I was creating those horrid flower beds." He pointed at some overgrown mounds. "I found strips of what I thought were animal."

Eliote was intrigued. "I'll let the scene of crime officers know of your discoveries so they can log it for excavations later." Once again thanking him, Eliote left Oliver Broome in the hands of Day while he went and prepared his team.

Outside, Flick and her team were eager to get started. Eliote walked with her to the overgrown flower bed and asked her to start her forensic search there. Grabbing some equipment, they began gently scraping away the layers of soil. It wasn't long before the female pathologist's trowel, scraped a hard object. Taking out a brush from a metal case, she started to brush away the soil from around the object, slowly revealing the features of a skull.

"Eliote, over here!" she shouted over to the detective, who was talking with Day.

He walked quickly towards the doctor. "What you got, Doctor?" She beckoned for him to look into the hole and the skull protruding from the soil. "How long do you think it has been in the ground?"

"It's hard to say, Chief Inspector," Flick replied moving slightly out of the way to allow a photographer to take a couple of pictures. "I will know more when we do a thorough examination of the bones back in the lab."

"Can you at least tell me what sex it is?" Eliote urged her as he rubbed his eyes after being blinded by the flash. She took a smaller brush from her box and carefully brushed away the soil from around the eye sockets and the rest of the face, revealing a slightly pointed chin.

"I'm not an anthropologist, but even I can see that this is the skull of a female." Using the end of the brush she pointed to the skull, "There are no brow ridges, and if you look at her forehead, it is slightly more rounded, male foreheads slant backwards."

Eliote and the doctor were beckoned to another part of the flowerbed where another SOCO was working. "I've found what would appear to be part of another skull," he said, as they approached him.

Eliote glanced down at the skull and then remarked to Flick, "You have only just begun in a small place and have found two skulls." He looked at the rest of the garden. "How many skeletons are we going to find here?"

"If what my dad has found in Loughton is anything to go on, we may be here for a few days."

"I agree," he paused and walked towards the house.

"Where are you going?"

Eliote turned back. "I'd better get on to Brightly. We are gonna need a bigger team." He headed for his car.

"I'm glad you have rung, Chief Inspector," his superior said, when she picked up the phone. "I have had Johnny Gittings' solicitor in my office, demanding to know why he has been in custody and not interviewed."

With everything that was going on, he had forgotten about Johnny. "Sorry, Ma'am, he can go for now, but I will still need to speak with him."

Brightly didn't seem happy. "The solicitor has referred this case to the IPCC."

Eliote acknowledged this. "Okay, Ma'am."

"You've placed me in a dire position, Chief Inspector. They could have both our hinds for this," she breathed heavily.

Eliote looked over at his team working hard. "I will take full blame for this, Ma'am, just let me finish these cases."

There was silence, and then Brightly spoke, "Okay," she paused. "Anyway, what can I do for you?"

After his long call to his boss, Eliote walked back into the house and approached the sitting room. He opened the door and found Mr Broome sitting, talking to Sergeant Day.

"Mr. Broome, I am here to ask if we can dig up the whole of your house. We have unearthed two human skulls. We think that there may be more underground."

He looked shocked. "Those bones I found weren't animals, were they? I was touching his murder victims?"

"I am afraid it would appear that they were human," Eliote spoke calmly.

The man turned white and drank some sugary tea, which had been made for him by a constable. "You have my blessing to dig up the lot. Never liked the way the garden was anyway." He smiled, and Eliote smiled back.

"Is there anyone we can contact, so you can stay with them for a few days?"

"My daughter, Rebecca." He gave Day the number, and Day left the room.

"What do you know about the previous occupiers of the house?" Eliote asked, sitting down opposite him.

"All I remember is Mrs. Green sold me the house. It had belonged to her husband's ex-wife, and when she had died of cancer, she'd left it to her son. The family were allowed to live in the house until Anthony turned eighteen."

Eliote poured himself a cup of tea. "Have you an address for Mrs. Green?" Mr. Broome stood up and approached a side board. Taking out an address book, there under 'G' was the address:

'GREEN, GEORGINA, 145 HIGH STREET, GLAYTON.'

There was a knock at the door, and Day returned. She approached Eliote and whispered, "They have found another skull."

Eliote looked at her and replied, "I'll be there shortly." She also whispered that Oliver's daughter was on her way. "Okay. When she gets here, let her in." Day nodded and left the room.

A short while later, there was another knock at the door, and Eliote answered. Oliver's daughter had arrived and took her father away from the house. Once he had watched them go, Eliote approached the back of the house and found several white tents had been erected by Flick's team.

Eliote was now told to wear protective white overalls and shoes, and after dressing, approached the taped off area.

Flick saw him and walked towards him, trying not to interfere with the other teams.

"Report please, Doctor?" he ordered.

"Well, so far, we have counted six skulls and several other bones. Two are female, three are male, and one of the skulls will have to be examined more closely. I'd say the ages range from early 20s to 30s. All of the bones have extensive knife marks, as if they had been prepared for butchering."

Eliote looked at the tents where the SOCOs were working. "Are there similarities to the ones your father found?"

"Without looking at the bones he discovered I cannot confirm or deny any similarities, but, and this is only speculation, I believe that these victims were all killed in the same way. Whether by the same person, that is what you are going to have to find out."

Eliote nodded. "Thanks, you don't make it easy for me do you?"

She smiled warmly. "It's in the Strong family DNA. You should know that by now."

He smirked. "Oh, I do." He moved away from the tape. "I'll let you get on. Keep my team informed of any new discoveries." She acknowledged him and carried on with her work.

Eliote took off his protective clothing, and went and found Day. "Sergeant, you're in charge here. I'm heading over to the first site."

"Righto, Gov!" Eliote headed for the Saab, but as he left Hectors close, a large gathering of press and residents had gathered. Even Edward Pierce was there and gave him an evil stare as he passed. The press were taking photos and several tried to stop him. The uniformed officers pushed them away as he drove away.

When he arrived in Loughton, Eliote parked his car next to the squad cars. Potter allowed him under the tape. The Sergeant walked with him towards the several tents that had been placed around the bodies.

"How many now, Potter?"

"Ten, sir, and still counting." The new CID recruit continued, "Seems that a couple of years ago, the people living next door asked if they could buy some of the land between the two houses to make a way through to the back of their home. Strong and his team are beginning to dig there next. Also, some others are re-examining the cellar floor."

Eliote patted him on the back. "Well done, Sergeant. See? It's better being in CID than uniform," he said, smiling, and left him to find Strong, who was scraping away some earth from under the empty path. "Doctor!"

Strong turned and offered Eliote a grim smile. "Eleven now, as Penny has just this second discovered another one hidden under a flower bed." Eliote looked around and saw several SOCOs working hard in every part of the garden. "Some of my team are investigating the garage area." Strong stood up and stretched his back, remarking, "It reminds me of the Cromwell Street affair, some years ago."

"I always missed those cases. I went after the criminal gangs and…" He paused, as if about to spill some secret and looked at the earth, annoyed at himself. "How could someone kill and bury all those bodies, and never get caught?"

"Like most killers who bury their victims, I have no clue."

Eliote sighed. "All I know is it's going to take extra man power and resources to find out half of the people buried here and at Hectors Close." Eliote turned and could see Strong looking at him. "What?"

"You're not as strong as you first made out, are you, Chief Inspector?"

"No, let's just say something happened a couple of years ago, which has affected me."

As Potter approached, Strong remarked, "About Potter… It was good of you to take him under your wing. The ex-DI didn't like him."

Eliote watched Potter get closer to their location. "I like to give people a second chance."

Strong smiled. "Do I get a second chance?"

Eliote smiled back. "I don't see why not," he paused. "Especially if you buy me that pint after work."

"Now you're talking!"

Potter interrupted Eliote, "Sorry to bother you, sir, but I've just had Day on the phone. She's reporting Flick has found another three bodies."

Eliote excused himself from Strong and walked back with Potter towards the Saab. "You're with me. I think it's time we met Green's mother." Potter nodded and told another CID detective he was in charge. They headed for the car, and the two detectives drove away from the scene, once again passing rows of press.

Strong smiled as he watched them go, and then he carried on scrapping at the ground, but as he did, he found another bone. "Oh bloody hell."

Penny looked over from her trench and asked, "What's wrong?"

After cursing the sky, he replied, "I've found another one."

Eliote parked the car outside the house on the high street. Potter and Eliote approached the Victorian house. He glanced over at Potter and remarked, "Same as Hectors Close. Actually, I'd say it was almost identical."

Potter nodded and explained a little history to him. "These homes, and the ones at Hectors Close, were built about the same time, and by the same contractor."

The two officers walked to the front door and pressed the buzzer. Deep within the house, they heard footsteps, and a lad, about twelve, answered, "Yes?"

Eliote showed him his badge and asked. "Can I speak to your mum, please?"

The boy sighed and turned. "Mum, it's the police."

Eliote and Potter heard the boy's mother shout loud from the kitchen, "What have you done now?"

Eliote interrupted her, "We are not here because of your son, Mrs. Green. We are here to talk about Anthony Green, your stepson."

A middle-aged woman with brown hair and blonde highlights walked out of a kitchen area and approached him. "Well, you'd better come in, Detective."

Mrs. Green led them into the front room where the lad had connected his PlayStation 3 up to the television. She turned to the lad. "Can you go and play upstairs while I talk to these officers?" The lad nodded, and after turning off the device, he sauntered upstairs to his room.

"Mrs. Green, we are investigating your step…"

She interrupted, not giving the detective time to finish. "…What's the point? He's on death row."

Eliote continued, "We have discovered several skeletons in the back gardens of a house in Loughton, several in his house in Hectors Close, a body buried under a stone on Chelmesbury's main golf course, and two bodies up a path near the Millennium Green."

Mrs. Green looked shocked, and for several seconds, didn't speak. "Detective Chief Inspector…"

"Simon Eliote."

"DCI Eliote, I loved Anthony as my own son, but it doesn't surprise me. He would invite some of his friends around to our house, and we wouldn't see them again. He was always a loner and getting himself into trouble. He was what you would call a troubled soul."

"Can you name any of his friends, Mrs. Green?"

"No, I am sorry. Like I said, he didn't have friends long."

Eliote remembered what Mr. Broome had said. "But according to people who knew him, he was one of the 'in crowd'?"

She shrugged her shoulders. "I can't answer that. When he was here, he was quiet, and would lock himself away in his room and listen to his music, very loudly."

Puzzled, Eliote looked over at Potter. "Ok, Mrs. Green. We will keep in touch."

She smiled and followed them out. After Eliote and Potter had left, the young lad came down the stairs and looked at his mother. "Why do the police want to have information about Dad?"

She glared at him and he bowed his head. "It's almost dinner time, so go and get washed." He skulked away, but she shouted after him, "I'm going out tonight, so your Nan is looking after you," This excited him, and he ran up the stairs and into his bedroom. Georgina watched the Saab disappear down the road, and then she went back into the kitchen and prepared lunch.

On their way back to the station, Eliote and Potter talked. Both were under the same impression that Mrs. Green wasn't telling them everything.

"Potter, when we get back to the station, I want you and Pickington to do some checks on our Mrs. Green. I want a lot of information about her." Potter wrote down the instructions. "Also, send Frashier all the information we have gathered." Potter nodded, and then they headed back to the station.

***

When Angels Feast

By
Kevin Bailey

CHAPTER TWENTY-EIGHT

Inspector Frashier awoke to the sound of his door being banged severely. The sound went straight through him, and he looked at his watch on the side table. It was seven in the morning.
"Oh blast," he cursed. Rubbing his eyes, he went to the door and looked through the peephole. There, in all his glory, was Markovitch, and he didn't look happy. He opened the door, and the American detective walked in.

"You're not ready yet, Inspector?" he said in his American tones, and Frashier apologised.

"Sorry had a late night. Painted the town every colour of the rainbow."

The American looked at his watch. "Unfortunately, it's going to be a long and hot day today, thought you might want to get to Green early." Frashier went into the bathroom, and Markovitch continued, "Seems that Green didn't have a good night either."

Frashier looked at the detective through the mirror. "Go on."

"He trashed his cell, and had to be restrained."

Frashier popped his head out of the bathroom, his toothbrush in his mouth. "Why?"

Markovitch went to the window and opened the curtains. "Seems one of the guards mistreated the pictures you gave him."

Frashier took out the toothbrush. "Those were my bargaining chips. I was using them to get him to talk to me, so why did they do it?"

Markovitch shrugged his shoulder. "You must understand that things are a little different here in The States, Inspector. Green killed one of us. I know it's wrong, but there are some who want revenge on him. I am including myself on that list."

Frashier walked out and glared at the American. "The man's going to pay the ultimate justice, death by lethal injection, isn't that revenge enough?"

Markovitch shook his head. "No, he deserves to suffer."

Frashier returned to the bathroom and remarked, "You want to be careful. An old Chinese proverb says, when you first seek revenge, you must dig two graves."

Markovitch approached the door. "We'll be in the lobby," he said, ignoring the quip and leaving the room. Frashier cursed and dialled the number for the station on his mobile and asked for more pictures. He then got dressed.

Markovitch was waiting for him in the lobby. As Frashier passed the receptionist, she handed him some papers. He thanked her, and the two men headed for the Ford, which was parked in the car park.

The journey to the prison was silent because Frashier was still angry at the way Green was being treated. He sat in the back, going over all the information Potter had sent him to use against Green.

After going through all the security procedures again, Frashier prepared the room once more. The other door opened, and in came an unresponsive Green.

The first couple of hours, the interview went slowly. Green just stayed up against the wall and wouldn't speak. Frashier felt like he was banging his head against a wall. He looked down at some of the information he had received from Chelmesbury CID, and tried to prevail with Green.

"I have been told of the discoveries in the two gardens. One in Loughton." This seemed to make Green's ears perk up. "And at your old home in Hectors Close. Seventeen bodies at last count…"

Green finally said something. "…So you have found my little graveyard." Now he had Green talking, he felt happier.

"We also found this?" He showed the prisoner a photo of the two bodies found near the Millennium Green.

"That place has really changed," Green remarked. "When I was there, it was a swimming pool. Where do they swim now?"

"At the Academy school," Frashier answered quickly. Before he was interrupted, he asked, "So who are they?"

Green smirked. "Doesn't my father look bony," he said, laughing. "But then again, he always was a skinny man."

"You killed your father?" Frashier shockingly asked, and Green nodded still slightly laughing.

"Yes, and his lover. I cut out and ate her clitoris and parts of her breasts." He licked his lips. "Yummy. They were so juicy. I could see what my father saw in her."

Frashier was appalled. "Why kill your father?"

"After he left my step-mom, I followed him home from work," he paused, reminiscing. "I saw my Dad and his slapper enjoying a picnic. I waited until he went for a slash, and then I slit his throat, and went back and slit hers. It was a gift for my beloved!"

"And what of the others?"

He looked coldly at Frashier, sending a chill down his spine. "The others were just strays, homeless people. I gave them a good meal, we had some fun, and then I killed them."

"But we counted men and women?"

Green shrugged his shoulders. "It doesn't matter what sex they are Inspector. To me, they are just food, and, boy, didn't I have a wonderful meal!"

Frashier was starting to feel sick at the thoughts going through his head, and he knocked at the door.

"What's wrong, Inspector?" he smirked. "I thought you, of all people would understand. Having a murderous beast living within you, who is trying to get out?" Frashier glared at his prisoner, who just smiled and approached the glass. "Obviously, you can't handle the truth." The door opened, and Green immediately started to laugh.

Frashier walked out of the room. As he walked down the corridor, he could still here him laughing. Going into a cloakroom, he looked at the mirror and splashed water on to his face.

What Green had said kept going over and over in his mind.

Markovitch walked in and stood up against the basin top. "You finished with that piece of scum?"

"Yep, I have finished with him for the time being."

"Ok, I'll have him removed from the room. Oh, some food has been prepared for you in the guard room." After Frashier's contact with

Green, he wasn't that hungry, so declined. The American detective looked worryingly at his British counterpart. "You okay bud?"

Frashier shook his head. "Nope, it's just something that Green said."

Markovitch patted him on the shoulder. "Ignore his outburst, William. He is close for the table, and he knows it. He's just trying to get below your skin."

Frashier nodded, and then splashed some more icy water on to his face. "When is he scheduled to be executed?"

"Well, with your investigations still on-going, the Governor has postponed the execution until you are finished with him," Markovitch answered.

Frashier thanked him, and Markovitch patted him on the back again, and then left the room. Frashier examined himself in the mirror. His eyes looked tired and bloodshot. What did Green mean when he had said that there was a murderous beast behind his calm Italian complexion? Maybe the American detective was right, and Green was trying to wind him up. Frashier had never hurt anyone, not even when he was growing up. Even with all the bullies who had picked on him, he had just ignored them.

But then, from deep within his sub-conscious, a voice, which scarily sounded like Green, replied, 'What about the day you lost it? That day you could have been a murderous beast.' The voice laughed, and the memory came flooding back…

1986
Shrewsbury C of E Secondary School

The school was a typical secondary school, with its unique elder buildings, and it new state of the art facilities, which comprised of a swimming pool and several indoor football pitches.

The young man who would become Detective Inspector William Frashier walked towards his form room. As was typical, he heard the usual taunts from the other children about his name sounding like he was from a foreign country.

After being told off by his last teacher for not handing in his homework on time, and another one calling him lazy, he wasn't in the best frame of mind, and so stopped and shouted out, "I was born in this bloody town, and not some foreign country, you bastards!" A group of tall students surrounded him, and he cowered.

One of the boys, who was a little older than Frashier, walked through the crowd and looked at the cowering boy. "You're pathetic. You use adult words, and yet cower when threatened." Frashier tried to push a path through the crowd, but the elder boy walked to him and pushed him into a bin.

Deep within the younger Frashier, something snapped, and he grabbed the bin and literally pulling it from the ground, threw it directly at the taller boy knocking him to the ground. Frashier, with all the anger inside of him, pounced and continuously punched the lad making him cry. Even though blood splashed across his face from the lad's nose, he didn't stop. The group of other students seemed to be frozen to the spot as they watched the younger Frashier pulverize the lad until he stopped crying, and went into a comatose state.

Frashier wanted to keep hitting him, but was pulled back by another pupil...

Frashier looked at the face in the mirror, and was shocked to see his younger self looking back at him. It was then that he remembered who it was who had stopped him from killing that boy: Alex Boyd, the man he owed so much too.

He touched the glass, and the memories came flooding back...

...Alex held him tightly, and the crowd dispersed. He looked around at their scared faces and realised they were now frightened of him.

The Head Teacher ran to Frashier. Boyd had let him go, and he had ordered the white-faced pupil to get help. Frashier was nearly dragged into a room, and was continuously asked, 'what had happened?' but Frashier just kept saying,

"Piss off. I told you that I was getting bullied, but you did nothing about it. You told me to just ignore it, and I tried, goddamn it I tried, but then, I had enough and turned on that bully. Now I've probably killed him." He started to cry. "Which means that I won't get to be a copper, even though I have worked so hard to get the right qualifications." He collapsed onto the table.

There was a knock at the door, and a skinny nurse walked in.

"Mr. Bryant," she said, ignoring the young Frashier. "The child is in a critical state, but doctors have told me that he is expected to survive. He is being taken to the intensive care unit at Copthorne."

Mr. Bryant smiled at her. "Thank you, Carol." He turned to Frashier, and with disgust, said, "Did you hear that, boy?" Frashier nodded. "I am going to ring your foster parents, and get them to come and collect you." The teacher stood up and glared at the young student. "You are now hereby suspended, Mr. Frashier." He walked out of the room, and Frashier sat there crying, 'What have I done?' This would now be on his file for the rest of his life.

Looking up, Frashier saw his older reflection looking back at him, tears now trickled down his face. He wiped them away. As he splashed some more water on his face, Markovitch walked back in.

"Just checking with you again, whether you want something to eat?" Frashier nodded and grabbing his belongings. He was escorted to a small clean canteen.

After grabbing some coffee and a ham salad sandwich, he sat down at a table and read some more of the files, preparing for that afternoon's interview with Green. He sat back to drink the coffee, and he remembered what had happened next at his school…

He had been off school for about two months, the only connection was his frequent visits by Alex, but his foster parents prohibited them from seeing each other for very long as he had been grounded and was being forced to study hard for his GCSEs which wasn't going as well as it could have been. Frashier hated not being at school; he missed the extensive library, and the few people whom had befriended him over the three years he had been at secondary school.

As he was going over World War Two and how it started, he heard the phone in the hall way starting to ring and his foster mother answered,

"Shrewsbury 345," she listened. "That's great news." She replaced the receiver and shouted up to Will, "Will, the boy has been allowed out of hospital, and when asked what happened, he took all the blame. He said he barged into you on purpose, and he deserved the beating. You have been allowed back at school, but even though you will be watched, this incident has been erased from your files." Frashier smiled and hugged his foster mother.

"That's great news." He ran up the stairs, fell on his bed, and burst into tears of joy.

Somewhere deep inside, the voice fell silent, and he finished off his sandwich. A smile appeared on his face. It was if a huge weight had been lifted from his shoulders, and now, it was time he made Green suffer, and do the job he had come to do.

After lunch, Frashier walked calmly into the room, and saw Green smiling at him, but soon that smile was wiped from his face as Frashier began to take down the pictures of Shropshire and started to rip them up.

"No, please, don't! Please," Green begged, but Frashier just looked up at him and then ripped another picture in half.

"You've been playing with me, Green, and now it stops." He ripped the same picture again and glared at the prisoner. "I came here for one purpose, and one alone, to discover the truth. You've been giving me little snippets of information, just keeping me interested and yourself alive."

Green watched him throw the ripped up pieces on to the floor and take another down. "Please don't. I'll be a good boy, and tell you what you want, but don't rip anymore of those pictures."

It was Frashier's turn to smile. "You'll tell me what I want to know?" He started to rip the photo, and Green nodded quickly.

"Yes, yes, I'll talk."

Frashier placed the photo on the table and looked at the file. "I want to know everything, so bloody talk."

WHEN ANGELS FEAST
By
Kevin Bailey

CHAPTER TWENTY-NINE

The afternoon went by quickly and Green spoke without conviction, scared that the Inspector would rip up another of the pictures. Frashier gathered so much new information to pass to CID, he was soon out of paper in his notepad, and the tapes ran out.

Markovitch knocked on the door, and the shattered Inspector looked up and watched as the American detective walked in. Green hissed at him once more, but the detective ignored him, and instead spoke to Frashier, "Hey buddy, it's time to call it a day." Frashier nodded and signalled the staff in the hall. A group of guards came in and restrained Green, taking the tired looking prisoner away. Frashier yawned, and Markovitch looked at him.

"I think you did damn well this afternoon, buddy." Frashier smiled. "Did you get all the info you wanted?"

Frashier yawned again and then nodded. "I still think he is hiding something from me. What that is, I don't know."

Markovitch patted him on the back. "There is always tomorrow!" Frashier nodded, and the two detectives tidied the room and headed for the car.

Back at the hotel, Frashier looked at all the files across the bed, and then saw the piece of paper with Jeanette's number on it. With a new-found burst of confidence, he dialled the number. "Hi, it's me. Do you fancy doing something tonight?"

***

After the tired Green had received his evening meal, which comprised of soup and a main course, the black guard came to escort him to the shower block. For their protection, the other inmates had already been taken. With his head bowed in silence and secured in manacles, he was physically pushed down the corridor, a towel and soap in his hands. Soon, the guard he despised more than any of the others walked around a corner and approached him.

Both glared at each other, and the guard pulled out his baton and aimed it directly at Green. "On your way, Green."

Green looked coldly into the guard's eyes. "Go on then, hit me, or do you just do it behind closed doors."

"Don't know what you are talking about," he said slightly twitching. This was when Green attacked.

With the reflexes of a cat, and with the manacles still attached, the condemned man grabbed the baton from the guard's hand, turned it around, and smashed it down, time after time onto the head of his victim.

The guard who had escorted him down the corridor watched the scene unfold, almost frozen to the spot, unable to stop what had happened. When he did come to his senses, he pressed an alarm bell on the wall, and guards came from every angle and jumped on to Green. With a thud, the group landed on the floor, and Green let go of the baton and looked over at what he had done.

Blood gushed from a large wound on the guard's head, and when they checked to see if he was okay, they discovered he was dead.

Green was led away, he triumphantly cursed, "You got what you deserved, you bastard. I hope you rot in hell." He was silenced by another guard, who rammed his baton into Green's stomach.

Another guard quickly went to a phone and dialled a number, speaking with a strong Texas accent. "You'd better get on to the Warden. We got a bit of a situation down here!"

***

Frashier sat at the hotel lobby bar and waited for his new love interest to arrive. As the time passed, he had a couple of whisky and cokes to calm his nerves, which made his waiting even worse. The room had begun to spin. He began to feel sick as, every time the door to the bar opened, he would look up, expecting to see her smiling face.

Eventually, Jeanette did appear. She looked a little flustered, but was looking ravishing in a flowery, red figure-hugging dress with cropped up hair. He eyed her up from top to bottom, and could have taken her there and then. She spotted him looking at her, and she too wanted him.

"How do I look?" Before he had time to answer, she continued, "I've had another crap day, so I am glad you invited me out tonight. It will be my chance to let my hair down,"

Frashier agreed with her. "I've had a crap day too." She sat down, and he looked into her sparkling eyes.

"What would you like to drink?"

"I think a Malibu and coke." The barman nodded, and Frashier ordered a coke.

"Not drinking tonight?"

Frashier pointed to some empty glasses. "As you can see, I've already had a couple before you came. I needed to relax."

"What we like, eh?" she said, taking a sip of her beverage.

"That's always been my problem. I can't relax properly."

"I'm sure I can get that out of your system," she said flirtatiously and winked at him.

He swallowed a large gulp of coke and quickly changed the subject. "So, how was seeing your other family? Was it as boring as you made out last night?"

"Oh, it was worse. My Grandmother can't hear, and so kept quiet. My Uncle has just separated from my Aunt, so he was also quiet. I wished I'd never come here."

It was time for him to flirt with her. "Yes, but if you hadn't, then we would never have met."

She smiled, took a sip of the drink in her hand and winked at him. "And that would have been a shame."

Markovitch walked into the hotel lobby, escorted by another officer. They didn't look very happy. When they approached the receptionist, he asked if she could buzz Frashier's room. The receptionist said there was no point, and pointed to the bar. When Markovitch entered, he saw Frashier entertaining Jeanette. He walked up and interrupted the pair. "Sorry to intrude, Inspector."

Frashier glanced up and smiled. "Ah, Markovitch, come take a seat, and join us for a drink."

The Detective remained standing and looked seriously at Frashier. "If the situation were different, I would join you, but we have an incident on our hands, and I need to talk to you in private." Frashier went to say something, but the American looked coldly at him. "It's important and concerns Green." Frashier looked at Jeanette and then at Markovitch.

"Ok, I am coming. Can you just give me a second?" Markovitch nodded and left the bar. Frashier looked at Jeanette and kissed her passionately on the lips. She was taken aback, but wasn't shocked. "Hopefully, this will not take long." She smiled at him and watched him leave the bar.

Outside, Frashier was looking angry at being disturbed, and he demanded to know why. Markovitch calmed him. "William, I came to inform you that the execution of Anthony Green will take place in the morning…"

"…Why, what changed?"

Markovitch directed his gaze to the floor. "After we left, he was being escorted to the shower block when he attacked and killed a guard. The Governor, of course was informed, and has signed the execution papers." He inhaled deeply. "Time, I am afraid, has run out on…"

Frashier looked through the glass door at Jeanette and demanded, "…Get me to the prison. I need to find out why he has done this."

Markovitch looked over at Jeanette. "You want to see Green, instead of spend the evening with a beautiful woman?"

"I have to find out," he responded. "Get the car running. I'll be out in a minute."

"Okay, buddy, you're the boss," Markovitch said sarcastically, and left Frashier in the lobby. He watched them go, and walked back into the bar and grabbed his coat.

Jeanette saw what he was doing and demanded, "What's going on?"

Frashier explained that he had to go and interview Green, and that it could be the last time. Even though she understood, she was still sad. He couldn't apologise enough, and told her to book anything she wanted to his room.

"I think I'm gonna order the biggest feast I can imagine," she said jokingly, and once he had kissed her again, he made his way to the two American detectives, who were waiting in the car park.

When the car pulled into the car park at the prison, Doctor Guanine approached followed by one of the guards.

"I am sorry, Inspector, but we have not prepared him for you."

Frashier looked at him in disgust. "I don't bloody care how he is, I just want to have a last interview with him." The doctor looked over at the guard and nodded he was escorted to the stone wall.

A couple of minutes later, Green was brought in, his face looked bruised and battered. Undisturbed, Frashier approached the glass. "Why did you attack the guard?"

Green looked at him and smiled. "I was hungry!"

Frashier hit the glass with his fist. "No, you weren't!" He dropped his hand to his side. "You knew it would cause the Governor to bring your execution up to date, why?

Green tried to be all innocent. "I told you. I was hungry," he snapped.

Frashier walked to the back wall, counted to ten and then turned and glared at the condemned man. "If you were hungry, why attack him in the corridor, you could have waited until he was alone and then attacked, just like you did with Alex." Frashier suddenly looked at the bruises on Green's face, "Was he the guard that used to beat you up? Was he the one who ripped up the photos I gave you?" Green kept quiet. "He was, wasn't he?"

"I don't know what you are talking about?" the man said softly.

"Bollocks," Green was taken aback by his outburst. "You could have claimed he was abusing you, and that you acted in self-defence."

It was Green's turn to get angry. "And you think that these bastards would have believed me?" He returned to the wall. "They are such a tight knit community. If I had reported that bastard, they would have stuck together, and it would have been my word against his. So what was the fucking point?"

"You don't know that," Frashier said softly, but in his heart, the detective knew Green was right. "Okay then," he said, changing the subject. "I ruined a date with a beautiful and ravishing woman," Green licked his lips, "to finish our interview."

The condemned man glanced over at him. "Now, why would you do that?"

Frashier approached the glass and looked at the man behind it. "Because I think you are hiding something from me," Green shrugged his shoulders, and Frashier screamed, "Tell me!"

Green smirked. "I ain't hiding anything…" Frashier smashed his fist on to the table, breaking it in half. Green was once again taken aback.

"…You're lying." A door opened and a guard came rushing in, Frashier turned and glared at the guard. "It's alright a little accident, leave us alone please." The guard reluctantly nodded and left.

"Bravo, Inspector," Green triumphantly exclaimed. "I made the beast surface."

Frashier stared at the smiling man, "Well now it's released, shall we sod the execution tomorrow." He could feel the evil inside of him building, and his good side struggling for control. "And I'll come in there now, and beat the living daylights out of you." He paused, and glared at Green. "And I won't stop this time," he reared, "until you die." Green could see all the evilness in Frashier's eyes, and for the first time, was a little frightened of the inspector.

"I can see that," he said, watching his protégé. "But I cannot allow you to kill me, Inspector," he said, calmly. "And I will not be pressing charges against your outburst. If I did, it would cost you your job and send you down. No, this is my gift to you," he said, staring into Frashier's eyes who immediately came to his senses and realised his fists were clenched. Instead, he walked back to the outer wall and counted once more to ten.

Green watched him. "Unlike the others in your profession, you have been kind and helpful, but I am afraid that this is the end of our friendship." Frashier turned and saw warmth in Green's eyes. "All I ask of you, my dear friend, is that you go and tell my Stepmother that I have died. I want you," he pointed at Frashier, "and only you to go personally to her." Frashier nodded, and, after saying his goodbye to Green, he left the room.

Markovitch was waiting for him outside. "Are you okay?"

Frashier shook his head, physically exhausted and angry at himself for letting the anger go.

"Can you get me back to my hotel, as I need to rest before I go home tomorrow."

Markovitch nodded. "Ok, William."

***

Jeanette had got tired of waiting for Frashier, and had booked a room for the night. She was just about to turn the lights off, when she had a phone call from reception.

"Miss Hastings, I have a Mr. Frashier in reception. He wonders if you like to have a late dinner in town." She didn't know what to say. "He says the meal and drinks are on him."

Jeanette smiled and replied, "I'll be down in a bit."

Half an hour later, which seemed to feel longer for Frashier, Jeanette came into the lobby and smiled at Frashier. "Will I do?"

"Yep! Let's go, partner," he said, with a horrible American accent. She scowled at him, and then they both began laughing and left the hotel.

WHEN ANGELS FEAST

By
Kevin Bailey

CHAPTER THIRTY

Simon Eliote walked into CID and carried the transcripts from Frashier's interview with Green. Approaching his office, he noticed Day was already at her desk.

"Morning, Gov." He acknowledged her and continued on his way. Once in private, Eliote began reading the files.

After a while, he entered CID, and it was no quieter, as detectives were running about chasing leads and new lines of enquires. This was the part of the job Eliote loved. As he watched, he saw the enigmatic Doctor Strong walk slowly into CID, and everyone turned and clapped him in appreciation of the job he had done in Loughton. He had removed fifteen full skeletons from the ground, as well as the remains of at least another six.

"Oh, please!" he said, going red with embarrassment, and handed Eliote the files.

The detective patted him on the back. "Well done, Doctor. Quite an achievement."

The doctor looked down at his muddy fingernails. "Oh, it was nothing," he said modestly. "Flick will be sending you her reports when she has finished. Last count on her dig was twelve full skeletons, plus the remains of another two." He opened his own report. "Looking at the skeletons and pictures my daughter has sent me from her excavations, I would say that this killer was very skilled at butchery. You could perhaps look into that employment field."

Eliote smiled and sarcastically rebuffed, "You trying to do my job now, Doctor?"

Strong pointed to himself. "What, me? Never! You're too good a detective. You've probably already…" Eliote lifted a file that Day just gave him and saw a title on the first page, reading, 'List of Abattoirs and Butchers in the Area' "…Ah okay." The Chief Inspector handed the file back to the Sergeant. Strong turned and, like some ham actor, pranced off.

Eliote watched him go, and then looked seriously down at Day. "So I've just finished Frashier's report from the interview with Green. From reading most of the transcript, he sounds like a bit of a psychopath."

Day slyly remarked, "Who, Green or the Inspector?"

Eliote glared at her, and she sobered. "I want you and the team to go through there with a fine-tooth comb. Try and see if we can identify the victims. Also get onto the missing persons unit, top priority." She nodded, and Eliote returned to his office.

After getting a cup of tea from a machine, he began looking at all the relevant information on the killings of Nigel Pugh and Nicky Waite. 'Am I missing something?' he said to himself. Suddenly, as if he'd had a premonition, he thought about the safe and who else would use it. A name came into his head, and grabbing his coat, he headed for the Saab.

Twenty minutes later, Eliote walked towards the house of Mary Gittings and rang the bell. She answered, and after showing her his warrant card, she allowed him in. "You'll have to excuse the mess, Chief Inspector. I don't really want to do anything."

Eliote smiled. "And I don't blame you, Miss Gittings, especially after your loss."

She turned the kettle on. "What can I do for you?"

"Your boss informed me in her interview, that you are one of the people who are authorized to use the safe?"

Mary nodded and sat down. "Yes, I place the account books in there, and anything important from bank statements to wage slips. Everything goes in there."

Eliote sat down in front of her and pulled out the picture of the Beretta. "Have you ever seen this gun before?"

"Sorry, I haven't. Why?"

Eliote returned the picture to his pocket. "After the fire, it was found in the safe. Analysis of the gun has confirmed this was the weapon which killed your fiancé."

Mary seemed a little shocked. "And it was in the safe?" He nodded. "I would just open the safe, throw in the documents, and close it. I never really knew what was in there. It was like a Tardis, bigger on the inside." She went white. "That was really the murder weapon?"

"Now, you're certain you haven't seen it before?"

"I said no, Chief Inspector," she said, almost angrily. "Sorry, I still can't understand why anyone would want to shoot Nicky." She grabbed a tissue and blew here nose.

"It's okay, Miss Gittings" He changed tact. "As Rachael's secretary, can you think of anyone who would want the place to go up in smoke?"

"No. I've always received lots of brilliant remarks about the company."

"What of Nigel Pugh?" He glanced up at her. "Did he have anyone?"

"What, Nigel? Never! He was a fantastic boss, always looked out for me and Johnny, and even gave us a few shares in the company." Her smiled faded. "I will admit, though, he has been a bit weird the last couple of years, especially since he became the company's new rep. When I have conversations with him on the phone, he is sometimes a bit of a wally."

Eliote looked confused. "Why would you say that?"

"Well, he would sometimes forget my name, or even how I sounded. I just assumed he was too busy to remember."

Eliote rummaged in his pocket and pulled out the pictures of the skeleton. "This is going to come as a shock, but these are the remains of Nigel Pugh. He was buried under the main office about five years ago."

She looked at the pictures, mortified at the fact this was Nigel Pugh. "It can't be. I only spoke to him last month."

Eliote pulled out another photo. "You spoke to this man, Edward Grant, otherwise known as Teddy."

She looked at the picture. "This isn't Teddy. He was skinny as a rake."

Eliote looked at her with remorse. "Your boss informed me she found Nigel shot dead. She rang Teddy and your fiancé, and they buried him. Teddy, then, took his place." He replaced the picture into his coat pocket. "It was all about greed."

She stood up and walked to the sideboard. "No, my Nicky wouldn't have done something like that, especially not to someone who has given us everything."

Eliote pushed her for more. "What do you mean?"

She looked at him, tears in her eyes. "Well, he paid the deposit on this place."

Now, he was intrigued. "Why would he do that?"

She was at first slow to answer, but he just stared at her until she finally broke. "Because he is the father of one of my children!"

Eliote was taken completely by surprise at this outcry. "Did Nicky know?"

"We'd had a big row, and had split up for a month. In that time, I became lost and alone. Nigel comforted me, and one stupid night, we…" She stopped abruptly, and Eliote got the picture.

"Right."

Mary seemed to crumble before his eyes. "We both agreed it was a big mistake. However, soon after, I discovered I was pregnant. Nicky assumed it was his, and I carried on with the lie, but I knew my child was Nigel's and not Nicky's."

"Did anyone else know…?"

"…Of course not," she scoffed. "It was a secret." She put a cup on the side and then turned and glanced over at him. "And I want it to stay that way."

"Your secret is safe with me." With the interview concluded, Eliote rose to leave, when another question entered his mind, "Oh, just one more thing. Did you know Nicky was having an affair with Rachael?"

She slammed the cup on the side table, and with her eyes full of hate, she screamed, "GET OUT OF MY HOUSE!" She snorted in disdain. "How dare you say anything to taint my Nicky?" she said, crying. "How dare you!"

Eliote took that as a 'no.' He approached the front door. As Eliote departed, he heard her sobbing. "I'm sorry," he said, sadly as he opened the door and headed for the Saab, but when he got there, he heard his phone ringing. Cursing, he quickly opened the door and grabbed the phone. "Eliote." It was Pickington. "What is it, Constable?"

"Gov, the phone we found with other belongings in the safe at Gold Security…"

"Yes, spit it out, man!" The chief inspector heard Pickington sigh.

"Well, sir, I contacted the network, and they have told me a name."

Eliote sat in the seat, a little anxious for the constable to get to the juicy bit. "Well?"

"It's registered to Nigel Pugh. The operator I spoke to told me it was taken out five years ago. It's a contract phone, and is paid in full every month by direct debit." Pickington came to the heart of the matter. "But, get this. It's paid from a bank account set up by Gold Security in the name of Johnny Gittings."

Eliote started the engine of the Saab, and it roared to life. "Well, I think it's about time we had that little chat with Mr. Gittings, don't you, Constable?" Eliote quickly finished the conversation with a final request. "And can you ask our uniformed friends to meet me at his address?"

Eliote got out of his Saab at 105 Belvedere Road, just as two squad cars skidded to a halt outside the house. As he was ordering the officer to locations surrounding the building, he heard the sound of a back door shutting. He ran down the alleyway between the town houses and emerged just as Johnny jumped over a panel fence. Giving chase, he was followed closely by Pickington, Potter, and several uniformed officers.

Johnny pushed over bins to try and elude his followers, but they continued not wanting to give up on their suspect. The officers jumped over the obstacles that had been thrust in front of them. As he approached a tall fence, he spotted the railway line and a dead end. So he turned and faced his followers.

"Right, Copper." He pulled a knife, and looked coldly at Eliote, but as they sized up to each other, a train went rushing past and it knocked Johnny off guard. Eliote kicked the knife out of his hand, and then, the pursuing constables pounced and arrested him.

They led him to the squad car, and drove back to the station, leaving Eliote and Pickington to investigate his home. As they were putting on surgical gloves, both detectives watched the officers outside beginning to cordon off the house and alleyways with tape.

When they opened the front door, they were greeted by a mess. Items of clothing and personal effects were strewn across the floors and split out of boxes. It was a similar state in every room they entered.
Eliote stood and decided they needed help. He took out his mobile and asked Strong to send some SOCOs over to help. As Pickington began to investigate the bottom floor of the house, the Chief Inspector began upstairs.

The constable opened a door into what was an office and saw a personal computer. Its desktop showed the image of himself and his sister outside Gold Security. He could see that there were files in the recycle bin and so double clicked on the icon. Inside were several files, and he wrote down the names on a piece of paper, before undeleting them. Once he had found the files, he opened them, and was shocked at his findings.

"Gov!" he shouted, and Eliote walked into the room.

"What have you found, Constable?" he pointed to the screen.

"It would seem that our Mr. Gittings has been playing around a bit with other people's money to buy up shares in Gold Security."

Eliote rubbed his chin. "So that corroborates what Miss Walker said in her interview about Johnny wanting to buy her out." He looked around the shabby room. "But from these accounts, he wouldn't have had enough to buy it all, so how was he planning to get the money?"

Pickington scrolled through more of the deleted files, when Eliote spotted an account labelled Gold Security. "Let's have a look at that." Pickington nodded and clicked on it. The two men examined the results, "So that's how he was doing it, stealing funds from the company to buy the company." Eliote looked at the screen. "What a crafty bastard!"

He pressed down on the mouse to reveal the amounts taken from the business accounts. "What if somebody found out about this, maybe Nigel or Nicky, and were going to spill the beans? Perhaps he had to silence them?"

Pickington gazed in admiration at his superior. "It would be a pretty strong motive, Gov."

Eliote nodded. "And maybe he then set the building on fire. It would eradicate the evidence."

Pickington didn't buy it. "Yes, but if he had killed Nigel, surely he would have realised that after the fire, we would have found the body under the cellar?"

Eliote looked patronizingly at his younger companion. "Yes, but in Rachael's interview, she said that it was herself, Teddy, and Nicky, who buried the body, and that Teddy then became Nigel. So he wouldn't have known about the buried body, would he?"

"True," Pickington replied, scratching his head.

"I'm missing something here, Constable." He started to walk backwards and forward across the room, thinking, 'If he had set fire to the place, how would he have found out, who would have told him?' It suddenly twigged in Eliote's mind. "Mary," he said out loud.

The constable glanced at his superior. "Gov?"

"She could have warned him." Eliote turned and saw a family photo on a fireplace. "Yes, as a private secretary and the user of the safe, Rachael would tell her," he paused, "well, almost everything. Mary would be in a position to go and tell her brother." In Eliote's mind, it made perfect sense. 'Well, they do say blood is thicker than water!'

"It's a good theory, Gov," Pickington said, bringing the Chief Inspector out of his slumber. "But can we prove it?" Their conversation was disturbed by a knock at the door, which spooked both officers. Eliote headed for the door and slowly opened it. Standing in the doorway was Flick.

"Sorry to scare you, Chief Inspector, but when I got here, I got straight to work and began in the shed in the back garden, and I found these." In her hands was an evidence bag full of clothes. "From the smell, I'd say they were soaked in petrol. Could they be any help to you?"

"I think so." Eliote looked back at Pickington. "If we can prove that Johnny and these clothes were at Gold Security that night, we can nail him." Pickington agreed, and Eliote looked at Flick. "Can you do an analysis on the clothing? See if you can place the clothing at the scene of the fire."

"Ok, Chief Inspector Eliote. I'll get to work when I get back to the lab." She disappeared out of the room.

Eliote ordered Pickington to unplug the computer, and take it back to the station for analysis. Pickington nodded, and Eliote left him to his job and carried on his search.

***

In the cells back at the station, Johnny was going through loads of things in his mind, trying to think of a way out of the mess, he'd got himself into. Why had he pulled a knife on that copper? He knew he would go down for that, and that alone.

But across the pond in America, another condemned man was about to face his fate, and unlike his British counterpart, the outcome would be death.

WHEN ANGELS FEAST

By
Kevin Bailey

CHAPTER THIRTY-ONE

Anthony Green walked with a priest, who was reading from the Holy Bible. Four guards walked several paces behind him towards his destination, the execution chamber. Sat watching from behind a curtain, which hid the chamber was Detective Markovitch and several relatives of his dead colleagues.

One of them looked at the detective and asked. "Do they administer the injection with a machine?"

Without any emotion, he answered, "They do have a machine," he caught a glimpse of the curtain twitching, "but they've been having problems with it. I understand that they don't want any errors with this one." The relative seemed happy with this news, and waited for the execution to commence.

In an adjoining preparation room, Green was led to a trolley and was strapped to it with lined ankle and wrist restraints. One of the execution team inserted two Intravenous tubes, one in each arm, before placing a sheet over him.

"Thanks for tucking me in," he said in good spirit. And then he was taken into the chamber. Whilst a saline solution began coursing through his veins, the curtains were drawn back, and Green spotted Markovitch and some of the relatives of his two American victims. "Gosh," he said to the priest. "All these people coming here to watch little old me die." The priest ignored him, and began to read more quotes from the scriptures.

From behind another door, a man in a smart black suit came in. Green looked up at the priest and asked, "Who's that?"

"That, my child, is the executioner," the priest replied calmly.

"Oh," the condemned man said, and looked over at the man who was carrying a folded piece of paper. He watched as he opened it and started to read.

"On the thirteenth day of July, Mr. Anthony Green, of sound mind, was sentenced to be executed by lethal injection." Taking a breath, he concluded, "Today, in the sight of God and in front of friends and family of his victims, that sentence will be carried out." The executioner looked at Green, "Do you have any last words?"

Green scanned all the faces and smirked. "It was fun," he then said his final word, glancing at Markovitch as he did. "I'll see you on the other side."

***

At that precise moment, Frashier boarded the British Airways flight back home. He was tired and fed up. Even though he'd had a productive visit, had met Jeanette, which should have excited him, the dread he felt, as he prepared to go and tell Green's Stepmother that he had been executed for his crimes overwhelmed him.
The idea of an execution was something he, as a British bobby, thought he would never have to deal with.

Frashier knew as he was escorted to his seat in economy Green had kept some secrets hidden from him. As he sat down and thought of what was taking place in the prison, he knew those secrets would now go to his grave.

"Would you like a pillow for your flight?" an attractive stewardess asked, bringing him out of his thoughts.

"Yes, please," he politely replied, and she handed him an engraved pillow which he placed against the cabin wall. Closing his eyes, he went to sleep.

***

Left alone in the chamber, Green looked down at the lines which were attached to his restrained hands and saw a different colour liquid flow into his body, he began to feel as if he was drunk.
The aches and pains in his body seemed to just drift away with every heartbeat, and for the first time in years, he felt at peace.

Those witnessing the death from the seated area, saw him drift in and out of consciousness, waiting for the end.

In Green's twisted mind, he saw his beloved mother calling out to him to come home.

"Coming, Mum," he said, trying to hold out his arms but when he looked down, he saw large metal chains were somehow wrapped around them, stopping him from grabbing her. "Mum, help." He began to cry out, but there were no tears. "What is happening to me, Mum?"

His mother looked cross. "You've been a naughty boy, Anthony. You shouldn't have stolen those apples. God is going to be angry with you."

Green begged for mercy. "Please, Mum, it wasn't me, it was…"

Back in the real world, a different coloured liquid headed towards Green's hands. "NOOOOOO!" Green whimpered and fell still. His breathing slowed, and then stopped. After another flush out with the saline solution, the final poison made its way down the tubes and into Greens arteries. Finally, his heart stopped.

Moments later (which felt like hours to Markovitch and the others, who had been sat watching the execution), they saw a doctor come into the chamber and check for any signs of life within Anthony's body. He looked at the executioner who had re-entered the room and nodded. Turning to face the witnesses, the executioner read out another official note.

"The time is eleven sixteen. The sentence has been carried out in accordance with the laws of the state of Texas." Then, the curtain was pulled shut.

Markovitch escorted the families and friends out of the seated area, and before he left, he looked over at the curtain and could only imagine what was going on behind. Satisfied that justice had been carried out, he went and joined the others in the corridor.

***

Back in Chelmesbury, and unaware of events unfolding in Texas, Simon Eliote prepared to interview Johnny Gittings. The file in front of him was from Flick, who had been in touch with the Fire Brigade. It confirmed the fire was indeed started with petrol. This was the first bit of real evidence he had against Johnny. He would have to use his experience to get him to confess to the murders, which he was adamant he had committed.

Eliote took a couple of sips of the warm tea on his desk, put on his jacket, and walked to the interview room. Day was waiting for him.

"Mr. Gittings has requested no solicitor."

Eliote smiled and walked in. Johnny sat drinking a cup of tea. He was unshaven and looked as shabby as his house. "Hi, Johnny. Sorry for keeping you." He sat down next to Day, who had a file already open in front of her. He scanned a piece of paper in his hand, wasting little time before enquiring, "When was the last time you saw Nigel Pugh?"

Johnny placed the cup back on the table, and without looking up he replied, "I was picking up my sister from work, and I had to prise her away from him. He was like some leech." He grimaced. "The man who had murdered my mother was trying it on with my sister."

Eliote turned a page in the file. "I think it was more than that. You see, Nigel was the father of Mary's last child."

Johnny flared up "YOU'RE A FUCKING LIAR!" He pointed at the detective. "She wouldn't have done anything like that! Not after what he did!"

Day ordered him to calm down, and Eliote continued, "She wouldn't have known that Nigel killed your mother. To her, he was a kind and considerate man. She needed someone like that, especially as she told me that she and Nicky had split up. Nigel was her shoulder to cry on. One thing led to another…"

Johnny looked down at the table and screamed, "…NO!"

Eliote could see the betrayed look in Johnny's eyes. "I'm sorry, Johnny." The man kept looking at the floor. Eliote shifted tactics and turned the file to the accounts which was found on his computer. "So, what is your involvement with Gold Security?"

Johnny spoke softly, "I used to do their accounts, and could see the potential in the business. So I tried to buy it, but Miss Goody-Two-Shoes Walker wouldn't sell me her shares."

"How did that make you feel?" Day asked.

Johnny glared at her. "Pissed off!" He sat forward. "I'd made a reasonable offer for the business…"

"…Yes, using money you had siphoned from the firm." He showed Johnny the findings they had recovered from his computer.

He shrugged his shoulders. "Yeah, so? She would never have found out because I would have owned the business, but," he seemed bitter, "she told me where to go."

"When was this?" Eliote asked, as Johnny sat back in the chair.

"About a year ago. Since then, I have been buying up the remaining shares Rachael doesn't own. I now own about thirty percent of the shares, and when Mary gave me her shares…"

Day stopped him. "…Mary has shares?"

Johnny nodded, but Eliote answered for him. "She was given a load by Nigel. You too, I'm told, is that right?"

Johnny shrugged his shoulders. "Yeah so…"

"…But if you hated him so much, why did you take the shares?"

He fell silent, as if trying to weasel his way out. Finally, he answered, "We received those as children, and as Mary is Rachael's personal assistant, she received more in lieu for all the help she had done for the business."

Eliote looked shocked. "But Rachael was having a relationship with Nicky Waite…"

It was Johnny's turn to butt in. "…Was. It ended when Mary fell pregnant."

"I respectfully disagree," Eliote said, grabbing a statement from the file in front of him. "According to this, the relationship went on a lot longer."

"No," Johnny cursed. "He promised me, on his daughter's life, that he had ended it."

Day asked, "When was this?"

"Not long after the baby was born. I had him up against a wall, and he swore to me," he again repeated his outburst. "He swore to me."

"And you believed him?" she asked.

Johnny just nodded. "We were best friends, so of course I believed him."

Eliote nodded and then asked, "I'll repeat my first question." Eliote tried to catch him out. "When did you last see Nigel Pugh?"

"Like I said before, as I was picking my sister up. Why won't you guys believe me?"

Eliote turned his head towards Day. "Sergeant, can you go next door, and ask Nigel the same question?" He then looked back at the unshaven man. "See if it corresponds."

She nodded, and as she was getting up, Johnny asked, "How can Nigel be next door? I heard through the grapevine he had been found dead?" Eliote looked apologetic and passed over a photo, and Johnny examined it. "No, it can't be," he said to himself.

"Oh, he's alive alright," Eliote said, as he glanced at the photo which had been taken in the next room. He showed him several others just to prove it. They were, of course, Teddy and several of Eliote's team, including Day.

"No, this can't be Nigel!"

Eliote just stared into the cold eyes of Johnny. "I'll bring him in if you want?"

Johnny stood up, and with his eyes wide with anger, he screamed at the two detectives, "YOU LIE! HE IS DEAD! I KI…" He stopped talking, went to a wall, and hit it disgusted at himself. Eliote, on the other hand, felt triumphant, and he smiled at Day, before speaking to Johnny.

"Because you killed Nigel, didn't you? You used a weapon you knew well." He took out the picture and placed it onto the table. "This is the rusty berretta your father, Edward Pierce, got for you as a child?"

Day was about to question Eliote, but was silenced as Johnny replied with gritted teeth, "Yes, I did it for her!"

"For your mother?" Eliote could see him nodding. "For the record, Johnny Gittings is nodding."

The man turned and was smirking. Day asked, "So, how did you know how to switch the firing pin?"

He turned and sat back down, and with pride replied, "Come on, Sergeant Day, keep up. You know all about my past, as you and the delightful Inspector Frashier arrested me, remember?" He heard the watch on Eliote's wrist tick. It seemed to be ticking towards his own judgement. "I didn't just do the accounts for good people you know. There were a few bad ones in the basket." He stared at her. "A couple of criminals wanted their books looked at…"

"…Like who?" Eliote asked, but Johnny just sat there shaking his head.

"Like I'm gonna tell you." He smirked once more. "But like you and the Sergeant," he said, looking at Day, "I asked a question and afterwards…" He paused making a gun silhouette with his right hand. "BOOM!"

"Shall we start at the beginning?" Eliote requested.

"Yes, let's."

Day asked the first question. "How long had you known Nicolas Waite?"

He didn't look up. "Like I told you, Sergeant, we were best friends. Have been since we were part of the 'in crowd,' at school." Eliote sensed Johnny was being cocky.

"What was he like?" she asked.

"He was a womaniser, but a damn great friend," he paused and drank some of his water. "When we were at school, I was always his shadow, his protector. I got his rejects when he had finished with a girl and picked another. The girls didn't seem to care." He paused once more. "He was the best looking lad in the year, and he could pick and choose who he wanted."

"So, when did you come out of his shadow and start running the accountancy business?" Eliote asked.

"I had a lot more GCSEs than many of the people at school so I went to college, and then on to university." He drank some water. "My foster father, Wayne Gittings, had been in business for many years, and so paid for me to start up my own company. Nicky was jealous, and we fell out, but when I discovered he was seeing my sister, we reconciled and became firm friends again. I got both Nicky and Mary jobs with one of my customers…"

Eliote butted in. "…Walker and Pugh Security Services?"

"Yes, they were bigger then than what they are now, with branches all over the Midlands, with clients all over the world, but Rachael's father squandered the business, and as their accountant, I pushed it back on track. I sold many of the businesses to competitors, but Rachael blames me for the ruin of her father."

"Ruin?" Eliote enquired.

"He was nearly bankrupt. I'd put him and Nigel together, not realizing he had killed my mother, and had been sent down for raping Rachael."

"When did you discover that little titbit?" Day jokingly asked.

"When my real father, Edward, came looking for a job, and while he was waiting to be interviewed by Rachael, he'd seen me and Nigel walking happily down the corridor." He drank a little more water. "After the interview, he enquired who I was, and came and found me." Eliote and Day both looked at Johnny, who was looking once again at the floor. "He then spilled the beans. I confronted Nigel, and he just laughed at me. Then, I knew." He threw the cup in a bin in anger. "As I was leaving, I heard faint noises coming from the cellar. Sneaking down, I discovered a secret."

"You found Rachael and Nicky?" Eliote said picking up a pen and moving it between his fingers.

"They did not see me. So I quietly left them making love and returned to my car, angry at the betrayal of my two trusted friends. I lusted for their blood, like they lusted for each other."

"And that's why you killed Nigel and Nicky?" Johnny nodded. "Did Mary know about the affair?"

Johnny glared at him. "What kind of sick copper are you?"

Eliote looked coldly at him and raised his voice as he asked, "Did she?"

Gittings paused for a second and then replied, "No, even though she had suspicions he was seeing someone. He denied everything, and for years, they were happy, but then he began changing, coming home late, smelling of cigarettes, spending their life savings, but wouldn't tell her where the money had gone to. She didn't know at the time it was Miss Goody-Two-Shoes! She found that out years later."

"How?" Day enquired.

"Because I told her!" Eliote sat back in the chair and threw the pen onto the table.

"You told her?"

"Yes, he was preparing to marry my sister, and I found out he was still having an affair with that bitch Rachael."

Eliote looked at Johnny and demanded, "So, what happened?"

> *Johnny drove his car down the narrow back streets of Chelmesbury and decided to drive past Gold Security. It was a business which he had always wanted to own and ruin, like Nigel had ruined his life by killing his mother.*
>
> *It was also a chance to get one over on Rachael, who had been a childhood sweetheart, but as she'd got older, they had drifted apart.*
>
> *He slowed as he saw the large Gold Security sign, and in the car park, he spotted a familiar car hidden out of view. There was also lights emanating from an upper floor office. Checking in his rear view mirror to see if anyone was behind, he stopped, got out, and discreetly climbed up a wall to look in through the window.*
>
> *What he witnessed made him angry, and he almost fell off...*

"What did you see, Mr. Gittings?"

Johnny glanced up. "You're an adult, Chief Inspector. Guess..."

"...Enlighten us." Eliote raised his eyebrow. "For the record?"

"Okay, if you want the sordid details, I saw Nicky performing oral sex on Rachael, and they were both obviously enjoying it."

"How long did you watch?" Day asked.

"I'm not some perverted individual, Sergeant!" He dragged his fingers through his hair. "But I did watch them for about five minutes, and then after, they began fucking each other. I climbed down and returned to my car."

"Then what?"

"I sat angrily for a while contemplating what to do. It was then I decided to drive around to my sister's house, and tell her what I had seen."

"How did she take it?" Day requested.

"You can imagine how she reacted." He looked over at the sergeant. "At first, she didn't believe me, and we had an almighty big row. For the first time in years, she even threatened to throw me out the house, but when I explained in explicit details of everything I had seen, she burst into tears." He looked at the table, saddened he had upset his sister. "Both of our fears had been realized." Eliote had seen the reaction when he had spoken to Mary, but she had lied to Eliote. He picked up the pen and wrote something down on a notepad and passed it to Day.

> *'Get Pickington and Wright to bring in Mary for questioning.'*

She read the note and exited the room. Eliote looked back at Johnny. "What happened after she found out?"

Johnny sat forward and smirked. "World War Three is what happened."

WHEN ANGELS FEAST
By
Kevin Bailey

CHAPTER THIRTY-TWO

Mary Gittings was sat in the kitchen of her home drinking a large cup of tea when the Vauxhall Insignia drove into the estate and parked outside. She got to her feet, almost spilling her drink, and watched as the two detectives got out and approached the front door.

On hearing the doorbell, she took a couple of deep breaths and answered. "What do you lot want now?"

Wright looked seriously at her. "I'm sorry, Miss Gittings, but we need you to come with us and answer some questions."

She didn't look happy at this request. "What about?"

The detective looked into the house. "Are the children here?"

Mary slightly glared at her and answered bluntly, "I don't think that's any concern of yours."

"Are your children here?" DS Wright demanded.

"No!" she retorted, "It's my friend's eldest son's birthday, so they are round there at the party."

Wright slightly smiled. "Is there anywhere they could stay tonight?"

"Why?" she demanded.

"Just answer the question please."

She didn't answer, but simply grabbed her portable home phone and dialled a number. "Hi Carla, it's Mary. I have to go to the…" She paused and looked at the two officers. "…somewhere, and I may not be home until tomorrow." She listened. "Cheers, hun, I owe you one." After she had grabbed a set of keys, she threw the phone onto the sideboard and was escorted to the car.

Pickington opened the back door and lowered her into the back seat, as Wright got in beside her. He jumped into the front seat and drove back to the station.

***

Eliote watched as Johnny began recounting the story. "She phoned him, and asked where the fuck he was. He just replied that he was in the pub, and had been there all night."

"And?" Eliote demanded.

"Well, after she had told him what I had said, she heard the sound as if clothes were being put on quickly, and he said he would be home soon."

"What happened when he got home?" Eliote was beginning to get a little impatient

"Like I previously said, World War Three and Four," he said sarcastically, and paused as Day re-entered the room and sat down. "There was an almighty big argument, and she threw him out."

"Is that why he beat up your dad?"

"Yes, he was so apologetic the next day, saying he'd been angry, and had taken it out on the first person he had seen. That was, unfortunately, my dad. He even came to the hospital, but Mary refused to see him, and so he went to work. Not only did I know his route, I also knew he had a love of sports cars. I borrowed one off a mate, and waited for the best place to kill him, my second victim…" he said triumphantly.

> *Johnny watched as the familiar car drove past him. He could see Nicky in a world of his own behind the wheel. Pulling out of a parking space, he followed, and they both approached some roadworks and stopped at a set of traffic lights. Johnny drove the sports car alongside, and could see his friend admiring it. The passenger window opened, and Johnny aimed the gun at his old friend, with a slight tear in both men's eyes, they looked sadly at each other. When the workmen began digging up the road with some jack-hammers, that was the signal, and Nicky watched in horror as his oldest and dearest friend pulled the trigger, closed the window, and drove away at high speeds.*

Eliote took out the photo of the rusty Berretta, and then the photo of the clean Berretta.

"What about this weapon?"

Johnny looked at it and smiled. "Mary had found it years ago in the safe at Gold Security, and as I already had the rusty one hidden and needed some spare parts, I asked her to steal it for me. At that time, Mary was innocent and brought it to me. No one noticed it was missing. I cannibalised it, and she returned a useless weapon. My rusty gun was now ready for my first victim…"

"…Nigel Pugh?" Day asked, already knowing the answer.

"They say the first kill is always the hardest. You see it in all the books and on film, but he was easy compared to Nicky…"

> *Nigel Pugh stood at the bar and looked around at the clientele at Glossies' Night Club. He was a good-looking*

man with a receding hairline and blue eyes, but to the clientele in the club, he had lots of money and that could get him anyone.

He was smiling at all the females, and giving the males an evil stare. Eventually, he spotted an attractive woman with brunette hair and a long flowing red dress which showed her curves. As she sat alone at the bar, she was fair game, and like some wild animal, he targeted her and made her the prey for the evening.
Even though, at times, he could be a romantic lover, lavishing his conquests with flowers and expensive meals, when he saw her, he just wanted sex. After introducing himself, he took the woman back to the Gold Security offices in his Aston Martin, and soon they were having frantic sex on his desk.

But to him, she was just another notch on his extended waterbed. Afterwards, he paid her some money for a taxi and made her leave. He grabbed some paperwork, and began preparing for his early meeting.

He was disturbed by a knock at the door. Thinking it was the woman back to give him a piece of his mind, he approached the door and prepared to say something in his defence when he saw Johnny stood angrily looking at him.

"What do you want?" Nigel asked.

"I want to know the truth, Nigel. Did you kill my mother?"

Nigel looked a little shocked. "I don't know what you are talking about, Johnny. Now leave, or I'll get security to escort you off site."

Johnny didn't bat an eyelid. He simply stared at him. "You killed my mother because she wouldn't come away with you. You shot her with the berretta that you have in your safe."

Nigel laughed and walked over to the aforementioned safe and opened it. Pulling out the metal tin, he opened it, and removed the gun, aiming it at Johnny. "What! You mean this gun?" Johnny looked a little scared, and this made Nigel laugh more. "Oh, Johnny, your mother was a slut, and I could have just clicked my fingers, and she would have come running."

Johnny flared up. "How dare you say those things about my mother? She loved my dad, and she was coming to tell you she was staying with him."

Nigel just stood there, smirking. "Yes, she did tell me that, and so I told her if I couldn't have her, no one would. So, I killed her."

Johnny become even angrier. "Why?" he demanded

"Because I could, Johnny." He sneered. "And now, the same weapon that killed your slut of a mother will now silence you." He pulled the trigger. Johnny winced, but the gun stayed silent. It was Johnny's time to laugh, and he pulled out the rusty Berretta and aimed it at Nigel.

"Sit down," Johnny demanded, and Nigel approached his desk.

"What are you going to do to me?"

Johnny cocked the weapon and aimed it straight at Nigel. "How did you describe it before..." He remembered the line. 'To silence you.' He pulled the trigger.

"So, what about the fire? Did someone find out about you stealing money from the company?" Eliote said, disturbing Johnny from his memories, and he looked at the cold blooded murderer.

"I was getting to that, Chief Inspector."

Eliote glared at him. "Well, please don't keep us in the dark," he said, and Johnny smirked at the pun.

"Oh, very droll, Chief Inspector." Eliote continued glaring at him. "Okay, after I had killed Nicky, I drove the car I borrowed back to my friend's. I jumped back into mine. I drove near the shooting, and saw you all there with your flashing lights and your forensics experts examining the car. I drove down a side street, and went to my sister's house to see how she was coping. That was when your lot turned up to tell her about Nicky. After you had left, she told me that Rachael had begun to suspect someone was stealing money from the account, and as Mary was the only one who knew the account numbers, she blamed her. I told her I would deal with it, and I went home and waited until night…"

Johnny drove his friend's car to Gold Security, and after surveying the area, parked in a side street. Taking out some cans of petrol from the boot and the second gun, he closed and locked the car and walked over to the offices.

Seeing two burly security men in a hut, he avoided them, like he had done so on the night he'd killed Nigel by keeping close to the building, and disappeared into the darkness.

As he approached a side door, he took out a set of keys Mary had given him and located the safe. He opened it with the code she had given him, and then took out the relevant documents.

He went to the petrol cans and doused the place. After checking he had covered enough, he walked out of the office, and removed his gloves. From outside, he lit a match and threw it into the room.

There was an almighty big whoosh as the petrol ignited. Outside, the security guards came running, as did the security patrol. They all tried in vain to enter the offices, but the flames were now too high, and they ran to call the emergency services.

This was the chance the watching Johnny needed, and he headed back to his car and drove away.

"So, where did you go then?" Day requested.

"I went home and hid my clothing in the shed. I had meant to burn them in the incinerator, but time was against me."

Eliote looked at Day and nodded. She pulled out the clothes they had found at Johnny's house and placed them on the table. "Are these them?"

"Yes."

"Does Mary know about any of this?" Eliote enquired.

"No, I told her I was going to buy the company, and that was why I would need the keys and the safe code." He looked up sadly. "She made a deal with me. She said that she would give me the keys and codes, if I made her my partner in the business when I brought it. Because I needed both, I agreed."

"Okay," Eliote stood up and looked at Johnny. "Johnny Gittings, I am charging you with the murders of Nigel Pugh and Nicolas Waite, plus the arson of Gold Security." He read him his rights, knocked on the interview room door, and a constable walked in.

"Yes, sir."

Eliote looked at the young, blond constable. "Take Mr. Gittings to a cell." The constable nodded and led him away.

"Interview of Johnny Gittings terminated." He looked at his watch and read out the time, then he pressed stop on the recorder and gathered all the evidence, placing it in a cardboard box. Day wrote on the box and took it away.

***

Detective Inspector Frashier arrived back in the UK, and took a connection to Chelmesbury, arriving later in the day. His first port of call was the station, and when he entered the unit, he found the teams working hard on figuring out who the victims of Green were.

Day greeted him warmly, "Inspector, is it nice to be back?"

He sighed heavily. "Yeah, it feels like I never left the place." He headed for his superior's office, and knocked on the door.

Eliote looked up and beckoned him in. "Evening, Inspector. Good trip?"

Frashier looked at him and shook his head. "Yes and no," he paused. "Found out a little bit of information before Green was executed. He just said his victims were loners…"

"Yes, they may have been loners, but they had families who would like to know where they are." Frashier nodded, and Eliote reported, "I've got Day and the team hunting to see if we can identify any of these victims." He looked at his number two. "What about Green?"

"He was complicated. One minute, I thought I was breaking through. The next, he would go silent, but what I can't work out is why he would attack that guard, which would bring his execution forward?"

Eliote shrugged his shoulders. "He was a strange man," Frashier nodded in agreement. "So what now?"

Frashier handed over his last file to Eliote. "I have to go and tell his Stepmother that he is dead. That was his last request."

Eliote smiled. "Ok, how are you holding up?"

Frashier was shocked at this sign of affection. "I'm okay, Gov. Like you said, it's gonna take some time to come to terms with the deaths, but I can't just sit around at home and mope. I'll be back on duty Monday morning, bright and early."

That was what Eliote wanted to hear. "It'll be nice to have you back, Will." The two men stared at each other, and then Eliote ordered, "Ok, I'll want your full report on my desk as usual. Got to keep her ladyship happy." He smiled. Frashier returned the smile, and left Eliote alone in the office.

***

Frashier turned the grey BMW into the street, and parked in the only available space and grabbed the piece of paper on which he had written the address. He got out and walked up the pavement to the plain looking house. Nothing about the structure made it stand out.

He approached the door, and could hear music somewhere behind the unimpressive door. He pressed the doorbell, but no sound came from it. He knocked hard several times and waited. He then heard the music stop and faint footsteps approach. But when the door opened, he was in for a surprise.

"You?" he said with shock.

"Hello, Inspector, I've been expecting you. Won't you come in…?"

***

WHEN ANGELS FEAST
By
Kevin Bailey

CHAPTER THIRTY-THREE

Feeling exuberant at bringing Nigel and Nicolas killer to justice, Eliote walked triumphantly from his office to Day's desk. As he neared her location, he heard his superior shout to him. Brightly beckoned him out of CID, and into the courtyard that ran around the circular building.
"Walk with me to my office, Chief Inspector." He obliged and as they walked across the yard surface, she began talking. "I hear congratulations are in order."

"Yes, Ma'am. Both cases have been dealt with. Frashier has a few lose ends to clear up, and then we are done." She stopped in her tracks and glared deep into his eyes. She was so close he could smell her perfume.

"You are very lucky that it turned out that Johnny Gittings was the killer."

"Ma'am?" He furrowed his brow, confused.

"I mean, the case against you has been dropped. You're now off the hook."

He smirked. "Thank you, ma'am."

She moved away, but before leaving, remarked, "You ever put me in a position like that again, I'll make you a constable before you have chance to say, 'What!'" Brightly placed her hands on her hips. "Do I make myself clear, Chief Inspector?"

"Ma'am."

Eliote watched her walk away, and like that first day at the station, he thought she looked good in a uniform. Once she was out of sight, he headed for CID.

***

Brightly hid around a corner, and peered out to see if Eliote was still there. He had just begun to turn and disappear back to the circular building. She realised he must have been watching her walk away from him. She smiled cheekily and resumed the path to her office.

As she walked she felt like a silly school girl, who'd got a crush on the head boy. The thoughts she had were electrifying, but they couldn't ever come true, could they? She hoped not. She had always said she would never get into an affectionate relationship with a junior officer, even one as smart and good-looking as Eliote.

Trying to push her erotic thoughts away, she quickly ran to her office, told her secretary that she wasn't to be disturbed, quickly she drew down the blinds, so that she couldn't see the CID unit, and began looking through the files on her desk.

***

Eliote found the newly promoted Inspector Miranda Day clearing out her desk. The happy feelings he had since seeing Brightly turned once again to remorse. Now the cases were finished, his best detective was leaving for pastures new. As he neared her desk, he tripped over a box.

"What's this?" he asked, picking up the box from the floor and placing it on the empty desk next to Day's.

"It's all the belongings from Green's cell." She grabbed some more of her stuff and placed it into some storage containers. "Frashier wanted me to go through it to see if there was anything in there that could answer some of the questions he still had. He could then hand them to his stepmom."

Eliote picked up an important looking document. "No I wasn't talking about that crap. I mean, what's this?" he said, holding the item in his hand and waving it around.

"Looks like a wedding certificate, Gov."

Eliote handed it to her. "Yes, but look who it belongs to, Inspector."

She spotted the name. "Oh my god," she proclaimed. "It's Anthony's."

"Yes, it's between him and Georgina, but look at the name of the bride's mother."

Day examined the name, but was none the wiser. "Should I recognise the name, sir?"

Eliote almost ran to his office. Rummaging through all the files on his desk, he came to the file Frashier had given to him concerning the death of Jane Boyd. He ran back to Day. Sifting through the pages of neat notes quickly, he came to the Inspector's interviews at St. Augustus Nursing Home and handed it to Day.

"I've been getting it wrong. Georgina wasn't Anthony's step-mom." He cursed under his breath. "Look at the age. She would have been too young, I reckon about fifteen, no!" he said bluntly. "Someone else was his stepmom, and if that is correct, I think Frashier could be in a lot of trouble."

***

"I can't believe it," Frashier said, mortified. "You're Anthony's stepmom, Mrs. Cook?"

"Oh, please, Inspector. Call me Gladys." She ushered him into the home. "I'm not at work now." She escorted him into a sitting room, and sat down opposite him. "I wasn't just his stepmother. I was a lot more than that," she said proudly. "Lover, friend, confident, oh, and of course, his mother-in-law."

***

Eliote, Day, and a smattering of other CID and uniformed officers raced outside to the vehicles. Eliote swiftly gave his instructions.

"Our colleague may be in danger. When we get there, I want the house encircled. No one goes in or out, got it?" The team nodded in acknowledgement, except for Day, who was trying in vain to ring Frashier's mobile.

"WELCOME TO…" She hung up and tried again, but it continuously went straight to the answer phone.

Eliote approached her. "Any luck reaching the Inspector?" he said, getting into the black vehicle. She shook her head, and got in beside him, a worried look on her face. "Well, let's just hope we can get there in time!" he declared and sped off.

***

Frashier looked at the elderly lady. Her white hair shone brightly from the spotlights which encircled the room. She looked like an angel, and Frashier was beginning to think maybe she was an Angel of Death.

"So, Inspector, what brings you to my door?"

He began to look sombre. "This will come as a shock, but Anthony was executed yesterday morning."

"He's, he's dead?" she said, stuttering.

He nodded and tried to be tactful as he informed her. "He attacked and murdered a guard at the prison in Texas. The Governor brought the execution forward. I am so sorry."

She went as white as her hair and looked angrily at him. "You're sorry? That can't bring him back, can it?"

"All I can say is that before he died, he asked me to come here personally and tell you." The anger left, and she started to cry.

"Thank you!" she said softly. Out in the hall the grandfather clock began to strike, she looked up at him. "Will you excuse me? I have to prepare for dinner." She got up and headed out of the room.

It was then the inspector noticed an opened parcel. He got up quietly and approached to examine it. It was for Zilpaterol Hydrochloride, and it was addressed to the nursing home. Something in his mind clicked, and he cursed.

"Oh my god." He heard her returning, and quickly sat down and asked, as she entered the room like a queen, "I understand you have a daughter and a grandson. Would you like me to contact them?"

She looked at him and gave a small smile. "That will not be necessary, Inspector…"

"…If I am to call you Gladys, you must call me Will."

"Of course, Will. My daughter and her son are hanging out with friends down the road. I'll let them know when they return."

Making out that he believed her answer, he asked, "So, what happened to Antony's father?" She looked puzzled at his request. "Oh, it's so we can inform him."

"Oh, he ran off with his secretary years ago. That was when I met my third husband, Arthur. He was, and still is, a decent man," she replied regally.

"Is?" Frashier enquired.

She nodded. "Yes, unfortunately, dementia caught up with him, and he is at the home I run." He took out his notebook and wrote this info down. As he was doing so, she spotted the drug's name in the notebook. She was also keenly aware of the package on to which he kept gazing at.

"Oh, how rude of me. I haven't offered you a drink. What can I get you?"

He placed the notebook back into his pocket and replied, "I'd love a coffee."

She stood up, and as she left, she grabbed the package. In the corner of her eye, she could see him looking and knowing it would look suspicious, she turned and explained, "It's for my grandson. He has bad asthma. I'd read up somewhere on the internet this was used as a treatment. I showed it to his mother, and we ordered some through the nursing home." Frashier once again pretended to be convinced, and she hurried from the room.

***

Eliote drove like a bat out of hell down the main roads of Chelmesbury, sirens blazing overhead. He felt like a racing driver on a circuit. Even Day was shocked at his driving, and held on to the door handle for dear life.

The police vehicles behind were struggling to keep up with the Saab, but as he swerved around a corner nearly missing a cyclist who wasn't paying attention, he knew that time was running out. If Mrs. Cook was the killer, Frashier could be next for the pot!

***

The house fell silent which placed Frashier on alert. Checking down the corridor that she was out of sight, he thought he would check the rest of the place out. He came out of the lounge and opened the door opposite. He found an unmade double, a single bed and a cot. The two smaller beds had teddy bears and pyjamas neatly placed on the pillows. He spotted two large sports bags containing children's clothes, and a chill ran down his back when he lifted a picture frame. The picture was of the woman he loved and her precious children. Eve smiled warmly out of the picture at her father.

He examined Eve. He could see his own mother hidden deep within her face. He touched it warmly, but was distracted by a door shutting somewhere deep beneath the house.
Taking out his phone, he took several pictures of the room, and its belongings and tried to send them as a message to Day, but had no signal.

"Shit!" he cursed and tried another spot to send the pictures, but as before, the error message kept coming up on the screen.

Putting the phone back into his pocket, he headed for the kitchen which was at the rear of the property. As he walked up the corridor, the silence was shattered by the sound of a grandfather clock which ticked neatly to the steps he made.

He cracked the kitchen door open, and he found it empty. The only sound was from the kettle on the stove whistling. On the sideboard, next to the kettle, were two cups all prepared. He was about to shout out to his hostess when he spotted light flickering from behind a large cupboard door. Intrigued by this, he approached. Just as he got near the door, it opened, and out came Mrs. Cook, who pretended to be shocked at finding Frashier standing there.

"Will! You startled me!" He apologised and looked into the darken cellar. She could see what he was doing and distracted him. "I noticed there weren't any teabags in the jar, so I went to get some from the cellar. It's where we keep the food, as it stops my grandson from stealing it." She turned off the stair light and closed the door, firmly locking the bolt.

After she had made the drinks, they both returned to the lounge. She spotted that the door opposite the sitting room was slightly ajar. Frashier returned to the chair, sat down, and began to drink his coffee. It was hot and sweet, just the way he liked it. Suddenly, the room began to spin and he felt drowsy. He looked up at Mrs. Cook, who was sipping her own tea and smiling at him.

"What is ha, ha, ha, ha, ha, happening to me?" he said, stuttering.

She just sat there and smiled. "Sssh now, my dear," she said, placing her finger to her mouth. "It's just a mild sedative, she calmly placed her cup on the coffee table and approached him. He tried to throw the cup away, but she just took it from his shaking hands. He tried to push her away, but she stopped him and kissed him passionately, then remarked, "Soon, it'll all be over." He pushed her away once more and tried in vain to stand. She helped him up, and he tried to take out his mobile, but she just shook her head, tutting, "Naughty, naughty. You won't be needing that, Inspector." She carefully took the phone, turned it off, and placed it on the table.

"What are you go, go, go, going to do with me?" he asked gingerly.

She just smiled evilly, and then led him by the hand back to the kitchen, whispering her reply into his ear. "Anthony sent you to me. He said he would send me someone if he died."

"What the, the, the hell are you talking about?" Frashier said, slurring his words and feeling like an idiot.

"He sent you to me," she paused and licked her lips. "For my own pleasure. I suppose he told you to come alone." He nodded reluctantly, and she looked up at the cellar door. "As you were so interested in what was behind that door, why don't we go and take a look?" She smirked.

When they arrived, she unlocked the door and pushed him through. He fell down the stone stairs and landed in a heap at the bottom step.

***

Eliote hand-braked the car to a stop outside the house. He and Day almost jumped out. The other officers arrived, and the Chief Inspector told them to pan out around the house. When the swat team arrived and approached the front door, he gave the order.

"Go, go, go," he barked, and he watched as an officer with a battering ram broke down the door. Mrs. Cook looked up in surprise as officers emerged into her home; their guns were aiming straight at her.

"This is the police!" One of the front line armed officers proclaimed. "Put your hands behind your head and get on the floor." She did as was instructed, and an armed officer placed handcuffs on her and led her out to Eliote.

"It's over, Mrs. Cook." She spat at him, and was led away.

"Gov!" Day shouted from the house and Eliote briskly walked into the kitchen as directed, where he found her looking down into the cellar.

"Phew," he said, holding his nose. "That's smells as bad as Loughton." Eliote looked at the bottom step, and saw Frashier on a heap on the floor, blood gushing from an open wound on his head.

The Chief Inspector carefully walked gingerly down the stairs and looked at his fallen comrade.

"Frashier?" He knelt at his side, touching his shoulder. "Will?" Eliote shouted up to Day, "Miranda, man down! Call an ambulance!" She turned and rang the emergency number, then looked at Eliote and gave him a thumbs up.

Eliote waited for Day to come down and stay with the inspector. He found a light switch and turned it on. He was appalled at what he saw. The place was as eerie as Loughton, and he could see fresh blood stains on the walls. "My god," he said, as he saw Georgina and her son, Frank, hanging upside down from hooks. They were both naked and their throats had been cut. He also noticed Georgina had a stab wound to her chest and Frank's final shocked expression.

Turning away from the horrific scene, he spotted several large freezers similar to the ones that were found in Loughton. After placing on some gloves, he walked over and taking a couple of deep breaths. He opened them expecting the worse, but unlike the previous ones, they were almost empty, except for some chickens and a piece of beef.

He closed the lids and continued to examine the cellar. Up against a wall at the far end, he saw that the floor had been disturbed. Grabbing a shovel which was leaning against a wall, he started to dig away at the soil. Before long, the top of a male skull came into view.

WHEN ANGELS FEAST
By
Kevin Bailey

CHAPTER THIRTY-FOUR

Eliote, Day, and a drugged up Frashier sat in Interview Room One. In the Inspector's eyes, the room was still spinning. 'Maybe I should have gone to hospital,' he thought to himself, but he needed to know what had happened to his beloved Jane.

Mrs. Cook kept glancing at Frashier. "Don't worry, my love," she said caringly, as if tending to a patient. "The symptoms won't last long. You'll soon be feeling ok."

Eliote made her look at him. "How many people have you killed, Mrs. Cook?"

"I couldn't say. When the Angels feast, no one cares about the numbers, just the gorging."

Eliote took out a report from Strong detailing what he had found. "Thirty-five victims at last count, but the teams are still searching all the properties to find the remains of anymore of your brethren's victims."

She raised an eyebrow. "Blimey, but then again, we did enjoy the feast," she said smirking and patting her tummy.

"How did you choose your victims?"

She sniggered. "You really think we choose them at random? Ha! We planned everything, right down to the last detail. Our targets were worked on for weeks before we pounced, and that includes the detective here." She pointed at Frashier.

"What do you mean by that?" Eliote demanded.

"We had the inspector closely watched, but when we found out he was a copper, we switched to another victim. Whoosh! He ended life as a burger."

Day looked like she was going to throw up. Eliote addressed her, "You okay, Inspector?" Day nodded, and Eliote continued with the interview. "Okay, so you'd choose them, torment them like a cat does after it's caught a mouse, and then what?" She didn't answer, but simply remained silent. "Was it all about food, or would Anthony kill them out of jealousy for sleeping with you?"

"Oh, come on, Chief Inspector, really? You don't think that my sweet Anthony killed all those people, do you?" She sat forward in the chair, her eyes almost bulged out of her head. "I did!" she whispered and sat back. "He wouldn't have hurt a fly," she smirked. "He was too good. There was never nastiness in him."

Eliote sat forward and remarked, "He killed several people, including an American police officer."

She remained reclined back in her chair. "He did it to protect his family; to make you lot leave us alone. It would point the finger of blame at himself. I believe that is why he killed that guard, so he would take our little secret with him to the grave…"

"…But, he's dead, Mrs. Cook. The secret is out, and you will pay the price."

She looked mortified. "Yes, so?"

"So," Eliote asked. "Anthony never killed those people we found buried in the ground?"

"No, he never killed for the cause."

Eliote turned a page in the file, and saw the picture of the skeletons found by the old swimming bath site. "When did you last see Anthony's father?"

"What has that got to do with this?" she snapped, staring coldly at him.

"Just answer the question please, Mrs. Cook." He demanded

She tried to remember. "The day he left me, no, sorry, us." She frowned. "He just walked out of the door and disappeared, never to be seen again."

Day took out the picture of the two skeletons found near the Millennium Green. "What's this?" Mrs Cook asked the two detectives.

Eliote remained silent, so Day continued on, "We have reason to believe these are the remains of your second husband and his secretary." She read the name from the file. "Mrs. Rebecca Swinbourne,"

Mrs Cook looked shocked and touched the pictures. "No, you're lying. He wouldn't do anything like that. It wasn't part of the plan. That woman found at the golf course was to have been his first kill, but he couldn't do it. So while she relaxed, I did the dirty work. He helped me bury her, and we gorged on the flesh like crazed wild animals, and then we made love next to where she lay." She placed the photo back on the table and looked up at the detectives. "So, why would he have done this? It was out of character."

Eliote placed Green's statement on the table, and she read it.

> *'I saw my dad and his slapper enjoying a picnic. I waited until he went for a slash, and then, I slit his throat, and went back and slit hers. It was a gift for my beloved!'*

This passage seemed to make her smile. "My dear sweet boy." She looked up at the three detectives; a warm smile was etched on to her face. Then, as she returned her gaze back to the photo, she divulged a secret. "I did contemplate killing Anthony, but when we made love, it was gentle and very loving. I realised I was falling in love with him. I just couldn't give him what he wanted, which was a child of his own."

"How did that make you feel?" Day asked.

The smile was wiped off her face and she looked saddened. "It was horrific having to watch the man you love be with another woman…"

"…but he fell into the arms of your daughter," Eliote pointed out.

"At first, it was weird, but soon the three of us became a team. We would hunt together and share the rewards."

Eliote looked at the smile which had reappeared. "So what was 'the hunt' like?"

"Oh it was perfection, a pure feast. Georgina or I would get dressed up and either go out or go online to find a victim. Then, as the weeks progressed, we would go on a date. Anthony would always be there following us in the shadows. Then, when the person we had targeted had looked away, I would place the same sedative as the one I used on the Inspector," she looked over at Frashier, "into a drink. We would go outside for some fresh air where Anthony was waiting and would take him or her back to our 'den.' There, myself, Georgina," she looked up at Eliote, "or sometimes Anthony and the victims would have fun." She raised her eyebrow. "I would be the one to kill them. We would then hang them to drain overnight, cut them up in the morning, and place them in the freezers, ready for feasting." She licked her lips.

Frashier, who had been silent for most of the interview, looked over at the boastful women.

"What about Jane?" He glared at her. "Your friend."

"We didn't have friends. They were all food to us…"

Eliote interrupted her. "…What about the patients at your nursing home? Aren't they food?"

She glanced over at him and scolded him. "I could not hurt them, Chief Inspector, that's absurd. They are the elderly."

"But you killed all those people, never giving them a second thought?"

"Of course. They were young and tasty…"

"…WHAT HAPPENED WITH JANE?" Frashier snapped keeping his eyes fixated on Mrs. Cook.

"I tried to fatten the skinny cow up…"

"By using the Zilpaterol Hydrochloride, a drug used in The States?" Day asked.

"But I think she saw me and Georgina preparing a meal. The next thing we heard was the door slam shut, and she and the two children were gone. I tried to find her, worried she would go to the police, and you would come to investigate the place. We watched the station, and of course, you, Inspector, but she didn't show. We breathed a sigh of relief. Our secret was safe for now." She made eye contact with the solemn looking Inspector. "I was happy and saddened when I heard on the news what had become of them."

Frashier struggled to stand. "Not as saddened as me, Mrs. Cook!" With Day's help, he walked out of the room.

Eliote sat back in the chair and looked at the woman in front of him. He was not afraid of her, like those victims would have been.

"So," he asked, "why did you stop using the bungalow in Loughton?"

The woman shifted in the seat. "I used to look after old Mrs. Southwick, and was allowed to use the place any way I wanted. I got Anthony in, and after we had made love in her bed, he erected a partition in the cellar," she reminisced happily. "I had found the old coal shoot, and we created steps to enter the hidden area. It was a way we could slip in and out without the old woman seeing."

Eliote stopped her. "You didn't answer my question, Mrs. Cook!"

"Mrs. Southwick died in my arms, Chief Inspector, and so we had to move the operation to Anthony's house. We couldn't get the freezers full of meat out in time, especially with that nosey neighbour, Mrs. Lock, about. We would sneak in, grab some, and sneak out," she breathed heavily. "Unfortunately, we had some bad luck. Anthony got arrested in Scotland as he bundled me onto a train." She looked up as Day returned.

"What were you doing in Scotland?"

"Looking elsewhere in the country for victims. We couldn't keep taking the people from Chelmesbury and the area. It would have made you lot a little suspicious."

"Didn't Georgina come with you to Scotland?" Day asked.

"No, as time progressed, she would hardly come out on 'the hunt'…"

"…And why was that?" Eliote tapped his pen against his hand.

"She had Frank to look after."

"Did you resent her?"

She glared at him. "I did." She turned up her nose. "She had given him something I couldn't, and it hurt like hell, but as the years progressed, I began to adore the child. He was my boy."

Day looked puzzled. "If he was 'your boy,' why did you kill him and his mother?"

Looking over at Day, she answered, "He was a bright and very inquisitive lad, and after finding that his mother had left the cellar door unlocked, he went and investigated. I found him looking white and frightened. He'd opened the freezer and found the skull of a man staring at him. He wanted to call the police, and so I had to silence him."

"And his mother?"

This question upset Mrs. Cook. "She'd come home and found him hanging on a hook. We had an almighty big argument, and she was crying, as a mother would. I had to silence her, before her screams brought you lot here. I grabbed a knife and stabbed her in the heart."

Eliote looked at the heartless killer. "She fought you, not only because you had just killed her son, you had killed the only link to the man she truly loved. Did she know?"

"It came out in the argument. She kept saying he was hers, how could I do that to her."

"She was acting like any wife would, protective of her husband…" Day responded

Mrs. Cook stood up and snapped, "HE WAS 'MY' ANTHONY, NOT HER'S." She slumped back into the chair and quietly said,

"And now, they are all gone." Eliote went to say something else, but she held up her hand to silence him. "You can do to me what you must." With that final sentence, she fell silent.

After a constable had led the deflated Mrs. Cook away, the two detectives were feeling triumphant in the fact they had put another 'Deathly Angel,' behind bars. They tidied up the interview room.

Day looked over at Eliote. "What do you think will happen to her, Gov?"

Eliote looked at the empty chair. "She will probably be sectioned under the Mental Health Act, and never be allowed out of a mental hospital, except in a wooden box."

She smiled at him. "Right, good night, Gov."

"Good night, Inspector Day," he said with a wry smile. With that, she walked out of the interview room. Eliote gathered up all his files and walked to his car. He looked at the old part of the station and smiled. Dorothy Brightly was looking at him. She waved and he waved back. He then jumped into his Saab and drove away.

***

At a large, quaint, medieval house on the outskirts of Glayton, the sound of a phone ringing disturbed the peace and quiet. An oak door opened, and the middle-aged cigar smoking man walked to an old style phone and answered.

"Hello."

He heard the silent tone of a younger man. "Sorry to bother you, Father, but we may have a problem."

The man placed the phone onto the table, went and closed the door, and then returned to the receiver. "Report, my child."

The caller gulped heavily. "Alex hasn't delivered on his promises. He didn't do his homework, as the site was unavailable to sell." There was silence. "Father?"

Placing his Cigar in an ashtray, he fumbled beneath his green jumper and pulled out a large gold medallion. The picture engraved depicted an angel behind which were two crosses, one on top of the other, the bottom cross was upside down. Inscribed on the bottom cross were the words *'Church of the Sacred Angel'*

After touching the angel's face and praying for forgiveness, he tucked the piece of jewellery back beneath his clothes and took a couple of puffs on the cigar.

"To say I am not disappointed is an understatement, my child. I'm guessing you are dealing with this in the usual way?"

He heard the caller swallow a drink and then reply, "I've contacted our friend…"

"…I don't want to know. JUST GET IT DONE." He hung up, and the oak door opened. A woman about the same age as the man, wearing expensive clothes and a green hairband holding up her slightly grey hair, stood looking at him.

"Everything okay, dear?"

He nodded and after kissing her on the head, remarked, "It's just church business, darling. Go back to the film. I'll be along in a moment." She nodded, and left him to his thoughts.

***

Outside Alex Boyd's house, a high performance Jaguar engine came to a stop. A smartly dressed man in a long navy coat got out and walked in the shadows up the long drive. He approached the front door and rang the bell.

Deep within the house, he heard swearing, and a television went quiet. Hurried footsteps approached the door. The door quickly opened and Alex spoke angrily, "It's about bloody time you re…" He was stopped in his tracks by the face of the man in the dark suit, who stood on the shadowy doorstep, a bible under his arms.

"Hello, sir," he said, in a calming fashion. "I'm sorry to bother you, but…" He smacked Alex in the face with so much force he flew down the corridor and into a heap on the floor.

After checking that no-one had seen what he had done, he entered the house. Locking the door to the outside world, he grabbed his shocked victim off the floor, and threw him into the sitting room, smashing him into a cabinet with a thud.

The stranger walked casually into the room and approached the window, looking through the net curtains, he closed the blinds, and approached Alex, who was begging for his life. The attacker wasn't listening, and Alex was once again thrown against the wall.

"You betrayed our father," the attacker snarled. "And now, you must pay for that betrayal."

Alex tried to protest. "Tell him I'll work harder to get the land, I promise!"

The suited man shook his head. "It's too late. Father has other plans, and they don't involve you!" He made Alex's last minutes of life painful without breaking a sweat. He begged for his life again and again, and this made his attacker angry. "Alex, you have insulted me and our father with your begging, so please be silent." He smacked him across the face, and Alex collapsed onto the floor. The suited man leant down and whispered into the blood-stained ear, "It's time for you meet our maker." From inside the Bible, he took out several ties. Alex watched as he tied the ties together and formed a noose. Tying the rope to a door handle, he threaded it through a chandelier, placed the noose over Alex's head, and with some inner strength, he pulled his victim off the floor and stripped him of his clothes.

"Please tell our father I…" Alex begged once more to his attacker, but was silenced by the suited man. He was pulled up the door. The ties cut into his neck, and he tried to remove them, but time was running out. The suited man simply turned and walked out of the room, shutting it behind him, leaving Alex to die.

An hour later, the suited man walked out of the house, did the sign of the cross, and headed for the Jaguar and drove off.

The house became quiet, except for the sound of a dripping tap in the kitchen.

Two hours later, the silence was shattered by the ex-Russian nanny Tatyana Avilov who was heading towards the house. She placed her key in the door and opened it. What she found was disturbing. The house was unusually clean and tidy. She closed the door and shouted, "Alex it's me, I just came to say sorry for being angry with you?"

The house was quiet. She shouted again. "Alex, where are you." There was still no sound, and so she headed for the kitchen and could hear strange noises coming from the front room. "Are you okay?" she said, opening a back door entrance into the front room.

As Tatyana walked slowly into the front room, she became aware of something tied to the other door. It was Alex, and he was hanging, his face was staring at his naked groin. She ran out into the street screaming.

***

When Angels Feast

By
Kevin Bailey

EPILOGUE

Chelmesbury Railway Station

William Frashier stood on the platform and waited. Down the line was a tunnel, which would soon light up to announce the arrival of his new love, who had agreed to spend the weekend with him. The butterflies in his stomach intensified as the minutes to her arrival ticked by. As he looked at his watch, he spotted specks of blood on his cuffs.

"Damn," he cursed. "I knew I should have changed." His thoughts were erased as he heard the rails vibrate. He glanced over at the tunnel and saw it brighten up. Above his head, he heard the announcer.

> "The train now approaching platform one is the nine-forty service from Hereford..."

Listening to the words, Frashier began to walk towards the oncoming train. It was then that he felt the iPhone in his pocket vibrate. He took it out and saw it was the station. As the train pulled up, he contemplated answering it. Then he saw Jeanette waiting at the door for the train to stop, so he placed it back in his pocket, and walked towards her.

***

Eliote drove his Saab up the narrow street and approached the gate to a bedsit. As he parked up and got out, Harry's middle aged landlord came out of his workshop, wiping down some engine part with an old rag.

"Can I help you?" Eliote took out his warrant card and showed it to the landlord. "Bloody police! Can't you leave the poor sod alone? Ain't he be through enough?"

Eliote stood at the gate. "I am here to inform him there has been a terrible miscarriage of justice, and I am referring his case to the Independent Police Complaints Commission."

"It's about bloody time."

"Is he in?" Eliote asked, and the man shook his head.

"Nah, he went out this morning, and I don't know what time he'll be home."

"You don't know where he is?"

"Sorry, I don't," he said, lying. Eliote thanked him for his time and returned to the Saab. Pausing in thought, he instantly knew where Harry could be.

Nearing the Millennium Green, the Chief Inspector parked the car in a space. Taking off his jacket, he walked over the bridge, and headed for the clearing up in the woods.

As he neared the clearing he heard Harry talking to someone whose voice he recognised. It was Charlotte. They both seemed to be happy in each other's company. He stopped in his tracks, deciding that maybe the time wasn't right, and he turned and walked back to the Saab.

As he got close to his beloved car, he heard his phone ringing. Quickly opening the door, he grabbed the phone off his dashboard and answered. "Eliote."

It was DS Wright. "Sorry to bother you, Gov, but Alex Boyd has been found hanging at his home. Strong's first impression is he was attempting autoeroticism, but when he dug deeper…"

"…He should be good at that by now," he quipped, but Wright ignored it and continued.

"He is beginning to think the scene has been set up to look like it was an accident." Eliote sighed, and then looked up into the woods, and thought of the two lovers enjoying each other's company. How he missed that feeling of longing.

Saddened by his thoughts, he answered. "Okay, inform Fras…"

Wright interrupted him. "…The Inspector has got the weekend off Gov, as he's got a friend coming to stay."

Eliote cursed his stupidity. "Of course," he said stuttering. "I'm on my way." He got into the car and taking one last look towards the forest, he placed the car in gear and drove away.

THE END

BUT SIMON ELIOTE WILL RETURN…

Printed in Great Britain
by Amazon